friar TUCK

Cameron Taylor

www.friartuckbook.com

AuthorHouse™ UK Ltd.
500 Avebury Boulevard
Central Milton Keynes, MK9 2BE
www.authorhouse.co.uk
Phone: 08001974150

© *2010 Cameron Taylor. All rights reserved.*

No part of this book may be reproduced, stored in a retrieval system, or transmitted by any means without the written permission of the author.

First published by AuthorHouse 4/28/2010

ISBN: 978-1-4520-1493-7 (sc)

This book is printed on acid-free paper.

for Peter Groenink & Miss. Green

Friar Tuck ~ Chapter 1

The three primeval unities:
One Divinity; one truth; one point of liberty.
Triads of Bardism

Fountaindale Abbey, Advent 1199.

The arched oak door banged open with an almighty crash. The silently dining monks sprang to their feet, ready to run.

"Brother Michael Tuck." The Sub-Prior swept in with a tight grin. "The Abbot wishes to see you. Right now."

Under his tonsure of nut-brown hair, Tuck's auburn eyes turned dark with dread.

"I've never seen the Sub so happy. You're in for it, Tuck. Stay steady." The friendly whisper from one of his brothers set Tuck's hands trembling.

The brethren sat, muttering in annoyance and relief, while Tuck slid out between their bald pates to answer his summons.

Early twilight hazed golden-marine through the open cloisters as the Sub-Prior hurried Tuck towards the chapter house. Tuck scuttled along, scrambling for his wits.

They fairly raced across the empty scriptorium, then down a tight corridor to the Abbot's office. The Sub-Prior knocked two loud raps, shot Tuck a withering glance, then flung open the door.

The Abbot of Fountaindale Abbey sat bolt upright behind a broad desk of plain timber, deeply engaged with a large, curling letter. A purple ribbon hung from its cracked wax seal. The flame-topped tallows of a three-armed candelabrum guttered high on the right, fluttering warm yellow light over the old stone walls.

The Sub-Prior stopped just inside the door, and nodded for Tuck to advance alone.

The Abbot folded his letter with a snap.

"Brother Michael." The Abbot cut Tuck to the quick with a flash of his stern blue eyes. "You know why you are here. Please explain yourself."

Tuck's excuses turned to dust on his tongue. He had no idea which of his mischiefs had been discovered. Mindful of past successes with this tactic, Tuck adopted his best shamed-face.

"Father Abbot, a wicked devil tempted me, and I was not strong enough to resist. I beg your forgiveness."

"Your confession will help you in heaven, Brother Michael, but not here." The Abbot's prayer-sharpened gaze turned over every stone in Tuck's soul. "My forgiveness is not what you need."

Tuck's toes tingled in alarm. The Abbot usually went for sensational rollickings, not grim resignation.

"Father, actually, I'm not sure what-."

"Stealing from the Abbey stores."

"Oh, but Father Abbot!" Tuck's voice quaked with relief. "I haven't stolen from the stores."

The Abbot cast a blistering look over Tuck's shoulder.

"Brother Michael," the Sub-Prior spoke up loud and clear, "I personally witnessed you, this morning, passing Abbey supplies to peasants over the back gate."

The words pierced Tuck's ears like hate-driven nails.

He'd almost forgotten.

On his way to the kitchen after Matins, he'd come across a half-frozen little family begging at the Abbey gate. Moved by their need, he'd not thought twice about sharing from the brethren's surplus. Of course, he hadn't asked permission, but never imagined it theft. Stealing from the Abbey was stealing from God.

Tuck's guts twisted.

"Father Abbot," Tuck appealed with all his heart, "those people had *nothing*. This harsh winter-."

"This winter has been harsh on us all." Sadness shaded the Abbot's voice.

Tuck quailed.

Practiced at finessing misdeeds, justifying goodness flummoxed him. He'd expected punishment for the brewery behind the chicken coop, or helping a brother slip out at night, but not this.

The Abbot stood to pronounce judgment, a dour crease on his brow.

"Brother Michael Tuck, for robbing Fountaindale, you are sentenced to 50 strikes of the lash, and immediate expulsion."

Tuck couldn't breathe. He'd lost everything, ruined by an act of charity.

"Father-." Tears leaked from Tuck's eyes.

"Michael, I will not hear your appeal." The Abbot held up a broad, flat hand. "You are no longer a coenobite of this Abbey. You are a gyrovague, a vagrant monk, of no interest to me. May Our Lady show you the mercy I cannot." The Abbot stared down at his desk, implacable.

The Sub-Prior approached from behind, righteous satisfaction ringing in every step.

"But Father-."

"Father Abbot has spoken." The Sub-Prior took a tight grip of Tuck's elbow. "Brother Michael, come with me."

Tuck wanted to throw off the Sub-Prior's grasping hand, but shame sucked the air from his lungs, leaving him too weak to resist.

In charge of rich holdings and a ready labour force, Abbots often ensured monthly returns before heavenly rewards. Fountaindale's Abbot was one of the honest few, a true spiritual Father. To be judged a thief by the man, curdled Tuck's soul.

The brethren gathered in witness on the far side of the whipping yard. Their habits hung ghostly in the cold slanting dusk, faces obscured under full cowls. Tuck wanted to call to his friends. Fear of none answering, deadened his tongue.

Disaster tore at Tuck's heart.

As one of Fountaindale's coenobites, Tuck enjoyed close-knit community, a strong roof over his head and at least two proper meals a day. Life at the Abbey had filled all his future.

Expelled, he had only his habit to protect him from the wicked winds of the world. Rootless and unwarranted, vagrant monks were notorious for living by wit first, and sanctity second. Tuck would be cursed out of every tower and town in Christendom.

Tuck's thoughts focused in immediate terror of the lash as a stout pair of brothers tied his hands to the time-worn whipping post.

Friar Tuck ~ Chapter 2

The three obligations of humankind:
To suffer; to change; to choose.
Triads of Bardism

Tuck regained consciousness deep into the night, slow with cold. Sawing blades of pain sculled his back when he lurched to his feet, his hands still bound. A scurrying wind flew freezing fingers over Tuck's bruised body, triggering bouts of violent shivering.

The high heavens held a scatter of winter-brittle stars, echoing the exile in his soul.

Then, a cowled monk stood beside him, tenderly untying Tuck's hands. Without word, the brother took off his cloak and wrapped Tuck firmly into its warmth. Tuck was formulating his thanks when the mystery monk shoved a heavy bag into his arms, and hustled him toward the Abbey's gate.

Tuck reeled through the portal in a fog of pain and confusion. Seeking direction, he looked back.

A trick of moonlight revealed the Abbot of Fountaindale's cobalt eyes under the mystery cowl. He gave Tuck a subtle smile, then shut the Abbey door.

Tuck thought of thumping and shouting until they let him return, but couldn't summon the will to raise his fist. He'd be banging 'til doomsday.

Holding back a wretched sob, Tuck reached into his bag to adjust its weight, and discovered a sack of wine. Grateful beyond measure, he swallowed three swift gulps. The bursts of blackberry and vanilla in his mouth were sure signs of the Abbot's private recolt.

Gathering all his courage, Tuck took two large paces, then stopped short. His first instinct had been to head for the closest village, but he would only be a burden there. Tuck cast about, seeking what lay in each direction of England's dreaming lands.

The thick December night reduced the surrounding fields to a series of swells, bleak as the North Sea. Beyond them lay only foreboding.

Nearby, a bare, black oak swept up from the earth. Its broad limbs spread wide, then high, splitting into scores of branches that ended invisibly in the wind-stripped sky. Tuck shuffled over a patch of crackling, frozen mud to lean against the tree's rippled trunk. His back ached terribly as he remembered his blind contentment at dinner, scant hours before.

Tuck shed a tear that iced his eyelash. The pain would pass if he could rest, but he needed to find shelter. The cold tugged at his toes like river fish.

Taking plentiful nips of the blessed wine to keep warm, Tuck tried to assemble some options. The only place he could think to find food and firewood was a forest. Tuck withdrew what turned out to be a venison pastry from his miraculous bag, and munched it in meditation.

Venerable Sherwood began a few miles to the east, but hunting there was strictly forbidden. The woodland belonged to the King, and Sheriff's patrols enforced the Royal privilege. Tuck wondered if he dare break the law on his first night as an outcast. His hands chilled to numbness as he stalled, but no other way forward presented itself.

Tuck prayed that a quiet tread would keep him safe, clasped his cloak and belted his bag.

The wind harangued him, homeless and forlorn, across the clodded dales, blustering through the twiggy hedgerows as it gusted. Tuck clamped down on his rattling teeth. If he stopped before he found cover, they'd find his corpse silver-shrouded in icy Advent dew.

Tuck squinted into the pre-dawn distance. Sherwood's sentinels beckoned with arms of pewter against the slated sky.

A drop in temperature muffled the stars as Tuck closed the final half-mile. With false-dawn turning the edges of the world to white, he clambered over the boundary-fence, then pioneered between the trees.

The ground melded into a crisp carpet of old leaves crunching underfoot. The falling rays of the rising sun revealed the forest in soft-edged shades of black and tan. Tuck trudged on, his eyes bright.

Already, the old stone Abbey with its solid certainties and comfortable community seemed no more real than Camelot. Seeking asylum in the arboreal arms of Sherwood, existence itself fundamentally changed.

Tuck followed any trail leading farther into the woodland, stopping at noon to catch his breath on a rise above a fast-flowing stream. The trees strode and gaited away on all sides, trunks and branches turning tones of old amber against the centuries-green humus. Tumbles of sunbeams breathed up steamy twists of dew from the damp earth, filling the air with a misty golden silence.

Tuck let his feet follow the stream-bank to a natural ford, casting a happy smile over the fat fish frolicking under the water.

Crossing the melodic shallows on three flat stones, an unusual firmness braced Tuck's soul. The reality of his destitute situation didn't shock him anymore. Where he'd come from was gone, and the future in heaven's hands. With a lift of his chin, he dedicated himself to the present.

Near mid-afternoon, Tuck paused to shake the last drops of wine from his sack. Here in the deepwood, trees spired from foundations broad as three good men, flying boughs as buttresses to Saxon-arched branches. Oak and elm grew so close, their roots twined before gnarling beneath the loam.

Framed by the sable pillars was a luminescent emptiness. It reminded Tuck of Lincoln Cathedral at Easter. His ordinary senses detected only air between the trees, but his spirit thrilled to the surge of the Sacred Breath.

With the splendour of Sherwood rising all around, freedom's exhilarating invitation buoyed Tuck's tiring legs. He tramped on with the sun swinging westward, low into streamy clouds of caramel-cream.

A pair of deer capered onto Tuck's path, sliding to a stiff-legged halt when they caught his scent. He marvelled at their thick winter coats, then the nobility in their huge, hazel eyes. They were the first living creatures Tuck had seen since leaving Fountaindale, and his heart opened in spontaneous friendship.

The lead deer, a young male, lowed a great call and stamped the ground. The second, a sleek female, nibbled at leaf-fall, glancing up as if in invitation to share. Tuck chuckled at the idea, startling the deer into bounding away.

Smiling as darkness crept over the cloud-knuckled sky, Tuck looked for somewhere to spend the night. Straight-standing maple spaced this spinney, but a thick copse of dogwood clustered nearby.

Tuck squeezed between the trunks to find a natural covert three paces wide. Animal traces indicated the place was occupied during summer, but there was nothing fresher. He shook off his cloak and put down his bag, already right at home.

Feeling lucky, and therefore blessed, he gave thanks to the Holy Mother for her care. Gathering a swift armful of kindling, Tuck also gave a grin for his capability.

The campfire's first flames warmed his toes magnificently.

Friar Tuck ~ Chapter 3

The three things that is Divine in all things:
What is most useful; what is most necessary;
what is most beautiful.
Triads of Bardism

Over the following days and weeks, Tuck's mind plunged into the liquid quietude that exists far from human doings.

Using skills his fingers remembered from boyhood, he set noose-traps for rabbit and wood-rat. To supplement his diet, he fished the frozen-edged streams of Sherwood for rainbow-tinted trout.

The season's mid-afternoon sundown saw Tuck collecting firewood as he ambled back to his covert. There, he'd built a nesty bender, complete with buried fire pit at its mouth.

During the long nights Tuck fed his fire, laughing and brooding over his life, sometimes singing to himself.

Living for survival, and finding abundance, transformed Tuck's faith. The routines of religion fell away. Instead, prayers leaped to his lips, and the Divine occupied all his thoughts. Advent passed with each breath tasting like sacrament within the peace-vaulting, winter-fresh forest.

Tuck's contemplative state shattered on an overcast, January afternoon. He was walking to keep warm, skin sodden under his soaked clothes, when a sound that wasn't natural to Sherwood tickled his ears. Tuck stopped, head tilted like a puzzled dog's.

Through the swaddling drapes of misting rain, the jingle of a horse's harness, more than one, and muted hoof beats, carried between the trees. The metallic jangle and hollow stump grew louder, seeming to come from everywhere at once.

Tuck disappeared into the nearby foliage of an evergreen yew, just as a company of Sheriff's Foresters came into view.

The Foresters warded the King's hunting rights like guards in a tree-barred jail. Ancient laws empowered them to penalise, torture and kill without need for evidence, court or judge. Even the innocent avoided their patrols at all costs. They'd find a gyrovague guilty of everything.

Tuck gasped to see them in the backwoods. They usually stayed on the outskirts of Sherwood, as poachers are easiest to catch on their way home.

Wrapped in greased skins against the drizzle, five Foresters trotted their horses along a sunken chase, cradling heavy crossbows.

Tuck hunkered onto his heels as they ambled by, ten yards in front, the blunt heads of the horses hanging parallel to the ground. Three horses passed Tuck's position without catching his scent, but the fourth reared as if stung. The beast brayed out a sharp staccato, then lunged straight towards Tuck's hiding place.

Tuck was dashing away before the rider shouted his surprise.

Tense twanging syncopated the thwack of a foot-long crossbow-bolt slapping into the side of a nearby chestnut. Tuck lifted his robes, picked up his knees, and ran like Holiness was a foot race.

The Foresters spurred their horses up the side of the chase, and onto Tuck's tail. The riders crouched low over their saddles, eyes fixed on Tuck's retreating form. They couldn't fire crossbows from this hunting half-gallop, but were catching up fast.

Tuck jinked clumps of tangling brake, keeping a vital few yards ahead of his pursuers. Splashing across a sudden stream, he spun right to hare up a boulder covered slope. Close behind, the horses surged over the water, sending black divots waking into the air.

Halfway up the slope, scrambling past a boulder the size of a house, Tuck was too shocked to scream when something snagged his ankle. He crashed to the ground, then was hoisted backward under the boulder. A pair of bony hands clamped over Tuck's mouth, and a bearded face glared into his frantic eyes.

The sounds of pursuit rushed around the hidden hollow, the horses' hooves hammering overhead, then faded as the Foresters crested the hill, and tally-hoo'ed away.

The hermit peeled his hands off Tuck's mouth, but scowled at him to keep quiet. Tuck lay motionless as the hermit listened intently for a long time, his face rigid.

"*You're* the idiot who lights a fire every night, aren't you?" The hermit finally whispered, unmistakably furious.

Tuck's jaw dropped open.

"You're the one who brought them this way. *Idiot.* I've been here three years, and the Foresters haven't ever come this close. *You* arrive, and they follow quick as pestilence to a corpse!"

Tuck made to reply, but the hermit bristled his chest-long beard in perfect outrage.

"Shut *up*. You don't have the right to speak. *Idiot.*" The hermit poked his head above the rim of the hollow, listened again to the silent woodland, then slithered his skinny form free.

Tuck stayed still a moment more, confounded, then followed, squeezing through the gap on undignified heaves of his elbows.

"Sure, now you'll need a mug of wine to steady your idiot nerves, won't you?" The hermit stood proudly, as if the boulder-strewn slope were his ancestral hall.

Tuck pulled bits of twigs out of his hair, catching up to events. Giddy, but finally given a chance to speak, he determined not to be out-done.

"Not only idiots' nerves are soothed by wine," Tuck pitched his voice low and friendly, "but only a fool offers what he does not have."

"*Ah,*" the hermit replied with a sneaky grin, "but *only* an idiot looks a gift-horse in the mouth, and insults it to boot."

Tuck's wit deserted him: "You mean you *do* have wine?"

The hermit's ringing laughter sounded off the boulders as he traipsed down the slope, waving for Tuck to come along.

The hermit's long strides took the men into Sherwood's deepest recesses, dusky and moist, dotted with stag-headed oak, and wolds of split-trunk hazel.

"In summer, it really is very pleasant here." The hermit waved an airy hand, as if presenting an unseasonal garden. "And over there," he motioned definitively to his left, "we have the wine cellar."

Tuck didn't know what to make of this outlandish figure. The hermit appeared more or less out of his wits, but he was a bit too sharp *with* his wit to be completely mad.

The hermit took Tuck to a grove of tall ash. The trees encircled an innocent-looking pile of rotted leaves and wind-fallen branches.

The hermit reached a long arm beneath, and pulled out a swollen wine sack.

"What did I tell you?" He guffawed at Tuck's stupefied expression. "You're an idiot."

The first slug of wine curled Tuck's tongue tight, pickled his tonsils, and scorched down his throat to set his belly ablaze.

"Now, that's forest wine if I ever tasted the like!" Tuck sputtered. "What d'ye make it from? Nettles?"

The hermit looked at Tuck as if he was beyond salvation.

"If forest wine could be sold for what this cost, we'd all be rich." The hermit poured a long arch of ink-red ichor cleanly into his mouth. *"This,* my forest friend of unfortunate taste, is the finest French mountain wine money can buy." The hermit smacked his lips. *"C'est un premier cru du Château Mas, qui enrobe Le Pic Saint Loup comme un poème."*

Tuck eyed the hermit dubiously at the sudden French, but didn't refuse the offered wine. The second abrasive mouthful quenched better than the first. By the third, Tuck thoroughly enjoyed the spicy attack on his senses.

Handing back the sack, wanting to laugh in relief at their escape, Tuck was overtaken by deep affection for his rescuer.

The hermit took the wine with an indulgent squint of his eyes as he caught Tuck's mood.

"Aye, well," the hermit rattled his beard, "since the All Merciful looks after idiots and drunks, you can be thankful for your double blessing."

Tuck laughed from deep inside, mainly at himself, but also for the forgotten pleasure of sympathetic company. A tear or two threatened to escape alongside his chuckles as their merriment faded away.

The trees stretched up to divide the eastern sky into sets of early stars. The architectural perfection of static-lightning limbs and straight-laced trunks stitched Heaven to Earth.

"I was serious about your camp." The hermit stood, gesturing Tuck to follow. "The Foresters only care about those who hunt the deer ... Or, who are too stupid to be ignored. You can stay with me tonight, but will have to find your own way tomorrow."

Tuck accompanied the hermit with a spring in his step, wondering how the forest air could be so dark, when the ground glowed beneath his feet.

The hermit led Tuck past a snagging thicket and into a countryman's snug. In a trice he'd lit a fat beeswax candle, its flame dancing blue and white. Tuck took another long pull of wine as the hermit busied about.

Sturdy log walls sloped at a low angle toward the rear. A packed-earth roof nestled above, complete with pale roots dangling around the neat smoke-hole in its centre.

Flourishing each dish, the hermit presented a late dinner of finely-roasted wood-pigeon and wild onions, finished by shrivelled summer fruit, tart and delicious.

"How long have you been a guest of Sherwood?" The hermit's curiously formal tone caused Tuck's ears to twitch.

"Ah, not more than two months."

"Hm. So, you won't have seen the Lords and Ladies yet?"

Tuck wondered if his drunken ears had deceived him.

"Lords and Ladies? In Sherwood?"

"Yes." The hermit jutted out his beard. "The Wild Hunt? The Tuatha Dé Danann? You know, *The Little People?"* The hermit dropped into a raw-edged whisper. "Aye, an' have ye never shuddered at the sound of the full moon carried on the wrong wind?"

Tuck gave a solemn shake of his head.

"Nor seen the colours at midnight?"

Tuck shook his head again, superstition tickling up his spine.

"You *must have* come across the hilltop mushroom rings."

"Yes, I have seen those!"

"Idiot. The mushrooms are *playthings."* The hermit's eyes bulged fearsomely above the roiling coils of his beard.

Unnerved by his host's swerves of emotion, Tuck looked for the right answer.

"Err, do you mean fairies?"

The hermit convulsed as if gripped by a piercing torment.

"Sweet *Mother.* Don't *ever* call them that. Especially not *here."* The hermit swiped the wine sack away. "Idiot! Don't you know they *hate* being called that?"

Tuck stared open mouthed, then remembered his manners. His guestly duty required he accept his host's eccentricities as graciously as he received his vittals.

"Ah, no. I didn't know. I'm sorry." Tuck applied his most polite tone. "So, when did they last pay you a visit?"

The hermit went beetroot with rage, then flung the wine sack back at Tuck.

"*I'm* not the idiot here. You would do well to remember that." The hermit's eyes sank into the shadows above his craggy nose. "*If* you manage to survive a few more months ... You'll be alone in the weald ... Late in the waxing ... And with abomination gnashing at your very soul, *you will witness the Tuatha Dé Danann for yourself!* Call 'em what you want then, but sure, it'll be respectful."

Harrumphing at the general impertinence of the world, the hermit lay down in disgruntled silence. Robbed of words, Tuck decided to settle to sleep as well. He quietly laughed off the hermit's strange stories, but his dreams were phantasmagoric.

Tuck awoke with a start soon after dawn, somehow already knowing he was alone. The hermit had left the half-full wine sack as a gift, and Tuck picked it up with a soft smile. Remembering his eldritch dreams with a shudder as he made his way out of the snug, Tuck resolved not to drink too much of the stuff in any one go.

His good humour morphed to dismay on reaching his homely covert.

The hermit had been right. The Foresters had smashed a horse-sized hole through the encircling dogwood branches. Tuck found his bender trampled to the floor, the fire pit filled with faeces. He shed a desolate tear. While not much more than a convenient arrangement of sticks, the covert had been his first shelter away from Fountaindale.

Gathering his few belongings, Tuck sent a prayer for mercy into the cloud-cluttered January skies, and headed for the heart-woods.

Friar Tuck ~ Chapter 4

The three things that bring victory over evil:
Knowledge; love; power.
Triads of Bardism

Winter loped through February to savage March with unseasonable cold, tightening belts everywhere.

From his hides within the densest copses of crab-apple and hagberry, Tuck watched the weather force many new-comers into Sherwood. Most came quietly creeping for food and firewood. A few carried a hunger only booty and bloodshed could satisfy.

On a day like any other, pacing embowered acres, marvelling at Creation's bounty, Tuck received his first personal lesson in evil.

A man's corpse swayed from the bough of a sessile oak, his stretched neck strangled in a noose of old rope. The smell told Tuck the corpse was fresh.

The victim had been a peasant, youngish and strong. He'd been stabbed several times, hung, and disembowelled. This barbaric killing wasn't the work of Foresters, but outlaws, monsters in the guise of men.

Moved to pity, Tuck recited the Rites for the Dead. The liturgy shone in his memory, the words and gestures natural extensions of his prayerful consciousness.

Furious anguish battered at Tuck's soul, as if the victim's ghost had stayed to rage the glade. Tuck continued his prayers, bringing every effort to bear in wishing the trapped spirit to Peace and Saint Peter.

Compassion opened Tuck's wisdom-mind, launching his benediction heavenwards like a catapult.

Tuck's normal consciousness resumed as a shock of wind rocked his body. Gripped with awe, he traced the wind radiating outward through the nearby canopies, then a serenity that exists beyond objects settled into the spinney.

Tuck had no blade to cut the body down, so searched out a sharp stone. He came across delicate, parallel lines drawn in the forest floor instead.

Tuck's belly clenched. They were the heel-marks of a woman being dragged away.

Tuck got to his feet, thinking deeply, then set off at a trot.

He knew just what to do.

Tuck flowed like a fox, staying on track whilst looking out for a mature rowan. Soon enough, Sherwood provided a stave of straight hardwood. He hefted the three-foot shillelagh, thinking of strong Saint Patrick overthrowing pagan idols.

Tuck padded fast through the forest, a few yards to the left of the tracks. His ears, fully alert, picked up sounds that barely vibrated the air. His eyes, always moving, analyzed every nuance of stillness, colour and shade.

Inside a clearing between two stands of ash, he came across the remains of a campsite. The fire had been wastefully large, with smoking, half-burned boughs scattered all about. No woodsmen had inhabited this place. A colourful scrap of cloth caught in a thorny shrub marked the start of a fresh set of drag-lines.

Tuck scouted out this trail, praying for the Holy Mother to protect the kidnapped Jane.

He heard the snide laughter of the outlaws before he saw them.

"S'Blood and hatchets! That last bastard had more guts in him than a donkey." Hacking cackles lifted across the woodland.

Tuck glided into place behind a broad maple. His cassock had matured from woollen gray to woodland brown, blending perfectly into the finely tinted bark.

"His wife's stubborn as one too."

More laughter, venal and vile, jarred in Tuck's ears.

"How much is left of the loot, you filthy dogs?" This loud voice was coarse with corruption.

"Plenty to last until the hangman takes ye!"

Raucous uproar and angry shouts greeted this last remark.

Tuck eased around the outlaws, catching brief glimpses of their camp through the ground-sweeping branches of an elder yew.

Three simian men in sheepskin jerkins sat on a fallen tree, passing a wine sack. Weapons lay within easy reach of them all. Beyond the group crouched the kidnapped Jane, bound hand and foot, face bruised green and purple.

Tuck's anger focused into determination. He marked the place in his mind, took a few noiseless paces away, then ran as fast as he could. He headed for the widest trail he knew in the area, the best spot to find a handy company of Foresters.

After five hours of useless waiting, the sun passed beyond the horizon. A chilling darkness coursed among the trees, drowning Tuck's hopes.

Dismay and resolution fought in his heart.

He'd planned to use the Foresters against the outlaws. It had seemed so straightforward and glorious. Now, he was on his own, and driven to act, sure the Jane would be dead before sunrise.

Tuck didn't feel glorious at all as he tacked his way back through a coppice of bare birch.

The outlaws were drunk, arguing furiously around an oversized fire. One held a strong knife, the second a heavily notched longsword, the last a snaggle-bladed axe.

The fire blazed eight feet into the air, lighting up a large, jagged-edged area around the camp.

Hot yellow reflected in the outlaws' eyes as they swore and swaggered with the currents of their argument.

"*The devil take you!*" The knife-man swung his weapon toward the axe-man. "I can see in your face you've the French disease. If you think I'm going after you, this'll right your boozy brain."

"*What?*" Longsword's coarse tones slurred every word. "Poisoned sprogs. I'll have no Neapolitan bone-ache infecting my pleasures! It'll be me first, by the very bastard bawd who sired me."

"I'll have you know that these are the marks of proud canary, not the pestilent clap. My axe is clean enough anyhow, clean enough to split your craven heads!"

The Jane, still tightly bound, sobbed in despair.

"When there's throats to be slit, or guts to be cut, I find you behind me." Longsword sliced his blade about. "When there's cleaving to be done, d'ye believe I'll stand astern?"

The trio heaved around the fire, mocking and feuding. For all of their threats, none looked inclined to actually act on their words.

Instead, the outlaws kicked burning logs at each other, prancing and weaving in the scattering light. From the way they yelped admiration or derision at the flaming footballs, it was obviously a favourite game.

Tuck edged closer, discarding desperate plans as soon as they formed.

"I want the woman." The knife-man sheathed his weapon in hard emphasis.

The outlaws focused on their captive.

"A'right my pretties." Longsword's voice grated in debauchery. "We agree we love gold as much as women, eh?"

His companions howled their approval.

"Then, let the gold decide who gets the female first."

The outlaws drew a hemp bag from a shadowed nook. Wrapped in the bag was a smooth wooden chest. All three snatched at the chest, causing it to drop to the ground. Its lid cracked open, spilling a few silver coins.

The outlaws each chased one down, then held it up to the others in challenge.

The Jane's sobbing sounded loudly in the menacing quietude.

"Best of three! Nearest to the wench, wins." Longsword pitched his glittering coin through the air to land six inches from the Jane's feet.

"By the devil, you've got a game." Axe-man threw his coin too far, landing it in a clump of bushes.

Knife-man laughed nastily, and lobbed his coin a neat two inches from their victim.

"That round's mine." He called with depraved glee.

The outlaws cursed each other mightily as they retrieved their coins, then began the next round.

A bony hand clamped over Tuck's mouth from behind, smothering his involuntary cry.

"Shut *up*." A fierce but familiar voice hissed into his ear. "Idiot."

The hermit's bushy face appeared in the corner of Tuck's eye, smiling.

Tuck ripped the hermit's hand off his mouth, but kept hold of it to drag him a few yards away.

"What in the name of all that's Holy are you doing here?" Tuck demanded in an impassioned whisper.

"That's my wine they're drunk on." The hermit pointed an indignant finger towards the outlaws. "Thieving bastards. What are you doing here?"

"Rescuing the damsel." Tuck replied, his mind whirling, but still trying to formulate a credible plan.

"Hm. An idiot for a rescuer. Some hope she's got." The hermit snorted.

"Don't you start-."

"Well, all I'm saying is, she doesn't look very rescued to me." The hermit waved his hands to calm Tuck down, then leaned in close. "I mean, were you planning to cut her free *with that stick?*"

Tuck lost all rationality and swung an enraged punch.

The hermit dodged nimbly, but almost fell over a treacherously low bush.

Avoiding the obstacle with three impossibly unbalanced steps, he failed to get his gravity in order, and ended up on his hands and knees, clearly visible in the firelight.

The outlaws stopped their game, weapons rising faster than birds breaking cover.

Tuck only had a moment to think, then came charging in.

He aimed his shillelagh straight for the hermit's raised rump, and gave it a resounding whack.

The hermit yowled, grasped a buttock in each hand, and sped off around the leaping flames. Tuck set after him, swiping at the hermit's head with his shillelagh.

The outlaws exploded with laughter, too drunk to wonder why the forest had provided this unexpected entertainment.

On his next circuit of the fire, without breaking stride, the hermit slipped a slim knife out of nowhere and jabbed it into the neck of the axe-man.

Tuck, only a pace behind, whipped his shillelagh smartly across the heads of the other two.

Knife-man collapsed at a satisfying crack on the crown, but Longsword parried the knockout blow, smacking Tuck's shillelagh out of his hands

The hermit dodged in, but had to tumble away as Longsword hacked his blade towards his face. He was swaying from the drink and breathing heavily, but seething with danger.

The hermit stayed at a distance, his stiletto no match for the outlaw's three foot length of hardened steel.

Tuck had nothing at all to hand.

"*Spayed mongrels,*" Longsword snarled, standing above his cash chest, "you'll have my soul before my money, an' fight the devil first for either!"

The hermit glanced at Tuck, then at the Jane.

She'd slumped, trying to blank everything out, certain her life would soon meet a ruinous end.

Tuck nodded, and the hermit shuffled sideways toward her.

Longsword focused his aggression on Tuck, jigging nervously in front of him.

"*Come on* you scum diver." Longsword shifted in readiness. "I'll spit your skull through your ears, an' boil your brains in beer!"

The hermit reached the Jane, and began to cut at her bonds.

Tuck knew precisely what heroism called for.

"*Heathen son of blasted ancestry!*" His voice swelled with sermonic power. "You're nothing but a drunken, cut-rate, cut-purse."

"By all the weeping widows murder ever made!" Longsword bellowed. "I'll have your fat buttocks fried for breakfast chops."

"Ignorant idolater! I'll squash your unrepentant head in my hands like a rotten turnip." Tuck demonstrated a convincing crush.

"Swinish Friar! I'll carve off your feeble arms, an' force feed 'em to you. Fingers first!"

"Prurient sinner, the rod of justice is poised *to spank you down.*"

The hermit helped the Jane stand free, and they edged out of the firelight.

"Prurient?" Longsword repeated in confusion, caught between defending his coins and his kidnap.

Tuck seized the moment, and ran.

Friar Tuck ~ Chapter 5

The three things ever increasing:
Light; understanding; soul.
Triads of Bardism

The sun slunk edgewise through March of 1200, loafing and languid over the winter-bound land.

The hermit visited Tuck at irregular intervals, bringing aromatic wine and tall stories. The pair traipsed amongst the trees, sharing company and Sherwood's secret places.

Lying on their backs to properly digest a roast rabbit supper one evening, the men admired the miraculous band of the Milky Way emerging from the pitch-blue of the doming sky.

"Tuck, d'you know enough of your stars to see it'll soon be Festival of the Trees?"

The hermit never failed to astonish. Frequent eruptions of French pointed to Norman ancestry, and his manners to nobility, but he had education in every sphere. Without his hot-to-trot humours, the man's learning would have been the wonder of Britain.

As it was, Tuck regretfully considered him to be a classic case of *malus libri*.

"No," Tuck smiled up at the heavens, "which of those beauties told you that?"

"Idiot. The stars don't speak, they *show*." The hermit encompassed half the Universe with an expansive hand. "I've already explained, it's *trees* that talk, and water that sings. You just don't know how to *listen*." The hermit fell silent, caught in another of his infuriations.

"What's the Festival of the Trees, hermit?" Tuck asked after a respectful pause.

"Hrrrmph. *Lady Day* is all it is." The hermit's beard bloomed with indignation. "The day when Sherwood is invaded by every man Jack and maid Jane for five crow's miles *is all it is.*" The hermit waved his hands in exaggerated dismissal. "Oh yes, nothing for you to be concerned about, my belly-brained brother."

Tuck sat up.

He was used to the insults, but the news hit him like a shock of cold water.

"What do you mean, *invaded*? People aren't allowed to come into Sherwood! What are you talking about? This better not be another of your nonsense stories. Tell me quick."

"*Alban Eilir* is how the Irish call it." The Gaelic rolled lovingly on the hermit's tongue. "It is the time when day and night are equal, reaching toward light. The Festival of the Trees is dedicated to the dawn, and sacred to the Great Mother. Its action is planting, its meaning is rebirth, its symbol is-."

"*Fine*, but what's that got to do with the forest being open?"

"Sherwood isn't ever *open*, idiot. It belongs to the King. Don't you even know that? But, even Kings bow to tradition. The people feel when they must come to the woods, and man's law would be fool to stop them. During the Festival of the Trees, the Foresters find themselves ... Occupied elsewhere." The hermit ruminated, pulling on the end of his beard. "The old folk believed the land sometimes needs help to break into spring. It certainly couldn't hurt this year."

"But why come into the forest?"

"The common folk come to revel what they call Lady Day, but there are some who know *what lies behind*. The earth will quicken under spiral dances, the trees awaken to bell and drum, and the ardour of renewal kindled by vigorous, open-air, wide-ranging, love-making!"

"WHAT?"

The hermit chortled with pleasure. "*Don't you worry,* my chaste friend. If those festive Janes come a-frightening you with their batting eyes and cooing lips, you can always use your other staff on them!" The hermit collapsed into hysterics, slapping his thigh.

"Maids don't frighten me, hermit." Tuck replied, full of affronted dignity. "I simply have an honest man's respect for the gentle sex, something which you lack, amongst other things. And I choose to remain faithful to chastity, I am ... No longer ... Bound to it."

The hermit's head snapped round. "Oh ho, so why d'you wear those monkish robes, then? *To keep warm?*"

Tuck's habit was undeniably warm, but his attachment to it wasn't entirely practical. The robe was the only thing that gave him identity in the primeval timberland.

Without it, he felt he'd disappear.

"I'm sorry, brother," the hermit continued, seeing Tuck's abashed expression, "I was only ribbing. Let me tell you about the most important events of festival, for we are sure to witness them." The thrill in the hermit's voice drew Tuck out of his maudlin mood. "Yes, my friend of fine sensibilities, for you and I will go to the revels, and see the dances!"

A whirling excitement passed into Tuck's blood, overcoming the fear of change throbbing his body.

"Gamwell's the place for us." The hermit clapped Tuck on the back. "Best ale south of Hadrian's wall, *and* musicians who can actually play. Even we forest dwellers have a holiday, and the Festival of the Trees is it."

Tuck grinned.

He'd almost forgotten that outside Sherwood's immutable realm lived a whole wide world.

"It sounds just grand, but you'll have to do something about your whiskers, if you don't want to scare the young'uns."

"*What d'you mean?*" The hermit's eyes flared with protective instinct. "I'll have you know my beard was once the admiration of all Paree."

"I don't doubt it. Those Frenchies are infected with even stranger notions than you are." Tuck shook his head in despair. "But if you don't do something, it'll be the laughing stock of Gamwell an' all!"

The hermit harrumphed his displeasure through Tuck's chuckles, but couldn't stay distempered for long.

The air was warmer than it had been for months, the trees content at the end of their long sleep, the stars large above.

"For the first time in your life, you may be right, monk." The hermit sounded mystified. "Never mind the young'uns. *I wasn't joking about the Janes.*"

Come festival day, Tuck woke to a majestic clarity of thought. Smooth air braced his face like angels gliding on clouds. Lark-song lifted a light-yellow sun into the freedom-filled, sapphire skies.

He met the hermit at a certain oak, and late morning saw them strolling the easy road to Gamwell. Beyond a last stand of beech, Sherwood opened to ploughed fields, rippling bay and beige under a parhelion sun.

Tuck stepped from the cover of the forest with all the shame of a gyrovague heavy on his soul. He imagined the villagers greeting him with scorn, and his courage withered. The confidence he'd established by surviving the winter cracked in an instant. In misery, Tuck recited prayers to calm his mind and ask for support.

To his supreme astonishment, a torrential rush of strength unfolded through his faith, surging into every corner of his troubled soul.

During his months in the wilderness, Tuck had prayed, often and ardent. Living the way of the wood had also planted the touch of true peace in his heart.

Sincere devotion from a peaceful heart was the method given for Divine communication, and in this moment, actuated by practice, Tuck marvelled at the secrets of Scripture.

The hermit nodded as if he could read Tuck's thoughts, then whistled out the first bars of a merry jig. The rhythm carried a playful sway that illumined the open countryside to perfection.

Tuck joined a tentative counter-point to the theme. The hermit skipped three paces, and with a *hip hup ho* was at dancing speed.

Tuck caught up on the next refrain, and by the first return the two men were soaring in improvised, inspired symphony. The melody was speckled with birdsong, its harmony delved from true friendship, the twirling tune o'er-joyed at the prospects of the day.

The happy pair arrived on the festive village green amidst a clutch of capering children and welcoming offers of free ale.

After a fine time sharing lunch at a long table of holidaying Gamwellians, the hermit led Tuck around the green, past where man-Jacks and maid-Janes were preparing for the evening's events.

Separated by a wattle partition, both camps were in mayhem. Bells and drums crashed in random clamour, and a barrage of bawdy remarks turned the air blue. Gales of laughter greeted any particularly licentious one-liners.

Tuck noted with consternation that most of the best ones were coming from the female side of the divide.

Cackling festively, the hermit led them to an ancient alder, loftily balanced at the side of the sun-sparkled village pond.

Tuck sipped absently at his ale, floating in a bubble of contentment, until an impossible vision made him choke.

Snorting beer out of his nose, Tuck elbowed the hermit squarely in the ribs.

"What the blazes d'you do that for?" The hermit yelped, trying not to spill his jug at the jolt.

"A Bishop." Tuck replied faintly.

Striding across the greensward, stole flapping and mitre bobbing, came the tall Pontifical, dispensing benediction with relaxed undulations of his arm.

An appreciative crowd of locals had gathered closely by the time the Bishop halted his progress, as if by chance, in front of the brew-stall.

"Many Blessings on you all!" The Bishop declared in a curious accent, casting his eyes about with abundant goodwill.

Suddenly he stooped as if struck, one hand rising awkwardly to catch his mitre before it fell, the other flung out in disbelief.

"But what do I see before me? *Sinners at the very Gates of Hell*, on Gamwell Green!" The Bishop jabbed a disbelieving finger toward a table near the rear of the stall.

It held a goodly assortment of monks, fair shocked out of their cups at the sudden attention.

"*No doubt* the fires of damnation will burn *doubly hot* at the devil's delight in your *degenerate* souls." The Bishop straightened in wrath. "Come forth churchmen! Bishop Guignol, of Holy Roma, calls to you."

The villagers, awed by the Bishop's professional melodrama, yelled out encouragements and less savoury remarks to the hesitating monks.

The Pontifical turned to his audience. "Oh, you faithful ones. *Witness* the array of sin set before us, unashamed on this God given day!"

The crowd, pleased to be on the side of the angels, swiftly jeered the unfortunate monks from their table to face Bishop Guignol.

"Oh, *renunciates*," Guignol lamented, "you are feasting on a fast day."

The crowd hissed and booed.

"In public sight of all these good people." Guignol motioned to the crowd in dismay.

The villagers responded with cat-calls for their offended sanctity.

"At a pagan celebration!" This capstone sent Guignol into a flurry of defensive cross-signing, the guilty churchmen wailing onto their knees, and the crowd into a rambunctious frenzy.

"Not only this, my scroyly sinners," Guignol's accent wavered unevenly as he raised his voice, "not only this, but behold!" The Bishop plucked a well-presented Jane out of the crowd. *"Is not temptation all around you?"*

The crowd roared its agreement, the maiden curtseying to one and all with a corky smile.

"See the unrestrained innocence of this maiden! *She is not for you to look at.* Her legs, no doubt given their divine shape from hours of prayerful kneeling, are not to be lusted over!"

The Jane raised her skirts to the height of her thighs for a moment, and put on a pious expression. The crowd's temperature broke boiling point, producing two more lovely lasses in support of the Bishop's sermon.

The monks fixed their eyes despairingly to the ground, stammering Latin avowals and plausible denials.

The Bishop admired the worthiness of his new recruits, cast his eyes meaningfully over the penitent churchmen, then picked up a jug and took a long draft.

"By the heavens!" The Bishop exploded. *"This is strong ale."*

The crowd yelled and applauded, hats flying into the air.

"Strong ale! The peril of all holy men... ."

Guignol's audience jeered once more at the cringing churchmen.

"And, I am told, *even the holy women* of this Blessed Isle."

Loud confirmations came from the crowd, Gamwell's beauties taking up jugs and draining them in suffrage.

The entire village was now gathered in high spirits around the extraordinary Italian Bishop.

"Oh, but we are a *merciful* Church." Guignol folded his hands on his finely embroidered tunicle. "We must, I say, *we must*, find a way for our brothers to redeem their sins."

The crowd yelled colourful suggestions for atonements, provoking pitiful laments from the monks.

Guignol paced about, nodding in appreciation, then raised his arms for silence.

"Good people, we can forgive the breaking of a fast day, can we not?"

The Gamwellians grumbled their reluctant agreement.

"We can even overlook their fleshly lustings."

The crowd agreed more easily, their own consciences appeased at this mercy.

"But drunkenness at a pagan celebration! *Wickedness such as this requires swift penance.*"

The monks bowed their heads, hopes raised and dashed.

"*On your feet*, my lost lambkins. I have the solution that will *save your souls*. To discharge your sin, we will sing Ave Maria 25 times, in unison."

The monks leapt up, more than ready to sing their way to salvation.

Then the Bishop finished his proclamation: "And to prove *sanctity* stronger than *insobriety*, any sinner not in perfect time will sink a jug, and *start again!*"

Half the choir had succumbed groundward to the ale before Guignol whipped off his mitre, and a riot of laughter boomed from the crowd.

The hermit, who had gone to take a closer look, hurried back to Tuck with a delighted grin and two more brimming jugs.

"It's the mad-cap Earl!"

"Wh-who?" Tuck stuttered, anxious he may yet get tangled up in these Churchly events.

"Robert Loxley. He's famous in every ale house for ten crow's miles. I should have known it was him." The hermit gave a great laugh. "Didn't I tell you Gamwell was the place to be?"

"You mean he was *impersonating a Bishop?*"

"Yes! Idiot. Drink your ale, maybe it'll grow you brains as well as guts. He did a damn fine job of it too, I must say." The hermit sighed in happy satisfaction. "Robert Loxley. *What a scoundrel.*"

Friar Tuck ~ Chapter 6

The three concords that uphold all things:
Love and justice; truth and imagination; Divinity and occurrence.
Triads of Bardism

The festival afternoon lengthened time over Gamwell green, mellowing the villagers into happy pods of neighbour, kith and kin.

As the friendly sun eased behind the thatched-roof cottages, Tuck left the hermit spouting preposterous European tales to a group of enthralled Janes.

Tuck traced his unsteady way back across the expectant fields to the green-fringed forest. He touched the first shoots of an awakening hazel with a delicate hand as he passed into the evening bronzed tranquillity of the weald.

Tuck halted in wonder at the nearby groves.

Everywhere, woven wreaths of early budding twigs and bright flowers hung from lower branches. Red and green ribbons, the colours of life, wrapped the trees in fancy extravagance.

He meandered through the festivallized forest, the antics of the Jacks and Janes echoing all around. The cries of wild-hearted youth sounded naturally, inducing not invading.

The last of the sunshine swam in diffuse sparkles amongst the trees, like diamant grains suspended in the hallowed air.

Tuck followed his own paths into the deepwood, and with sunset flinging burnt orange spires across the sky, dipped into a hollow for a well-earned rest. Laying down, he smiled, wondering what trouble the hermit would have got himself into by the end of the night.

Tuck woke to the darkness of late night. Nothing moved, and there was no sound, yet something had disturbed his sleep.

He sat up, then an odd discomfort made him stand.

Tuck climbed noiselessly out of the hollow, unafraid, but cautious. To his left grew a tight spinney of crackwillow, so Tuck crept to his right, into a widely spaced holt of oak.

No abnormal resonances came to his senses, yet the hairs on his arms were stiff with warning.

A dash of purple light flittered in the corner of his eye.

Tuck lunged with remarkable speed into tree-shadow, his presence less discernable than a cat's.

A yellow flash repeated twice to his left. Spinning round, he caught another gleam of bright green to his right.

Tuck hurtled through the holt, the ground rising under his feet, and dived into stand of trusty yew. He cursed himself as an idiot for not having his shillelagh.

His curses turned to fearful prayer when three tall figures slid past, heading for the top of the hillock. A blistering instant of golden light silhouetted a dozen more elongated folk already assembled at the apex.

Swift as swallows, glowing orbs of indigo-blue, lime-green and radiant-red flipped over the hillock.

Tuck's guts turned to water.

The lights had revealed disjointed dancers, moving waist-high and widdershins around the tall ones on the crown of the hill.

Tuck took two paces backward, then careered helter-skelter away downhill.

A massive black dog with blazing malachite eyes bounded over the crest of the hill. The beast dipped it's head, long tongue lolling to taste the air, then unleashed a hideous howl.

Tuck sprinted for his immortal soul.

The eldritch animal caught up in a blink.

Tuck choked on a cloud of sulphurous vapours as the dog pounded in, then its full weight slammed into his legs. Tuck was smacked off his feet, flew three screaming yards, and smashed into a young holly.

He ended up on his side, winded, stunned, blinking back tears of mortal terror.

"You're out late, priest." A glacial voice stated from a pace behind.

Every fear in Tuck's life clutched simultaneously at his heart.

The sharp pressure of a sword point pressed into his ribs.

"Why would a priest come in secret to the Gable of Si'ir?" The questioner's sleet-bitter breath was monstrous. "To overturn, burn, and shatter? Is *that* why you came, priest?"

"N-n-no." Tuck's body convulsed with primal horror. "P-please I, I was asleep ... I woke up and, and came the wrong way, and-."

"Ah. The wrong way." Each word came encased in ice, biting at Tuck's ears. "*Poor* priest. Did no-one tell you there are many wrong ways to find? And only one right way to lose? *Never return.*"

Tuck fled wherever his feet took him, not stopping until he'd reached the hermit's hide.

"So, you finally met them." The hermit took Tuck's shaking body in his arms, and hugged him tight. "Bet you didn't call 'em fairies to their faces, eh?"

Tuck felt the hermit smile, and was grateful his friend could find humour in the situation.

"Who are they? *What* are they?"

"Ah. Many men have asked that question, monk. And most have been lost forever to Elf-land." The hermit lit a few candles, and hunted out a half-full wine sack. "In Ireland, the seanachies taught three truths about the Elves: They come from Sidhe; they fear no evil; they know no good. The only other thing known is that it's wise to stay away from them."

"I can understand why." Tuck murmured.

They sat silent for a long time, sharing the welcome warmth of the wine.

"That's the other thing hermit!" Tuck exclaimed, remembering. "They were cold, *terribly cold*. Every word was like a snowstorm blowing in my ear."

"Ah, yes, that phenomenon has entered popular myth as Jack Frost. They really gave you a good scare, didn't they?"

"Hermit, I'm still terrified." Tuck held out his trembling hands as evidence. "I don't know if I can even stay in Sherwood after this. What happens if they come back? *What happens if I meet them again?* I don't think I can deal with it. It's, it's *ungodly*." Tuck's voice cracked. "I'm a gyrovague, *an idiot*. I can just about deal with Foresters and outlaws, but I tell you I'm not brave enough for this. I'm just not."

"Steady, monk. Steady! Hold yourself together." The hermit's eyes turned mysterious. "We're not completely defenceless against the Wild Hunt."

"I am! I'm completely defenceless. You don't know what it was like-."

"Be quiet. Idiot. I do know, damn well, what it was like. I saw them once myself."

"*What?*" Tuck's surprise caught his spiralling hysteria. "When?"

"When I was a student in the Old Country. I was almost a big an idiot as you, but thought myself very clever. I'd read Tam Lin's ballad of his time in Sidhe, and was curious beyond caution." The hermit shook his beard, not smiling. "I went to a bleak place in the west, where standing stones moulder amongst the peat bogs. There I waited two full months, living off seagulls. Quite tasty if you cook 'em right, your Irish seagull. Not stringy like the English ones at all. On the dark of the moon of the third month, I witnessed the Tuatha Dé Danann perform their rites amongst the stones."

"Did they catch you?"

"Oh no, like I said, I wasn't quite as stupid as you. I'd done my research. Always do your research, Tuck. And have another drink whilst I fetch something, it'll do you good."

The hermit came back hours later, holding a tightly wrapped package in his hands.

"I borrowed this from the library at Mur Ollavan, and, um, somehow, never got round to returning it."

The hermit revealed a simple wooden cross the length of his hand.

"Now then, I think it went like this... ." The hermit fiddled with the cross until it opened into two pieces.

Inside the cross-box lay a miniature dagger, its blade wrought from iridescent-blue metal. Its handle looked to be pure gold, with three emeralds glowing on the crosspiece.

"What's that?" Tuck was enchanted.

"This, monk, is a Star Dagger. It's one of only five ever forged. The gold and jewels are worth a hefty sum, as you can imagine, but the metal of the blade is beyond price." The hermit lifted the dagger, holding it between thumb and forefinger.

"The Irish call it mithril-silver, but it's not really silver at all, as you can see from the colour. They say the metal fell from the sky, and was smith'd by Wayland himself. It's a very dangerous weapon."

If not for the shattering events of the night, Tuck would have laughed.

The dagger spanned four inches, its blade not much more than a big needle.

"And *no*, you don't stab people with it." The hermit passed the dagger across to Tuck with a reverent expression. "It's what the ignorant would call a magical blade. Why don't you wave it near that iron cooking pot?"

Tuck glanced up to see if the hermit was joking, but he looked completely serious.

When Tuck brought the dagger within six feet of the pot, it leapt out of his hand, snapped across the gap, and stuck to the side with a musical clang.

He let out a yell and jumped backward in fright.

The hermit gave one of his most satisfied cackles. "Heh. Idiot. *See?* And that's just its most easily observed power. Good, eh?"

The hermit reached across and, with some difficulty, pried the dagger off the pot.

"But how does it help against the elves?"

"Ah." The hermit replaced the Star Dagger in the cross-box. "I can't explain how it works, I just know that it does work. If you're already in hiding, holding it makes you invisible to them. That's how I wasn't caught. Tam Lin also noted that if you get really close to an elf with a Star Dagger, they suffer incredible torment. *But,* I wouldn't try that if I were you."

"I won't." Replied Tuck with dread certainty. "I'm never going near one of them again."

"Here, wear it round your neck." The hermit thrust the cross-box into Tuck's hands.

"But I can't take this-."

"Listen monk, if it makes you feel safe, then you should keep it. And this way, if the librarian ever catches up with me, I can honestly tell him I don't have it."

Friar Tuck ~ Chapter 7

The three ways to know a person:
By their discourse; by their conduct; by their companions.
Triads of Bardism

Early summer of the year 1200 saw life erupting from every bole and hole in Sherwood. The days turned balmy, but the nights held nips of ice well into June.

On Midsummer's day, Tuck was sending up a grateful prayer for his morning's catch of trout when the stream carried a faint tread to his ears.

In a blink, he'd gathered his fishing gear, and leapt into the nearest bush.

A tawny headed huntsman approached from upstream, dressed in worn, finely-fitted leathers. He carried his longbow nocked, and moved gracefully amongst the trees.

Tuck narrowed his eyes, recognizing something familiar about the figure.

The huntsman almost passed Tuck's hiding place, but stopped as if on a whim, and sat down. He pulled off his cockily-cut hat, and ran a slow hand over his crop of thick brown hair. His emerald-green eyes were set like sparks in his youthful face.

Tuck watched with growing ill-humour as the huntsman unstrung his bow, pulled off his boots and lay back with a contented sigh.

Tuck relaxed, thinking he'd be asleep in seconds, but after a moment's silence the intruder reeled out a selection of ribald songs at the top of his voice. His singing was well trained, and truly rude, obviously that of a noble.

Tuck's legs had long gone into cramp from their awkward crouch when the huntsman sat back up.

"I think you've been squatting in that bush long enough, don't you, Friar?" The huntsman spoke facing the rushing stream, causing Tuck to hesitate.

"Come, come, I won't bite you. Or even beat you. And definitely won't eat you!" The huntsman laughed merrily, glancing sidelong at Tuck's hiding place. "You hide well, but late, my friend. Do come out. I'm hungry, and something tells me you and the good Lord have done well with the fish of Sherwood this fine morning."

Tuck emerged, scowling in his unfriendliest manner. A lunch guest had not been in his plan for the day, particularly one given to lewd music.

That his painful wait in the bushes had been a farce was also not best pleasing.

"Perhaps if you gave more thought to the good Lord, and less to corky couplets; He would bless your bow with better aim, and you could catch your own lunch."

"*Oh ho.*" The huntsman sprang to his feet with a happy smile, and placed his hands on his hips. "A forest Friar with a hot welcome! Let me see ... The Lord blesses those who practice, and those who pray. That's why I've no need of my bow today."

Tuck wasn't going to be seduced by the huntsman's playful grin, or outdone by his rhymes.

"This forest Friar is blessed with fish for two, it's true. But however I choose to share God's bounty, I'll wager it won't be with you."

"A sporting Friar to boot!" The huntsman laughed outrageously. "A wager you say? On a Holy day? Very well, my well fed Friarly friend - be warned, I'll play you to the *very* end. What had you in mind?"

The huntsman's mockery again struck a familiar chord, but Tuck couldn't spare the brainpower to think of why. He hadn't meant to offer a wager, but had no intention of backing down.

This ramping rapscallion needed a helping of humble pie.

"Alright." Tuck pointed to the tinkling waters. "I'll wager I can walk across that stream without getting my feet wet."

The huntsman gave the stream a lively examination.

The emerald current rushed by at some speed, four yards across and a good two feet deep, with no bridge in sight.

"Unless you're more holy than you look," the huntsman turned to Tuck with an inquisitive eye, "that's the stupidest wager I've ever heard of. You're on!"

"Fine. Come down to the side of the stream, so you have a good view of your trouncing, knave." Tuck kept his expression firm.

The huntsman strutted jauntily to the edge of the waters, and gave Tuck a low bow, fluttering out his hand in courtly invitation.

Tuck leapt onto the huntsman's back before he had time to straighten. In a trice, he'd hooked his arm round the huntsman's neck, and locked his ankles around his waist.

"By Our Lady!" The huntsman wheeled and teetered like a drunken pony.

Tuck gave the scoundrel a mighty whack on the rump. "Forward, knave! *On, on, on!* Carry me across like a good Samaritan!"

Tuck's forceful smack drove the huntsman to take a large pace directly into the stream.

Another cracking slap on the arse, and the man was traversing like a stubborn donkey. The water frothed around his knees as he struggled, turning turquoise before it splashed back into its element.

Six long paces and a brace of buttock-boiling blows later saw Tuck dismounting onto dry land. He settled his robe with pointed dignity, then broke into gales of laughter.

The huntsman clutched his lumbars with one hand, the other rubbing his throat as he panted for breath.

"Why, huntsman, where's your smile? We have crossed by walking, and yet my feet are dry."

"Well, my weighty brother," the huntsman stood upright with a groan, "it seems the old adage is true: see fox or Friar 'ere noon, and bad luck is your'n the whole day through."

Tuck was still laughing when the huntsman pressed the tip of his dagger amiably into his gut.

"Now, brother, I left my boots on yonder bank, and am overcome with tiredness. Perhaps you would be kind enough to carry me back?" The huntsman prodded Tuck encouragingly with his knife, grinning.

Tuck gave the huntsman a long, hard look, then turned, ready.

The huntsman bounded onto Tuck's back with an excited whoop, and they set off.

Relying on his dagger to discipline his steed, and revelling in the swift reversal, the huntsman didn't think keep a proper grip.

Halfway across, Tuck planted his feet in the sandy stream-bed and gave a great heave.

The huntsman flipped into the air and flopped into the water with a terrific splash.

He leapt up almost instantly, water cascading from all over, but Tuck was already on the far bank, laughing again.

"Pray for wits, not lunch, knave. You will be better served!"

The huntsman waded through the water against the pull of his wet leathers, distinctly not laughing.

Tuck retreated a pace, and picked up his shillelagh.

The huntsman squelched up the bank, hefting his dagger in his left hand.

"Friar, I'll laugh alongside any man-Jack who beats my wits, but you've assaulted my dignity, and for that I'll be having redress."

"Your dagger against my shillelagh? Isn't humiliation enough? Don't make me hurt you as well." Tuck was only partly bluffing.

The longer reach of Tuck's weapon gave him a clear advantage.

"Oh, I won't be using my dagger." The huntsman replied casually as he approached a nearby willow. "But this!" He grasped a thumb thick branch, and snapped it with a kick.

Cleaning the pole with a few swift flicks of his knife, the huntsman now held a serviceable seven foot staff.

Tuck knew his advantage was lost, but the temptation to knock some manners into this jackanapes was just too much. He brought up his shillelagh with a look his Abbot would have been proud of.

The huntsman raced forward, the tip of his staff dancing in deceptive arcs, and launched a fast one-two.

Tuck knocked the first attack downwards, and caught the second cross-wise, but the fresh willow bent around the shillelagh to connect painfully with his ear.

Tuck wrenched his head away, then advanced to return a good clout, but the huntsman batted him back with thrusting jabs and snapping side swipes. Tuck's arms were thoroughly bruised under the assault, but protected him well enough.

The huntsman made a deceptive move and jabbed again, this time catching Tuck square on the nose.

Tuck yelled in pain and snatched at the end of the huntsman's staff with his left hand, miraculously catching hold of it.

Using the staff for leverage, Tuck span and delivered a solid reverse thump to the huntsman's ribs.

The huntsman yelped an oath, then yanked his staff free and launched a series of strikes onto Tuck's head that ended with a snap as the willow staff broke in two.

The battering counter-attack had sent Tuck reeling, but now he emerged rampaging. The huntsman had not expected his staff to break, and careened away in dismay.

In the fury of melee he hadn't noticed his back was to the brook.

Tuck grinned wickedly as he stepped up and gave the knave a strategic poke in the solar plexus. The huntsman doubled over, lurched awkwardly, lost his footing on the muddy bank, and dunked backward into the water.

Tuck had already grabbed his things and was making his escape when the huntsman emerged from his second ducking, laughing merrily.

Tuck paused a few yards away, ready to fly, but curious despite himself.

"Most excellent fighting Friar!" The huntsman's smile lit up the entire scene. "I concede your valiant victory. But all this unhabitual bathing has given me an *unnatural* hunger. Hold a while. Have mercy. Have lunch! You've impressed me, and I'm in need of good counsel."

Tuck was suspicious of another trick, but the huntsman held out his hands to show they were empty.

The flattery was also rare as relics.

"I know you from somewhere." Tuck commented as the pair licked their fingers clean of stone-baked trout.

"Oh damn, we haven't been presented, have we?"

"Er, no."

"That's alright then. I never remember anyone I've been presented to." The huntsman gave a broad smile. "May I offer my broken willow to your service, Friar? My name is Robert Loxley."

"The mad-cap Earl!"

"Well, some folk call me that ... But rarely to my face, it must be said." Loxley gave Tuck an injured look that twisted instantly into amusement. "Your honesty is refreshing good brother, almost as refreshing as that stream."

Both men laughed, and Tuck wondered at the warm feeling in his chest.

Loxley had a way about him that was enthralling. He acted like a younger brother, foolish, rakish and rude, but was so easy in his smile that mischief was just part of the package. Even fighting with him was fun.

Robert regarded Tuck expectantly for several seconds before he realized what was wanted.

"Ah. Um. I am, er, Tuck." He hunched sheepishly. "And I'm not a Friar. I'm a … A, a vagrant monk." It was the first time Tuck had admitted his status to anyone, and it stuck in his throat. Shame coloured his cheeks and his heart pulled in sorrow.

"Friar is what we called the French brothers on Crusade." Loxley responded, glancing with understanding into Tuck's vulnerable eyes. "And you're unlike any gyrovague I've ever met."

Tuck felt a piece of his heart lift, and fell in love with Robert Loxley at the same moment.

"You said you needed counsel, Robert." Tuck was overcome with emotion, so kept his voice lofty.

Loxley leapt to his feet and began pacing.

"*Yes*. I'm in trouble, Tuck. Big, big trouble. I need help, help of all kinds. I just don't know what I need help to do. To live as Loxley, and die as a traitor? Or die as Loxley, and live as a coward?"

"Well. You'd better tell me all about it." Tuck sat, powerfully present, creating a space in which the Earl could speak his mind.

Friar Tuck ~ Chapter 8

The three parts of every action:
Thought; word; deed.
Triads of Bardism

King Richard, Lionheart of England, sailed for the Third Crusade limned in the blue light of dawn, March 15th, 1190. Richard led a formidable army, sanctified to fight, like the very angels, for gilded Jerusalem.

The ranks of armoured knight and practiced archer, tenacious piker and sly sapper felt doubly determined as a salty Nor'easter projected their disciplined flotilla across the Channel.

Amongst the pennanted knights eager for glory rode 16 year old Robert Loxley. Under his family colours of forest-green and mellow-gold, the young knight's muscles throbbed with a puissance to beard the very devil.

On the enchanted isle of Cyprus, the Lionheart's men joined armies raised from across Europe to answer the call of Crusade. These oft-time enemies advanced to battle led by a scintillating squabble of Emperors, Kings and Dukes.

For his part, Salah al-Din Yusuf idn Ayyub, victor of ten thousand battles, and current Sultan of Jerusalem, made ready to again rebut invasion from the north.

From the first exhilarating charge, Young Loxley was noted as a precocious talent. Where the fighting was fiercest, there his green and gold would fly rampant.

Havering in the spitting chaos of carnage's acres, men instinctively rallied to lucky Loxley's shining blazon. They knew this knight would fight with them all the way to Heaven or the Holy Land.

Within weeks, Robert had earned his dreamed-of place amongst England's finest.

Advancing through the wastelands of outer Egypt, this muscular exertion against the foes of God settled into dull slaughter.

Living cheek by jowl with 9,000 sweating British soldiers plagued by digestive disorders and the pox bled life of all its mystery. Robert's boyhood faith in his Saviour drained into the barren sands not long after.

After a year of campaigning, Young Loxley was so keen to see an end to war, he threw himself headlong into every conflict. He dealt death as fast as he could swing his sword, only that Jerusalem, and peace, be the length of one corpse closer.

The Crusaders enjoyed a run of victories as Saladin fought town to town on a retreating front. The Sultan was buying time to gather an overwhelming force from the four corners of his vast territory.

Crusader victories brought treasure looted from sacred tombs and ancient palaces, some of it extraordinary. However, every bag of gold weighed on the uneasy European alliance.

Trust amongst the leadership was quickly lashed away by avarice, old rivalries surfacing like snakes seething from a hole. Their common enemy held the alliance together in Holy Land, but all swore scores would be settled back in Europe.

Breaking through a breach in the bricked defences of a nameless desert stronghold, Robert Loxley leapt off his horse to engage the fleeing enemy. The soldiers skirmished their way forward, driven by their officers, hunger and lust.

Robert broke down a promising looking door with the help of two burly pikemen. The door splintered with a sharp crack, and the invaders piled into a jewellery-maker's workshop.

Young Loxley held his heavy-edged longsword extended downwards a foot in front of his armoured face. With his fingers clenched tight under the pommel at the height of his forehead, the lethal steel was ready to slice in any direction. His left hand, tucked in at waist height, held a shorter, thicker, blade for stabbing forward or parrying sideways.

The dust of their forced entrance cleared in an instant, and the pikemen unsheathed their short swords. The Welsh steel blades, first cousin in design to the efficient Roman gladius, swung towards the old man crouching agilely in front of a woman and two children on the opposite side of the room. The enemy's dark eyes flared keenly above his scimitar, curving in the dim lamplight.

Professionally quick, the defence was overcome, objectives liberated, and the next target acquired.

With no faith left to fight for, Robert stayed on Crusade for the love of his King, but May 1192 saw him turn back for England. He'd been wounded so many times in both body and soul, he could no longer usefully ride a horse into battle. Bone-weary, the knight took seven months to return to the dulcet environs of Castle Loxley.

Pernicious events, and evil news, had travelled far faster.

Months earlier, King Richard's younger brother Prince John had been illegitimately acclaimed by the people of London, and seized the throne. After a brief parley, William Longchamps, Richard's Chief Justiciar, had retired to his Bishopric at Ely, unwilling to invoke the horrors of civil war.

Hearing of John's actions, King Richard had cut a deal with Saladin, and torn away from the Holy Land. Needing to cross treacherous Europe with all haste, the Lionheart had put on a disguise, and made a bold dash for home with a minimal escort.

Leopold V of Austria, a man Richard had quarrelled with many times on Crusade, had discovered the King dressed as a pilgrim, having dinner near Vienna. Leopold imprisoned Richard, then delivered him in chains to The Holy Roman Emperor, Henry IV.

Emperor Henry, an old adversary, imprisoned the Lionheart in impregnable Trifels Castle. As well as humiliating England, Emperor Henry was chancing for a windfall to fund his Italian wars. The Emperor set the King's ransom at a record 150,000 marks.

The breathtaking price for the King's release had reached England's shores only days before Robert. With the full resources of the English crown it would take many months to amass the money. With the Exchequer locked in the tight fist of Heir-Presumptive John, it would take years.

His final illusions shattered, Robert swore to stay away from politics forever.

The knight healed in body, but could never again wear full plate armour. Robbed of his landed right to fight steel-wrapt on horse, Robert took up the weapons of his people, the long bow and long staff.

Unwilling to leave the bucolic peace of his family seat, Robert Loxley spent his days practicing archery on the common paddock nearby. The long whisper and solid thump of his ash war-arrows marked out the passage of time as it waned over his scars.

In the evenings, Young Loxley took to visiting the inns and pubs of his father's shires. He soon won the love of the drinking halls, always arriving laden with fresh game and ribald wit.

Old Earl Loxley was often in London, fighting for the family interest against the hostile intrigues of John's interim court. Being a close friend of Longchamps, and vocal lobbyist for Richard's ransom, Loxley was a natural target for the Heir-Presumptive's ire.

Although the Earl's pragmatism protected him from direct threat, only cold cunning kept his privileges intact. Many of Loxley's allies at court were not so fortunate.

It took three years for Richard's ransom to be raised, but finally the cream of loyal England gathered at Dover one rain-swept day in 1194, to greet the ship of Royal liberty.

From their first glimpse of their returned King, the loyalists knew Merry England was yesterday's dream. Richard, gaunt and embittered by his long incarceration, was a sight to turn the patriotic heart to dust. A lacklustre Lionheart entered London a few days later, cursing the rain that had followed him all the way from Dover's quelling cliffs.

Within months, fed up in every sense, Richard declared John official heir to the throne, and decamped for sunshine and sieges in France.

Thus the status quo was established until the Lionheart's death five years later, at the hands of a vengeful child, on April 6th 1199.

On May 27th, England's Royal Court was riven and recast in the tempest of King John's coronation.

Friar Tuck ~ Chapter 9

Three things whose greed will never be satisfied:
A sea; a cemetery; a king.
Triads of Bardism

"Sweet, weeping, *Saviour.*" His Majesty, King John I of England, stood unsteadily from his coronation table.

Albion's trusty crown sat askew on the monarch's thin brow, shining dully in the red firelight.

The papers freshly delivered by spy from Paris fell from his hand in disgust.

"We are not crowned a day, and Our bubuckle'd brother's imposthume issue Arthur of Brittany has allied with that puffed-up, gawdy giglet, Philip of France, against Us!" John swept his ruthless gaze around the suddenly quiet celebrants. "By the *very rotten* back teeth of Hades! The devil's deboshed dam littered those malapert mongrels on a nayward night in hell. *Vacuous, vain, pissant, puking pretenders.*" His Majesty was drunk beyond all reason, his anger swift catching up. "All Our gentleness towards France is *banished.*" John raised his fists in inconsolate rage. "We will *destroy* these distemperate, derogate, diseased, doltish doxies. Maul them and pike them!" The King gesticulated with psychotic realism. "Stab them and scathe them. Burn, be-mete, ballow and beat, bodkin, bow and bilbo *until they beg to basimecu!*" John's voice vaulted across the polished granite of the state room in London's Tower. "Here is Our answer and gage:

England will reave French skies black by bodkin arrows, and grind those Galliards gasting into the *gangrenous jaws* of gaping Gehenna."

The elder Barons cast doubtful looks at each other as John Plantagenet stomped about the mouth of the double-hearthed fireplace, ranting and swearing in equal measure.

The rest of the noble assembly shuffled their booted feet anxiously under the wassail table.

"We'll need money." John was stalled by this thought, and swung his flushed face towards his vassals. "And *lots* of ships." The flames roared high behind the King of England as he strode forward to slam his hands onto the table top. "Filthy, phantasmic, painted offspring of the devil's overscutch'd arse!"

Late the following morning, the King was huddled irascibly in his library, attended by two of his best men. Neither were Barons, or even knights, but valued Crown servants nevertheless.

The first was John's Treasurer, Andrew Thompson, widely rumoured to be a black magician. The second was James Focsal, a ship-builder so skilled they said saltwater tided his heart.

"My most gracious Liege, in answer to Your Kingdom's need, may I present the Exchequer's findings?" A persistent tick tugged Thompson's mouth into a half-smile every few seconds.

John gave his Royal assent with a terse nod.

"The Barons are annually, feudally, bound to supply knights to Your service. 27% of said knights are poorly equipped, and badly trained. The Exchequer concludes that England would be better served by gold than these half-knights."

"How much better served?"

"To determine the benefits of such a progress, the Exchequer suggests a cost for supplying a knight per annum. Multiply said figure by the number of knights provided per Baron, per annum. Followingly, convert, for parity, 30% of the resultant production into a cash-indexed sum. Such modernization will yield significant benefits, *and*, continental mercenaries would off-set the military shortfall on a favourably seasonal basis."

"Now, *that's* proper fiscal planning." John muttered, doing a few quick calculations of his own.

"Additionally, my Liege, Exchequer experts will confidently predict an average Baron can expect an opportunity saving per knight, per acre, per year, year on year, after the first two years."

"Hell's gleaming teeth! You're a genius, Thompson. Have you got a name for this entirely sensible, what did you call it? *Modernization?*"

"My Liege, the Exchequer proposes it be called 'scutage', in honour of the absent knight's blazons."

"Make it so, Thompson! We wish *scutage* introduced to Our Northern Lords before Midsummer. If fruitful, We will extend it across the rest of Our fecund land."

The Treasurer hurried off to draw up the paperwork.

"Master Focsal, your report?"

"Good news, Your most Royal Highness, good news." James Focsal took two ornately embossed books from a nearby shelf, and unrolled the large parchment he'd been cradling with both arms.

The King looked on dubiously as his treasured, paired edition of Monmouth's *Historia Regum Britanniae* was employed for paperweights.

Focsal bent excitedly over the technical plans drawn across the face of the parchment, attracting John's interest with a wave of his hand.

"Your Majesty, with Your approval of this proposal for Portsmouth, we will build four strong fighting galleys every year. In addition, many of the innovations can be replicated in Your other ports. At the far end of up-scaling, England could float 40 new ships in a single year."

King John's gaze glittered with dreams of power.

"We'll learn France to respect Us more than she ever did Our father! Master Focsal, begin at once. We decree Portsmouth home to the new Royal Navy. If your shipwrights succeed, you will be appointed Admiral."

Treasurer Thompson presented scutage to the Court under King John's avuncular gaze soon after Beltane.

The protest was all too predictably led by the Earl of Loxley.

"My Liege, I beg your leave. Provision of money is not the same as provision of knights. What are the sons of our landed families to do if they cannot enter the knighthood? This *scutage* does not sit well with our traditions."

"Earl Loxley, are you saying you cannot *modernize* your fief to Our Kingdom's service?" The Court fell silent at the King's venomous placidity. "Times have changed, Loxley. Mark well that England must change with them." The King's features stiffened with sudden fury. "Damn your insolent bones! The undernourished, half-clad, bumpkin-knights Loxley has provided of late are exactly why We have implemented this measure."

"Loxley's knights were good enough for King Richard, *and your father before him!*" The Earl shot back, offended beyond reason.

Without seeming to move, the other courtiers shifted away.

Too late, driven to carelessness by his scandalized passions, Old Loxley realized he'd been baited into an unwinnable fight.

King John glared down from his throne while Loxley considered his position.

"Your will is law, my Liege." The Old Earl hung his head low.

One dismissive flick of the King's colubrine eyes was enough to drive Loxley from the room.

King John swore in his soul that the example he made of this upstart Earl would ensure the smooth adoption of scutage by all.

Unable to do much more than mooch pessimistically around his fief awaiting the King's displeasure, a pleurisy took hold of the Old Earl.

Six months later, in November 1199, 25 year old Robert Loxley watched disconsolate as his father's body was entombed in the castle chapel, his coat of arms carved deep into the sealing stone.

Friar Tuck ~ Chapter 10

The three beauties of any land:
The granary; the smithy; the school.
Triads of Bardism

Earl Robert of Loxley scanned his mother's resigned features.

"But mother, all our fortune was put to Richard's ransom. We simply can't afford to pay cash instead of knights to that bastard John." Robert crushed the warrant for the King's scutage in his fist. "It'll drive Loxley into starvation." The young Earl's eyes condensed to dark pits. "By Our Blessed Lady, the castle's almost falling down from lack of repair, the people are buckling under this infernal winter, and our threadbare knights are already the wonder of London!"

"My son, what you say is true." Lady Loxley held up a pacifying hand. "It is also true that you cannot oppose the will of the King. Your father knew this, and protected our privileges. You must seek to do the same." Lady Loxley's features creased with love. "However, as you know, with no husband, I have no desire to remain in worldly affairs. Robert, by dedicating myself to the nunnery at Rubygill, I entrust Loxley and your life, alongside mine, to the will of God." She reached across to lightly grip her son's wrist, her eyes merry and wry. "You will do as you see fit. You are a fine heir, and well beloved. Remember to serve your people before yourself, and come what may, you will be happy." Lady Loxley stepped into the waiting carriage, and turned a final time to her only surviving child, her expression sharpening. "And find yourself a wife. As your father always meant to say: *An Earl needs his Dame.* Our Lady bless you, my son."

From the day his mother joined the Sisterhood, Robert Loxley's old life was knocked on its bucolic arse as surely as if he'd been stuck by a thunderbolt.

January of 1200 found Earl Robert receiving a never-ending series of peasants and tenants, each looking for succour from hardship. February was full of tough decisions.

Come the ice-wimpled ides of March, Robert experienced his first headache. Every step he took as Earl impacted in several directions, often wrong-footing his original intentions.

It wasn't just Loxley that was suffering. Decades of Plantagenet scheming and fruitless war had bled England's reserves dry. The unusually long winter had delayed the rural cycle of renewal, and things were at breaking point.

Worrying over his finances late into the dismal drizzles of April, Earl Robert was haunted by the sound of barrels scraping empty. Farm stock had been whittled down to rag and bone, and wild game was as rare as had never been seen. With hunger prowling the shires, a host of other problems were brewing.

Nearby, the King's under-hunted forest of Sherwood was tempting many peasants to poach. Stealing from the King's larder was ordinarily a hanging offence, but not knowing what else to do, Earl Loxley turned a blind eye.

He just hoped everyone else would too.

More trouble stirred among the surplus scions of Loxley. Instead of boistering about London learning how to be knights, the best men of the shires chafed uselessly under their fathers' roofs. Already, the knightly economy of squires, ostlers and blacksmiths had collapsed under this mortal blow to their trade.

Most were leaving for richer domains, and Robert couldn't blame them.

Despite everything, with hard work and a little luck, he had confidence his fief would make it through, were it not for scutage. The tax had to be paid in cash, and in advance.

Without yet having shorn and traded this year's wool, the Estate would be crippled. Additionally, Loxley reinvested most of its revenue in the locality, providing gains across the board. Surrendering the wool-gold to the King in scutage would breed only poverty.

Waking from a subdued May Day feast, with disaster looming on every side, Robert sat at his father's desk and wrote a thinly veiled refusal of scutage. Glad to be taking decisive action, he saddled for London to personally petition the King's mercy.

Two days later, His Majesty King John was notified of young Earl Loxley's arrival and request for audience.

Remembering the trouble Old Loxley had caused him, John decided to show the boy who was boss, right from the start.

All day long, the Royal Court hubbubed with patronage, politicking and persuasion. Ambassadors, courtiers and petitioners gained their audiences, but Loxley was left waiting in outer chambers of London's Tower.

Late in the afternoon, Robert's impatience boiled over, and he pressured one of his father's old friends to present him.

"Ah *yes*, Earl Robert of Loxley." The King's voice was pitched low, as if holding a private conversation, although they were in open Court.

"Your Majesty." Robert bowed elegantly, as he'd learned to do on Crusade.

"I trust the inheritance of verdant Loxley suits you well?"

A barb behind the question pricked at Robert's pride.

The Earl gave his King a hard glance.

"My Liege, Loxley is a fine fief, and as loyal to Your crown as it was to Richard's before you."

King John nodded slightly, his expression unmoving as Robert looked him in the eye.

Frustrated by his long wait, and emboldened by the King's attention, Loxley blurted out what was on his mind.

"My Liege, I come in all honesty, to beg this year's scutage be waived."

A tide of silence swept through the Court.

King John almost smiled, and Loxley's instinct twitched with danger.

"Robert Loxley!" King John's voice lashed like a rope snapping. "*You dare* present yourself before your King for the first time, and defy your Country's need in the same breath?"

"My Liege, I-."

"Silence." The King hissed, then turned to his nearest courtier. "Loxley's son has learned *nothing* from his fencing father." Smirking, John refocused on Robert. "Are you telling Us, Loxley, that you are incapable of inheriting to the benefit of England?"

Robert couldn't think of an answer that wouldn't damn him, and his face turned very hot.

"Loxley, Loxley... ." King John shook his head in disappointment.

Robert dared to interrupt, rage and fear of failing his fief making him reckless.

"My Liege, I speak for the people, not myself. The Church inflates its tithes as much as the Crown raises its taxes, and those at the bottom suffer every increase doubly. Your Majesty, *I beg you*, hear the plea of England's shires." Sincerity shone though Robert's voice, stirring the hearts of the Court.

King John's features dissolved into fury.

"*Insolent Earl*, Ours is the very voice of England, and England *demands*." The King almost rose from the throne as he yelled down on his vassal. "Bring Us Our scutage by Midsummer boy, or forfeit your inheritance!"

Robert stumbled from the court, shocked, ashamed and deeply, deeply, angry.

Thundering across the drawbridge of Castle Loxley, he was filled with the awful anticipation of having to report his failure.

Jumping from his saddle, Robert realized that there was no-one to report his failure to, and experienced a moment's relief.

Then he felt horribly alone.

Robert had a month to find the tax money. He knew he would do better at the end of the rainbow than in Loxley's strapped shires.

Friar Tuck ~ Chapter 11

The three roots of evil:
Covetousness; falsehood; arrogance.
Triads of Bardism

From the western tower of Castle Loxley, Robert watched Midsummer's dawn enamel the horizon with white gold before the stars faded into cloud-framed vistas of the freshest blues.

The Earl had been unable to sleep during the short night.

By selling everything not nailed down, forward bargaining the wool, and calling in every debt and favour, Robert had amassed close to the amount needed to pay the King. Another month, two at most, and he was sure he could gather the rest. Loxley only hoped the King would wait.

At midday, Robert was in the castle courtyard organizing the evening's deer roast, when a boy ran over the drawbridge.

"Lord Loxley! My Lord!" The lad slid to a halt. "There's riders come from London."

Across the courtyard the people stopped what they were doing.

"What's that, boy?" Robert called out, coming forward.

"Master Bardolph of the Blue Boar sent me, my Lord. My name's Much, and there's riders come from London, my Lord, aimed for Loxley."

Robert raced up the steep stairs to the battlements.

The summer lands of Loxley patch-worked away in sunlit shades of honey and moss. Leafy Sherwood, three crow's miles to the East, glowed supermarine. A few figures moved across the landscape, dimmed by distance, but none on horseback.

Then, at the far end of the Nottingham road, a cloud of way-dust drifted into the air.

Doom clenched Loxley's heart.

Turning back to the courtyard below, Robert realized everyone was looking up at him.

"Good people," Robert flashed his most brilliant smile. "That deer won't roast himself! And give Much a mug of ale, by Our Lady, before he thinks we've no manners."

A few yeoman laughed, and the people returned to their tasks, but a dark mood ran in undercurrent.

Robert was arranging prizes for the Midsummer games when a drumming of hoof beats swelled through the castle's gateway.

A troop of twenty riders crescendoed into the courtyard, scattering people to the sides as the horses snorted and pawed at their sudden stop.

Robert stood in the centre of the yard, mightily displeased. The troop's unannounced entrance could only mean they came as sanctioned enemies.

A large, arrogant man spurred his charger a few paces from the throng.

"Earl Loxley?"

Robert gave a curt nod.

"My Lord, I am Sir Guy of Gisburne. I carry the Treasurer's greetings, and this letter." Gisburne swung down, then offered a folded parchment in a gloved hand.

He was dressed in London finery, his loose, embroidered shirt a contrast to Loxley's leather jerkin. The severe cut to the courtier's black hair, however, hinted there was more to Gisburne than foppery.

Robert broke the Treasurer's seal, already knowing what he would find inside. Gisburne waited impatiently for Robert to read the missive, his troop shuffling their horses behind.

The people of Loxley stayed in the corners of the courtyard, transfixed by events.

"My Lord," Gisburne stated loudly, "Treasurer Thompson requires an immediate answer."

Loxley bit back his anger. "Come with me."

Gisburne nodded for two of his men to attend, and followed Robert into the castle.

In the seneschal's office, the Earl opened the chest that contained Loxley's scutage.

"Almost all of it is here. You can tell Thompson that Loxley will send the rest to London before Lammas."

Gisburne eyed the chest, then signalled to his men.

The men-at-arms slammed the lid, slid the bolt, and hefted it back to the courtyard.

"Ah, my Lord." Gisburne's tone was gratingly courteous. "Perhaps I should have said. The Treasurer specified an immediate *and full* answer."

Robert's blood thundered. The scutage chest had been filled with pain, coin after coin leeched from Loxley's already aching arteries.

Gisburne was treating it like a Christmas stocking, nothing more than a few dry apples and a lump of butter.

Robert knew that this money, enough to feed his peasants for half a year, wouldn't last a day in London.

He had a vision of King John frittering the cash on frivolity, and his temper broke.

"My Lord? Your answer? A second chest perhaps?" Gisburne didn't hide his sneer.

Loxley gave the courtier a venomous glare, and stormed back to the courtyard, pulling his father's longsword off the wall as he passed.

The men-at-arms were binding the scutage chest securely to the back of a pack horse.

Every Jack and Jane had guessed what it contained, and were glowering at the legalized robbery.

The horses stamped and whinnied, snapping at each other as the riders stayed bunched protectively together.

The already tense atmosphere turned explosive when Robert re-appeared in high dudgeon.

"YOU THERE." Loxley's voice was battlefield loud. "*Unbind that chest!*"

The men-at-arms looked at each other, then complied.

"Leave that chest exactly where it is." Gisburne stepped past Robert, his tone promising brutality for disobedience.

"Gisburne, tell your men to return my money. *And Thompson that I'll see him in hell.*"

"Loxley, this is the King's business, and you are tax deficient. Don't tell me you're as foolish as gossip suggests." Gisburne goaded, placing his hand on the pommel of his sword.

"Gisburne, if we heeded to gossip, the Treasurer is a sorcerer, the King a changeling and your mother a huswife."

"*Duel*, mad-cap, for your insolence!" Gisburne unsheathed his sabre in a singing sweep.

Robert found his sword in his hand, its tip testing out the air between him and his opponent.

Gisburne smashed downwards onto Robert's blade with all his force. The ringing tightness clanging from the swords ignited Loxley's most violent instincts.

Robert whipped his weapon through a wide arc, sword-edges rasping, and shoved Gisburne in the face.

The courtier was driven backward three paces, cursing as he brought his blade back into play.

The duellists exchanged a few rapid bouts, taking the other's measure, then separated, ready to fight in earnest.

Gisburne settled behind his glittering wand of sharpened steel, side on, comfortable and calm.

A chill entered Robert's gut as he raised his pommel to his forehead, then swung the sword point downwards. He hadn't fought sword to sword since Crusade, and his memories ran with blood.

Gisburne flung himself into a series of ferocious strikes. Multi-coloured sparks blazed from the ringing, clashing, flashing blades.

The shrieks of skittering metal shook Robert's arm, the sensation sending his mind sliding back to the Holy Land.

Gisburne was a natural swordsman, strong, accurate and fast. His refined technique was more than a match for Robert's war-sired skills.

Where Loxley had trained for the chaos of multiple opponents and the protection of armour, Gisburne was a nimble fencer, skewering and evading with diabolic concentration.

Loxley was already fighting for his life.

Gisburne's unrelenting assault left no room for attack, screeching his sabre all over Loxley's last-split-second parries.

Robert did his best to rally with a few heavy chops, but ghosts sapped at his puissance.

Gisburne slid to the side, and launched a combination of cruel cuts.

Unable to defend in time, sensing he was fatally out-matched, Robert was forced back one step. Then he had to immediately give two more to avoid a homicidal overhead hack, and knew he was lost.

Gisburne suddenly reversed his grip and swatted Loxley's last riposte aside.

Robert's guard was sundered, everything from head to hip unprotected. He watched, helpless, as Gisburne re-orientated, winding up for a deadly lunge.

"STOP." A commanding voice cried above the combat.

Cursing through locked teeth, Gisburne touched his sword-tip to the ground.

Robert's sword arm was flung out where Gisburne had knocked it, his body cringing in anticipation of a mortal wounding.

"Earl Robert of Loxley! As King's Justice, I order you to *yield and submit.*" The Sheriff of Nottingham jutted his head out like a paunchy, pugnacious bulldog.

Robert stooped with utter defeat.

The Loxlians began a loud muttering that soon turned threatening. They knew the Sheriff well, and hated him better.

The soldiers disciplined their spooking horses, hands moving to weapons as the mob advanced a few steps.

"Loxley, I am warranted by the King to bring you in, *alive*. You will submit. You will submit, or I will slaughter every Jack here. The Janes I'll leave to my men." The Sheriff's sadism sent a shiver down every female spine.

Seeing the despair of their gentle, humorous Earl, the Loxlians thronged, preparing to charge.

"*Good folk!*" Earl Robert pulled himself upright, knowing his people would be slaughtered in seconds. "Brave folk, I am your Earl, I will answer to the King." Tears twinkled in Robert's eyes as he implored his lovely mob. "We have nothing to be ashamed of. All will be well."

"They'll kill you Earl Robert!" A voice cried out, spasms of agreement rolling through the crowd.

"My people, calm yourselves. You heard the Sheriff, they want me alive. I'll tell the King we can do no more than we have already. The light of truth will sway him. I'll soon return to you, and all will be well. Trust me. Calm yourselves. All will be well." Robert hoped he sounded more confident than he felt.

The crowd teetered on the edge of riot, but Robert's reasoning had taken the wind from their sails.

They remained certain in their waters, however, that the light of truth wouldn't brighten the King's coffers.

"By all the babblers in hell! Stop this chatter and gather your gear, Loxley. We ride direct for London."

In minutes few, the troop trotted away, Earl Robert in their midst.

The Loxlians followed the troop's progress along the London road from the battlements, their Midsummer preparations long forgotten.

A crow's mile from the castle, Earl Loxley's roan hunter broke free of the pack. The horse was at full gallop in a blink, carving turf as he dashed East towards Sherwood.

Robert Loxley held the reins low and loose in his right hand, spurring hard. His left worked his long bow free of its sheath above the horse's shoulder.

The Sheriff's men were a furlong behind, and only just gathering pace, but Gisburne's charger had leapt to the chase.

"Halt, Loxley, and face the King's Justice, or die with a sword in your back!" The edge of Gisburne's raised blade refracted chrome-yellow in the sunlight.

"I bow to England's justice, not the King's. If that justice damns me, then so be it!" Loxley yelled back, nocking an arrow.

Robert gripped his roan's flanks with his thighs, turned his upper body entirely around, and loosed a warning shot at his pursuer.

The ash arrow split the distance in a streak of white feathers. Its fletching shrieked as it fluttered by, a hand-span away from Gisburne's throat.

Gisburne pulled on his reins, slowing his charger enough for Robert to gain half a furlong.

The Earl nocked a second arrow, whipping his hunter to greater speed.

Loxley leapt Sherwood's boundary fence, floating easily in his saddle, closely followed by Gisburne. Moments later, the Sheriff's troop hurdled the fence in a cluster of flickering weapons and flying hooves.

The riders stampeded across the spaciously pillared acres of the outer forest.

Half a mile in, yew and elm gathered closer, forcing all but the most foolhardy to slow down.

Riding at a breakneck canter, Robert Loxley risked a glance over his shoulder. Incredibly, Gisburne had kept up, and was preparing to hack at the roan's rump.

Loxley loosed his bow without thinking.

The arrow slashed across the gap to sink into the chest of Gisburne's charger.

Horse and man went down screaming, their bodies tumbling together until they crashed into a tree. The abominable squeals of the wounded animal rent Loxley's heart.

Robert raced on, flat in his saddle, until the Sheriff's troop had fallen far behind.

Run into the ground, the roan finally lurched to a stop at the base of a steep hill, whiffling with exhaustion. Spur-blood tarred its flanks, off-yellow foam frothed at the animal's mouth, and its eyes rolled in pain.

A savage rage blackened Robert's mind as he scrambled away on foot, deeper into the darkling woods.

Friar Tuck ~ Chapter 12

The three triumphs of the bards of Britain:
Learning over ignorance; reason over terror; peace over violence.
Triads of Bardism

"Well, I know what we need to do first."

"What's that, Friar?" The hint of a smile played about Robert's lips at Tuck's resolute tone.

"Pay a visit to Sherwood's wine cellars."

Tuck led the bemused Earl Loxley on secret ways, crossing impassable areas of gorse and thicket in three quick cuts.

Warm winds tossed leafy branches into the deep-blue shelter of the evening sky.

"Hhhrrrrmm." The hermit tugged at his beard judiciously. "Sure, I'd agree you're in big trouble, Earl Robert... ." Then, he cackled. "Your new best friend's an idiot!"

Tuck threw the winesack into the hermit's lap, causing him to exhale with a whoomph, choking on his joke.

Loxley looked from the hermit to Tuck and back again, then let out a peal of merriment that blew sleeping birds off their perches.

"Then my good Friar is in fine company!"

The trio's laughter washed away the bad feelings that had been cramping Robert's heart. Suddenly, he was fighting back tears, his soul soft with the fortune of having found folk of such good salt. And wine.

Morning saw a more sober crew padding through the summer shadows of Sherwood. The hermit led them, but wouldn't say where they were going.

Near noon, the trio penetrated an area of tall rocks hiding to a twisting canyon the height of two tall men.

Lines of red banded the sandstone walls. Miniature trees and flowering plants of all colours pocked the rocks.

"Why haven't you brought me here before, hermit? It's beautiful." Tuck glanced about in wonder.

"That's why, monk. Now, shut up. I'm trying to remember the next bit."

The sun hovered brilliantly overhead, raining light through the canyon in countless plashing beams.

The hermit examined each large rock they passed, cursing under his breath in what sounded like Gaelic.

Tuck was shrugging in mystification at Robert when the hermit gave a hoot of happiness.

"That's the blighter!" The hermit cleared overgrowth from a child sized boulder, revealing a labyrinthine carving in its side.

The pattern was engraved in one continuous line, curling back and doubling forth in a looping weave.

"The Endless Knot." The hermit grinned proudly at his bemused companions. "Robert, you sit there."

The hermit pulled Loxley to the side of the canyon and sat him facing the knot stone.

"Tuck and I are off for lunch. We'll be back tomorrow at midday with yours."

"What am I supposed to do until then?"

"Isn't it obvious? Sit there, and look at the knot. Idiot. You need to figure out what to do, don't you? Well, meditating on the stone will help." The hermit thrust out his beard. "And don't move. *Whatever happens.* Don't move."

"But... ." Loxley's mouth opened and closed a few times.

"He's an idiot." The hermit muttered sadly to Tuck as he hustled them away.

Robert Loxley was left surrounded by birdsong and radiant verdure, rather nonplussed at the turn of events. He made to get up, but a curious weight in his belly kept him seated.

With nothing else to do, Robert let his eyes trace the whorls in the knot stone, and his conscious mind faded into the endless pattern.

Tuck and the hermit returned the next day as promised, to find Loxley seated where they'd left him.

"Well?" The hermit demanded. "Anything?"

"I'm very thirsty." Robert replied, clearing his throat.

"*Is that it?*" The hermit's eyes bulged with outrage. "Tuck, give this idiot a drink of water. Loxley, we'll be back tomorrow. This time, *keep your concentration.*"

Loxley almost protested, but Tuck motioned him to stay in place.

Tuck knew of labyrinths, and the effect on their walkers. The Church had used them for centuries. He'd never seen one like this, but the principle remained.

Robert followed the figures of his forest friends away up the canyon with dubious eyes. At wit's-end after his escape from the King's men, he'd been willing to submit to the hermit's cockahoop idea, but now he was hungry.

Loxley swore a few oaths under his breath, then turned his attention back to the knot stone. He fixed his eyes on the turning pattern, determined not to be made a fool of for a second day.

The hours passed terribly slowly until Tuck came back, this time on his own.

"Right, Friar, I'm all done here. I've seen what I must do. I'm going to whack that hermit a good crack on the head, then get riotously drunk, and stay that way 'till doomsday." Loxley gave Tuck a look that showed he wasn't joking.

"Ah." Tuck sat down, offering water. "You'll have to wait until tomorrow to crack the hermit a good 'un. He'll be back then."

"*Is he completely mad?* What are we supposed to do until then?"

"The hermit said to tell you to stop being angry with the stone, and listen to it instead."

Tuck flinched as Robert almost punched him.

"And what are you going to do?" Loxley barked.

"Erm. I'm to sit next to you. If you don't mind."

Robert gave Tuck a long glare, then a grin peeked between his lips.

"Keeping an eye on me is he, the bearded baboon?" Loxley looked thoughtful. "He's a sly one that hermit, I must admit. A cunningman they'd think him in Scotland. The Welsh might name him Ovate ...

65

But I know the clear-eyed Irish would recognize him as a *thoroughgoing smartarse.*" Loxley turned to the knot stone without another word.

The moon had waxed full over the last two nights. This third evening, she hove above the canyon like a wanton pearl, raising night light out of earth and stone.

Just before dawn, with Tuck snoring gently at his side, Loxley experienced an extraordinary flash across his consciousness.

Like an argent fish leaping, he saw not what he would do, but who he would be.

Robert was deeply engaged with the stone when the hermit returned at midday.

"Ah *ha*. I don't need to ask how you are, Loxley. Lunch will be over here when you're ready."

The Earl came out of his reverie, and glanced at Tuck.

Robert's verdant irises were blasted wide, like he'd been staring at infinity.

A movement occurred in Tuck's mind, a force that had no focal point, yet acted, and the gyrovague knew he'd found his calling.

Clear as a story being told, Tuck saw how the temptations of a lawless life would pervert Robert's personal power, creating a demon of the woods.

The same qualities in the man, if inspired to live by faith, could make him legend.

Tuck chuckled at the idea of a wandering monk turning outlaw minister, then an endless plain stretched out in his spirit.

In its golden crop he witnessed a pattern that spoke to the beginning and to the end, everything in its place. Tuck's heart bloomed with joy.

Then he wondered how on earth he was going to cope.

Oblivious to everything except food, Loxley wolfed down his lunch.

At the end of the meal, the hermit presented a small bottle in formal toast.

"This is *Uisce beatha*, the water of life." He announced reverently.

The sharp brew breathed of pungent malts and peat, and was so cold it left a freezing trail from gullet to gut. Gasping, the men passed it around until empty.

"That was a real treat!" The hermit smacked his lips in appreciation. "It's been cooling in the stream all morning, but I got it last night, under the full moon, from a pregnant hedgehog."

Tuck and Robert locked shocked eyes, thoroughly unsure if the bearded madman was joking or not.

The hermit ignored their expressions. "So, Robert Loxley, what's the plan?"

"No plan, except to be truly myself." The Earl's voice sang with strength. "I did my best within their laws, and I'll do the same outside their laws. I'll be the finest outlaw England's ever seen!"

"You'll need a new name." Stated the hermit.

"And a moral code." Quickly added Tuck.

Loxley gave a great call of laughter. "Then hermit, you shall provide my name. And Friar, you my moral code."

"Robin, after Goodfellow." The hermit answered. "And Hood, for your face is monstrous to the law, and you'd be wise to cover it."

"Robin Hood!" Robert Loxley moved boughs with the force of his lungs.

"*Do Good* shall be your moral code." Tuck avowed. "We'll fill in the details later."

Friar Tuck ~ Chapter 13

The three things the humble will gain:
Plenty; happiness; the love of their neighbours.
Triads of Bardism

The autumn-tinted afternoon browsed drowsily in Friar Tuck's ears as he and Robin Hood moseyed through the weald.

The outlaws had spent the morning fishing, enjoyed a long lunch, and were now ambling homeward. Dragonflies, matte-black and lightning-green, zoomed between butterflies flapping royal-blue and dusty-orange.

Tuck couldn't think of a better way to spend a day, and thanked the Creator for His infinite blessings.

The happy pair approached the deepest stream in Sherwood, at least ten feet of fast current down to a pebble dashed bed. It was bridged by a fallen tree, so old its surface was worn flat.

Robin had taken two paces across the bridge, when a giant of a man appeared on the far side. Eight feet tall, and broad as a house, the giant held his head lowered, looking into the waters.

Robin had been itching for mischief all day, and Tuck's heart sank to see he'd grabbed his chance.

"What *ho!*" Robin called out with unnecessary volume.

John Little reared back, coming close to tipping into the stream.

"*By all that's Holy*, are you a knave? Or just stupid?"

"Some have said both." Robin gave a satisfied laugh. "And are you blind, or are there clouds up there, wrapping your mile-high eyes? I was crossing this stream and you, friend, got in my way. Please stand aside."

"You *are* stupid." Little sounded like he'd solved a tricky mathematic. "*You*, friend, are in *my* way. Return t'yonder bank, or by this staff it'll be you falling aside."

Little hefted a ten-foot ironwood staff in his huge right hand.

Tuck offered thanks the giant hadn't pulled out a sword, and sat down.

"*Oh ho*," Hood winged a merry glance at Tuck, who grimaced in return. "Wait right there, my brash boggler. I'll bring a bough to nay-say your sapling."

John Little planted his feet, and raised his eyebrows. He'd couldn't decide whether to be angry with, or laugh at, this prancing fellow.

Robin skipped off the bridge, and attacked a stout alder. After watching his friend wrestle vainly with a thick branch for a few minutes, Tuck sighed and went over to help.

In a trice, Robin jumped back onto the bridge furnished with a seven-foot alder staff, and a devil-may-care grin.

"So, have you remembered the manners your mama taught you? Like making way for your betters?" Robin twirled his staff, testing its heft and marking his challenge.

"No wonder you're so stupid! Your brains must be jelly from all the bashings you've invited."

Robin's answer was a quick triplet of strikes, each coolly deflected by the giant.

Little took up a new stance, and swung his staff up to hold it in both hands.

"That was just *silly*. Why don't you let your monkish friend take you home quietly? You clearly need looking after."

Robin spat, and swept the end of his staff insolently through the air. The giant lost his temper, and charged into battle.

Little's titanic torso turned at the waist as he advanced, spiralling his arms to set his staff threshing. Anything in his way would be mown down.

Robin crouched and poked his staff out in one hand. The tip of the alder whistled across the top of the bridge to catch at the giant's ankles.

Little skipped over the sly strike, but his progress was stalled. Flipping his grip, the giant thrust his weapon downwards, poling for Robin's head.

The outlaw skittered out of range, staying low.

John Little smacked his staff down again and again, so close the wind of its passage ruffled Robin's hair. Then the giant pulled his staff in, readying for another advance.

Robin propelled himself up and forward, unreeling powerful, popping blows as he came.

The giant stood his ground, and the fighters clashed in a blistering flurry of cracks and raps. Staff collided with staff five times a second, both men committed to proving his supremacy.

Tuck stood, concerned. This was no longer braggarts' banter taken to extremes, it was serious, personal warfare.

Back and forth across the narrow bridge the giant and outlaw attacked, blocked, jabbed and dodged.

Robin sought to get in close, spinning his alder in short fast arcs. John Little lashed back with tremendous lunges from the ironwood.

Sneaking low again, Robin slid inside Little's guard, and struck like a jumping snake.

The giant pushed his staff defensively sideways, but the narrow bridge prevented him twisting his body fully out of the way. The alder staff struck home, and Little let out a tree-shaking shout.

Robin had committed every force of weight and sinew, hoping for a decisive blow. The giant shook off the hit, let go of his staff with one hand, and wielded it like a hammer.

Tuck was impressed. The chap was big, but strength enough to swing a ten-foot staff like a walking stick was truly unusual.

Robin was still recovering from his last attack, body stretched out, unprotected over his front leg.

Little connected a thumping swat to the outlaw's back, dropping him flat like a squashed bug.

Tuck winced in sympathy to Robin's winded groan.

After a few seconds unmoving, Robin dragged his arms in, and struggled to his feet. Nobody spoke as he drew his legs back into a fighting stance.

Robin threw Tuck a jaunty wave, then bobbed into melee in a blur of flailing aggression.

Hood was magnificent, stubbing, bashing, wrenching and pounding at a velocity that set his staff humming. Little retreated, his staff darting close about his body, barely keeping the wood-wielding whirlwind at bay.

The giant was almost forced to the far bank, when he counter-attacked.

Robin's speed could do nothing against the bull-charge Little threw his body into. The giant suffered three hits to the head, but kept his staff set like a lance.

Too late, Robin realized Little had gone all or nothing.

The tip of the ironwood drove through Hood's defence to connect with his midriff, sending him hurtling off the bridge.

The alder staff span away gracefully, but Robin dropped like a rock into the middle of the stream.

Tuck rushed to the bank.

Hood had lost the surface, his arms flailing. The current thrashed him under the bridge, and threatened to send him whirling downstream.

John Little punted his staff into the stream, catching Robin's body as he passed. The outlaw grabbed for rescue with one hand, and pulled himself up for air. Little walked across the bridge towards Friar Tuck, dragging Robin at the end of his staff like a water-logged cat.

The outlaw clambered up the stream bank and hunched over, panting.

Gravely observing Robin's difficulties, John Little gave an apologetic shrug to Friar Tuck.

Tuck waved his hand airily in reply, as if to say these things happened every day.

"Well, Friar," Robin puffed painfully, "have you seen the size of the fish I caught today?"

There was a moment's silence, then everyone burst out laughing.

"Well met, big fish."

"Well met, fat badger." Little replied, liking the rotund fellow instantly.

Tuck carried an air of goodwill, like a rose-scented breeze that lifts the heart.

"Are you joining our outlaw band?" Tuck gave Little a searching stare.

"With what he's just proved he can do, he's got no choice." Robin cracked a belly warming grin up at the giant. "Unless he wants a choice, that is."

Little gazed down on his two companions, wondering how a quiet walk in the woods had turned into fisticuffs, and ended in enlistment.

John Little was a blacksmith by trade, but he'd been unable to work since spring, when his wife and child had died from fever. Their souls had taken the strength of his hammering arm with them to heaven.

He'd been wandering across England ever since, aimless and alone.

Little shrugged. That laugh had been his first since his family died. Joining these merry outlaws felt like the best offer he'd had for years.

Friar Tuck ~ Chapter 14

The three things necessary to enter an inn:
A strong head; a tough stomach; a heavy purse.
Triads of Bardism

At Robin's urging, he and Tuck would spend occasional autumnal evenings in low profile pubs, catching up on news and warming themselves by a late fire.

John Little tactfully offered to watch over the camp these nights. His size would always attract too much attention.

Summer had been short, with Lammas passing almost unnoticed in the struggle to gather sufficient crops. Now, at Wine Harvest, the pubs were full of bitter complaint and sorrowful stories.

Loxley's new Earl, Guy of Gisburne, had no feeling for his people, and less for the land. The outlaws heard how peasants were beaten to the ground for the slightest misdemeanour.

Many spoke of Gisburne and Nottingham carousing their nights in Castle Loxley, entertaining secretive visitors who never used the country inns. There was even a dark whisper of country maidens being kidnapped to serve in midnight bacchanals, but Tuck dismissed this as fanciful gossip.

The rear snug of the pub was home to a pair of musicians, their voices and lutes ringing out over the bustle of the public bar.

Tuck was enjoying their melodies, and taking possession of two last beers, when the door flew open.

"It's Loxley's men!" A panicked figure screamed into the doorway, then ran off.

Half the pub were up and heading for the back door before Tuck could draw breath, but it was too late.

A man-at-arms strode into the pub, tunic'd in Loxley's colours. Six soldiers trooped in behind, each carrying a loaded crossbow.

Tuck placed his beer mugs back on the bar, and glanced at Robin.

Hood was seated in a corner, green hunter's hat cocked low, part of the background.

"All right, you lot," the man-at-arms' voice was bored but brooked no argument, "outside. One by one. We've had a report of tax evaders round here, and have to make sure you're all good little boys and girls."

Nobody moved in the shocked silence.

"You!" The man-at-arms pointed to one sallow looking fellow near the front. "You first. Get outside. *Move it,* before I smack you to the floor and drag you by the hair."

The yeoman trotted quick time behind the man-at-arms and two crossbowmen out of the pub.

Four crossbowmen stayed inside, choosing the next person to be questioned.

A steady flow of people passed beyond the pub door, those inside wincing at the sodden thump of beatings being handed out. Very soon, most of the pub was empty, perhaps three people before Tuck was called, and only the two musicians between him and Robin.

Flicking his eyes over the last few pub guests, Tuck noticed the musicians had done their best to disappear into the snug. They looked as fragile as their lutes, and were obviously guilty of something.

Robin hadn't moved, but his very stillness made Tuck nervous in his waters.

"You, monk. You're next. *Outside.*"

Friar Tuck exited the building, unthinkingly closing the door behind him, praying with every particle for a miraculous intervention.

Gyrovagues were cursed by all, and Robin had been declared a traitor for escaping the King's Justice.

Outside, the man-at-arms greeted Tuck with a filthy look.

"Oh, for the love of all huswifes! A monk. What the bloody hell are you doing in there?"

"Err, drinking, good watchman."

"I'm not good, and I'm not a watchman, monk. But I think you are a monk. You certainly look stupid enough for the job." The soldiers cracked into hacks of laughter. "Go on drunk monk, bugger off before I smack you just for looking so dumb! Devil knows you deserve it."

Tuck nodded humbly and turned away.

"Next. NEXT. What the bloody hell are they doing in there?" The man-at-arms sighed in disgust. "You, go tell those simpletons to bring the next one out, and sharpish."

His crossbowman opened the pub door and hastened inside.

He was thrown back out a second later, landing in an unconscious mess at the man-at-arms' feet.

"*What the bloody-.*"

The two musicians charged out of the doorway, one wielding a pub bench, the other a broken lute. Close behind, grinning like a maniac, raced Robin Hood.

The second crossbowman swung round to shoot, but Tuck plucked the bolt neatly off his weapon before he could fire it.

"Oi!" Was all the crossbowman managed to say before Tuck followed up with a knock-out haymaker.

The man-at-arms reached fast for his sword, but the musician hurled his bench to catch him across the legs.

The man-at-arms went down hard, and in a flash Robin was at his throat with a wide bladed dagger.

"*Bastard.* I should kill you." Robin's eyes were black voids.

"I'm only doing my job! *Mercy!*"

"Your *job*? Your job is to protect people, not scare and batter them." Robin had taken a grip of the man's throat and was slamming his head into the ground at every word. "Which evil bastard do you work for? Which one is it?"

"*Gisburne.*" The man-at-arms blurted. "Gisburne sent me. He's the one you want. I'm just a soldier, a servant."

"Yes. Gisburne is the one I want." Robin glared at his captive, dagger loose in his left hand, then turned to Tuck. "Friar, should I kill this man?"

Robin's face was open, ready to follow his friend's guidance.

A sinuous power wrapped itself around Tuck's mind. The capacity to lead Loxley into good or evil was in his hands.

A judgmental part of Tuck wanted to see the man-at-arms punished for being a bully and the servant of dark masters. The knave had probably committed enough sin for twenty men.

Tuck's ego was seduced by the status Robin's trust granted him. If he played it right, allowed for a little ruthlessness, Robin's charisma would carry them both to fortune. He could even end up an Abbot.

No one would curse him as a gyrovague then.

An ashen tint stole over Robin Hood's face as Tuck regarded him. It bleached his cheeks, and hung a gray sorrow about the outlaw's temples, truly appalling compared to the usual radiance of his merry brow.

The Holy Spirit had revealed the face of worldly ambition, and Tuck's throat constricted.

Tuck concentrated his mind in prayer, and cast out his anger-driven temptations. "Killing him will do no good to anyone, Robin. There's a thousand more where he came from. We've got better things to do."

Hood tightened his grip on the dagger, but then broke into a grin.

"Yes. Like find our new friends a new lute. I swear they play so well, they knock audiences off their feet!"

Tuck laughed with relief as Robin's face normalized.

"Well met, excellent musicians. I am Friar Tuck, and this is Robin Hood, of Sherwood Forest."

"Well met, brother Tuck. My name's Will Scarlett, and this is Alan-a-Dale. He's the real musician, I was just helping out."

"If you'd seen Scarlett in there, Friar," Robin interrupted, "you'd know he's rather handy with his helpings out! By Our Lady, he's got a fast punch behind that handsome face."

Tuck noted Scarlett's long, copper-coloured hair, lean frame and hungry eyes. He was handsome, as Robin said, but the man smouldered with inner turmoil.

Alan-a-Dale flourished his lute and took a graceful bow.

"Thank you, bold Robin of Sherwood, and merry Friar Tuck. Alan-a-Dale: Minstrel, actor and traveller, at your service, gentlemen."

Under his mop of sandy hair, Dale's features were curiously difficult to catch, as if every expression belonged to a different man, but his dark-blue eyes were crisp with intelligence.

"You've a choice, my friends," Robin's face glowed as he captured them with his charm, "you can go that-a-way, and take your chances with the Sheriff; or come with us into Sherwood. We've everything except riches, and nothing save liberty!"

The band hastened across a newly-shorn field, skipped over the rivulet at its edge, and ducked back under Sherwood's overarching boughs.

"I do have one question." Scarlett murmured to Tuck, as they followed Robin's whistling form through piles of fallen oak leaves.

"What's that?"

"Is he for real?" Scarlett nodded in Robin's direction.

"Why do you ask?" Tuck raised an eyebrow.

"Back at the pub. I've never seen anything like it. When your man Hood was called, he looked quiet as lamb. Then, he jumped three tables and dropped two crossbowmen with his fists. The other two succumbed to my lute." Scarlett's expression grew incredulous. "Thing is, he was declaiming in rhyme the entire time!"

Tuck snorted back his laughter, and patted Scarlett on the shoulder.

"Oh, yes, you be quite sure Robin's for real. A terrible poet, but completely sincere."

Friar Tuck ~ Chapter 15

The three primary contemporaries:
Man; liberty; light.
Triads of Bardism

Michaelmas of the year 1200 saw Friar Tuck creating a permanent base in the hermit's canyon. Five men would leave an obvious trail if they stayed in a series of temporary bashas.

Besides, after almost a year in Sherwood, he was in sore need of a few home comforts.

Alan-a-Dale and Will Scarlett helped establish the new camp, then sorrowfully announced they had to take care of some business outside the forest. The pair promised to return as soon as possible, and join the band permanently.

John Little had to have a quiet word before Tuck realized they'd been talking about women, which set him thinking about many things.

To Robin, the whole thing was a great adventure, the Earl taking to woodland life like a duck to water. In truth, Hood added little in a practical sense to their daily tasks of survival. The outlaw's boundless humour, however, turned the overcast October backwoods into a crucible of cheer.

Robin Hood spoke to his men around a succession of camp-fires, endlessly discussing plans. Even if Hood's ideas were somewhat map-cap, his sense of purpose brought meaning to the outlaws' structureless existence.

"We can't go attacking Loxley Castle!" Little cried one night after Robin had outlined an audacious coup. "Even if five men could overcome the walls, 50 guards, 20 servants, various nobles and other knaves, what do we do then? Nottingham will come down like a ton of bricks, backed up by King bastard John. And what do you want with a castle anyway?"

"I don't want just any castle, I want *my* castle. And it's Gisburne I really want, not the stones of Loxley." Robin took a deep breath. "*But,* I see your point. We'll just have to start smaller, and work our way up."

Ever since the incident at the pub, Robin had been chafing to be more active against the oppression of his people. Tuck had counselled strongly against leaving their hideout, at least until after Epiphany, when the forces of law would have retired to their barracks for the winter.

What they would do for the next three cold months was another question.

"Working our way up sounds good, Robin. What do you suggest?" Tuck handed out healthy portions of his highly-regarded Sherwood stew, to welcoming grins all round.

A bony hand reached in from the mahogany twilight of the weald and intercepted Robin's bowl.

"*Idiot.* Why ask him that?" The hermit appeared, sputtering over his beard. "How can he possibly answer you?"

"Here's a man who understands me!" Robin Hood waved his arms in relief.

"Of course I understand you. You're an idiot." The hermit giggled loudly and, on a roll, swung round to John Little, looking to include the newcomer in his insults.

Taking proper stock of the size of the man, the hermit had a slurp of stew instead.

"Sweet *Mother.* That's fine stuff, Tuck … As fine as the new outlaw you've got there! Where d'you find the giant?"

"Robin fished him at the river." Tuck replied deadpan, his fellows creasing up with laughter.

"*A Mhuire Mháthair,* a giant in an English wood! The fellows of Mur Ollavan will never believe me." The hermit stroked his beard at this tall story in the making. "So, who is Robin Hood?" The hermit swung a winesack over with the question. "What's his first act of liberation?"

"Actually, hermit, you've given me the clue." Robin's broad smile lit up the band's faces. "I'm going to see my old mum. I need some *sensible* advice."

The following morning, Alan-a-Dale returned from visiting his sweetheart, and the outlaws bantered their way to the Priory of Rubygill.

The sun was hot but the air cold, a sublime time to be walking under the open-topped canopies and ocean-blue skies. Tuck hurried along, keeping pace with Robin's jaunty step, Dale's swaggering gait and Little's enormous stride.

Over the last few weeks, Tuck's wisdom mind had become aware of a joyful motion in the most subtle folds of silence. Immersion in prayer, faith and the forest had nurtured a new perception of Spiritual life in his soul.

Ministering to his little congregation was also rewarding, but rather less contemplative.

After a couple of mischievous incidents almost went too far, Tuck had established a few camp rules. These rose out of necessity, but he also knew his best chance to bind virtue into the band, was whilst it was taking root. Then, the fruits would be good.

Trying to graft precepts on later would be painful for all concerned.

Additionally, Tuck was all too aware Robin had a dark side. The outlaw's soul had been afflicted since Crusade, and recent events had not improved his sense of humanity.

Hood was obsessed with power and righteousness. He was adamant force birthed right. Everything he'd experienced showed the strongest arm always won. At the end of a cold, rainy evening outlawed in Sherwood, none of Tuck's Biblical refutations sounded very convincing, even to his own ears.

Guiding the battle-hardened outlaw to see further than immediate consequence was proving tricky.

The Priory of Rubygill stood encircled by a high earthen wall, in turn secured by a deep ditch. Daubed in the otherworldly greys of a winter sunset, the convent house loomed like judgment day.

The Priory gate was studded with bolts for strength, and surmounted by a cross for sanctity. From the expressions on Little's and Dale's faces, Tuck noted he wasn't the only one feeling nervous.

Robin, as breezily confident as ever, rapped smartly and called out an irreverent halloo.

"Who arrives at Rubygill? And what do you seek?" A voice announced from nowhere, causing Dale to jump in fright.

Tuck looked up, and there, beside the cross, was a young nun's face staring down.

"Robin of Sherwood, blessed nun. I seek my mother, and a roof for the night." Hood sent a brilliant smile up to the nun, who seemed quite taken aback, then disappeared.

The heavy door swung open to reveal an iron-faced lady dressed in a simple woollen robe.

Robin switched his debonair grin for the glitter of boyish innocence.

The Prioress narrowed her eyes and tightened her lips as she examined Robin in his Lincoln green leggings and tunic.

Sensing a disaster brewing, Tuck swiftly stepped forward.

"The Lord bless you and Rubygill, Mother Prioress. I am brother Tuck, lately of Fountaindale, now conscience to Robin of Sherwood."

"He looks like he needs as big a conscience as he can get." The Prioress replied doubtfully, turning her penetrating gaze onto Tuck. "Fountaindale, you say? I know the Abbot there. How is my friend? Does he still suffer from his knees?"

"Er ... I'm sorry, Mother Prioress," Tuck replied, embarrassed, "Father Abbot never spoke to me of his knees."

"*Ha.*" The Prioress didn't smile, but her eyes grew a shade less ferocious. "Only a real monk would give that answer. Right, I'm allowing you in." The Prioress waved her hand impatiently. "But, I warn you, brother Tuck: Your friends are here on your conscience, as you say." The Prioress fixed him with a daunting stare. "I'm holding you *personally* responsible for them. Understand?"

"Fully, Mother Prioress. As it happens, I think the Good Lord has had much the same idea."

This time the Prioress did smile. Slightly.

"First things first. All of you will wash before taking a step farther into my Priory. Pray the filth in your souls is as easy to clean." The Prioress herded the subdued crew into the lavatorium, then swept from the room, leaving a distinctly sober chill in her wake.

The merry men set to with barely a whispered joke between them.

In the empty refectory, the Prioress had set out a large tureen of vegetable soup and a loaf of fresh bread. She stood at the head of the table, arms crossed, as the band meekly took their seats.

Robin Hood tried a gallant smile, but it faltered on the glare the Prioress returned. The outlaw kept his face in his bowl for the rest of the meal.

Tuck revelled in the atmosphere of a religious community. He savoured the broth, almost identical to one he used to particularly enjoy at Fountaindale.

He only hoped his Father Abbot never found out a certain brother Tuck had supped here.

The men sighed with gratitude as they pushed their bowls away. After their long walk, they felt like princes finely feasted.

"You said you were looking for your mother." The Prioress unfolded her arms. "Whom did you mean?"

"My mother, Mother Prioress," Robin's expression held more humility than Tuck had ever seen, "is the former Lady Loxley."

"Ah, Sister Beatitude. She's *your* mother?" The Prioress looked faintly shocked. "Well. I will ask her to attend to you. If she wishes. Tonight you will sleep in the dorter. It's right there." The Prioress pointed to a study looking door with a sliding bolt on the outside. "You may wonder where my nuns are. *Don't*. They are all fully occupied in communing with God. And staying away from you." The Prioress eyeballed each man. "Understand?"

The merry men nodded like their lives depended on it.

"Oh, Robert, I'm happy to see you, but it's a sad story you came to share." Lady Loxley, now Sister Beatitude, took her son's hands in her own.

Robin looked at his gently enfolded hands, guilt-wracked. To his mother's eyes he didn't doubt he'd failed in every sense.

"At least you've made some nice new friends in the forest, dear." Sister Beatitude smiled indulgently at the band, each man returning his best smile.

"Yes, they're a good crew." Robin's voice dropped to a stage-whisper. "But the monk's a bit of an idiot."

Little and Dale collapsed into giggles.

"And you've kept your humour, I see." Commented Beatitude with an understanding smile at the scandalized Tuck. "I'm not sure what I can do help you, my son, except to pray, as I always will."

"I wanted to tell you that I aim to get full redress from these bast-, er, knaves."

"*Vengeance is Mine!*" Beatitude yelled out in a voice of storm and sea. "Saith the Lord." She continued quietly. "That means: If you chase revenge, you will have a miserable life. No, Robert, leave vengeance to God. He's better at it than you are. Anyway, it seems to me you should have enough to do, looking after your people. Just because your title's been taken, doesn't mean you've been let off your chores."

His mother's stern tone warmed Robin's heart.

The King's judgment had stripped Loxley not only of his privileges, but of the role he'd been reared to fulfil. It was soul-theft, leaving the Earl wayward and ashamed.

His mother had always *been* Loxley to Robert. She knew everyone, was involved in everything, and presided over the seasons' turnings like Gaia. Beatitude's words unlocked a barred gate, and Robert's duty spoke again to his spirit.

Robin Hood woke the merry men just after dawn with a shout.

Tuck sat up with a start, Little swung out of bed ready to take the head off the first person he saw, and Dale scuttled beneath his covers.

"They've locked us in!" Robin rattled the door handle. "Don't they trust us or something?"

"They don't trust us." Tuck replied around a yawn.

The merry men were fed breakfast under the watchful eyes of the Prioress, then ushered firmly to the gatehouse.

"Brother Tuck, I wish you Our Lady's Blessing. And Her Fortune. You're going to need both with this crew, if I'm any judge."

Tuck hid his smile with a bow.

The Prioress reached out an elegant hand and tapped Tuck lightly on the crown of the head with her forefinger.

Tuck almost fell over at the electric blessing that shocked through his skull, sparked down his spine and melted into his hips. He glanced up at the Prioress in astonishment, but she'd already moved onto other business.

"*You.*" The Prioress closed on Robin with uncanny speed. "Sister Beatitude needs to work. And you, with that slippery smile, are quite clearly a big boy. I don't want to see you round here for at least a year, understand?"

Hood nodded through his shock and awe.

"Our Lady's blessing on you all. And for Our Saviour's sake, *do* behave."

The Priory gate closed with a thud that vibrated in the soles of the men's boots.

"Well, I hope that was worth it." Alan-a-Dale declared as they walked away. "I don't think I'll ever say another bloody swearword in all my life."

Tuck was well pleased with their visit. His pervading fear of Spiritual community was reduced, and more practically, he'd noted the Prioress' man-taming technique.

"Yes." Replied Robin. "But let's talk about it back in Sherwood. I want the hermit's wisdom on this. And his wine. Did that Prioress chill any of you fellows to the bone too?" Robin's expression of frosted horror set the men guffawing.

As they fell into their league-eating walking rhythm, each man celebrated camaraderie in their hearts, but none more so than Friar Tuck.

Friar Tuck ~ Chapter 16

The three things that cannot be obtained:
Poverty from charity; wealth from robbery; wisdom from riches.
Triads of Bardism

Sherwood's lofty denizens welcomed the merry men home with birdsong overhead, and soft loam underfoot.

John Little prepared a feast for their return, baked woodcock and roasted quail, followed by honey and nut cake.

"I used to make the nutcake for my daughter." The giant replied proudly to the compliments of the men.

Little's face held the memory, then his lip quivered, and he collapsed into bewildered grief. "I used to call her Squirrel." Tears trickled from his hopelessly sad eyes.

"Poor little John." Murmured Tuck, placing a sympathetic hand on the giant's arm.

He sniffled, blinked a few times, then sniffled again.

Then a tiny smile crept to his lips.

"My name's John Little, Tuck Friar."

Subdued laughter jockeyed round the campfire as the hermit materialized out of the forest like a bearded revenant, eager to hear the band's latest stories.

"Sweet *Mother*. The formidable Prioress of Rubygill herself!" The hermit broke into a fond smile. "Dear Sister Brighid." He tugged at his beard in happy memory. "I knew her, back in Ireland. Before she took on the Priory job, of course. *What a woman.* On a good day she had half of Meath running up Tara, and the other half running down!"

"Yes, she made quite an impression on us too." Robin muttered.

Tuck fixed the hermit with an inquisitive look, wondering, not for the first time, exactly who he really was.

The hermit giggled at Robin's chagrin, then shot Tuck a glance that made his hair stand on end.

"What are you staring at, brother? I can only hope you didn't embarrass yourself in front of my good Prioress." The hermit's tone suggested Tuck was capable of anything. "Sure, I'd never live it down if she found out you were my student."

Tuck gaped, caught midway between indignation and surprise.

The merry men collapsed with laughter, even Little unable to stop his chuckles breaching his melancholy.

The hermit's sky blue eyes, however, held Tuck's attention rapt.

Tuck's mind leapt across the fire, entering the hermit's heart. The hermit welcomed him with awakened love, libraries of wisdom arrayed either side of his soul.

Tuck felt himself kneel, although his body didn't move. The hermit made a mysterious pass with his right hand, his fingers held in a particular fashion, and nodded very slightly.

Tuck's consciousness returned to his physical body, and time resumed.

"Humpph." The hermit shifted in his seat. "Maybe you didn't make a complete idiot of yourself after all, monk. Right, Robin, the question remains: What's to do? *Where's the action?* How are you going to set all England ablaze? Inspire the courage of Arthur in every man Jack? Stir the spirit of Albion in our dear ladies Jane?"

"By Arthur. *By Albion.* By the salty fruit of England, our good men and sweet women! My name is Robin Hood, my roots are the trees and my aim is true. This I swear ye: I will act by right, for right." Patrimony fired the merry men's blood. "Force makes Right. But the force of our band will not make Robin's right. No. With Our Lady's blessing, the outlaws of Sherwood will make justice right, prosperity right and freedom right!"

"By my strength, I'm with Robin Hood!" Little John raised his gigantic fists to the star spangled heavens.

"By my faith, I'm with Robin Hood!" Tuck's heart pulsed with joy at Robin's Holy call.

"By my witness, I'm with Robin Hood!" Alan-a-Dale sang out, his minstrelsy magnifying his words into the triumph of ten thousand men.

"By the Sweet Mother, a miracle!" The hermit cried in ecstasy. "Someone's gone and blessed our boy with brains!"

The days of Advent bloomed with the clear light of clean skies, but most mornings found Sherwood's groves glowing under scatterings of fine snow.

Will Scarlett re-appeared late one evening in mid-December, road-stained and carrying tales of merciless oppression. With Nottingham's support, Guy of Loxley had tightened the screws on his fief, mining the very marrow of the people.

Scarlett's report set a tiger pacing in the breasts of the outlaws, tightening their revolutionary resolve.

Two days before Christmas, they put Robin Hood's first strike for right into action.

Little John, Friar Tuck and Will Scarlett emerged from the outer reaches of Sherwood, driving an empty cart along the main road to Nottingham. The band was dressed as monks, the morality of which Tuck was still debating.

Scarlett at least suited the cloth, in the style of an ascetic. Little John was another matter entirely. His habit had been hastily sewn together from three normal men's robes, and looked like it.

The giant had gamely offered to play a hunchback for the raid, but Tuck had discreetly quashed that idea. The only thing that would attract more attention than a giant monk, was a giant hunchbacked monk.

Castle Nottingham dominated the land for miles around, elevated on sheer cliffs over 100 feet high. Established by the Norman conquerors, and strengthened by Henry II, this fearsome fortification was the seat of Royal power over middle-England.

Below the cliffs spread the new town of Nottingham, pleasant wooden houses and workshops, built by craftsmen with a rare eye for planning.

At the foot of the cliffs began the old town, carved directly into the sandstone rock. A few main entrances gave onto branching corridors and splitting tunnels pocked with round-ceilinged rooms or buttressed caves. The dwellings, craft holes, brewer's basements and tanning dens wormed every which way into the rock, with some pipes and chimneys leading all the way to the castle above.

The outlaw crew browsed their way idly through the milling streets of new town. The only danger came from Scarlett's popping eyes when Nottingham's milk maids sashayed by.

At the foot of the rock, Tuck enquired after a certain establishment.

"The Pilgrim? Of course, good monk, it's a bit farther round, can't miss it."

The Pilgrim pub joined old and new Nottingham. Its spacious wooden front room stood proud of the rock, but behind the public-bar, stone-cold brewery-rooms and beer-cellars sprawled far into the sandstone. The Pilgrim held the grant of brewing the castle's beer, and provided the services of an inn for travellers.

As well as being the best pub in Nottingham, the outlaws had chosen The Pilgrim because it had a good-sized chimney leading directly from the brewhouse below, to the castle stores above.

Hoisting man-sized hogsheads of ale up a hundred feet was infinitely preferable to squeezing them through the pub, rolling them up the long hill, and then having to negotiate the narrowly built castle. Bringing empty barrels down was also a good deal easier.

Tuck's crew booked a room for the night, then settled comfortably into the back bar, over pints of dark ale, cool and tasty.

Tuck heaved a sigh of relief after his first sip. The set-up had passed without a hitch.

Friar Tuck ~ Chapter 17

The three gifts of charity:
Food; sanctuary; instruction.
Triads of Bardism

Robin Hood and Alan-a-Dale trotted through Sherwood's outer acres on two fine chestnut mares, dressed in the manner of lower nobility.

Hood had grown a tight beard over the preceding months, and under his floppy-brimmed hat only the sharpest eyes would know the face of Robert Loxley.

Alan-a-Dale strummed a folk melody from his broad bellied lute, singing in a voice that reflected in ochre lusters off the pillaring oak:

> **Let me bring you songs from the wood!**
> **To make you feel much better than you could know.**
> **Dust you down from tip to toe,**
> **Show you how the garden grows,**
> **Hold you steady as you go.**
> **Join the chorus if you can, it'll make of you a merry man.**
>
> **Songs from the wood make you feel much better.**
>
> **Let me bring you love from the field!**
> **Poppies red and roses filled with summer rain.**
> **To heal the wound, and still the pain,**

As we drag down every lover's lane.
Life's long celebration's here, I toast you all in penny cheer.

Songs from the wood make you feel much better!

Let me bring you all things refined:
galliards, and lute songs served in chilling ale.
Greetings, well met fellow, hail!
I am the wind to fill your sail,
I am the cross to take your nail.
A singer of these ageless times, with kitchen prose and gutter
    rhymes.

Songs from the wood make you feel much better!

Robin joined the chorus with abandon, then the riders spurred their horses into a free-spirited canter for Castle Nottingham.

By the time the outlaws were within a half-mile, the sky had filled with snow clouds readying themselves for their nightly work.

The pair skirted new town, then slowed their horses to a walk as they neared the lower gate of the Sheriff's castle.

"We've come for the party!" Proclaimed Robin in a drunken Scot's accent.

Alan-a-Dale swayed in his saddle, played a dissonant half-chord on his lute, and pulled a sloppy smile.

The three guards posted in the lower gatehouse took one look at the inebriated aristocrats, and waved them through.

Hood and Dale trotted up the long slope to the towers of the castle. The thick stone casements perched with dingy majesty against the steely skies.

Arriving at the upper gatehouse, Robin flourished what looked like an invitation, and declared himself to be son of the Clan Chief Douglas. As proof of their lineage, Alan-a-Dale hammered out a lively reel, declaiming an indecent limerick for lyrics.

The guards chortled at the song, and motioned the capital pair on.

Hood and Dale were welcomed by liveried doormen, presented with cups of wine, and shown to the wassail hall.

Castle Nottingham's main hall heaved with the sound of two hundred men getting drunk. Long tables were set out in a U, straining under the weight of fulsome feast and celebratory cup.

Robin pulled Dale into the nearest gap, loudly greeted their bench mates, and joined in with the relish only mischief can bring.

The pub grapevine had it that Nottingham was celebrating a bumper year for rents, leases and taxes. This wassail, profligate beyond the dreams of peasants, was only the first of three to be hosted by the Sheriff over Christmas. The lower orders were being feasted today, proper nobles on Christmas Eve, and the highest ranks would wassail Christmas Day. The King's Justice was investing in friends in high places.

The evening passed in a blur of succulent boar, stuffed venison, serving wenches and sweet wine.

Not too late, and not too early, Hood and Dale rose from their bench. They weren't faking their drunkenness now, their disguises pissed perfect.

The pair wished the Sheriff a cracking good health, which went unheard above the din, and titubantly followed a page to a turret room reserved for guests.

"I'm not sure I should have had that last one." Dale commented, gloomily holding his stomach.

"Last what?" Robin did his best to focus on his comrade. "Wine? Boar? Wench? Wine?"

"You said wine twice!"

"That's because I'm seeing two of you. Stay still, will you, Dale. You're making me queasy will all that jigging about."

"I'm not moving." Dale looked down at his banding legs. "At least, I'm not doing it deliberately."

"By Our Lady, that's the strongest wine I've ever had!" Robin laughed hysterically. "I think we should add a couple of barrels to our little heist. What d'ya say, Dale? Eh? *Dale?*"

Alan-a-Dale had sunk into a snoring heap.

Three hours before dawn, Robin Hood woke Alan-a-Dale with a friendly kick.

The minstrel moaned, but didn't move. Robin kicked again, a little harder.

"By the hot hammers in my head, Robin, stop kicking, *please.*" Dale pushed himself off the floor, then vomited copiously into the corner.

"Come on, Dale!" Robin clapped his man cheerily on the back. "We've dark deeds need doing."

Dale stood pitifully upright, his eyes bloodshot. "I'm never getting drunk with you ever again, Robin Hood. Never."

Hood worked hard to suppress his glee as the outlaws stealthed down the spiralling stairs. Reaching the ground floor, the pair creaked across the entrance hall, and entered the servant's quarters.

Candles burned in widely spaced sconces on the walls, but nothing stirred. Robin Hood threw Dale a look of such excitement, the minstrel almost forgot his hangover.

The first room the outlaws arrived at housed the kitchen. The outlaws scuttled through, into the store rooms. Here was the aim of the heist.

With so many strangers coming to the castle, ordinary riches would be double-locked and triple-guarded this Christmas. The poorest peasants also had no use for gold coins. If they tried to spend them, questions would be asked. But food and drink spoke currency enough for any Jack or Jane.

Hood had gambled no-one would think to secure the vittals.

The outlaws heard snoring coming from the far end of the storeroom, and moved in to measure up their opposition.

A boy was asleep on a bed of rags, his small mouth emitting a rumbling snore every few seconds.

"I pity the lad's wife when he's grown." Alan-a-Dale whispered in Robin's ear, causing the outlaw to bend double as he restrained his laughter.

Regaining himself, Robin shook an inficete finger at Dale, then snuck up to the sleeping boy.

The lad woke with a start, Robin's leathery hand tight against his mouth.

The outlaw leaned in close.

"No noise, understand? We've wenches in the next room. Understand?"

The boy's eyes shrank from pools of terror to slits of cynicism as he caught up with the situation. He nodded.

Robin took his hand away, and turned it palm up. Revealed were two pennies, a good month's wages for this gallopin.

The boy disappeared the coins without seeming to move.

"What's your bidding, master?"

"Get lost 'til after dawn."

The boy dashed from the room.

Hood and Dale set to, piling provisions helter skelter into strong canvas sacks. The outlaws dragged the sacks to a wide hole in the floor, then pushed them in.

A hundred feet below, a dull thud announced the arrival of the first bag of loot.

Friar Tuck and Will Scarlett, in position at the base of the Pilgrim's beer chimney, pulled it out and passed it to Little John. The giant snuck it away, onto the waiting cart.

Thud! THUD! Two more bags dropped, Tuck and Scarlett heaving them away. Little took a bag in each hand, and skipped back to the cart.

"That man is even stronger than I thought." Scarlett marvelled as they waited for the next arrivals.

"Oh, that's nothing," Tuck murmured, "I once saw him rip a hawthorn straight out of the ground, roots an' all."

Robin Hood and Alan-a-Dale filled sack after sack, dumping them down the chimney. The storeroom, so recently brimming with a fortune in victuals and vittals, was almost bare when the outlaws ran out of sacks.

Lost in the task, Alan-a-Dale bent to drop in a raw deer's carcass, but Robin stopped him with a chuckle.

"I don't think they'll appreciate that below, Dale. We've got enough. Let's take a bow before the kitchen boy comes back."

The outlaws scurried through the servants' quarters, and dashed out the back door.

A mighty rampart and palisade enclosed the castle courtyard. High clouds emerged white from the night as dawn approached.

Robin Hood unwrapped a hook and long rope from around his body, and had it secured to the top of the palisade on the first throw.

Dale shimmied up, then sat on top as Robin scrambled into place beside him. The sun's rim blistered on the horizon, exuding apricot in an unfocussed hemisphere across the sky.

The outlaws looked over the cliff side of the castle walls. Their ascent up the palisade had been a good 40 feet, but their descent would be over triple the distance.

Dale unbound a second rope, fixed it to the first, and let the line drop. Hood was over the edge and rappelling down to new town in a trice. The outlaw landed lightly and stood aside.

In front of him, looking greatly surprised, was an aged ox-herder.

"Good morning, dear fellow," Robin doffed his hat, "looks like a dandy day ahead, what d'you say?"

Dale appeared out of the skies in a rush of oaths to land on his arse at Robin's feet.

The ox-herder stepped back with a horrified expression as he regarded the foully swearing arrival. Then the old fellow looked up to see if God had decided to cast any more nobles out of heaven.

From round the corner of the cliff came a heavily laden cart, driven by three monks madly grinning. When the herder saw one was the size of a house, he pegged off at all speed.

The outlaws bounced and jounced back to Sherwood in the over-laden jalopy. Sacks of loot were piled in the rear, with Robin, Dale and Scarlett sat on top, singing.

Friar Tuck and Little John drove the paired ponies, laughing as they trundled through the magnificent Christmas Eve morning.

That evening, the merry men split up, visiting every pub for ten crow's miles.

In each, the story was the same: Anyone visiting a certain oak on Christmas morning would be gifted with food and drink to last the season.

The outlaws were met with stunned silence, mocking jibes and even offended outrage. No-one believed these fleeting visitors dressed in Lincoln green could be serious.

Christmas day, 1200, dawned in a tremendous detonation of golden light that flowed like honey into the upturned bowl of England's heaven.

The night's snowfall had settled into a crisp, clean cloth, revealing the Earth in innocence.

An hour after dawn, a lone yeoman arrived at the oak, and he was drunk. The outlaws loaded him with food, wine, and firm instructions to tell all his friends.

Two hours after dawn, the merry men couldn't keep pace with the throng of people arriving open mouthed. Each departed with full arms, calling double blessings on Robin Hood.

At mid-morning, the merry men forced an already over-laden Loxlian Jack to accept the last of the loot.

There was simply no-one else waiting.

"Hey, we forgot to keep any of that fortified wine." Exclaimed Robin as the outlaws headed lightly back into the trees.

"For which I am eternally grateful to Our Most Merciful Holy Mother, Robin Hood!" Dale answered to a broad round of jeers and laughter.

Friar Tuck ~ Chapter 18

The three things to be considered in all things:
Nature; form; work.
Triads of Bardism

The merry men's first strike for right proved a great success.

The Sheriff had been made to look the worst of fools in front of his guests, robbed in his own castle. The Christmas Eve wassail was a complete wash out, and despite buying up every scrap he could find, even the Christmas day feast was embarrassingly sparse.

While the aristocracy was in high tantrum, Robin Hood's name passed among the people like a magic charm. Alan-a-Dale promoted their success by going on an Epiphany tour of pubs and inns, singing of Robin Hood and his cause.

He gave copies of his songs to every minstrel, troubadour, pipe-blower and drum-monkey he met, and was sure to get the crowd singing along to his climactic choruses:

Robin Hood, Robin Hood,
    riding through the glen,
Robin Hood, Robin Hood,
    with his band of men.
Feared by the bad, loved by the good;
Robin Hood, Robin Hood, Robin Hood!

The fine Christmas season turned harsh come mid-January, sleet and freezing hail mauling everything from cinereal skies.

Instead of extending their activities as planned, the outlaws hunkered into their encampment, waiting out the weather like everyone else.

Candlemass dawned softly into a powder-blue firmament, bringing the first hope of spring.

It also brought the hermit.

"So, what have you been up to since the Christmas caper? Tweaking Gisburne's tumescent nose? Plotting another petard for the Sheriff's delight? Tell me *everything*."

"Well, hermit," Robin replied strongly, "we've obviously been very busy here, establishing our foundations and determining priorities."

"Idiot. Can't you do *anything* without me holding your hand?" The hermit sighed, his beard rising and falling with the depth of it. "Alright, listen up. Here's what you're gonna do. It's new, and it's called *distributive justice*."

Will Scarlett and Alan-a-Dale shared lunch at a pleasant spot by one of Sherwood's main trails. A spacious copse of beech extended over the area, lending their elegant forms to the beauty of the February morning.

Just after midday, a group of riders appeared, walking their horses along the track. Three men-at-arms on war-horses vanguarded an expensively-dressed Abbot on a glossy bay pony.

Scarlett moved into the middle of the track, and held up a hand.

The riders, 15 yards distant, pulled down on their reins.

"Get off the road! Make way for the Abbot of Doncaster."

One man-at-arms spurred his horse towards Scarlett, meaning to force him aside.

The others scanned the immediate area for ambush.

"Won't you join us for lunch, Father Abbot?" Alan-a-Dale's cultured invitation carried clean as a bell. "We have some fine canary here on picnic today."

The first man-at-arms slid his horse to a stop in front of Scarlett. His waters told him something wasn't right, but there were only two of the blighters, an empty forest all around, and the offer of lunch seemed very civilized.

The Abbot of Doncaster stepped his pony to overlook the picnic selection.

"Bless you. Canary, did you say? I could do with a damn drink."

Scarlett joined them, and soon all three were sharing a sack of the hermit's finest. The men-at-arms dismounted, and sat across the way for their own lunch.

An enjoyable hour later, and a good deal tipsier than he'd intended to get, the Abbot of Doncaster made ready to leave.

"Well met, my friends. May the Lord bless you. And your canary." The Abbot hiccupped a little laugh, and turned to his pony.

"Aren't you forgetting something, Father Abbot?" Asked Alan-a-Dale in a pleasant tone.

Doncaster turned back, patting his pockets and looking puzzled.

"No, I don't think so... ."

"Dinner in Sherwood has to be paid for." Scarlett stated stiffly.

"I'm sorry?" The Abbot tried to sober up as he registered the change of mood.

"Don't be concerned, Father Abbot, the price is the same for everybody." Continued Dale, speaking easily. "It's whatever you can afford."

"Oh. I see, well, er, I think I have a couple of pennies somewhere here."

"Ah." Scarlett stared daggers. "You've misunderstood. It's us who decide what you can afford, not you."

The Abbot looked to his men-at-arms, but it was too late.

Robin Hood, Little John and Friar Tuck stepped out of concealment, and walloped the guards to the ground.

"*Damn you all to hell for the filthy thieves that you are!* I'll see you hung and drawn for this."

"What have I found, ho?" Robin Hood called musically from next to the Abbot's pony.

"*You leave that where it is.* That's holy money!" The Abbot's cheeks turned white.

"Holy money?" Robin repeated with boyish curiosity. "*Holy money?* I've never heard of holy money. Have you, Friar?"

Tuck put on a thoughtful expression, then shook his head. "No, Robin. I've heard of blood money, funny money, dirty money, filthy lucre, ill-gotten gains, oh, and taxes, of course. But, I don't think taxes are actually *sanctified*."

Robin gave hoot of laughter and lifted a hefty chest off the pony's rump.

The outlaw jaunted over to where Scarlett was holding Doncaster.

"How much did our fine-drinking Abbot say he had to offer for his woodland repast?"

"Two pennies." Replied Scarlett darkly.

"I've got the answer, Friar! This holy money is *heavier* than normal money." Robin swung round to give the Abbot a corky grin, then back to Tuck. "You should feel the weight of our Abbot's tup'pence! By Our Lady, *it's a miracle.*"

The merry men had tied the Abbot loosely to a nearby beech, and dissolved back into Sherwood long before the first man-at-arms recovered consciousness.

"Those hell-bound criminals have got to hang for this. *And fast.*" Doncaster yelled his choler into the Sheriff of Nottingham's depressed face.

"By all the outlaw bones in hell. With robbery rife in Nottingham, bandits in bloody Sherwood is all I need." The Sheriff knocked back a cup of wine and flung his mug to the floor. "*Of course we'll hang 'em.* Want 'em quartered too?"

"*Yes!*" Yelled the Abbot. "Halved. Quartered. Eighth'd! I don't care as long as it's excruciating. I'd collected all my loans from the last twelve-month in that damned chest." The Abbot's voice shot up an octave. "*With exorbitant interest.*"

"I'll get Gisburne on it right away. He'll string up those damned hugger-muggers in a trice."

Friar Tuck ~ Chapter 19

Three things incapable of change:
The laws of nature; the quality of truth; the Triads of Bardism.
Triads of Bardism

Gisburne's men invaded Sherwood the following day. 20 mounted men-at-arms with crossbows flanked 20 footsoldiers armed with spears and short swords. He'd sent his most trusted knight, Sir Ralph Montfaucon, to captain the hunt.

Montfaucon was the ambitious younger son of London gentry. He'd entered Gisburne's service during the Welsh uprisings, where he'd displayed all the cruelty an aspiring noble could wish for, and a lot more sense.

Walking his black stallion snorting into Sherwood, Montfaucon fought the feeling he was entering a tombyard. The open range of black oak soon gave way to tight copses of barren crab-apple and bare elm, their wintering limbs pricking about the cloud-piled sky.

The footsoldiers were clustered together by overgrowth, and the riders gradually pushed many yards to either side by the trees. Several miles into the timberland, Montfaucon noticed his riders were spread over half an acre, while the footmen were treating this mission like a walk in the park.

The knight called the soldiers together to ream them out.

"Don't you realize these are *dangerous criminals* we're tracking?" Montfaucon's stallion reared at his master's villainous tones. "You lot! Stay together. You lot! Keep your bloody distance, or you'll end up spearing each other. *And find me some damned thieves.*"

Two crow's miles farther into Sherwood, the merry men were putting the final touches to the day's lunch.

Will Scarlett had raced into camp an hour before, breathlessly relaying that a party of unprotected nobles were on their way through the forest. The band had sprung into action, high on their success of the day before, and happy to have a reason to chase away the damp.

Hood did a final check, then waved the merry men into hiding. Right on cue, the sound of riding chatter arrived on the breeze.

Passing between a brace of oak, six nobles trotted graciously into the trap.

Robin Hood stood to the side of the forest road, at the head of long table set with white linen and candles.

The plates and mugs were wooden, but Little John had added sprigs of holly and yewberry that gave the ensemble a certain rural chic. In the place of honour, couchant, was an ash roasted boar, tusks an' all.

The nobles were so engaged by their repartee, Robin had to cough politely to get their attention.

"Oh, Harold!" Cried a shapely maiden in a purple-bodiced longdress. "Is this one of your diversions? *It's marvellous.*" The maiden dipped daintily off her horse, clapping her hands in wonder.

"Sweet maid," Robin gave a low bow and rose with a rakish grin, "may I bid you the warmest of welcomes to the bowers of Sherwood. A blessed day indeed, to have you dine with us."

"NO, Kate wait!" Harold yelled in a panic-pitched voice.

Kate turned in confusion, and the rest of the nobles jumped off their horses.

The group gathered hastily together, uncertain as to what was going on, but giving Hood very hard stares.

"What do you mean with all this, my good man?" Harold puffed his chest out.

"I mean lunch." Robin stepped aside to properly present his table.

"Oh, I'm *starving* Harold." Kate implored. "*Can't* we eat at Sherwood's bower? Are you *sure* this isn't one of your adventures?"

"Kate." Another lady stepped forward. "Come here please."

"What? *Why?*"

"NOW." The lady's command cracked across the space, and Kate jumped to it.

Hood glanced with interest at this interloper, and was thunderstruck.

The lady's hair was ringleted in shades of midnight, bunching staphyline about her sternly held features. Her black eyes sparkled with the same spirit as the stars, her nose was cute as a kitten's, and the lady's lips, to the outlaw's enraptured gaze, were simply superb.

Hood lowered his eyes, his body an electric weave as he took in her healthy figure. He knew she was the most enchanting woman he'd ever beheld when he registered her apple-green riding-jacket, with matching breeches slipped into high horse-boots. A jauntily feathered hat set off the outfit.

Robin sighed in appreciation. He'd always had a weakness for hats.

"Who *are* you, Sir?" The lady's tone made clear what she thought of the outlaw's personal inspection.

"By Our Lady, I'm so sorry! My name is ... Robin Hood. Of Sherwood. My Lady." The outlaw gathered his wits, and thrust his most seductive smile to the fore. "Please, beautiful blessing, would you please tell me your name?"

"*Certainly not, Hood.* You look like a common thief to me, a rascal and brigand. Stop this gaming at once, it will go easier for you."

Robin was astonished, and impressed, at her boldness.

"Now now, there's no need for any unpleasantness." Interrupted Harold. "We'll just get on our horses and ride on. How's that, Hood?"

Robin gazed at his viridian vision, lost to everything but her.

"*Hood*, you should know my companions are all fencing champions." Harold placed his hand on his sword pommel.

Having watched Robin's theatrics with steadily worsening humour, Tuck signalled the merry men into play.

Scarlett and Dale stepped out from the hollow of a venerable oak, brandishing staffs.

Tuck quietly took hold of the horses, and Little John circled round.

"Fencing champions, eh?" Replied Robin, regaining his poise at the appearance of his men. "That's a commendable achievement. Well done. Now, please, I really must insist," Robin indicated the table, "my good Friar has been roasting that boar all morning!"

Two of the nobles reached for their swords, but Little John placed a heavy hand on each of their shoulders from behind.

The sight of the giant was enough for them to surrender to Robin's invitation.

The outlaws settled the nobles, and soon had them enjoying the feast, except for the black haired lady.

She sat in stony silence, and slapped Robin's hand, hard, when he tried to slip a perfect morsel of roast-boar onto her empty plate.

Robin retreated, all wide eyes.

"Hey, Hood!" Called Kate from the other end of the table. "Her name's Marian of Arlingford."

Marian's scandalized fury battered around Hood's ears as he bustled over to Friar Tuck.

To the smitten outlaw, her imprecations sounded sweet as a storm in heaven.

"Friar! I've got double urgent business. For Our Lady's Sake, just keep them here until I get back. Keep. Them. Here."

Robin Hood sprinted off between the trees.

Tuck's heart sank. From the joyous lope of the outlaw's legs, it was sure a monstrous mischief was brewing.

Little John stood guard over the horses whilst Dale and Tuck hosted the guests. Will Scarlett kept look-out.

The nobles were approaching dessert when Scarlett heard a stomach-chilling sound.

Unbelieving of his ears, Scarlett crouched and rested a palm on the forest floor. Then his waters reversed.

An army was heading their way. At least 20 horses, and platoons of men. Scarlett snapped upright and whistled the three tone danger signal.

The merry men scattered top speed into Sherwood's shadows.

The outlaws moved so fast, the lunch party were still wondering what to do, when Montfaucon came into view at the head of his soldiers.

"Thank the Lord!" Harold cried. "You've saved us!"

Montfaucon leant over his pommel in disbelief.

The foot-soldiers spread out behind him, focused behind their spears. The mounted men-at-arms trotted through the trees, their half-seen forms encircling the lunch table at a distance of 15 yards.

"Saved you from what, *exactly?*" Montfaucon eyed the lunch table with wary cynicism.

"Brigands, bandits and outlaws!" Cried Kate.

The soldiers shifted into battle formation.

Montfaucon glanced at Kate, then around the other rosy faces at the table.

"What did they do to you, *exactly?*"

"The bloody scoundrels forced us to have lunch." Harold snapped.

"Very politely though." Kate presented her full wine-cup in evidence.

"Kate. Be quiet." Marian brooked no quibbling.

"They almost assaulted us." Harold stated loudly, scrabbling for dignity.

"Well, I'm appalled." Montfaucon sat upright in his saddle, holding back a grin. "What kind of villainous, wood-crazed lunatics would do such a thing?"

Marian gave a short laugh, and plucked a tasty twist of flesh from the roast. "Smart ones, my good knight."

"We'll be leaving." Harold marched over to his horse.

"Hold a moment." Montfaucon cast a look around the quiet woodland. "Where did these outlaws go?"

"Every direction!" Kate jumped in. "One minute they were here, then *poof.* Gone, like willow-the-wisps."

Montfaucon smiled at the exuberantly tipsy, charmingly bodiced maiden.

"Well, my lady, thank you. Be assured we'll greet these wassailing willow-the-wisps with whipping cheer!"

Robin Hood sped merrily back towards the lunch table, clutching a finger ring in his hand. The outlaw owned no ring of gold, but Sherwood had provided.

He'd stripped and bored a branch to the right size, cut off two slices, and waxed them with duck fat. The first ring he attached to his neck chain, the second was for Marian of Arlingford.

Hood was so wrapped up in planning how he would present his gift, he ran straight in the back of Montfaucon's mounted men-at-arms.

The outlaw staggered wildly to the right as the spooked horse bucked its hind hooves, throwing its rider.

A crossbow bolt whacked into the tree Robin had caught himself on, then another speared agonizingly into his left calf.

A third whooshed by, two fingers above his head.

"By Our Lady!" Hood tumbled away, looking for brake or yew to hide in.

Only oaks stood in this part of the forest, ancient and widely spaced.

Montfaucon swung his stallion to face the fracas, and spurred.

The beast sprang like a deer, then ripped a gallop out of the forest floor.

"*Kill the thief!*" The knight's shining longsword swung high with bloody intent.

The footsoldiers fanned fast into the forest, the men-at-arms wheeling to get a shot. Montfaucon had the outlaw in his sights, 10 yards and closing.

Then an arrow came whispering out of the forest, catching a man-at-arms in the throat.

A second, a third, then a fourth ash arrow slammed into a soldier.

The footmen crouched for instant cover behind trees. A second volley of arrows whirred in, and more men fell.

Montfaucon yanked on his reins after an arrow thudded into his saddle. The black stallion howled at the pain in its mouth.

Terrible cries echoed back, like half the barbarians in Wales were about to erupt from the weald.

A third volley of arrows sank into body and limb, and the soldiers routed. Montfaucon twisted his stallion's head, and followed.

Harold and his party of nobles had just regained their saddles, when Sherwood discharged Montfaucon and his men in a flood of oaths.

A fourth volley of arrows chased through the air after them.

Friar Tuck appeared next to Robin, quickly followed by the rest of the merry men.

Scarlett and Dale were loosing shaft after shaft, Little John prowling for enemies like an irate bear.

Robin grabbed the bow out of Dale's hand.

"Little! Lift me up. Lift me up *now*." Robin jumped into the giant's arms.

Little John hoisted Hood into the air as the merry men stared in bewilderment.

"Stay steady, Little. Stay steady, goodman John."

Robin fiddled with his arrow, then drew the bow. He took careful aim through the wind-dancing, winter-bare woods, and let fly.

"*Go! Go! Go!*" Robin hollered, banging Little on the head.

The merry men scarpered, Little John with Robin Hood riding on his shoulders, laughing like a loon.

Montfaucon was rallying his men with dire threats, and Harold hurrying his friends away, when Robin's arrow came gliding through the air in a gentle arc.

Marian felt a tap on the top of her head as her horse broke into a canter, and thought it was low branch.

It was only after her party returned to Arlingford, that she realized an arrow had lodged in her hat.

"By Heaven's Mercy!" Harold gasped. "Those outlaws almost *murdered* you, Marian."

"What's that, behind the arrowhead?" Asked Kate, reaching out inquisitive fingers.

Marian brushed Kate's hand away so she could see for herself.

Tied to the shaft by a thread of Lincoln green, was a gleaming oaken ring.

Friar Tuck ~ Chapter 20

The three foundations of true law:
Order; justice; peace.
Triads of Bardism

"I'm in love, Friar!" Robin declaimed as Tuck bandaged up his calf wound.

"*What?* Are you sure you aren't confusing Cupid with that crossbowman?"

"This is no time for joking." Robin grabbed Tuck's shoulders. "Can you do marriages?"

"Can I *do* marriages?" Tuck waggled his head in disbelief.

"My mother would love her. And even if she didn't, I still would. Marian! Of Arlingford! Friar! Where is this blessed Arlingford?"

"It's about four crow miles north. Not to mention, five fathoms into fairy land." Tuck smiled despite himself.

"Monk, are you trying to tell me my love for Marian of Arlingford is impossible?" Robin Hood stood, tested Tuck's bandaging, then threw his legs akimbo, voice rising. "Unwise? Unrealistic? Undreamable? *Unredeemable?* Hah! My love will conquer all this, and more."

"Maybe she's just unavailable."

"By Our Lady, *I swear she's not.*" Robin clasped his hands. "I love Lady Marian. But God's truth is she's got a temper on her like a hornet stung wildcat. She's not yet met her match, mark me." Robin paced a small circle. "There's only one problem."

"Ah. Only one? What's that Robin?"

"We need more recruits. Today, Gisburne sent 50 men into Sherwood. Next time it'll be 100. We've got to be ready."

Tuck sought the quiet space from which wisdom speaks. He'd foreseen this moment.

Hood's outlaw crew had adopted a principled mission, now it was time to add some practical morality.

"Alright Robin, I know how to get recruits for our merry band. But, there's something you have to agree first."

"What's your need, brother Tuck?"

"Chastity in the forest."

"WHAT?" Robin girned absurdly. "Have you gone and had a conversion or something?"

"No, Robin." Replied Tuck patiently. "I've seen how you lusty men go la-la over women. If we allow shenanigans in Sherwood, it'll be the ruin of the band."

"But ... But, good Tuck ... Gentle Friar, *wise* friend, aren't women like wine? Gifts from our all merciful Lord, sent to soothe our days on this troubled earth?"

"No, Robin. Women are not like wine. Even I know they're a bit more complicated than that."

"But, *celibacy*... ." Robin pronounced the word like it was a Frankish malaise. "What will the men say? *By Our Merciful Lady,* what will I do with Marian?"

"Robin. Celibacy in the forest means you can do what you want outside the forest. When you're married."

Tuck had meditated long on the question, seeing not only the potential for trouble in the ranks, but also the danger to their female guests.

Forcibly extorting gold from the greedy in return for lunch was, according to the hermit at least, quite acceptable to God's laws. With more men in the troop, and no rule to contain them, Tuck knew that sooner or later someone would try for some fleshier booty.

That was totally unacceptable.

"Yes, I understand that, of course. But, isn't all-out celibacy a bit *extreme* Friar?" Robin spoke in a most convincingly mature fashion.

Tuck just shook his head.

Sir Ralph Montfaucon crossed the drawbridge of Castle Loxley, his features drawn in abominable disgust.

The knight had regrouped his men, and dived back into the forest after the rout, but hours of searching revealed nothing. Sherwood might as well have been empty.

As the sun set across the wintering shires, Montfaucon prepared to face Earl Gisburne's wrath.

"*Hellfire and Hellflame.* You had the bastards in your hands, and let them escape." Gisburne yelled across his dinner table.

"My Lord, there were at least 40 of them, armed with longbows! This isn't just a couple of chancers you've got carousing in Sherwood, there's a damned infestation of outlaws out there."

"An infestation? I see." Gisburne nodded as he filled his wine cup. "Then we'll just have to send the exterminators in, won't we?"

"Aye, my Lord."

"Aye, Ralph." Gisburne lifted the cup in cheer. "My dear Montfaucon, you know I trust you. If you could have got the outlaws' heads for me, you would have. Have a mug of wine, it's really quite good. We can gather 100 fighting men between Nottingham and Loxley, and raise a militia of 50 more from the shires." Gisburne sat back, his face shining unhealthily with drink. "That should be plenty to deal with the vermin."

"My Lord, with 150 men, I'll bring their thieving heads back in baskets."

Gisburne penned a swift letter, then summoned his seneschal.

"Get this to Nottingham, and send word through the shires that I want volunteers to form a militia. They're to report here on Lady Day. *And no old codgers.* I'll personally kill any codgers that come. Understood?"

"Yes, my Lord."

The merry men sat with unaccustomed gravity around their campfire.

Tuck had just finished explaining chastity.

"The Friar's quite right, fellows." Robin declared into the silence. "More men means more rules, simple as that."

"Ahem. It's not only chastity we need to establish."

"By Our Lady, *I knew it.* No, Friar. NO. I am NOT having sobriety in the forest." Robin waved his hands in absolute denial.

"Thank you, Robin, I hadn't considered the merits of sobriety." Tuck relaxed internally, praying to the Holy Spirit, and let his wisdom mind speak. "To grow in weal, this band needs strong roots. Robin Hood must have legitimacy. *He is henceforth King of Sherwood*, Lord of All Outlaws!" Tuck's voice rebounded among the rocks of the canyon. "With a King comes justice, and leadership. Robin Hood will be our common father, our root, under tree, and under God."

The merry men swayed to the forces of fate and faith quaking the air.

"Second. *Charity.* The riches we steal will be fully redistributed to the needy. The band will live only on what we can hunt and gather. Third. *Chivalry.*" Tuck's face took on a new light, expressing the essence of this idea directly into his flock's minds. "Our power will feed the hungry, and protect the weak." Tuck gestured strongly with his right hand, his voice ringing with prophetic charisma. "These will be our laws. Keep them, and live in victory. Fail them, and the merry men shall be cursed for ten times ten centuries."

"King Robin Hood! Crowned of Sherwood. Blessed be the Lord of All Outlaws." Little John's voice rumbled the Earth.

"Charity!" Cried Will Scarlett, his usually closed features transported with joy.

"Chivalry!" Alan-a-Dale's rendition of the word raised hairs on the back of every man's neck.

"Chastity!" Friar Tuck poured the every purity into the word.

Robin's band of outlaws had become his sons.

Like a dam breaking, his lordship, stymied since he'd lost his lands, bathed his soul.

"I will lead you." Robin's voice was humble, resolute. "I will lead you, as I am led. By God and my good Friar!"

The merry men exploded into cheers, hugs and triumphant laughter.

"Now, good Friar," Robin grinned, "where do we find our new recruits?"

"Ah, I know you're going to like *this*." Tuck replied with a broad smile. "Plenty of men handy with a bow, *and* a chance for good King Robin to impress our tempestuous maid of Arlingford."

The merry men chorused with catcalls and whistles, which Robin accepted with courtly bows and little gestures.

"There's an archery contest, to be held this Lady Day. Every Jack old enough to nock an arrow will be there. If we can't find a goodly crew of mischief-makers amongst them, then I'm a nun."

"By Our Lady, that's brilliant! But what about Marian?"

"The competition happens to be in Arlingford, and can you guess, Outlaw King, who could be handing out the prizes?"

"BY OUR LADY," Robin roared, "thank the Lord! *For Friars, for longbows, and Maid Marian.*"

"For Friars, longbows and Maid Marian!" Toasted the merry men.

Friar Tuck ~ Chapter 21

The three things never at rest:
The heart; the breath; the soul.
Triads of Bardism

Lady Day 1201 dawned crisp and fresh as Robin Hood, King of Sherwood, woke his not so merry men with an excited jig.

"Up, you blessed crew! By Our Lady, we're Arlingford bound."

The band pulled on their disguises with good-natured grumbles. After realizing it would curb their feast day options, no-one was going as a monk. Friar Tuck sent up a prayer of deepest thanks for this mercy.

The merry men set out in fine humour, Robin skipping ahead like they were off to his first ever fair.

The trees had budded earlier this year, flourishing in congregations of sap-rich shoot and verdant leaf.

Alan-a-Dale launched a sprightly air:

Have you seen Jack-In-The-Green?
With his long tail hanging down.
He sits quietly under every tree,
In the folds of his velvet gown.

It's no fun being Jack-In-The-Green,
No place to dance, no time for song.
He wears the colours of the summer soldier,

Carries the green flag all the winter long!

He drinks from the empty acorn cup,
The dew that dawn sweetly bestows.
And taps his cane upon the ground,
Signals the snowdrops it's time to grow.

It's no fun being Jack-In-The-Green,
No place to dance, no time for song.
He wears the colours of the summer soldier,
Carries the green flag all the winter long!

Arlingford was a thriving market town set by a slow flowing river. The brisk March morning had mellowed into a true spring day, bringing out throngs of people in celebration.

During the competition, Alan-a-Dale would sing his songs of Robin Hood. Little John and Will Scarlett would keep an eye out for sympathizers, and get chatting. If they proved of the right mettle, they would be invited to meet at a certain oak on Easter day.

Robin, of course, would be fully engaged in the contest. Tuck had decided he would be fully engaged keeping Robin out of trouble.

Alan-a-Dale wandered across to the brewer's stall, tuning his lute. Will Scarlett and Little John trailed a distance behind, already identifying a few likely looking lads.

Tuck watched Robin present himself as a competitor, and the heats began immediately.

The top end of the village green had been set with archery targets. In the first round, five archers drew at a time, each with three shots. The best of the five passed to the next round.

The crowd greeted the teams of archers with encouraging shouts as they came and went, their arrows swishing the air. Robin easily won his group.

Tuck cast an inquisitive glance through the crowd to Scarlett, who gave a positive nod in return. The recruitment drive was going well.

Round two of the competition saw 40 archers assembled before the prize table.

Set out on a sea-green cloth were three open boxes. To the left was the third prize, a large crate overflowing with victuals. To the right was the second prize, a small coffer filled with copper pennies. Held in a presentation case in the centre was the first prize, a silver arrow shimmering in the sunlight.

The crowd rippled tipsy, eager for entertainment, squashing Tuck up into the front row.

"Good people!" The Mayor of Arlingford stepped in front of the prize table, wearing festival clothes set off by a tall crown of woven twigs. "Doughty archers! We have three more rounds of competition to play, each more challenging. *The prizes are stupendous… .*"

The spectators yelled their appreciation.

"But I'm sure everyone agrees, the greatest will be the winner's kiss from our very own Lady Marian."

The crowd sent up a sky-shaking whoop as Marian stepped into view.

The maid was dressed in a form-fitting gown of dusky-blue, her midnight curls bunched under a delicate circlet of spring flowers.

She paced formally across to the mayor, her black eyes flashing greetings to the crowd.

"Arlingford *ho!*" Marian called in a boisterous tone. "It's true I've offered a Lady Day kiss to the boldest Jack archer… ."

The audience heaved with licentious good humour, calling out their approval of their lady's game spirit.

Marian broke into an amused grin. "I just pray: *May the best man win.*"

Laughter rocked the crowd as a team of boys hauled the targets to 200 yards, and the competitors stepped up to their marks.

Longbows were drawn, then arrows sliced across the distance in slivered streaks, thudding strongly into the targets.

The villagers competed amongst themselves to shout the loudest cheers for winners, and the most inventive insults for losers.

The second-round archers shot in eight groups of five, and again only one man from each went forward. Robin won his group by a solid margin, attracting much praise.

For the third round, the targets were shifted to 250 yards, and more spectators gathered from every side.

Eight semi-finalists stood before Lady Marian and the prize table.

"My most excellent archers. The targets are set at 250 yards. You will compete in fours. The best two in each group will enter the final, to shoot it out at a distance of 300 yards. Good luck!"

The archers stepped forward, eyeing each other fiercely as they selected their arrows.

The first group shot, and the winners raised their arms in jubilation. Robin was in the second group, and scored highest, but only by a few points.

Tuck acquired a mug of ale from a passing vendor, and settled in for the final.

The crowd's exuberance condensed as the four finalists presented themselves to Lady Marian's benign gaze.

Each man stood firm, intimidating his rivals, but their tension was palpable.

"Men, you have handled your weapons with skill to make a lady swoon."

The audience took a collective in-breath, then let out a roar that must have been heard in London.

"*But we were only playing before*. All I'm looking for now is pricked bullseyes!" Marian raised her arms, a figure to rival Boadicea. "*Boys,* set the targets. *Men,* choose your arrows. Our Lady's blessing on your bows."

Robin's grin danced with challenge.

The first archer, a rangy fellow, drew his bow. His arrows vibrated as they flew the long distance to smack into the target. He scored one bullseye, which the crowd rewarded with a good cheer.

The second finalist stepped up and shot. His superb technique scored him two bullseyes, and he received his rapturous applause with a happy bow.

Robin Hood strutted like a bantam to the firing point, and took up a wide stance.

The crowd jeered and cheered this cocky Jack in equal measure, then settled to watch him perform.

The outlaw's bow creaked in the silence as his first arrow flew.

Thhhhhhhhhwack! Even at this distance, the arrow buried its head firmly in the bullseye.

The outlaw's second arrow drew whispers and oaths as it joined its mate in the bull.

A heady pressure built amongst the people, Robin's heroic features inspiring them as much as his skill.

Robin Hood nocked his final arrow and swung the longbow into place. His left arm was steady as a mountain as he drew with his right. The focus in his eyes burned an almost visible path through the air to the target.

The audience erupted with amazed shouts as Robin's third arrow bulled for a perfect score. Tuck found himself dancing a jig with a buxom maiden, laughing at the top of his lungs.

The fourth finalist calmly took his place whilst the crowd were still delirious from Robin's feat. His first arrow silenced everyone with a deep thud as it landed dead centre.

The competitor drew again, his concentration total, and sent the next arrow hammering home.

"It's Gilbert Whitehand!" A Jack next to Tuck exclaimed. "The King's Royal Archer. He must have come up from London. The local boys won't like this one bit, no way, no how."

Without seeming to be aware of the throbbing excitement of the audience, Whitehand drew his last arrow.

The King's Archer stood for five long seconds at full draw, the air thickening around him as he prepared to fire.

The arrow flickered away, its passage illuminated by the sun, to pierce the bull with a sharp *whack*.

The crowd raised a clamour to wake the dead.

Robin went still.

His victory, and Marian's kiss, had been ripped from his hands.

"Our Lady has blessed you both!" Called Marian above the hullabaloo. "A knock out round will be played. Each archer has two arrows. The distance will be 350 yards. *Gentlemen*, only bulls count. *Boys,* prepare the field."

The Arlingford lads placed the targets on the banks of the river, the crowd spreading down the range to get better sight of the competition.

Will Scarlett brought Tuck a large jug of ale.

"Alan's packed it in for the day, Friar. We've got more volunteers than we know what to do with, and everyone's watching the contest anyway." Scarlett nodded across to the competitors. "How d'you think Robin's holding up?"

Tuck was worried.

Sherwood's King stood like a statue as Whitehand advanced to draw.

For a moment, Tuck was angry Robin could hold a game in such importance. Then his eyes drifted to Marian, and he sighed. Glancing back to Robin, Tuck found himself staring into his friend's forested eyes.

The outlaw's gaze was glassy, and his expression rigid. Hood had shot to the limits of his ability, and with victory so important, the challenge of the moment was overwhelming him.

Friar Tuck reached out and made the sign of blessing, which the outlaw returned with the briefest of smiles.

Gilbert Whitehand loosed his first arrow in a grand arc, the flight floating through the air to thud into the target just a little off the bull.

The crowd called out its consolations.

Robin's rival drew again, chose a diminished trajectory and with prayers on his lips, loosed.

This arrow slapped into the bullseye like a salmon leaping.

The lines of spectators broke into waves of admiring cheering.

Tuck reached for the internal stillness of his spirit, humbly seeking a boon in the name of love. From far away, he watched Robin take up his stance.

Tuck felt the shaft in his own fingers as the outlaw nocked, the strain in his shoulders as the outlaw drew, and the passage of air as the arrow flew.

It thocked square in the bull in time to a beat of Tuck's heart.

The crowd fell silent. Anticipation drummed the atmosphere.

Robin Hood chose his final arrow, and sighted down its length, rotating it slowly. He tweaked its fletch, then nocked.

Tuck's consciousness dissolved into the energies of Creation. His prayer powered blessing touched Robin's forehead with a cool finger.

The King of Outlaws raised his bow, drew and let fly in one unbroken motion.

The arrow accelerated in a shallow arch, slowing steadily on the crest, regaining speed as it fell.

Tuck's Divine interconnection faded as the missile swooped, leaving him gasping as he followed its fateful descent.

Sssssssssslam! The arrow buried its head next to its brother in the bull, and the audience went out of control.

For once, Robin looked as surprised as everyone else at his achievement.

The three champion archers approached the prize table.

Marian cheered the runners-up along with the tumultuous crowd as they collected their winnings.

A hush fell as Robin gave Marian a low bow.

Lady Marian's expression was just turning suspicious when the outlaw took her in his arms, and joined his lips to hers in an intimate, passionate kiss.

Time seemed to stop, then the couple broke apart.

A riot of enthusiasm rose from the crowd, but Tuck heard every word as Robin accepted the silver arrow on one knee.

"*You*. You're the outlaw who nearly murdered me!"

"What? *By Our Lady,* I'm sorry. I was being romantic-."

"*Romantic?* You dunderhead. You call almost skewering my brains for the sake of this ring, romantic?"

Marian showed the oaken ring on her finger, her face furious.

Robin broke into the biggest grin Tuck had ever seen, and let out a triumphant yell as he hefted the silver arrow into the air.

"Marian of Arlingford, you are the blessing of my life. Will you marry me?"

"Are you *completely* mad?" Marian's eyes went wide with shock.

"Is that a yes?"

"Hmmph. You don't know what you're getting into, outlaw. Take my advice, go back to your forest larks."

"M'Lady's wish is my command, but promise I can see you May Day?"

"I can't stop you visiting Arlingford." Marian put on a frosty smile, then made a big show of clapping Robin.

The King of Sherwood turned to the crowd, raising the silver arrow once again to thunderous applause. This time though, Robin walked over to Gilbert Whitehand, and lay the prize in his hands.

"You deserve this more than me, my friend. It was fate that guided my last arrows, not skill."

The festival crowd toasted the victor's generosity well into the night.

The merry men rambled home late in high spirits.

"Did everyone get what they came for?" Robin was particularly merry this evening.

"Aye, Robin," replied Dale, "there's three score boys, men and codgers who will be at the oak, Easter midday."

"Three score? Tuck! Be thankful we're recruiting Jacks and not Janes, Dale would have had the woods swimming with women!"

"Ah. Actually Robin," the minstrel smiled, "there's another two score goodwives, widows, and maidens who wouldn't take no for an answer...."

"By Our Lady, Friar. What on *earth* are we going to do with all these Janes?"

"Treat them with respect, Robin, treat them with respect."

Friar Tuck ~ Chapter 22

The three foundations of learning:
Seeing much; studying much; suffering much.
Triads of Bardism

Lady Day had also been busy at Castle Loxley. Instead of preparing feasts that morning, Gisburne and Montfaucon were inspecting troops.

Nottingham had sent 50 footsoldiers. Their short swords and round shields glinted under the changeable March sun as they stood to attention. Loxley's own force of 50 fighting men ranked their spears in disciplined formation.

Next to them stood a loose mass of Loxlians, armed mainly with farm implements. These country-men had been forcibly volunteered for the militia by their shire-lords. None had seen battle, and few had ever swung a weapon in anger.

Worse, they knew Gisburne placed no value on their lives, and were dreading what might happen in the shadows of the outlaw wood.

"Hellfire Ralph, would you look at this sorry lot." Gisburne pouted with distaste. "No wonder my taxes are so poor. These men wouldn't scare a sheep."

"No, my Lord. And they'll run at the first chance they get. We'll have to keep them in the centre of the soldiers."

The company of troops set out at mid-morning, and followed the main road into Sherwood.

Entering the forest, Gisburne reined his horse in hard.

"Flaming hellfire, what's *this?*"

"This, my Lord, is the commoner's way. They decorate the forest for pagan reasons. I believe they call it the Festival of the Trees."

"Didn't we burn all the witches?"

"Yes, my Lord, but this is the work of the people. I find it rather charming, in a backward sort of way."

"You've spent too long in London. After a season out here you'll have had all the backward you can stomach. Look at the bloody men for example! *What are they doing?*"

The Loxlians were weaving flowers and twining branches as they walked, swinging them up into trees as they passed.

"I believe the peasants call it 'festivalling', my Lord."

By mid-afternoon the company had come across nothing more substantial than rabbit droppings, and Gisburne had lost interest.

"You lead the men, Ralph. I can't parade around the woods all day, I've got business to attend to." The Earl cantered for Loxley and a large cup of canary.

Montfaucon eyed his Lord's back, then rallied his men.

"Right. We're not going home until we've killed some outlaws. If you don't want to spend the night in Sherwood, get hunting."

Just before sunset, the sky dusted mauve, a hue and cry sounded from Montfaucon's left flank.

The knight slipped out his sword and spurred his stallion.

"Sir, we caught these four hiding behind that stand of elm."

Montfaucon eyeballed a group of frightened looking Jacks, each with twigs woven into their hair.

Several had large bruises forming.

"Please, my Lord." Stammered one, falling to his knees. "We're not outlaws, we've come for the trees."

Some of Nottingham's soldiers laughed, but the Loxlian militia-men looked grim.

"Where's the outlaw camp?" Frustration flipped Montfaucon into a blind rage. "*You know where it is.* Tell me, and I'll let you go."

"Please," another Jack fell to his knees, "we don't know anything, we're from Edwinstowe."

Montfaucon nodded to one of his soldiers, who clouted the Jack to the dirt with his spear butt.

"Sir." A grave voice spoke up from amongst the militia. "I know that boy. He's Ian Tanner, a good lad, not an outlaw. They're in Sherwood for the Janes, not robbery. You must let them go."

Montfaucon's face turned bright red at being commanded by a farmer.

"You." The knight indicated another soldier. "Take the militia searching to the East."

The Loxlians were loath to leave the scene, but a few military jacksie kicks got them moving.

"Right. I'm asking again. Where is Hood? *This time,* if I don't get an answer, one of you loses his head."

The Edwinstowe Jacks dissolved into tears, wailing their ignorance.

Montfaucon leapt off his horse, the pleading of the peasants driving into his brain like spikes. He sliced the head off the nearest Jack without even really meaning to. His sword arm just followed the banner of his anger.

The other Jacks tried to scramble away, and a red mist covered Montfaucon's vision. The knight ravaged amongst them, swinging his sword left and right, taking off heads with each monstrous blow.

Montfaucon came back to himself swathed in silence.

The twitching corpses spouted blood in every direction, but the soldiers had their eyes fixed on their Captain. Most had seen battle, and some had witnessed slaughter, but none had witnessed butchery this despicable.

There was no way those festivalling boys had been outlaws.

"Right." Montfaucon re-sheathed his sword with a satisfied schlack. "Now we've killed some outlaws, we can go home. You! Gather the heads. You! Gather the company. *Move it,* you mincing morons, before I really lose my temper." The knight pinned a parchment to a nearby tree with his dagger, and spurred his stallion away.

The militia was dismissed at the gates of the Castle Loxley without thanks. The men weren't certain of what had happened in the woods, but dispersed across the shires carrying the rumour of bloody murder to their hearths and pubs.

The merry men reached the woods long after the new moon had been and gone.

Not far within, near a wide track, an unusual odour came on the breeze.

"Quiet." Will Scarlett stepped forward, sniffing.

The outlaws were instantly alert.

Nothing seemed out of place in the gloom.

"Can you guys smell anything funny? And no, I'm not joking."

The band had come to realize Scarlett was more sensitive than normal men, all his senses crisper. He was the first to hear danger, had eyes that could see for leagues, and his nose almost took the fun out of hunting.

"I'm a bit pissed, but something out there doesn't smell right." Scarlett whispered. "Let me get my bearings a minute."

Will rubbed his face vigorously, breathed all the air out of his lungs, and paused a beat. Then he took an impossibly long inhalation, nostrils flaring like bat's ears.

"There's fresh blood, a lot of it, about 200 yards that-a-way."

The merry men rushed to the scene of Montfaucon's murdery.

Hood wept when he identified the victims from their clothes as Loxlian Jacks.

Friar Tuck began the Rites for the Dead, a discomforting ache where his heart should be. Little John wordlessly broke off a wide branch, and dug shallow graves, while Dale and Scarlett swung the corpses into place.

Robin knew precisely who was responsible. He could feel the hand of Gisburne smearing Sherwood with evil.

"Hey," called Alan-a-Dale, "what's this?"

Dale pulled Montfaucon's dagger out of the ash and handed the parchment to Hood.

The King of Sherwood held it up to catch the starlight, and made out one word:

Outlaws

"By Our Lady." Robin sighed, his heart rending. "They've been killed because of us."

"No." Tuck replied immediately. "Nobody could mistake these Jacks for outlaws. They're wearing festival gear, for pity's sake! They were killed for us, not because of us. This is a message, Robin, a very direct message."

Friar Tuck ~ Chapter 23

The three things most precious to human kind:
Health; liberty; virtue.
Triads of Bardism

With spring in full swing, nobles, clergy and merchants took to the roads of England

All the quick routes between London and the North passed through Sherwood, and the merry men applied distributive justice with dedicated zeal.

"The only thing is, dear Friar, the richest travellers are too well protected for the five of us to handle." Robin mused after another long day lunching. "Everything keeps telling me we need more men."

"Come Easter we'll have a good 50, Robin." Tuck replied, licking his fingers free of dinner.

"50's enough to begin with, but not to end with. We need *overwhelming* force. Our enemy is strong, Tuck. Entrenched."

"Yes... ." Tuck gave Robin a careful look, troubled by a sense of something amiss.

Easter's sun strove, resplendent, for zenith as the merry men made their way to the meeting oak.

They didn't know what to expect, but carried enough food to feed an army.

They needed every morsel.

Robin Hood and Friar Tuck looked on in awe as nine score men and women gathered under the spreading boughs.

Dale, Scarlett and Little John handed out food left, right and centre.

"Well, you got what you asked for, Robin."

"Yes." Replied Hood, overwhelmed. "I guess that's a good thing, right Friar?"

"Now's not the time for a cold belly. Once they've stopped munching, they'll want talking to. Be inspiring. Be bold! Tell them about the rules."

"Right. Good news first."

"Always." Tuck nodded serenely.

"Got it." And Robin Hood, King of Sherwood, stepped forward.

The assembly quietened.

There had been a hundred stories of folk gifted with food or coin by the mysterious outlaw, but many disbelieved them. Times were so tough, helping others was a luxury few could imagine.

It had been the songs of Robin Hood and his merry men that stuck in the people's hearts, feeding their hunger for a hero.

"Good people. Thank you for meeting with us. I am Robin Hood. There is Little John, Friar Tuck, Will Scarlett and Alan-a-Dale. We five have taken a stand." Robin strode to the edge of the crowd, his figure golden under the benign canopy. *"A stand against tyranny and poverty."*

The people leaned closer, caught in Robin's charisma.

"Yes, I am an outlaw. Yes, I rob. But I am an outlaw from tyranny, and I rob those who inflict poverty. We few, merry men, want you to stand with us. Each of you. Stand with us! Together, we will overthrow tyranny. Today, we make our freedom in the forest, and with God's blessing, together we'll bring freedom to all the shires!"

Jacks and Janes cheered with wholehearted approval, codgers danced jigs, and children bounced in wild joy.

"For we work with God's blessing, good people." Robin's battlefield voice flew like a cloth over the heads of the jubilant crowd, settling them. "By joining the merry men, you accept Sherwood's laws. I am Lord of Outlaws, human justice rests with me. We are self-sufficient in the forest, everything we rob goes to others. Finally, under bough and branch we are disciplined. In Sherwood, men and women remain chaste. Our success will be measured by the strength of our commitment. These few rules mean an end to tyranny! An end to poverty! Freedom for us, and freedom for all!"

The assembly rose to their feet with a roar. More than Robin's powerful charisma, plentiful lunch and potent reputation, the rules made everything credible. Jacks recognised a structure behind the man they could trust. Janes felt confident and valued.

"Robin Hood, King of Sherwood, you have our allegiance. Swear us to your oath!"

"My people, the merry men have no oaths of fealty. Freedom means just that. You are here because, in your hearts, you have decided to work for the good of the shires. *The King of Sherwood needs no oaths from ye.* Your hearts are full strong enough for me!"

The merry men paraded into the forest, the hermit's canyon accommodating 185 boisterous outlaws as comfortably as it had five.

Robin Hood and Friar Tuck interviewed every Jack and Jane, giving each a length of Lincoln green cloth to disguise their faces when robbing.

Little John, Alan-a-Dale and Will Scarlett worked on expanding the encampment.

Sunset saw the happy band gathering around a large fire.

"My people. You join the merry men with a variety of skills, and lives outside the forest. I urge you as your King: As much as you apply your skills to advance the cause, do not neglect your other duties. If you have to go, *go*. We need friends *everywhere*. Robbery is only the beginning. We seek the overthrow of tyranny, and our example will raise the spirit of Arthur across Albion, to break the rule of wrong over the people, forever!"

Of the nine score new recruits, two score, the codgers especially, were tasked with providing safe havens and spreading the word. Another two score were Janes, best able to gather and relay information, leaving five score fighting Jacks.

Of these fighters, two score were suited to forest life. The rest would come and go, assisting as they could, ready to be called on at need.

Each new recruit was assigned to one of the original outlaws, now Robin's Captains.

The next morning, Robin Hood and Little John began weapons training. The sight of a hundred Jacks wielding synchronized staffs lifted everyone's hearts.

Will Scarlett and Alan-a-Dale set up communication chains and secret signs, working mainly with the Janes.

Friar Tuck passed among the people, embedding their sense of purpose with good humour and spiritual authenticity.

The merry men celebrated an Arcadian lunch in the company of two hogsheads of pale ale, honestly donated by local brewers; and three maple-roasted buck deer, absently donated by King John.

Outlaws old and new rejoiced that the battle against tyranny had begun as they filled their bellies under the lush leaves of Sherwood Forest.

"Merry men!" The Lord of Outlaws appeared between two oaks, raising his voice in comradely hail. "We strike together against poverty, for the first time - within the hour!"

Friar Tuck swung his head round in surprise, noting Little John and Alan-a-Dale looked equally spooked.

"A caravan is at this very moment entering the weald from the south. Soon it will be ripe for the taking. Rise up! Rise up! Go to your Captains: Little John, Friar Tuck, Alan-a-Dale and Will Scarlett. They will lead you in your tasks. Our Lady's Blessing on us all!"

The merry men heaved a cheer into the skies that shook the trees.

Sherwood's King corralled his leery Captains.

"Tell 'em, Scarlett."

"Fellows, it's a caravan of six carts. They're guarded by a score of mounted men-at-arms."

"*A score?*"

"Hush, Friar, let Will finish."

"I know what they're carrying! Nottingham often sends to London for wine and other items he can't get locally. This is his first supply train of the year, brimming with goodies. Thing is, this time, the Sheriff's also made use of the guard to escort up two chests of newly minted coins."

"That's quite a haul." Little John rubbed his hands together.

"And quite a guard." Added Dale.

"The new recruits have had five minutes training, and we barely even know their names! You can't take them robbing like its scrumping, Robin."

"That's where you're wrong, Friar." Hood had a look in his eye Tuck had never seen before. "You forget I was born to lead companies. I can go a heck of a long way with a hundred willing men." The outlaw's eyes darkened from pools of leafy green to points of deepest sage. "Now I'll show you what overwhelming *really* means. Captains!" The outlaw's smile steeled his men's hearts. "This *early strike* shall bind our crew together like nothing else could. It will also challenge each of you. Now, you must be leaders." Hood's fiery energy quickened his officers' courage. "Look to your co-ordinations, mark your tasks. *A quick advance:* lead your men by example; stay resolute. *A quick assault:* strike hard, there is no place on the field for dilly dally. *A quick clearance:* be like the ocean tiding, leave nothing and no-one behind."

Robin settled the men into ambush, his torturous experiences of Crusade redeemed. Loxley's military service gave Hood a capacity for leadership and strategy that would have been impossible any other way.

This stretch of road climbed steeply from the south, flattened into a clearing bordered by bushy crab-apples, then curved into a fork a little farther on. Where the main road continued north to Nottingham, only a few miles distant, the fork dipped west into an overgrown chase to nowhere.

Alan-a-Dale's and Will Scarlett's teams crouched concealed on the flanks, Little John lurked at the top, and Robin Hood was ready to cut off the rear. Friar Tuck was stationed at the fork.

The Lord of Outlaws sent his gaze flashing around the area, then ducked away, satisfied the company was invisible.

Five mounted men-at-arms noisily crested the rise in the road, carrying sword and shield, armoured in chainmail. Behind them rolled the six carts, large wheels creaking under low canvas tops. In line down each side rode five more alert men-at-arms, with the final quintet holding crossbows to ward the rear.

Dale and Scarlett's teams exploded out of the crab-apples, 20 men to a side. They had been hiding behind cut branches, which they now thrust into the horses' faces.

The flanking guards were thrown from their spooked steeds, and clouted unconscious. With four outlaws for each man-at-arms, it was short work.

Robin Hood's 20 men, archers all, peppered the group of rear crossbowmen, their heavy-headed bodkin arrows smashing through the guards' chainmail.

A second volley wasn't required.

Little John's platoon rushed the vanguard. The sight of a bellowing giant supported by a horde of green-scarved maniacs, set the remaining men-at-arms galloping hell for leather for Nottingham.

Tuck's team commandeered the carts, and drove them down the chase.

Little John and Alan-a-Dale cut their forces back to the canyon, whilst Hood organized the camouflage operation. Even a hundred men couldn't carry away such a haul in a hurry, so they'd decided to leave it in place.

Scarlett's crew disappeared the carts under heaps of brake, whilst Robin's platoon lugged a frame covered with crab-apple branches across the mouth of the fork.

The carts, and the fork itself, vanished from view.

Job done, Will Scarlett dashed away with the men, leaving Friar Tuck and Robin Hood alone to give the site a final dust-down.

Seeing everything was as it should be, Robin gave Tuck a merry grin, which he returned in full, and the pair hustled away.

The flanking guards were just coming to consciousness when the Sheriff of Nottingham thundered in at the head of a company of soldiers.

The snorting horses and battle-ready men milled and wheeled in tightly packed tension as the caravan guards explained what had happened.

"By all the powers of hell, *they can't have taken the carts far.*" The Sheriff shrieked. "They must have gone south!"

The troops whirled into formation, and charged down the slope of the road.

The Sheriff had galloped two pelting miles before wondering how six laden carts could have covered the distance so fast.

"They must have taken a side track." Nottingham forced his way back through the column. "Turn around, damn you. Spread out and search the forest!"

The Sheriff spent a fruitless afternoon combing the woods south of the ambush. Since he'd come from the north, it didn't occur to him to search there, especially not within 20 yards of the hijack.

As the sun set behind iron-shod lines of cloud, the Sheriff returned to Castle Nottingham, apoplectic.

By this action, the outlaws had invited every one of hell's damnations on their miserable heads. The Sheriff swore he'd race the devil to personally deliver them.

The six carts sat tranquil in the chase until midnight, when the outlaws stripped them to their axles, and bundled the whole lot away.

Friar Tuck ~ Chapter 24

The three kinds of knowledge:
The nature of each thing; the cause of each
thing; the influence of each thing.
Triads of Bardism

May Day 1201 dawned to a lightning storm of rare power cackling and crackling above Sherwood.

The bolts stayed high, throwing fantastic flashing forms silhouetting through the cloudscape. The rising sun brushed away the storm clouds with splays of platinum light.

After enjoying an inspired poached trout for breakfast, Robin and his Captains set forth for Arlingford in particularly fine humour.

The dawn storm had charged the air with the tang of mountains. The trees roistered upwards, their trunks creaking with juicy peristalsis. The weald was head over heels with spring, sparkling in bird-song.

Arlingford revelled in the festive spirit. The thatched cottages brimmed with bouquets of flowers, and the alders around the pond looked almost abashed under their weight of festive decoration.

A tall white pole stood in pride of place on the village green, multicoloured ribbons trailing from its top to flutter over the ground.

Festivallers thronged everywhere, greeting friends not seen since the year before, or gathered in loose circles on the grass.

Alan-a-Dale and Will Scarlett set off into the crowd to spread outlaw stories. Little John, Friar Tuck and the hermit collected frothing mugs of May ale. Robin Hood looked out for Marian.

Toward mid-afternoon, the May Troupe appeared on the edge of the green, to loud acclaim from all around. Musicians marched proudly, wearing festive tabard and trews, ringing out traditional tunes.

Then Lady Marian, dressed as the May Queen, led forth a gaggle of gaily-dressed dancers.

"By. Our. Lady." Robin gaped.

A long white gown flowed from the May Queen's bare shoulders, held by flashing copper clasps at the hips. A wide belt of woven wildflowers wrapped her waist, matching the delicate circlets sitting at ankle and wrist. Marian's headdress plumped with rose buds, succulent and tight in their bed of raven curls, and her feet were bare.

Little John pulled Robin back down to the bench he'd sprung up from.

"Easy, wildcat. Even the Lord of Outlaws can't interrupt the May Queen in the midst her duties."

At the May Pole, Marian lifted a ribbon into each dancer's right hand, moving sunwise.

Three times the Queen circled the pole, until all the ribbons were held by happy Jacks and frisky Janes.

"Our Lady's renewing blessing on our Isle!" Marian called with the voice of ten thousand women, and the dancers whirled into motion.

Weaving as they went, the Jacks and Janes wound their ribbons to the pole, then reversed and unbound. The music swelled, and the crowd swayed in rhythmical happiness.

Robin had to wait another hour before he could to catch a moment with Marian.

"*Well.* I wondered if you would show up." Marian was pointedly distant. "You've got some nerve, that's for sure."

"Marian, you've filled my every thought since Lady Day."

"*I doubt that very much.* You look better fed than when I last saw you, and if rumour's believed, have been robbing innocent travellers all the while."

"Ah. Yes. That. We don't rob the innocent, you know, only the rich."

Marian couldn't help laughing, and Robin dared a dashing grin.

"*Don't* think you can come to Arlingford and charm your way around, outlaw. *Phoof!* I could almost like you, if it wasn't for your princely airs."

"*Princely airs?*"

"Yes, like that cocky strut you wrap your legs with, that frankly, *wide,* green getup you clothe yourself with, and that indelicate wit you twist your tongue with."

"If *only* I had something else to twist my tongue with... ."

"You see! Uncouth. *And proud of it.* I've duties to attend to, if you'll excuse me, Prince Charmer."

"Oh. Can I see you later?"

"I can't stop you being by the alders at sunset, even if I am May Queen." Marian let a twinkle enter her eyes as her mouth formed a dignified pout.

Sunset found Sherwood's Captains content around a merry table. God was in their hearts, King sat with Queen, ale hailed belly, and friends shared the glory of the blazing colours lifting the night-bound skies.

Later, the Lord of Outlaws joined them in a mug of ale.

He was like a triple Robin, magnified by love.

"Listen fellows, when you're ready, head back to Sherwood without me, understand?" Robin glanced around, grinning.

"Right you are. My Liege." Replied Little John, and everyone cracked up laughing.

Alan-a-Dale sang the merry men home:

May I make my fond excuses for the lateness of the hour,
but we accept your invitation, and we bring you Beltane's flower.

For the May Day is the great day, sung along the old straight track,
And those who ancient lines did lay, will heed the song that calls them back.

Pass the word and pass the lady,
Pass the plate to all who hunger!
Pass the wit of ancient wisdom,
Pass the cup of crimson wonder!

Ask the green man where he comes from, ask the cup that fills with red.
Ask the old grey standing stones, that show the sun its way to bed.

Question all as to their ways, and learn the secrets that they hold.
Walk the lines of nature's palm, crossed with silver and with gold.

Pass the word and pass the lady,
Pass the plate to all who hunger!
Pass the wit of ancient wisdom,
Pass the cup of crimson wonder!

"Ah, Tuck," sighed the hermit as they strolled into the cool arms of the canyon encampment, "seeing Robin with Marian makes me feel young again."

"Heaven have mercy!" Tuck pulled a face of riotous fear.

"Not in that way." The hermit laughed. "Idiot. I mean, optimistic, y'know?"

Tears started to Tuck's eyes, and he clasped the hermit on the shoulder.

"Aye." The hermit chewed his beard, his eyes glinting. "Romantic notions always were my downfall!" The hermit abruptly stood back, and his voice deepened: "*Should Sherwood's King not rightly wed the May Queen, sorrow will fill the forest.*"

"What are you talking about now, you bearded jabbler?"

"Hush, Tuck. That wasn't me speaking, at least, not the normal me."

"The *normal* you!" Tuck cried in wonderment.

"*Hush*, I tell you." The hermit leaned in, more than slightly drunk, but also very sober. "Sure, that was a *prophecy*."

Tuck pulled a dubious look.

"You're going to have to keep a watchful eye on this whole Robin and Marian *thing*."

"What? I'm a *monk* in case you'd forgotten."

"I'm sorry, I'll be a bit clearer." Replied the hermit with sarcastic patience. "For reasons too arcane for your idiot ears, Robin must not do *you-know-what* with *you-know-who* until they're wed."

"*What?* Hermit, that's the craziest thing you've said yet!"

"You're not in kindergarten anymore, monk. There's more at play here than you might imagine."

Tuck stared at his teacher, caught between drunkenness and confusion.

The hermit gave a short-tempered sigh. "This *thing* between Robin and Marian just has to be *done proper*. See? Simple enough for you?"

"But what am *I* meant to do about it?"

"You'll think of something." The hermit shrugged, then brightened. "You'd better, brother. It's in your hands, so it's on your head."

"Well, that's just dandy." Tuck muttered as the hermit disappeared into the weald, whistling a carefree air.

Then Tuck remembered that Robin, right at that moment, was with Marian. Alone.

The couple wandered in glorious sympathy through the spring-raptured trees. Oak hunched playfully, and crab-apple bushed in joyous plenitude.

Robin paid no attention to where they were going, his feet finding heaven in every step while his eyes gazed on Marian.

The May Queen glided weightlessly, a light smile curving her lips, enjoying Sherwood's rustling welcome.

The ground rolled through a copse of flourishing beech, then they passed a set of faithful yew to find themselves at the top of a hillock.

Stars paraded in intense clusters above their heads. A half moon ranged the vastness, so cleanly cut that its ebon side showed as stark as its silver.

Robin took Marian in his arms, and they kissed.

When the blissful lovers broke apart, they were surrounded.

Little People compassed the hilltop. At cardinal and sub-cardinal points stood 12 cloaked figures, the height of Little John, but a fifth of the width. Three more tall Strangers stood close by, faces hidden under curved hoods, emanating an unearthly chill.

Marian clutched Robin's hand, a grip he returned strongly.

The outlaw didn't sense an immediate threat, yet the hairs on the back of his neck were rigid.

"Greetings, guests of Sherwood." Robin stated courteously.

"Greetings, lovers of Si'ir." The voice came on a breeze of snow-cold air.

Marian opened her mouth to speak, but a flying globe of vibrant purple-pink light took her breath away. The ball cast a soft illumination over the scene as it drifted over the hilltop. Another globe, of virulent yellow, then another, of vivid green, sallied through the air, then a fourth materialized above their heads.

Where the others had been lustrous puffs of solid colour, this one's surface was aqueous with the hypnotic tones of a moonlit sea.

"King of Sherwood, Queen of May, Beltane is a night for lovers. Si'ir is a Gable for lovers. Our Green King and Merciless Queen celebrate as you, and the worlds will meet!"

The Little People began a spiral dance, stepping delicately as they hummed an occult melody.

Ardour flared in Robin's belly, and he grasped Marian's waist. The May Queen succoured the outlaw's soul in the depths of her star-smeared eyes. Her lips plumped for kissing, sending her sweet breath to play on Robin's face.

The curious light, the enchanting song, the turning earth, throbbed in the lovers' blood.

Marian grasped the back of Robin's head, drawing her fingers through his hair, drowning in desire. Robin tore a hand through the bronze clasp above Marian's left hip, revealing a fructifying beauty of thigh.

The lovers dove deeply into their kiss, their hands roving passionately.

"*Robin Hood,* what on earth do you think you're doing?"

In a flash, the music stopped and the lights went out.

The lovers were disentangling themselves when Friar Tuck appeared out of the sudden gloom.

"Er, Tuck, I know you're a monk, but it's called kissing. *And it's private.*" Replied Robin in a rough voice.

"I know that, but you're in the forest. You know the rules, Robin."

"What? *By Our Lady.* But... ." The Lord of Outlaws was speechless.

"What rules, monk?" Asked Marian, her body buzzing with liberated femininity.

"Chivalry, my Lady Marian. Charity, and-."

"*Chastity.*" Robin spat out the word like a bad apple.

Marian glanced from the bashful monk to the frustrated outlaw, then pealed into fits of laughter.

Tuck tried to mask a chuckle, then collapsed into uncontrollable giggles.

Robin Hood looked from the laughing monk to the guffawing Queen, and was swept into the torrent of hilarity.

Tuck escorted the lovers home, their encounter with the Hilltop Strangers fading like a dream.

Friar Tuck ~ Chapter 25

Three things that lay waste to the world:
A king without counsel; a judge without
conscience; a son without reverence.
Triads of Bardism

The merry men were delighted to find Marian joining them for a long breakfast. None of them made any jokes about her having slept next to the monk.

At midday, with the sun warm around fluffy May clouds, Little John got ready to accompany Marian back to Arlingford. Scarlett had reported the arrival of a rich-looking batch of unprotected nobles, and the other outlaws had to go to work.

Robin gave Marian's hand a charming kiss, which she accepted with a sensuous smile.

"Outlaw King, Arlingford will welcome your next visit."

"My Lady May, I promise you only one thing: It will be soon." Robin dashed off, Dale and Scarlett running with him.

Their figures hazed into the spokes of sunbeams shafting through the dappling canopies.

Friar Tuck shook Marian's hand, giving a little grin of apology.

"Dear Friar," Marian took Tuck's hand in both of hers, "thank you. If the King breaks his own rules, the people will never stick to them. You are a true friend to Robin, and thus to me. I love him."

"Dear maid," Tuck bowed with mischievous grace, "I also promise you one thing: I will see you wed as quick as the Good Lord allows!"

Tuck followed Robin with Marian's surprised laughter playing about his blushing ears.

This small job didn't need more than a tight crew, and the new recruits were busy at the encampment, so Robin had brought only his Captains. It felt good to have the old team together, capable and carefree.

Hood grinned as the outlaws got into position, darting from elm to yew, ash to elm, oak to oak.

Ten yards in front, a well travelled forest path opened into a spacious glade. It was a great spot for lunch, and the merry men had used it a couple of times already.

Will Scarlett appeared from the right, waving that their guests were approaching.

Soon enough, four young noblemen appeared, whistling a snappy tune as they strolled into sight. Each was dressed in the latest London style, with over-long sleeves and colourful jerkins under festooned hats.

Despite their dandified appearance, Robin noted their striped leggings outlined muscles of significant strength.

The whistling died on a half-note when the Lord of Outlaws emerged from Sherwood like a phantom Maitre D'.

"Welcome to the bower, my noble friends. Here you can eat and drink as much as you like, and all at one generous price!"

Friar Tuck laid out a cloth on the grassy knoll, whilst Will Scarlett and Alan-a-Dale unpacked tempting victuals from a basket.

The guests stared at each other with such perfect amazement, that Robin let out a good-natured laugh.

"Yes, my city-bred friends, this is how we do it in the country."

The guests regarded Robin, then the merry men preparing the picnic.

"Ah. In your country, you do it zis vay?" Asked a handsome fellow with a distinguished brow. "Ve are visitors here, from Saxony. Excuse us, ve do not know your customs."

"*Foreign friends.*" Robin indicated Tuck's picnic invitingly. "Here, you eat and drink. Simple, eh?"

The Saxons nodded their understanding.

"Then, you pay." Robin rubbed two fingers together, and gave a large, comforting, smile.

"But ve hav our own food." Each of the Saxons swung a shoulder bag into view.

Robin Hood blinked twice.

"Ah, in Saxony it is like zis alzo!" The leader cried with sudden enthusiasm. "You share viz us. *Ve share viz you.* Everybody eating togezer."

"No. You don't understand. You have to eat our food, then pay us, see?"

The Saxons held polite expressions for a moment, then confabulated in their own tongue.

"Yeeees." The leader turned back to Robin, seeking amiable clarity. "Ve eat *togezer*. Yes?"

"No, *no*. You eat, you pay, you leave. We give, we take, we leave. See? Everybody's happy. It's a good price, I assure you, and the food wonderful."

"Ve vould like to aczept your hozpitality," the Saxon leader replied with courteous dignity, "but ve hav no money. Ve came to ze vood for lunch, not spendings. You understand?" He shook his empty hands. "No. Money."

"Right." Robin drew out his longsword. "Will you just go and sit down, please."

The Saxons went still.

One, a stocky fellow, said something to another, taller chap. That one replied with three cynical syllables.

"Ve hav not our veapons." Stated the leader, pointing to his picnic bag.

"You don't need weapons. You need *mon-ney*. Look. Sit over there, and eat. Or I'll stab you. How's that? Got that? STAB." Robin thrust his sword obviously a few times through the air.

The Saxons didn't move, balancing on the balls of their feet. The tall fellow said something quickly to his leader, waving a hand at Robin, then the merry men.

Friar Tuck, Alan-a-Dale and Will Scarlett were gawping behind Robin, roundly dumbfounded at this unlooked for turn of events.

"Is zis an English joke?" The Saxon leader asked slowly.

"No, it is not a bloody joke. *Tuck!* Tuck, thank the Lord. Can *you please* explain to our guests what lunch is all about?"

"Er, right. You. Sit. Here." Tuck made highly illustrative sitting actions. "Then, eat." Tuck engaged the appropriate, if exaggerated, motions.

The Saxons nodded solemnly.

"Finally, pay." Friar Tuck reached into an imaginary purse and bestowed invisible coins on each of his guests.

Pleased with his international relations, he ended with a little bow.

The Saxons burst into billows of baritone laughter. Tuck's earnest pantomiming was just too hysterical.

Their giggles had just died down when the taller Saxon pointed ironically at Tuck, and jabbered a few lyrical words. The young men broke into a round of helpless ridicule.

Robin Hood stared hard at the ground, doing his best not to snigger. Will Scarlett and Alan-a-Dale had turned their backs, but their shaking shoulders couldn't be mis-read.

Tuck eyed the foreigners with particular ill-humour, causing them to bawl with laughter.

"Ve like your clown very much!"

"Yes. So do we." Robin kept a straight face. "However, now we've got to get serious."

Dale and Scarlett swung out longbows, nocked and ready, aimed steady.

Tuck hefted his shillelagh with unfeigned relish.

"Here, and here, and one for you, and here." Robin pressed a roll of bread in each of the Saxon's bemused hands. "Now you've got lunch. Where's your money?"

"I am sorry, VE HAV NO MONEY." The leader shook his head at his friends, as if the merry men were very possibly village idiots.

Robin pointed his sword at the Saxon's throat.

Dale and Scarlett drew their bows.

Tuck lifted his shillelagh.

The Saxons' faces came alive with courage.

"Ve have no money, but ve vill come tomorrow, bringing much wiz us." Volunteered the stocky one.

"Sorry. Tomorrow's no good, we've got other tables booked."

"His name is Hartmann auf der Lauer. You can trust his word, it is iron. My name is Freiherr Friedrich von Schönfels-Hohenstein. My word is stone." The Saxon leader gave the ghost of a bow.

"My name is Walther von der Gänseheide." Declared the taller one. "Hartmann speaks truth. My word is gold."

"My name is Gottleib Riemenschneider. Hartmann speaks truth. My word is pure."

Robin looked from one to the other, believing them in every respect, but disbelieving of the entire scene.

"Dale. Scarlett. Dear Friar. Pack up lunch, would you? Our visitors really don't have any money."

"Zank you. But may I ask who you are?" Inquired Schönfels-Hohenstein.

"Of course, I'm sorry, my manners are a little rusty. My name is Robin Hood, Lord of Outlaws. That is Alan-a-Dale, minstrel of a thousand boughs. With us today is Will Scarlett, tracksman and scowler. And of course, you all know good Friar Tuck." Robin sheathed his sword, smiling once more. "And my friends, I'm sorry to say none of us will be here tomorrow."

"Ah. Robin Hood, Outlaw Lord." Hartmann stated menacingly. "Ve vill come alone, and wiz much gold."

"Well in that case you corky little strumpet, *see you at twelve.*" Robin snapped, all his frustration rushing out in reckless challenge.

Hartmann smiled with satisfaction.

The Saxons sauntered back up the road, breaking into a round of loud chuckles before they curved out of sight.

The merry men packed up their picnic in thoughtful silence, then headed home, empty handed, and rather exhausted.

Friedrich led his friends to where they'd tethered their horses at the edge of a stream. Each was a gray charger 18 hands high, of impeccable pedigree, with pointed ears and expressive eyes.

Arriving back at Nottingham castle later that evening, the young men presented their odd adventure to the Sheriff.

"*The outlaws.*" Nottingham spat a gobbet of chicken across the table in outrage. "You met the thrice damned outlaws! You're lucky you weren't bloody killed."

The Saxons gave each other long looks.

They belonged to the Order of Teutonic Knights, on a tour of European Capitals, seeking knowledge and influence. The young men had come through Austria and France, and were officially visiting London. After spending a puzzling two weeks in King John's court, they had been invited to Nottingham, to see the famed English countryside.

Despite the cultural divide, the visitors had quickly appreciated the character of their host, and were not impressed. As well as being born to some of the best houses in Saxony, the knights were sworn to strict vows of temperance. The Sheriff's undignified debauchery had been doubly unappreciated.

There was simply no *Gastfreundschaft* to his feasting.

"But ve still don't understand, Sheriff, vat vas ze idea wiz ze lunching?"

"Those *evil* bastards give their victims lunch, so they can say what they do isn't stealing."

"Iz not stealing?" Asked Walther von der Gänseheide. "Vy iz zis important to Robin Hood?"

"The devil himself would be shamed at what I must tell you ... That outlaw Hood pretends to have honour! In truth he finagles the multitude with stolen goods. *The madman tells people they don't need to submit to the aristocracy.*" The Sheriff sat back, gone as far as he dared in voicing this heresy. "We, the elite, know it is our duty to protect the rabble from their own stupidity." The Sheriff gestured to include his guests. "After all, *we* know privilege is the very rock of civilization."

That settled it for the Teutonic Knights.

They didn't understand everything that went on in this extraordinary country, but they knew they weren't in any *we* with the Sheriff of Nottingham.

The young men were also secretly rather taken with the impossible romance of honourable robbers making merry in the deepwood.

"My forces aren't strong enough to roust them out of the forest, so I've sent to good King John for mercenaries." Nottingham squinted in drunken spite. "By all the hemp dancers in hell, I'll enjoy giving Robin Hood a full serving of the King's justice."

The Saxons retired early to bed, having decided to quit the ignoble Sheriff the following day. They solemnly agreed Nottingham didn't need to know about their personal lunch-time rendezvous.

In the cascading light of a magnificent May morning, the Teutonic Knights mounted their chargers in the courtyard of Nottingham castle. Draped in plates of painted armour and swathes of embroidered cloth, the horses pranced and blew like tamed dragons.

Freiherr Friedrich von Schönfels-Hohenstein lifted an armoured hand in farewell to the hung-over, and over-awed, Sheriff.

"Ve hav been unexpectedly called back to London. Ve zank you for your, ah, hozpitality."

"Goodbye, do come again. And relay my greetings to good King John!"

The Teutonic Knights sprang away in a tumult of pennant, hoof, armour and lance.

"This is stupid, Robin. Even if those jokers come back, they'll bring all of Nottingham and half of Loxley with 'em, and we'll be hanged." Little John paced around the forest glade, barely able to hold his temper.

"*By Our Lady,* John Little. I've already had an ear-bashing from Tuck. Don't tell me you're going to do the same." Robin peered along the track. "Pipe down. They'll be here, alone and with gold. I'd stake my hat on it."

Sure enough, Scarlett came running in from his look-out post a few minutes later.

"They're coming, and only four of them."

"See! What did I tell you?"

"But there's something you should know-." Scarlett stammered, but it was too late.

The Teutonic Knights hammered out of Saxon myth and along the forest path in a storm of Sturm and Drang. Clouds of dust rolled like an avalanche of raging titans in their wake.

The gray chargers slammed to a stop five yards from Robin Hood's gaping face. The sun broke brilliantly from between playful clouds to skitter fire-flashes over each knight's full mail battle-armour.

The knights pulled off their helms in unison, and shook out their shoulder-length, blonde hair.

"Gud Afternoon, Lord of Outlaws." Freiherr Friedrich gave a salute. "You vished to invite us to lunch, not zo?"

"Er, yes." Replied Robin, caught so unprepared he hadn't thought to call in the merry men.

The knights dismounted and clanked over to the picnic blanket.

Alan-a-Dale placed a mug of wine into each gauntleted fist, and took a nervous step back.

"Prost!" The knights toasted each other with gusto.

"Ah, now ve fight?" Hartmann auf der Lauer handed his mug back with courtly courtesy.

Robin Hood, King of Sherwood, gave a great whistle in reply.

40 staff-wielding merry men erupted from hiding, yelling at the tops of their lungs.

The knights swung up their swords as the wave of men crashed over them, swamped by an ocean of flailing staffs.

Then, incredibly, the outlaws were stalled in their advance.

Gottleib had gone berserk, taken hold of a merry man, and was using him to batter everything in range.

The other Teutonic Knights laid about with their weapons, but to Robin's astonishment, his men weren't bleeding.

The knights had kept their swords sheathed against the attacking peasants.

"*Onwards, outlaws!*" Hood commanded as he faced Freiherr Friedrich. "No blades, no bows. Let's bash some respect into 'em!"

Little John waded into the raging melee, aiming for Hartmann auf der Lauer. Alan-a-Dale and Will Scarlett took on the bonkers Gottleib.

Friar Tuck pushed through the heaving throng to square off against Walter Gänseheide, more than ready to fight for English dignity.

"Fritz, help!" Walter dropped his guard. "I cannot fight ze clown!"

In the midst of combat with Robin Hood, Freiherr Friedrich collapsed into fits of giggles. "Sing him a song zen, he vill like zat."

Walter von der Gänseheide sang in a soulful, ragged-edged voice:

Unter der Linde an der Heide,
(At the heath, under the linden tree).
Wo unser beider Bett war.
(Where our bed used to be.)

After the first verse, the rest of the Teutonic Knights joined in warm harmony, still fighting furiously.

Hartmann seemed a match for Little John, a rhinoceros against an elephant.

Dale and Scarlett couldn't get close enough to Gottleib to land a blow, merry men being knocked down like nine-pins all around.

Robin and Friedrich drummed up the heat of battle with the thumps of their scabbarded weapons.

Dort könnt ihr finden,
(There might you find,)
Beides, liebevoll gebrochen Blumen und Gras.
(Flowers and grass, picked in kind.)

Friar Tuck aimed a rain of hefty, enraged, swipes at Walter Gänseheide, which the knight batted easily aside with his sword.

Vor dem Walde in einem Tal,
(In a valley, before the wooded dale,)
Tandaradei!
(Tandaradei!)
Sang schön die Nachtigall.
(Beautifully sang the nightingale.)

By the time Walter finished singing, the merry men were on their last legs.

"Enough!" Yelled Schönfels-Hohenstein in a voice fit to silence the old gods.

"Enough!" Came Robin's matching cry a second later.

In contrast to the grinning Saxons, the merry men were scattered pell-mell across the glade. Most were groaning. The ones that weren't, were unconscious.

Little John extended a respectful hand to Hartmann, who returned the grip with a strong, friendly, gauntlet. Friar Tuck leant on his shillelagh, out of breath, and thoroughly disgusted at not having landed a single hit.

The Teutonic Knights regrouped, nodding to each other in appreciation of the battle, then remounted their horses.

The greys had stood untethered the entire time, nonchalantly watching the hoo-haa .

"Lord of Outlaws," called Freiherr Friedrich, "ve like you. And your clown! Train your men better. Ze Lord's blessing on your quest."

The knights fixed their helms, reared their horses and galloped away, pennants snapping gaily.

Something clunked at Robin's feet, and he looked down in wonder to find a large purse just rolled to a stop.

Friar Tuck ~ Chapter 26

The three things on which every person should reflect:
Whence they come; where they are; whither they shall go.
Triads of Bardism

"What's this out-of-nick nonsense about outlaws amok in Sherwood forest?" King John demanded of his High Constable.

"My Liege, it seems Nottingham can't control his peasants."

"Damn your stupidity. The Sheriff is pleading for *mercenaries*. He's got enough soldiers to deal with peasants. This is some other deviltry, listen! He speaks in this letter of*: Despicable criminals, assault and robbery* ... Yes, yes heard it all before. *Murder, sedition and outright rebellion* ... That's naughty! *Pagan blood rituals* ... Could be interesting. *Burning churches* ... Been tempted Ourself on occasion. *Deflowering virgins* ... That *is* interesting. *Hunting in the King's Royal Preserve* ... By the very black teeth of Hades, these battening bastards are boosting Our very larder!"

Two hundred Dutch mercenaries were duly engaged by England's military brokers on the continent. They would debark at Dover within two months. In the meantime, King John sent the Sheriff a band of entertainers, as a pick-me-up.

The band, famed across Europe, had enthralled the Royal Court for a week with their sometimes alarming *Magic and Alchemy* show. King John was sure they would liven up Nottingham's nights.

The merry men worked in tight teams all across the forest as the season waxed to Solstice. With Foresters patrolling in force, distributive justice became more dangerous, but was still rewarding work.

Friar Tuck kept the principles of chastity, chivalry and charity at the forefront of everyone's minds. Robin Hood embodied legitimacy, a beacon to his beleaguered people.

Little John trained the outlaws constantly, honing their rapid strike skills. Alan-a-Dale and Will Scarlett roamed the shires, distributing funds, embedding the support system, garnering intelligence and spreading the word.

Midsummer's eve ended with delicate elegance, the sky blushing silvery-pink before retiring to black-azure.

"Are we to Arlingford tomorrow, Robin?" Little John cried corkily.

"Aye!" The King of Sherwood skipped a jig. "To Arlingford's Midsummer festival, and blessed Maid Marian."

The outlaws joked and chatted away the drifting evening, Sherwood sleepily verdant after the long day.

Though satisfied with the progress of his flock, apprehension tickled Tuck's toes. The *thing* with Robin and Marian was yet to be sorted, but more generally, a number of merry men had been injured at recent lunches. Robbery was a losing game, and he'd started to wonder where Robin was leading them.

At some point the outlaws would have to leave the forest, and establish themselves in the eyes of England. As far as Tuck could see, nothing was being done to prepare for that day. He resolved to confer with the hermit at the next opportunity.

Robin's Captains accompanied their King to Arlingford, the main body of outlaws scattering to their own hamlets for the holiday.

The greenwood was abuzz with high summer, the trees abandoned to the long caresses of a languorous sun.

The merry men's voices shone with celebration:

All kinds of sadness I've left behind me,
Many's the day when I have done wrong,
But I'll be yours for ever and ever,
Climb in the saddle and whistle along!

So come on, I'm the whistler, I have a fife, and a drum to play!
   Drum to Play!

> **Get ready for the whistler, I whistle along on the seventh day!**
> **Whistle along on the seventh day!**
>
> **Deep red are the sun-sets in mystical places,**
> **Black are the nights on summer-day sands,**
> **We'll find the speck of truth in each riddle,**
> **Hold the first grain of love in our hands.**
>
> **So come on, I'm the whistler, I have a fife, and a drum to play!**
> **Drum to Play!**
> **Get ready for the whistler, I whistle along on the seventh day!**
> **Whistle along on the seventh day!**

Arlingford didn't disappoint the singing crew.

The village was packed with festivalling codgers, dancing children, roaming acrobats, ale-happy Jacks and sun-kissed Janes.

Marian met Robin under the alders by the pond, and they were inseparable for the rest of the afternoon.

Alan-a-Dale and Will Scarlett set off amongst the crowds, simply to have fun for once.

Friar Tuck and Little John sat yakking through the administrative affairs of the encampment, thoroughly enjoying their winding discussions over endless mugs of ale.

No-one noticed the horsemen approaching, at a fast gallop, along the riverbank from the west. Suddenly, Arlingford's green was surrounded by a snorting, stamping company of Loxlian men-at-arms.

Two score crossbows aimed into the stilling crowds.

A black stallion pawed its way onto the green, driving terrified festivallers before its flashing hooves.

"*Where is Robin Hood?*" Yelled Sir Ralph Montfaucon in a terrible voice. "Give him up!"

The crowd throbbed with fear and loathing.

"Run, and you will be killed." Montfaucon's cruel certainty stilled the heaving throng, leaving it mewling with trapped terror.

"I only want the outlaw. *Hood!*" Montfaucon's voice cinched in threat. "If you value these peasants' lives you will give yourself up."

A monstrous silence flapped over the green, the Midsummer sun blazing impartially over the abominable scene.

"You know me from the forest, outlaw. *Stand forth,* or we'll be having a Midsummer massacre!"

Friar Tuck's heart knifed with pain as the King of Sherwood stepped out from under the alders.

Little John was already up and rushing toward him, but Tuck grabbed his arm.

It was like trying to hold back a shire horse.

"No John, you'll be killed."

"*Robin's* going to be killed!"

"No, John, listen. They're not to going to kill Robin now, they'll want to judge him first. We'll think of something. We can't take on 40 crossbowmen. Please John, if we attack, they'll kill him immediately, and then the innocent people." Tuck's pleading stalled the giant. "We have to let him go."

"We'll get him back." John Little's resolve was granite.

Dale and Scarlett materialized out the crowd, alarm o'er-brimming their eyes. The merry men watched appalled as Robin Hood was bound and hoisted onto a horse.

Montfaucon's stallion reared like a thunderhead, then the company were away, their assembled power shaking the earth.

Tuck raced to the duck-pond, the merry men close behind. There, they found a devastated Marian.

Fat tears ran from the maiden's eyes as she fell into Tuck's arms.

"We'll get him back, don't worry, dear maid." He murmured. "We'll get him back, I promise. Safe and sound." As his arms held the weeping girl, Tuck was in the stillness at the core of his soul, raising prayers to the Merciful Mother.

"*Raging* hellfire, is it really him?" Gisburne peered into Castle Loxley's prison cell.

"Yes, my Lord. As you ordered, Robin Hood, trussed and ready for the hangman." Montfaucon replied with quiet assurance.

"You're a bloody miracle worker, Ralph! How did you know the knave would be at Arlingford?"

"I infiltrated the peasant's drinking holes. Gossip had the outlaw carrying on with some wench from Arlingford, so I stopped in on the off-chance. I got lucky."

"Ralph," Gisburne clapped his knight on the back, "with that kind of luck, you're going to go a long way."

Earl Gisburne led Sir Ralph to Loxley's main hall, calling for the best wine to be brought.

Robin Hood lay crumpled in the cold dungeon of his father's castle, beaten senseless.

Sherwood's Captains called an emergency council in the canyon. The merry men were chastened by the loss of their leader, nervy and argumentative.

The hermit arrived in the midst of a tense stand-off between Alan-a-Dale and Little John.

"We *have to* free Robin as quick as possible. He's probably being tortured as we speak! I say we go in, hard and fast, grab and run."

"We can't attack Castle Loxley, John. Even with a hundred men, we don't stand a chance. They're sure to put Robin on trial in Nottingham. There's a thousand tricks we can use in a town. We've got only one go at this."

"Much as I hate to leave Robin imprisoned for even one night, big fish, Alan's right." Tuck spoke in a calming tone. "Gisburne will have his men on full alert, and we'd need siege engines to get past the walls of Loxley."

"Then we'll build them!"

"We'll lose three-quarters of the band storming the castle, and even Robin wouldn't want that. They'll keep him alive for public execution."

"Brother Tuck is right." Stated the hermit. "More than ever, you must work together. Stop the arguments, even if they come from anguish. Merry men, your King is counting on you! *Rise to the challenge.*" The hermit's beard bristled with puissance. "Reclaim him from Nottingham, in full sight of the people, and from under the nose of their law. That way, even this disaster may yet be turned to the good."

The Sheriff of Nottingham was dancing for joy in the main hall of his castle. None of his retainers had ever seen the like, and were fearfully worried.

When he broke into song, even his bodyguards edged nervously away:

The scoundrel's in the jail,
The scoundrel's in the jail,
Hey-Ai-Eai-Eo,
The scoundrel's in the jail!

"Ha-ppy days! We'll throw a *sumptuous* trial. With the full pomp, might and majesty of the impartial law ... Then hang, quarter and draw the thieving bastard." The Sheriff knocked back a quenching mug of wine. "Seneschal. *Seneschal!* Send for the tailor, I shall need a new gown for this conviction."

"Yes, my Lord, and, my Lord?"

"Yes? Do speak up, or come closer damn you. By all the slack servitors in hell, what are you doing skulking over there?"

"Ah, thank you, my Lord. The Captain of the Guard reports a troupe of entertainers has arrived. They come with commendations from King John, my Lord, for your diversion."

"By the debauched djinns of hell! Good King John. Always *so thoughtful*. Seneschal, what are you waiting for? The devil to smack your lardy arse? Fetch me the entertainment!"

"Thank you, my Lord, but the troupe begs your indulgence. They ask to be given time to establish their *ambience,* as they called it. The troupe would be honoured to offer their first show this evening."

"Oh, must I wait? *How exciting.* Well, Gisburne and Montfaucon are bringing the criminal here in time for supper, so we can wassail these entertainers together. I'd better have me another little drink in the meantime. Ha-ppy days indeed! Tra-lala-lalala-la!"

Friar Tuck ~ Chapter 27

The three things that bring dignity:
Discretion; contentment; peace.
Triads of Bardism

That night, the Sheriff of Nottingham, Earl Guy of Loxley and Sir Ralph Montfaucon wassailed like it was Armageddon's eve.

The entertainers' ambience filled the far end of the hall. In the centre stood a tall tent, three paces in diameter. Mystic progressions outlined in sequins zigzagged its colourful cloth walls.

To the left and to the right, large copper braziers waited, unlit. An Oriental aroma wafted from the installation, spicy and mysterious.

The seneschal appeared as the sixth dinner course was taken away.

"My Lord High Sheriff, and honoured guests. The entertainment begins... ."

As the seneschal backed away with a bow, the braziers to each side of the tent bloomed with green fire.

The flames erupted like packs of emerald snakes towards the ceiling, then collapsed into foot-high tongues of faeric seaweed.

The whole thing gave the Sheriff a pressing case of heartburn.

Gisburne sat slack-jawed, and Montfaucon had his hand on the hilt of his dagger.

"By the scouring fiends of-."

The next spectacle cut Nottingham's oathing short.

A sinuous curtain of black smoke emerged from the stone floor a yard in front of the tent. Its tendrils drifted upward to conceal the tent, then an extraordinary figure emerged through the darkness.

A shimmering, bejewelled turban roosted lustily on the conjuror's head. His ebon robes draped to the ground in sinister folds.

The face between was prodigious with moustaches in the foreign style.

"My most noble Lords." The conjuror's basso profundo vibrated the dinner table. "We beg your leave to present *Magic and Alchemy.*"

Pooooooommmph! Cascades of yellow sparks fountained from the braziers, casting bright shadows around the hall.

Nottingham clapped excitedly, having settled his heartburn with copious mugs of wine.

Gisburne and Montfaucon exchanged mute glances, daunted by the sudden drama.

"Each night, our troupe will perform one, wondrous, feat of *Magic and Alchemy.* Behold: Tonight's fantastic experience!"

A scratching hurdy-gurdy droned and trilled as three assistants in tight-fitting spangly outfits emerged from the tent's enfoldment.

They moved with liquid grace, positioning themselves in a triangle around the conjuror. Strangeness perfumed the room. The hurdy-gurdy shrilled a note high enough to make the audience wince, then cut to silence.

A second passed, then another, tension mounting, black smoke drifting, the air feverish with dancing green light.

"*You must stay seated.*" Barked the conjuror, shocking the wassaillers nigh off their chairs. "The magical danger is extreme! I present to you: *The Flight of the Phoenix.*"

Gisburne let out a terrified yelp as the conjuror burst into a ball of fluid orange flame.

The Sheriff shot to his feet as the ball levitated into the air, spitting deep red globules of fire in every direction. He nearly screamed when two assistants grabbed him from behind, and forcibly plunked him back into his seat.

The Phoenix rose with awful majesty, unfolding a sinuous red neck and spiked yellow beak. Its wings expanded in flambant waves to each side, its tail a cascading freefall of crimson rubies.

The monstrosity stretched, howled a brain-freezing whistle, then ripped across the wassail hall in a streak of fire and smoke.

BA-BANG! The phoenix detonated in a stunning double-concussion above the heads of the dumbstruck audience, knocking them to the floor.

Nottingham, Gisburne and Montfaucon found each other, cowering, beneath the wassail table.

By the time the trio emerged, trembling, the entertainers had disappeared, the braziers were dead, and the conjuror's tent was covered by a plain drape.

Hints of unknown spices loitered in the lasts wisps of smoke sliding about the ceiling-beams.

"By the... ." Nottingham began, but couldn't think of anything to swear by, and fell silent.

"Quite." Muttered Gisburne, retaking his seat, thoroughly shaken.

"Ahem. Famed across all Europe did you say, my Lord?" Sir Ralph Montfaucon stared into the air.

"Yes, er, yes. Hrm. I believe so."

In Sherwood, things were tense.

Alan-a-Dale had summoned every sympathetic Jack and Jane in Nottingham to a certain oak.

Two score Nottinghamites had answered the call, listening quietly as the Outlaw Captains explained their part in the rescue plan.

Success hinged on the support of the people.

"I'm worried, hermit." Stated Tuck after the merry men had dispersed to their tasks.

"Yes, we all are."

"No. I mean about everything."

"Everything?" The hermit's eyebrows reached ridiculous heights.

"For once you bearded baboon, yes. Robin's rescue will be the first time the merry men act openly outside of the forest. We'll be directly defying the King's Justice. I can only see it leading to bigger conflict. I knew this was coming, but I don't think we're ready, and Robin's capture has forced our hand."

"Ah, yes. The Big Time." The hermit took a healthy swig from the winesack. "Welcome to it!"

The Sheriff of Nottingham looked in on his prisoner late the following afternoon.

The dungeon under Castle Nottingham was carved into the rock, with only one narrow passage leading in and out.

Robin Hood lay crumpled and bruised, his Lincoln green blotted with blood.

"By all the braggarts in hell, he doesn't look so big, eh, Gisburne? Your man did fine work, I must say."

"Yes, Ralph's that rarest of men: Loyal *and* competent. What are you going to do with the scoundrel?"

"By all the sluggards in hell, why wait? We'll hold court tomorrow, and punish him immediately."

"I always *did* like your style, Nottingham!"

"Speaking of which, I believe our entertainers have something special for us tonight."

The trio dined again in the wassail hall, anticipation rather spoiling their appetites.

At the end of the meal, plates were pushed away, and Nottingham nodded encouragingly at his guests, who smiled queasily in return.

"We're rea-dy!" Called the Sheriff.

The front of the ambience drew back to reveal a dimly lit, wizardly scene.

Behind a low table sat the conjuror, his head bowed in concentration.

"My most noble Lords." The conjuror's sonorous voice sent trills across Montfaucon's neck. "Tonight we travel into the future, and into the past. My Lords, I give you: *The Speaking Saracen.*"

The spangly assistants apparated into the tent carrying a metal tray, draped in a red cloth. An object shaped like a bird-cage was hidden under the cloth.

The audience leant forward, trying to get a better view. Lit only by two slim candles, everything in the tent wavered between half-seen and half-guessed.

The conjuror reached out his hand, suspended it in the air for a long moment, then whipped away the cloth to reveal a man's swarthy head.

Spontaneously, the braziers leaped to flaming life, this time burning claret, flinging bloody tints over every surface.

Gore puddled gloopily around the head's freshly severed neck, and despite being dead, its features contorted and writhed in unspeakable agony.

Gisburne swore the most obscene oaths. Montfaucon turned deathly pale, and the Sheriff clutched his table-top with both hands.

"Speak, Saracen, *speak!*" The conjuror's command released a sound like all the torment in hell from the Saracen's mouth.

"*By Melchior!* Silence, Saracen! *Silence.* Speak not in the tongues of the damned, but the tongues of men." The conjuror's voice shook the very walls.

"The dim-med future, my dead eyes see." Keened the severed head. "The dusty past holds no secrets from me. Ask whatever you wish to know. The answer on you, this slave shall bestow."

"My Lords," the conjuror's voice seemed fathomless compared to the Saracen's falsetto squeal, "the Speaking Saracen has been *necromantically enslaved* to answer one question from each of you. Question wisely. *Sir Ralph Montfaucon*, if you please."

Montfaucon, profoundly disturbed by the talking head, was roundly shocked to discover the conjuror knew his name.

The knight's mouth twisted into a cynical smile as he swallowed his fear.

"Saracen, answer me this: Where is my mother's ruby circlet?"

"In the place she lost it." Answered the Saracen in an acute whine.

"Was it lost?" Gabbled Nottingham, awestruck.

"Yes, but-."

"*Earl Guy of Gisburne and Loxley.*" The conjuror intoned.

"Saracen, answer me this: Who will win the next wars against France?"

"The wars will be won by those that name them." Squealed the severed head, gumming its lips.

A frisson of foreknowledge passed between Gisburne and the Sheriff as they locked eyes.

Montfaucon grew more and more dubious at the spectral spectacle.

"The final questioner, and the final question: *My Lord High Sheriff of Nottingham.*"

Nottingham quaked in his chair.

The question he really wanted answered, he hardly dare ask.

"Sar, Sara, Saracen, answer me this: When will I be made Baron?"

"The Sheriff will be made Baron," the Saracen's wail seared their ears, "when the sinner has paid his due."

The conjuror immediately dropped the drape over the severed head, the assistants tugged the tent flaps closed, and the scintillating carnelian flames in the braziers guttered to darkness.

"*Tell me what it means.*" The Sheriff leapt from his chair. "Gisburne, *do you know?* Montfaucon, *speak*, damn ye staring eyes."

"It doesn't mean anything, Sheriff!" Montfaucon gesticulated wildly. "*Nothing.* They're mountebanks. Mummers! I find their grotesqueries, well, *truly grotesque.*"

"But the Saracen knew your mother's circlet was lost."

"An obvious guess."

"And he predicted Guy's answer with dreadful certainty."

"A clever twist of words."

"And me ... A Baron, *when the sinner has paid his due.*"

"I should have thought it obvious." Drawled Gisburne. "The Saracen was speaking of the outlaw, Robin Hood."

"By all the slavering sooth-sayers of hell, Guy, you're right! The outlaw *is* the sinner. He will pay his due tomorrow, and generous King John will reward me for ridding the land of the rascal."

"My Lord Nottingham, I do think-."

Gisburne glared Montfaucon into silence.

"Sheriff, Ralph and I really should retire. It's a big day tomorrow, after all."

"Yes. Yes! Thank you, Guy. Another happy day tomorrow. Good night. Oh, court's scheduled for noon, and the hanging should start about an hour after. The punishment will probably take most the afternoon, so do make sure you pack in a hearty breakfast. Sweet dreams!"

Friar Tuck ~ Chapter 28

The three things that awaken a person:
Knowledge; good deeds; gentleness.
Triads of Bardism

The 25th of June 1201 dawned over a subdued encampment of merry men.

Friar Tuck had already been for an hour's walk, praying with every pace. The stakes couldn't be higher.

The entire company of fighting-Jacks had been rousted from the shires to defend the escape. Seven score men stood ready with staffs and longbows. The determined band filled Tuck with confidence as he passed them.

Will Scarlett and Alan-a-Dale were deep in conference with a core team of Nottinghamites, finalising details. The plan was daring, but simple. Their crew trusty, but untested.

Tuck only hoped Robin would be alert enough to react at the right time.

"*Merry men.*" Friar Tuck stood tall alongside Little John, Will Scarlett and Alan-a-Dale. "Our King needs rescuing! You know your roles, you have your disguises. If things go unexpectedly, *fulfil your tasks*. Today, each of you takes up arms in the battle against tyranny. Today, the merry men show our mettle to all England. Our Lady's blessing on us all. God's mercy on the King of Sherwood!"

"*God's mercy on Robin, King of Sherwood!*" The battle cry resounded through the greenwood.

The merry men advanced on Nottingham, 145 aggrieved outlaws, armed to the teeth.

Robin Hood woke with cold flush of rancid water thrown in his face.

"Wake up. It's your day to die." The jailer kicked Robin, hard.

The Lord of Outlaws struggled to his elbows, and received another kick for his trouble.

"Quicker, knave, or I'll whip you!"

Robin leaned against the wall, pulled himself to his feet, then wiped the dried blood from his eyes.

"There's water in the bucket, and a scrubber. You're to make yourself presentable for your trial. Then I'll give you breakfast." The jailer stepped very close, causing Robin to twitch in anticipation of a blow. "If you don't spruce up, there'll be no breakfast, and *I'll* wash you down. And you really don't want that."

The jailer stomped away, leaving Robin to slump back to the floor.

He'd been beaten so many times, his brains were mushy. His hands were useless after hours of being tightly bound. His guts ached from a hundred bruising kicks, and every breath sent a sharp pain through his ribs.

"How do you think this looks, seneschal?" Nottingham primped his new conviction gown.

"Fine, my Lord."

"Just fine?"

"Er … Wonderfully fine, my Lord. The colour really suits you and-."

"By hell's flatulence, seneschal, shut up! Have the carpenters finished?

"Ah, thank you, my Lord. Yes, my Lord. One Scaffold, one Quartering Table, one Judgment Table, one Criminal's Dock, one Witness Box and Stands for Two Hundred Spectators, my Lord."

"Have the grateful multitude massed for the trial of the thrice-damned thief?"

"Yes, my Lord, with visitors from as far as five crow's miles come specially. Certainly the whole of Nottingham is already assembled in the castle courtyard, my Lord."

"Is the criminal prepared for his trial?"

"Being prepared as we speak, my Lord."

"Ha-ppy day! That will be all seneschal."

"Thank you, my Lord."

"Guy, have you spoken with the Captain of the Guard?"

"A very capable chap. Rather than muck about, I've put all my men at his disposal."

"Good thinking, Guy. Yes, I recruited Captain Roland at the end of his mercenary days a few years ago. Terrible temper, but very *zero tolerance*, you know?"

"I would be honoured to personally guard the prisoner at all times, Sheriff." Volunteered Montfaucon as he strode into the room.

"By the jumping skeletons of Judgment day, you *are* an excellent fellow, Montfaucon! It shall be so. Bring the criminal from the dungeon, the trial will begin shortly."

The merry men reached the outer edges of Sherwood, staying back amongst the trees, staring at the towering cliffs of Castle Nottingham.

Little John kept six score men in the forest, arranged into tight strike groups. Each group would attack Nottingham's soldiers as they chased Tuck's rescue team, then withdraw and circle deeper into the forest. This way, a rolling ambush would leathalize the line of escape, making pursuit impossible.

Friar Tuck and Will Scarlett emerged from the trees, both in monkish robes.

Alan-a-Dale appeared minutes later with a score of merry men dressed as masons. The story was that they were visiting from the works at Lincoln Cathedral.

The new-town of Nottingham streamed with folk, all going to watch the trial. Tuck and Scarlett merged with a group of peasants as they passed the first castle gate, then stayed with them all the way into the courtyard.

The masons used inertia to sweep through the first gate, but were stopped and questioned at the second. Completely convincing as a Master Mason taking his boys for a big day out, Alan-a-Dale and the group were let through.

The castle courtyard thronged with people.

Wooden stands stacked to left and right, packed with seated spectators. On the far side stood the criminal's dock and the witness box, positioned to face the Judgment table. In the middle stood the gallows and quartering table.

Alert men-at-arms and soldiers were everywhere. Crossbowmen watched from guard towers, swordsmen milled amongst the crowds, and clusters of spearmen gathered at strategic points.

The resplendent Sheriff of Nottingham appeared at the Judgment table to a blaring of dissonant trumpets.

Sir Ralph Montfaucon shoved a bedraggled Robin Hood into the criminal's dock.

The Lord of Outlaws held himself up by leaning on his shackled hands, but didn't lift his head.

The Abbot of Doncaster arrived first into the witness box, glaring with undignified hatred at Robin.

"Father Abbot, do you recognize the outlaw before us?"

"Yes, Sheriff. I am certain this damned criminal is Robin Hood, brigand, skellum and catso."

"Is this the same Robin Hood who stole Church funds from your pastoral care?"

"Yes, Sheriff. That man there stole my holy money!"

"Thank you, Father Abbot. Next witness."

An astonishing parade of witnesses were called, none of whom Tuck remembered robbing.

A few were obvious plants to whip up the crowd, babbling about pagan blood rituals. Many were suspiciously professional in their testimony, soldiers dressed as merchants.

All damned Robin Hood.

"I call myself as the Crown's final witness." Boomed the Sheriff. "I recognize the criminal before us as Robin Hood, outlaw of Sherwood Forest. I personally know him to be guilty of a thousand crimes, including pernicious vittal-theft, and ruthless hijacking. I judge the criminal guilty on all counts!" He banged his gavel decisively.

Nothing happened.

"By every dull audience in hell." Nottingham sighed, the spoke up. "*I've stopped being a witness now.* I, as High Sheriff of Nottingham, judge the criminal *guilty!*"

Trumpets blatted, and soldiers converged on the criminal's dock, ready to take Hood to his doom.

"Hanging and quartering is the punishment. Sorry, no drawing today, we don't have the space. Sentence will be carried out immediately." The Sheriff gave a final crack of his gavel, and the merry men went into action.

Just as Robin's escort of soldiers dragged him from the criminal's dock, a mass of townsfolk bundled from the crowd.

Sheer weight of numbers swept the escort into the group of masons a few feet away. These good men reacted by ripping off their aprons to reveal jerkins of Lincoln green.

Loosed into the stumbling, shouting confusion were 20 fake Robin Hoods.

Montfaucon had been jostled away from the real Robin Hood, but thought he'd kept an eye on him. The knight ripped out his longsword and shoved a path through the rapidly degenerating situation, determined not to let the outlaw escape.

The clusters of soldiers mobilized but couldn't get past the bundles of pushing, yelling, fighting people.

21 figures in Lincoln green diffused in different directions through the mob.

The crossbowmen hesitated in their towers, not knowing who to shoot first. Men-at-arms and swordsmen came from all sides, making slow headway, aiming to cut off the escape at the nearest castle gate.

The Sheriff of Nottingham stared down on his courtyard, speechless. His Barony was sinking into a quagmire of heaving peasantry.

"Kill them all." The Sheriff shrieked to his crossbowmen.

The guard towers were rocking alarmingly under the shocks of the rampaging hordes, and the highly-strung marksmen hurriedly loosed a savage salvo.

Screams overtook the shouting as peasants fell in droves to the assault of the war-bolts. Five Robin Hoods were also hit, most struck from several directions at once.

The crossbowmen cranked weapons, sighting their next targets.

The entire courtyard surged with panic. Men-at-arms, spearmen, soldiers, Robin Hoods and townsfolk were propelled by the tide towards the first gate.

The beams of oak splintered like matchsticks.

The crossbowmen leaned out of their towers and unleashed a second salvo. The war-bolts thrashed into the crowds, killing tens, including six more Robin Hoods.

Then, the horde was free and streaming downhill, people of all kinds being ejected pell-mell from the sides.

The pandemonium hit the castle's lower gate with all the momentum gained from its downhill dash. The guards were thrown aside, along with their gate, guardroom and a good section of wall.

Friar Tuck and Will Scarlett, both praying for a miracle, were lifted like froth at the front edge of the charging mass. They were deposited as harmlessly as summer seeds at the base of Nottingham's cliffs, and immediately headed for the pub.

Hysterical people flooded in all directions, many wailing, some wounded, everyone looking to get as far away from where they were as quickly as possible.

Outside The Pilgrim, Tuck and Scarlett found four gasping Robin Hoods, none of whom were the real thing.

A moment later, two more appeared, carrying an injured Alan-a-Dale.

"Stay here." Tuck darted back into the chaos on the streets.

His normal mind had left him.

A terrible sense of danger had replaced it, as sharp as a dagger in his psyche. Tuck followed it like a smell, until he caught a glimpse of Lincoln green under the feet of the rampaging townsfolk near the lower castle gate.

Tuck laid about with his shillelagh, forging a path to where the Lord of Outlaws lay.

Sir Ralph Montfaucon was also forcing his way through the panic. The knight had already killed two Robin Hood's, chasing them down like vengeful lightning amidst a storm in hell. He'd lost all human sense in his fury at finding both to be fakes, but had not given up.

He'd just spotted his third Hood, lying on the ground nearby.

Friar Tuck didn't get a chance to hail Robin before Montfaucon slipped out from the swarming crowds, reaching in with his longsword for a quick kill.

Tuck smacked his shillelagh against the flat of the knight's blade, knocking it to the side.

Montfaucon reversed his flow, and swung in a neck-slicing chop.

Tuck ducked, and jabbed out for a winding blow.

The knight dodged, tilting his blade so the tip cut into Tuck's shoulder. Tuck ignored the wound, whipping a mighty swat towards Montfaucon's head.

The knight caught the attack across the edge of his sword with impressive dexterity, but cut through the shillelagh. The top section walloped into Montfaucon's face, obliterating his nose.

Tuck staggered as his weapon met no resistance, accidentally body-hammering Montfaucon to the ground.

Without pausing for thought, Tuck grabbed the unconscious King of Sherwood, and hot-footed it back to The Pilgrim.

Will Scarlett drove up in a twin-horsed farmer's cart, and everyone piled in the back. Tuck gently laid Robin Hood next to Alan-a-Dale on the floor.

The Sheriff of Nottingham grew incandescent with rage. His court had been made a mockery, his castle a bloody mess, and his Barony dropped from great height, into a particularly villainous privvy.

Guy of Gisburne thrashed out from the stables on his war horse, leading twenty Loxlian men-at-arms.

"By all the hatred in hell, bring me the head of Robin Hood!" Nottingham raved as the platoon raced by.

Those first riders were swiftly followed by a score more, led by Captain Roland of the Castle Guard.

By this time, the footsoldiers had organized themselves, and hastened off downhill as they formed up into ranks. Nottingham's crossbowmen appeared moments later, all the troops taking to the hunt with maximum prejudice.

The farmer's cart creaked like it would fall apart at any second as the merry men cut out of Nottingham's new-town. Scarlett took the last curve at such speed, the outlaws had to hold on with both hands for fear of being thrown out. Then, the escapees were a crow's mile down a straight road to Sherwood.

The forest spread before them with the deep green promise of sanctuary.

Friar Tuck ~ Chapter 29

The three resources of humankind:
Intelligence; love; prayer.
Triads of Bardism

The escaping farm-cart had rocked and rattled less than five hundred yards when Friar Tuck spotted the first plumes of pursuit.

Robin Hood muttered and moaned on the floor of the cart, but Alan-a-Dale made no sound at all.

Tuck quickly distributed the handful of long bows stashed in the cart. The outlaws had brought few weapons, needing every inch of cart-space for escapees.

During planning, this short ride to Sherwood seemed the simplest part of the plot. It had become their time of greatest vulnerability.

Tuck dared a glance over Will Scarlett's driving shoulders to see Little John come out of the wood, yelling encouragement at the top of his lungs. The giant's wind-driven voice lifted Tuck's spirits, but terror punched his heart when he turned toward Nottingham.

Guy of Gisburne and his men charged out of new-town locked into a tight arrowhead formation. Each man-at-arms held his longsword ready, the sunlight wavering over their wicked lengths.

The hunter-killers were closing fast.

The merry men loosed a hasty volley of arrows, then re-nocked, grimly waiting for Gisburne to get in range.

The brave cart had travelled only another two hundred yards, when Captain Roland and the Castle Guard thundered onto the road, galloping their chargers even faster than Gisburne's warhorses.

Tuck ordered the merry men to ready their second volley as Gisburne's troop approached to within a hundred yards.

The score of charging warhorses seemed to get quicker as they got closer.

Gisburne looked like the devil himself, eyes wide with psychotic aggression, screaming blue fury.

"Easy... ." Tuck beat back his fear. "Wait for it. Easy … Wait for it … Fire!"

Most of the volley went high or wide as the rocking cart ruined the archers' aim. Only one man-at-arms went down in a tumble of hooves.

The escapees waited until the pursuit had come within 50 yards before loosing their third volley. Three men-at-arms fell this time, others breaking the discipline of formation as they dodged the whispering slivers of death.

Captain Roland had almost caught up to the chase, his chargers flanking Gisburne's troop.

A fourth volley of ash arrows spat across the now 20 yard gap, every archer taking down a galloping man-at-arms, tripping those behind into cartwheeling balls of legs and longswords.

Captain Roland's guardsmen pushed their steeds harder, looking to get in front of the rushing cart.

Gisburne's troop locked on target, and closed to within ten yards, looming monstrously large in the eyes of the merry men.

Using their last arrows, the archers shot a rushed volley. Jolted about in the cart, the archers only took down three more men-at-arms. The nine surviving riders of Gisburne's troop achieved sword-range.

Captain Roland overtook the cart, his soldiers swinging in from both sides to close the road ahead.

The outlaws had advanced another three hundred yards, but Sherwood might as well be a hundred miles distant.

"Heeeeeee-Yaaaaaah!" Will Scarlett let out a tremendous yell as he cracked his whip above the cart-horses' heads.

The beasts jumped into a double-time trot, yanking the merry-men out from under the avalanche of swords Gisburne's troop were just unleashing.

Captain Roland's guardsmen blocked the road 30 yards in front, ready to mince the cart and everything in it.

Tuck frantically twisted his head to the front and to the rear, unable to act, unable to think, out of time, too panicked to pray.

Gisburne's troop reached in again, surrounding the speeding cart with swords hacking and hewing. Defenceless, the merry men took atrocious wounds on their arms and heads, several falling from the cart.

Tuck watched, devastated, as their corpses rolled floppily away from the trundling maelstrom.

With their backs to Sherwood, and concentrated on their victims, Captain Roland's guardsmen didn't notice Little John's approach.

Two score archers and staffmen came racing down the road with the giant. Little John outpaced the strike teams like a man amongst boys, his enormous feet thumping along as if shod in seven league boots.

The archers stopped at a hundred yards, nocked and loosed, nocked and loosed, firing in arcs.

The staffmen raced ever forwards, following Little John like cygnets to a swan. The outlaw arrows thrummed over their heads, then tore amongst Roland's pack of guards.

Little John arrived a second later, shoulder-ramming horses, tearing men from saddles, chanting invocations to the Holy Mother.

Then the staffmen piled in, thrusting, hammering, bashing and cracking with righteous fury.

Roland fought like a demon, but his guardsmen's morale had been shattered by this heinous invasion, and they were mauled to the ground.

Gisburne's men threshed in from all sides, inflicting butchery on the fleeing outlaws. The cart-full of merry men cringed hopelessly under the merciless attack.

Will Scarlett was struck down on the driver's bench, and the cart-horses stampeded in terror.

Friar Tuck held Alan-a-Dale's limp fingers in one hand, Robin Hood's twitching grip in the other, and reached for the peace of the Holy Mother. Tuck's faith steadied as the centre-light of his spirit remained unperturbed amidst the sense-shredding violence. He gave thanks for the blessings of his life, then an electrical snap shocked across his body as he recognized his readiness for death.

At that moment, the cart-horses collided with the whirling melee of Roland's disintegrating troop.

The farm-cart twisted along its axle and blew into a thousand pieces, flinging merry men in every direction, and scattering Gisburne's men-at-arms.

Captain Roland dropped like a sack of potatoes under the huge fist of Little John, and the few guardsmen still on horseback, took flight. Gisburne's men-at-arms rallied 20 yards distant, but then scattered under a hail of arrows.

Friar Tuck hoisted Will Scarlett onto his shoulder. Little John grabbed Robin Hood under one arm, and Alan-a-Dale under the other. The merry men sprinted for Sherwood.

Gisburne's troop was down to four men, retreating under the repeated volleys of outlaw arrows aimed their way. Roland's guards rallied out of bowshot, waiting for re-enforcements.

First to arrive were Nottingham's crossbowmen.

Two score gathered in a mass on the road as the merry men raced the final four hundred yards.

Then, the companies of Nottingham's spear and swordsmen caught up to the action.

"*They've not escaped yet.*" Yelled Gisburne through a welter of blood and dust. "*By Hellfire,* follow me!"

The 40 crossbowmen trotted out into a V formation, hungry to catch the merry men in their war-bolted jaws.

Two score spearmen and swordsmen broke into a charging run at the apex, keeping formation and covering ground fast.

The escapees reached Sherwood to the victorious cheers of four score merry men, as if the forest itself was with them. Janes took up the wounded, two to a man, and swiftly hoisted them off for succour in the deepwoods.

The main group of escapees, led by Little John, kept to the planned line of retreat. Tuck glanced up at the massive figure of the giant striding alongside him, his King and minstrel held as lightly as a loaf of bread in each hand. He didn't smile as he thought of the welcome the weald would give the Sheriff's soldiers, only seconds behind.

The first ambush team allowed Gisburne to lead the pursuit 20 feet into the forest, then unleashed a storm of arrows on their heads.

Before the crossbowmen could respond, the strike team had peeled away.

The trees swayed ominously around Gisburne as he halted in anticipation of continued attack.

Nothing happened, the silence of the woodland stirring dread in the hearts of the soldiers.

"*Keep on their tails.* They're down to their last men!" Gisburne sprang his horse forwards.

30 feet further in, another salvo of arrows shivered out from a patch of innocent looking brake, wounding seven men-at-arms, and scattering the rest.

A platoon of footmen charged thrashing into the overgrowth, but the second ambush team had already vanished.

Gisburne's company hunkered down, muttering foul oaths, crossbowmen spreading out to either side.

A ruckus on the flank left a further four riders dead, then a volley of arrows pierced amongst the spearmen in the centre.

The Earl used every threat he could think of to force another advance out of his men, only for his warhorse to stumble into a hidden pit.

Gisburne was thrown to the ground, and his soldiers decided it was time for a tactical withdrawal.

Retreating after his men, Gisburne sent his gaze burning into every part of the forest.

He saw nothing but lightly breezing summer trees.

Friar Tuck ~ Chapter 30

The three things pleasant to see:
The unhappy become joyous; the miser become generous; the lawless become legitimate.
Triads of Bardism

Celebration chimed through Sherwood Forest. The merry men had dealt a mighty blow against tyranny.

Robin Hood recovered within hours, broken and bandaged, but five times his usual self.

Even in the midst of rescue, Robin had thought the fracas accidental. To find himself amongst his people, under bough and under God, filled the King of Outlaws with a new sense of purpose.

Friar Tuck sat in a quiet corner of the encampment, between the hermit and Little John. The trio steadily passed a wine sack, not speaking much.

Will Scarlett came into his own, keeping the kitchens working all hours, throwing an interlocking web of look-outs across the timberland, and dispatching the news of Robin's miraculous escape to every pub for 20 crow's miles.

Alan-a-Dale had been struck by two war-bolts, one in the shoulder and one in the ribs. The shoulder bolt came out easily, but the other snapped, leaving its barbed head in the wound.

Dale's breathing rattled with ill-omen.

"Alan-a-Dale will die unless we get him to proper care right away." Declared a nursing Jane. "I'm so sorry. I've done everything I can. You need to take him to Rubygill, that's the nearest healing convent."

"Rubygill!" Scarlett was already rushing across to Little John.

The hermit, Friar Tuck and Little John left the camp minutes later.

The giant hurtled through Sherwood like a charging elephant, carrying Alan-a-Dale in his arms. Tuck and the hermit hurried along in his wake.

"Bring him into the Nursery." Prioress Brighid of Rubygill ordered after a purse-lipped examination of Dale.

By the time Tuck and the hermit arrived, panting, nuns had removed the minstrel's field dressings and were cleaning his wounds with wine.

"Tongs."

A nun passed a large pair of tongs that the Prioress inserted firmly into Dale's crossbow wound. The sides of the tongs screwed outwards, pushing against the edges of the bolt-hole.

Tuck's stomach queased as Dale's flesh stretched open.

"Pincers."

The Prioress' hand dived like a kingfisher hunting, dug around, then yanked the bolt-head out in a spray of glistening blood.

"Turpentine and poultice."

Two nuns stepped in, the first pouring a foul-smelling distillation liberally over the wound, the second slapping wads of honey-soaked barley on by the fistful.

The Prioress weaved a professional bandage around Dale's torso, fixing the poultice into place.

"What are you staring at, Reynold?" The Prioress didn't look up from washing her hands free of blood.

The hermit leaped out of his skin. "Ah! Dear Sister Brighid-."

"It's *Prioress* Brighid now, Reynold."

Tuck smothered his grin.

"Of course. Prioress. Ahem. Of course! How wonderful to see you again. How long's it been, let me see-."

"The last time I saw you, Reynold Fitz-Ooth, you were being run out of Ireland by the O'Shea sisters."

"Sure, that was a most terrible mistake-."

"Quite. I heard you'd mis-taken one sister, and then the other. Anyway, I'm glad to see your roguish face, even with that preposterous beard. At least you are in good company." The Prioress turned to Tuck with almost a sweet expression. "How are you, brother? And faithful Fountaindale?"

"Ah, Mother Prioress, this is our happiest and saddest day yet, but I am pleased to be here again."

"Follow me to the refectory. I need to know what's been going on."

"Prioress' pet." Hissed the hermit into Tuck's smug expression as they followed Brighid through the Priory. "You wait 'till I tell the old bat you were kicked out of Fountaindale."

"Don't you dare!"

A cold fury transfixed the Sheriff of Nottingham.

Guy of Gisburne sat blood-spattered to his left, beyond him a heavily bandaged Sir Ralph Montfaucon, and beyond him an even heavier bandaged Captain Roland of the Castle Guard.

"By all the cack-handed cacodemons in hell! How could you simpering dolts allow the sinner to escape? You! Montfaucon, failed in your guard. You! Roland, failed in your guard. You! Gisburne ... Just ... Failed." Nottingham's eyes were diabolic. "I'd do anything to get that bastard back in my hands."

"Bloody Sherwood protects them." Gisburne slammed his fists onto the table top. "*We did everything.* I lost more than half my men! They've got a damned army in that double-damned forest."

"My Dutch mercenaries are arriving in a month. *That's* a bloody army, Gisburne."

"Even 200 professional infanteers won't be enough. It's not just a case of force, don't you see that?" Gisburne pounded his fists until the table rang. "Hellfire and Hellflame, how do we defeat *Sherwood forest?*"

"I've thought of a way." Montfaucon's eyes shone above the wadding where his nose used to be.

"Another bloody brilliant idea from your pet knight, Gisburne?" Nottingham sneered.

"Shut it, Sheriff. Ralph, this had better be good."

"It is." Montfaucon pointed to the entertainer's ambience.

"By all the blazing buffoons in hell! We're going to be saved by mummers?"

"Yes. Those players hold powerful secrets over fire. I'll wager they can kindle a conflagration that'll force the outlaws out of Sherwood, and onto our swords."

"*Hellflame.* Ralph's right."

"I agree." Captain Roland's gruff tones silenced the Sheriff long enough for him to think a moment.

"The knight *might* be right. Seneschal? Seneschal!"

"Yes, my Lord?"

"Damn your bones! Why do I always have to call you twice? Fetch me the entertainers immediately. *And I mean right now.*"

"Thank you, my Lord."

The Magic and Alchemy team were shoved into the hall by four guardsmen.

The conjuror had no moustaches, and the svelte assistants were revealed as undernourished.

"By all the hare-brained harlots in hell, you want to trust our fortunes *to this bunch of comedians?*"

"What's your name?" Gisburne asked the conjuror.

"Alfred Hampstead, my Lord." The alchemist replied, sensing it was not a time for prevarication.

"Right, Hampstead, how would you go about burning down Sherwood Forest?"

Two days after his surgery, weak but enjoying the ride in Little John's arms, Alan-a-Dale was carried back to the encampment.

Friar Tuck and the hermit had spent an educative time with the Prioress, catching up on wider affairs in England.

Brighid had informed a stunned Tuck that observers across the land were following the progress of the merry men.

"Alan-a-Dale's songs have spread for hundreds of miles, and the powerful take note of popular poets, brother Tuck."

"Yes. But they'll really sit up now we've inflicted some poetic justice." The hermit sighed.

"That's the problem, Prioress." Tuck clutched his hands. "The merry men weren't ready for this, and now we're in the middle of it. We lost a lot of good folk, Robin's in no fit state, and we don't have any idea what to do next."

"Reynold? No clever suggestions?"

"Ah. For this time only, I'm fresh out."

"I can tell you the merry men have less than two moons before Sherwood will be attacked in force." The Prioress' eyes pierced Tuck to the quick.

"*Sweet Mother,* have ye been blessed with the gift of prophecy, Brighid?" The hermit looked impressed.

"No, you idiot. My Sisters in France have sent word that 200 Dutch infanteers are on their way to England. Final destination: Nottingham. And the merry men are the only game in town."

"Six or seven weeks. That's not long."

"Buck up, Tuck." The Prioress proclaimed. "It's plenty of time! What? Are you going to beg God for *more*?"

"Ah, not exactly, but-."

"But me no buts, brother. This is God's way of telling you to uplift your amply provided butt to the call of righteousness."

The hermit cackled loudly until the Prioress turned her flinty features his way. "Reynold Ryan Fitz-Ooth, redeem your years of capricious gallivanting, stop that ridiculous gibbering, and make yourself useful!"

The hermit's humour halted in full flight. "Of course, Prioress Brighid, what would you have me do?"

Guy of Gisburne, Sir Ralph Montfaucon and a score of men-at-arms cantered away from Nottingham castle three days after the trial.

They arrived at Arlingford as the sun set, the cool of evening already settled above the grassy swath of the village green.

"Her name is Marian. There can't be that many in a place this size. Go house to house." Montfaucon pointed his men to the peaceful line of stone-built cottages. "I want every wench who might be called Marian, aged between 16 and 60, assembled here in 15 minutes."

"We are on the King's business." Added Gisburne. "Soldiers, do what you must to fulfil your duty."

The men-at-arms tore through Arlingford in a whirlwind of brutality, wrenching almost every female in the village away from their husbands and families, dragging them to the duck pond. Those who tried to interfere were ferociously beaten, and one insistent Jack stabbed to death.

The terrified Janes huddled under the inhuman gazes of Gisburne and Montfaucon.

"All those called Marian, step forward."

The huddle shifted nervously, but no Jane came forth.

"*Hellfire and Hellflame,* if you don't do as the knight says, I'll personally cut the nose off each of your pretty faces." Gisburne slithered out his sabre and swung off his horse.

Two maids crept forward, and the Arlingford women began pleading the soldiers for mercy.

"Are there any more Marians," Montfaucon called eerily, "hiding amongst you Janes?"

Not a mother's daughter moved.

"I'm not sure we can trust you sneaky women." Montfaucon ripped a youngster out of the group and thrust her to the ground at his feet. "Now. Who knows this girl?" Montfaucon unsheathed his sword.

"I know her, my Lord." Answered a matronly figure from the front of the huddle. "Mary's her name, not Marian. Please don't harm her."

"Ah. Good. You, stand over there." Montfaucon gestured to his right. "MOVE. Now, who else knows dear Mary here?"

A goodwife stepped up, her face rigid with fury under her tears.

"I know the girl."

"Thank you. Go over there." Montfaucon gestured to his left. "Each of you will be asked how many Marians there are left in Arlingford. If there's any difference in your answers, or we think you are lying, Mary dies. Clear? *Good.*"

Gisburne approached the matron and got his answer.

The women of Arlingford shivered as the Earl's sadistic figure stalked the gloomy green to get his second answer.

Gisburne conferred with Montfaucon, and the two men nodded.

"Right. The good news for Mary is, we believe your representatives." Montfaucon readied to plunge his sword into Mary's little body. "The bad news is, there's one more Marian in Arlingford. Make yourself known, or the kid gets it."

Lady Marian broke free of the hands holding her back, coming forward with her head held high.

Gisburne grabbed Marian roughly by the wrist, threw her over his saddle, and mounted up behind.

Montfaucon's stallion flailed its hooves in every direction, then the raiding party were away like vampires into the deepening night.

Friar Tuck ~ Chapter 31

The three fountains of wisdom:
Youth; memory; genius.
Triads of Bardism

"By all Hell's succubi! She's a pretty one." Nottingham leered.

"You're not wrong, Sheriff. But she's got the tongue of a moon-mad shrew." Gisburne grimaced.

"Where's Hood's hideout?" Bellowed Montfaucon into Marian's bruised face.

"I don't know, knight, I just don't know! I've never been there." Marian yelled right back, black curls springing out in all directions from her fury.

Montfaucon walloped Marian with a back-handed slap, knocking her to the ground.

The maid bounced to her feet, shaking her bound hands at the knight.

"You knaves have crossed a line here. I am noble born! If my father was alive, he'd skin you for striking me."

"I don't care who your father was, wench. Answer me, and the beatings stop." Montfaucon leaned in hard. "Keep pissing me about, and it all gets a damned sight worse."

Marian shivered at the psychotic shadows swaying in the knight's eyes.

The bandaging across Montfaucon's mashed nose had stained with leaking blood, noisome above his hate twisted mouth.

"Whatever you do to me, I still won't be able to answer, you dizzard."

This time Montfaucon lashed out with a right hook.

Marian was flung against the wall and crumpled into a heap of red skirts and raven hair.

"Well. How's about a relaxing mug of wine, everyone?" The Sheriff suggested. "I'll wager our guest won't be answering any further questions tonight."

Marian of Arlingford was carried to the dungeon of Nottingham castle, and dumped in the same cell Robin Hood had occupied not a week before.

"How are Hampstead and his troupe doing with the necessary?" Asked Gisburne over his second mug.

"By all the false apostles in hell, they've spent over 20 pounds on, wait for it, *rare earths*. They've promised to show us tonight what they've come up with. If I don't like it, I'll have their mumming heads. Seneschal!"

"Yes, my Lord?" Came the swift reply.

"Bring me the wizard."

Alfred Hampstead and his assistants arrived, all dressed in heavy protective gear.

"By the howling mockeries of hell! Why are you dressed like that?"

"Standard alchemical precautions, my Lord."

"Show us what your stuff can do."

Hampstead guided his assistants to bring forward a small chest with utmost care, then produced a lump of yellowish mineral from his pocket.

"This is fool's gold. When struck against steel it flames, *like so.*" Alfred banged the fool's gold on the flat of his dagger with maximum drama, producing an abundant stream of sparks.

"What's that supposed to do?"

"Fool's gold, when powdered, is much more reactive. What do I mean, when I say *much more reactive*? Do allow us to demonstrate." Alfred motioned to his assistants.

The troupe gently scooped a cup of metallic, greenish-yellow powder from the chest, then poured it gingerly in a line across the floor of Nottingham's hall.

"You will note the argent hue of the pyrophoria. That's the added rare earths, direct from Sweden."

The assistants backed away as far as possible.

Hampstead approached the tip of the line with his dagger and fool's gold.

"I advise you not to look directly at what happens next, the reaction can burn out your eyes."

Turning his head away, Alfred again struck the fool's gold against the steel, causing a cascade of sparks to fall onto the line of pyrophoria.

WHAAMMMMM! The entire line of powder touched off simultaneously, emitting an intense flash of brilliant white light.

A reeking smoke was left cavorting in the superheated air.

Nottingham, having looked at precisely the wrong spot, rubbed furiously at his eyes.

Montfaucon and Gisburne were awe-struck.

"Hellfire *and* Hellflame. I'm rather impressed with that. What do you think, Ralph?"

"Er, yes. Very ... Impressive." Montfaucon gathered his wits. "But smoky explosions won't burn Sherwood. What will your alchemy do against the forest?"

"Ah, yes, *the application problem*. My assistants have developed a paste based on wood-sap. Should pyrophoria be mixed with this paste, it will form a sticky, um, *substance*. This substance can be applied to arrow heads, torches, and of course, smeared on trees."

"By the teeming tortures of hell, that stuff's *dangerous*. Make us up a hundred pounds by next week!"

"My Lord, that is impractical, not to say unadvisable. 100 pounds of pyrophoria would cost a fortune to produce. I also, personally, wouldn't go near any area that held more than a couple of pounds of it at any one time." Albert took a deep breath, and adopted his best tones of lectureship. "My Lords, *pryophoria is highly reactive*. What do I mean, when I say *highly reactive?* I mean, it has the tendency to trigger, for no good reason, all by itself. Our lives are currently hanging in an alchemical balance." Hampstead casually indicated the chest, at peace with the rigors of science. "Pyrophoria also combusts at very high temperature. What do I mean, by *very high* temperature? I mean it burns so hot, that water actually *fuels* the blaze."

Gisburne, Montfaucon and Nottingham stared at the powdered pyrophoria in the chest, not three yards from their knees.

"It will take us to the next full moon to prepare enough pyrophoria to immolate a good part of Sherwood. Not that I advise it, mind."

"By the ecstatic efreets of hell, *pyrophoria is the answer to all our prayers.*" The Sheriff cried. "Wait a minute, full moon's almost a month away. Can't you wizards work any quicker?"

Friar Tuck strolled along the bank of a stream, his consciousness absorbed in walking. His wisdom mind anchored internally, listening for the Divine Pattern.

Robin Hood had been a reformed character since his rescue, recuperating quietly and discussing sensible strategies for the future.

Alan-a-Dale, although still off his feet, kept busy writing rebel music.

Will Scarlett, once the distant loner, had proved an outstanding leader. He engaged every task with gusto, and got consistently great results.

Little John drilled and trained the fighting men with relentless conviction.

The merry men had taken the return of their King as an outward sign of God's blessing, and faith had soared alongside their morale. Tuck knew it wasn't quite so simple, but had gone with his congregation's enthusiasm.

Zephyrs accompanied Tuck back to the encampment, playing amongst the boughs of Sherwood, scented with warm bark and evening flowers.

He entered the canyon with the peace of prayer in his heart, his soul balmed by the beneficence of the trees.

"*By Our Lady,* Tuck! Tuck, where have you been?" Robin shook him violently by the shoulders.

The outlaw camp was in uproar, rash plans being shouted out, men grabbing weapons, Janes imploring the Holy Mother's mercy.

"Steady, what on earth's the matter?"

"Marian! *They've taken Marian.*"

"Little! Get the men in order. Scarlett! Get me the latest on Marian. Robin, will you sit down, shut up, and let me think for a minute." Tuck barked his orders, quashing the panic.

"My spies tell me Marian is in the dungeon of Castle Nottingham, badly beaten but alive." Will Scarlett reported towards midnight.

Robin Hood groaned, and held his head in his hands.

"Thank the Lord." Breathed Tuck. "What do they plan to do with her?"

"Nobody knows. Marian's noble born, so the Sheriff can't just murder her, but it looks likely she'll meet with a fatal accident."

"They'll keep Marian alive to lure Robin into their clutches." Little John sounded sadly convinced.

"Maybe not." Alan-a-Dale's gaze was bleak. "We know they're planning on sending mercenaries into Sherwood for us."

Hood groaned again, tears falling from his lowered face.

"Don't worry Robin, we'll think of something." Tuck's heart broke as he spoke. "We'll get the dear maid back, don't worry."

At the inconclusive end of the conference, Robin Hood staggered off into Sherwood's night, desolate.

The Lord of Outlaws wandered deep into the forest, the oaks attending him like mourners, the yew shivering in their spines.

Robin rambled such a distance that he entered an unfamiliar heartwood. These dense spinneys pocked Sherwood, the trees grown so tightly packed, the air flowed thick as pillows.

"King of Sherwood."

A chill breeze crossed Robin Hood's neck, and his skin crawled.

A vivid memory surfaced in his mind.

"The Hilltop Strangers!"

"We know what troubles your heart."

"*Marian*. How? What do you know? Tell me." Robin made out three tall figures, almost completely hidden in the night-shadow of a broad elm.

"We can help the May Queen."

"By Our Lady, *tell me how*."

"We require your help in return." A new voice spoke, its frigid tones coming from close by, causing his shoulders to flinch.

If Robin was sure of one thing in this weirdness, it was that no-one stood beside him.

"What would you have me do?" The outlaw cried, rent by hope and fear.

"It's not what you can do for us; it's what you can give us."

"I have nothing to offer you, Strangers. I am an outlaw." For the first time, Robin was ashamed of what he'd become. "I rightfully own nothing. I'm a criminal. I rob, I intimidate. I bring death to my friends, disaster on my loved ones! I live by force of arms ... Only in Sherwood can I pretend to a moment's peace. I am lost."

"We do not need riches, King of Sherwood. We need part of your very self." The voice coated Robin's ear in a film of ice. "Our grandmothers crafted The Gable of Si'ir as a Rainbow Bridge between worlds. Si'ir is very old, and we must replenish its power. Will you give us what we need, in return for keeping the May Queen safe?"

"Take whatever you want! Only help Marian, for the sake of our Sweet Holy Mother, *help Marian.*"

"So be it. Puck will cast a spell to protect the May Queen. In return, you will come to the Lover's hilltop on Alban Elfed, when day and night are equal, reaching towards dark. Come in secret, and come alone." The voice drifted far away, and the Strangers were gone.

"But Guy, she's an outlaw's doxy!" The following morning, Sir Ralph Montfaucon gaped at his boss in total astonishment.

"*Ralph*, if you ever speak of M'Lady Marian that way again, I'll run you through, and throw your corpse to the dogs."

"But, Guy, yesterday you said-."

"*Scathing Hellflame!* I don't care about *yesterday*, you fool. Yesterday's gone. I tell you I woke up this morning knowing *I love the girl.*" Gisburne raised his hands in rapture. "I dreamed an angel came to me! Cheerful little chap, curiously long nose. Gave me quite a fright as he climbed in the through the window ... But he glowed, Ralph ... He bloody *glowed.*"

Montfaucon threw an urgent glance at the Sheriff, who had just arrived for his breakfast.

Nottingham hesitated mid-stride, seeing from the knight's expression that something truly bizarre was happening.

"By all the necromancers in hell's abyss, what glowed, Gisburne?"

"An angel, Sheriff. Damned Cupid himself. *That's who it was!* He came as I was sleeping, and told me Marian was my one true love ... And when I woke up, I knew it was true."

"One true love?" Montfaucon stood in disbelief.

"Yes, damn your drooling mouth." Gisburne's voice mellowed around his love-struck smile. "I've already visited my turtle dove this morning-."

"*What?*" Montfaucon's shock set his nose bleeding again.

"Milady's eyes were like black diamonds, and her hair flowed as if t'were silk. Even her bruises suited her most prettily." Gisburne's smile dimmed a little. "Her tongue *was* in a most vocative temper, but the sweet cabbage will calm down once she heals up a bit."

"By the blistering blessings of hell, the man's in love!"

"Guy can't be *in love*," shouted Montfaucon as if the entire world had gone mad, "he only met the saucy bint yesterday!"

Gisburne leapt across the room, unsheathing his sabre as he came.

Yelling in fright, Montfaucon threw himself sideways to narrowly avoid a wild stab to the throat.

"Ralph! Damn me, you're my best friend, but if you ever speak of Lady Marian that way again, I swear I'll kill you."

"Gisburne! Guy," Nottingham waved his hands in a calming fashion, "*I know how you feel.* All that hot blood pumping around, eh? Heh. Good for you, but you must try to keep your temper, eh? Is that alright? Sir Ralph's probably just a bit jealous of your good fortune."

"I'm not bloody jealous!"

"Don't blame the poor fellow, Guy." The Sheriff clapped a comradely arm around Gisburne's shoulders. "The knight just needs a little time to adjust to this new relationship in your life."

"*S'Blood and S'Blood again.*" Montfaucon spat from between tight-clenched teeth. "I don't think I woke up properly this morning. This is all a dream isn't it? By the devil, tell me I'm still dreaming!"

"Yes, it is a dream! A peachy dream. Of long evenings by Loxley's fire with my tender Marian, the dogs at our feet, brats in the background..."

"Well," Montfaucon took a deep breath, "Guy, I don't understand any of this, but I guess once the wen ... She gives me the location of the outlaw, you can use her as you wish."

"Hellflame Ralph, *are you deaf?* Lady Marian told you yesterday. She doesn't know where Hood is. Don't tell me you're going to doubt the word of my fiancée?" Gisburne stared hard at his knight.

"*Your fiancée?*" Montfaucon grabbed his bandages as they tore loose.

"Oh, we're going to have a wedding! How *wonderful*. I'll need a new robe." Nottingham waved for his seneschal to take note.

"Hellfire, *yes.*" Preened Gisburne. "Not that I got the chance to pop the question to my thorny little rose this morning, but *it's understood*. We'll be married in Loxley chapel, and live happily ever after."

Friar Tuck ~ Chapter 32

The three schools for the fool:
The law; the consequence; the after-life.
Triads of Bardism

Robin huddled in despair, parading through his mind the merry men dead and wounded in the last few months.

Marian's kidnap crowned all the crew's suffering with thorns.

Hood's grand adventure had been gutted by the same barbed hook as Richard's Crusade. Greater force, not good intentions, defeated a strong enemy.

The secret hope Robin placed on the Hilltop Strangers lurked under his sadness. Striking a deal with the Lords and Ladies didn't surprise him. Hood knew the legends of the wood better than most. But, the outlaw waited for proof of power before truly believing in them.

Little John rehearsed a crack team of merry men for an impossible rescue, knowing with every command that it was futile.

Alan-a-Dale's lute suspended mournful notes along the rock walls, each blending into the last, like all the tears ever cried.

Friar Tuck tramped through the sombre woods, the hermit pegging along at his side. Neither had any fixed direction, just walking.

Tuck reached beyond the snapping despair of his consciousness, to his wisdom mind. Things didn't seem to be going well, his rational mind had to be conceded on that point. But faith affirmed that reversals had themselves been reversed; and the struggle to bring compassion into the world, always rewarded.

With the Divine his only refuge, and life raw in his hands, Tuck's theosophy had been stripped of the poses of religion. He'd lived close to the bone long enough for the Holy Spirit to have infused his experiential reality. He didn't regret a moment away from the comforts of Abbey life.

The hermit bathed his awareness in bird-song. Lapwing, yellow-hammer and mistle-thrush girdled the glades in snatches of half-remembered melodies. The trees swayed to the music like seamen in slow shanty, their leaves turning and bobbing in the evening breeze.

The contemplative pair made a wide arc and meandered back to the canyon.

They had not fixed the problems they faced that night, but were tranquil of mind.

"Tuck! Hermit!" Will Scarlett rushed past. "Follow me quick, you're never going to believe this."

"*Gisburne's going to do to what?*" Yelled Robin.

"Marry Marian, at Castle Loxley, in two days time." Scarlett repeated. "He's fallen in love with her!"

"It's a trap." Alan-a-Dale shook his head in denial of the news.

"Where did you get this information, Will?" Tuck motioned Robin to be calm.

"The Sheriff's seneschal's wife."

"She's lying." Sneered Little John.

"*She's making the bloody dress.*"

"But you *can't* go through Sherwood." Sir Ralph Montfaucon, for the second morning in a row, wondered if he'd actually woken up.

"My Lady Marian wishes to be wed as quick as possible. The only sensible route between Nottingham and Loxley is through the forest. *Ergo*, we go through the forest."

"But ... The outlaws ... She's-."

"Ralph Montfaucon! Not another word. *Not*. Another. Word. Lady Marian has said she's nothing to do with Hood. The rumours were wrong." Gisburne's eyes glazed with a preternatural light. "Get the soldiers ready. The Sheriff's bringing Captain Roland with us as escort. *Hellflame* Ralph, love hasn't rendered me completely stupid. The damned outlaws might try to rob us!"

A crisp morning-blue sky greeted the wedding party with high-piled clouds as they trotted away from Castle Nottingham.

Montfaucon and the Sheriff led 30 men-at-arms on fast chargers. A further 25 crossbowmen rode to each side, and Captain Roland brought up the rear with 50 foot soldiers.

Lady Marian rode body-guarded by alert troops, and a gambolling Guy of Gisburne.

When Gisburne had arrived in Marian's cell the previous morning with a flowers and declarations of love, the maid had thought it a trick.

Then, understanding Gisburne was sincere, she'd let fly every curse and insult she could remember, and many she made up on the spot.

The Earl had retreated, saying he understood how she felt. This sudden love was shocking for them both.

Lady Marian had almost torn her bonds apart in rage.

The following lonely hours had sunk despair into the Lady of Arlingford. The jail stank of fresh blood and old fear, her bruises were deeply painful, and only worse was to come.

In the end, Marian had hatched a desperate plan. Rescue from Nottingham's dungeon was impossible, but if she could get in bowshot of Sherwood, she knew Robin would not fail her. She asked for an immediate marriage at Loxley.

When Gisburne agreed without a second's hesitation, Marian had realized the extent of the Earl's madness, but didn't care.

Only now, riding towards her wedding with her hands bound firmly to her saddle, did she wonder what would happen if Robin didn't come.

"*They're doing what?*" Howled Robin into Will Scarlett's face.

"Robin, I know it's crazy, but Nottingham, Gisburne and a company of troops are coming through Sherwood. Right now. With Marian. I saw them *myself.*" Events had turned so bizarre, Scarlett had personally checked his look-out's story before reporting back.

"*MERRY MEN!*" Hood's summons exploded out of the canyon to sway the trees for a mile around.

In seconds few, Little John, Alan-a-Dale and two score outlaws had raced to their King, hefting weapons.

"Dale, summon the faithful. Little, get the men in battle order. Scarlett, set up an ambush at the crossing of the main tracks. Tuck, come with me. *We're going to free Marian.*"

The encampment erupted with action.

Tuck watched the merry men with a terrible feeling in his soul.

"Robin. I'm sorry, but we can't do this. It's not right."

"By Our Lady, Friar, you're sermonizing *now?*"

"No, I mean militarily. It'll take too long to get our fighters in place." Tuck's inner vision filled with a premonition of Sherwood dripping with outlaw blood.

"Damn your conscience covered cowardice, monk! I've taken action already, and by Our Lady, it's worked. I'm going to take my chances."

"Taken action? What do you mean?"

"Go help Scarlett set up the ambush!" Hood spun away to grab his bow.

Tuck's rational mind wanted to follow Robin's order, but the quiet voice of his spirit counselled against it.

Tuck's faith's was sorely tested, but in the end he rooted his feet to the ground.

"No, my King."

"Friar Tuck, *out of my way*. I'm going to get Marian, with or without you." Hood sank into his hips, his eyes black pits, readying to smash Tuck aside.

"Robin! *There's got to be another way*. Going head to head against Nottingham will only get you killed. What will Marian do then?" Tuck shivered with emotion, but his voice stayed rock steady, speaking from his sincerity.

Little John appeared at the head of the armed men, battle lust darkening their faces. For the first time, Tuck saw his flock as true outlaws, and his heart quailed.

Robin Hood's face grew fell as the giant stood alongside him.

"What ar't doin' fat badger?" Little John gave Tuck a very disconcerting look.

"Big fish," Tuck sighed, "put down your weapons. Please. We all want to help Marian, but this isn't the way. It's a trap, but not in the usual sense." Tuck flung a dramatic hand towards Robin, who was about to start yelling blue fury. "Look at our King! *He's mad with rage.* Is this who we are?"

The thunder cracking about Tuck's brow took even Robin aback.

"*That* is the trap. To act from rage, blinded by desire! Robin, with their officers leading them, *Nottingham's soldiers will fight to the death.* This is no merry grab and run. You're plunging into pitched battle! And even if we get the upper hand, do you think Gisburne is going to let you take Marian? He'll kill her before allowing that. There must be another way."

Little John's fists clenched with indecision, his every instinct telling him to rush to the rescue. The giant looked to his King for leadership.

Robin Hood gazed at Tuck with a devilish smile playing about his lips.

"By Our Lady, Friar Tuck, there *is* another way."

"By Our Lady, indeed." Agreed Tuck, his own grin breaking out. "Good King Robin, what mischief are you hatching now?"

Montfaucon held his sword ready, certain the outlaws would attack at any moment. The only reason the knight had finally agreed to this insane journey, was the chance to properly engage with Hood and his criminal crew.

Also expecting trouble, Nottingham stayed close to his bodyguards. Right from the start, the Sheriff had planned to use this outbreak of love to improve his chances of catching the outlaw. In about a month, his mercenaries and the pyrophoria would be ready. But if he could do away with the sinner before then, his Barony would come all the quicker.

The morning passed tensely as Gisburne's wedding party trotted along the main road to Loxley. Every oak seemed to hide a score of men, the dense yew perfect for concealing a horde of archers. The lyrical birds of Sherwood fell silent at their passage, and animals scurried away far in front.

Montfaucon scanned the soundless timberland to either side, gripping his glimmering blade in tight excitement. Although Hood remained the main target, the knight particularly watched for the fighting Friar who'd pummelled his nose. The knight would be disfigured for the rest of his life, and the wound made every breath painful. He'd planned, in detail, how to even the score.

At midday, and only a few miles from Loxley, the soldiers began to hope for a quiet run through the weald. Some had already met the outlaws, and all had heard terrible stories of their longbows. A few were even sympathetic to the cause. None wanted to fight them on their own turf.

Montfaucon, the Sheriff and Lady Marian were bitterly disappointed Robin hadn't yet appeared. Gisburne was oblivious, concentrated on composing serenades for his wedding night.

The timberland thinned steadily, leading from copses of oak, to groves of beech. The soldiers could now see a distance into the forest, but its empty spaces seemed even more threatening. Enraged peasants, ravening wolves, bellicose bears and every other nightmare of the deepwood stalked immanent in the deceptive bough shadow.

Friar Tuck and Will Scarlett sat 50 feet up an elm on the outskirts of Sherwood. They had left their King in the capable hands of Little John.

They knew if Robin saw Marian, he wouldn't be able to hold back from launching a doomed rescue. The outlaws stoically watched the wedding party come into view, then pass beyond the final trees.

Tuck gazed into the middle-distance, to where the white towers of Castle Loxley shone above harvest-heavy fields.

Suddenly, Gisburne sang:

Tra-la-la-lee, Marian you're for me,
Tra-la-la-loo, and I'm for you!

Reacting badly to the surprise, Montfaucon's stallion jiggered violently into the Sheriff's mare, and Will Scarlett jerked backwards off his branch, catching himself at the last minute with one hand. Friar Tuck couldn't help but chuckle at Will's doubly-aghast expression as he hoiked him back up.

The wedding party moved quicker as they pulled away from Sherwood, every soldier relieved at their safe passage.

Tuck's chuckles died in his throat as he watched Lady Marian throw a single, heart-searing, glance back into the weald.

Friar Tuck ~ Chapter 33

The three types of profit:
From producing; from investing; from good reputation.
Triads of Bardism

Robin Hood and Little John strained like hunting dogs at the edge of the forest, circling between the beeches in frustration.

The sun hovered on the horizon for hours, seeming immobile to the night-waiting outlaws. At last, the first motes of darkness stole over the landscape, and the merry men dashed out from under the trees.

In the fields near Castle Loxley, the outlaws hurried along an old straight track, then cut right, heading for a farmer's shed.

Robin's grandparents, like all forward thinking aristocrats, had built an escape tunnel from a basement chamber in Loxley castle. The route ran a crow's mile underground before coming out in these fields. Old Earl Loxley had built this shed on top of the exit, after a family of fiercely territorial badgers had to be evicted from the tunnel 40 years before.

Robin thought of his father with fond gratitude as he lifted the hidden trapdoor and dropped into the tunnel. Little John waited by the shed, ready to cover the retreat.

In the pitch-dark of the damp earthen tunnel, flying solo, Hood's cat-green eyes flared with adventure.

"You see!" Gisburne motioned his guests to be seated. "The course of true love *does* run smoothly sometimes."

Montfaucon scowled into his mug, as restless as his stallion. He and Captain Roland had scoured every inch of Castle Loxley, tightening security for the big day. Added to Gisburne's standing guard of 50, Nottingham's company of 130 soldiers rendered the castle impregnable.

The knight was satisfied the outlaws would enjoy a very warm reception if they came to the wedding.

"And wasn't Lady Marian brave? She didn't utter a sound all the way through that damned forest."

"By all the horns in hell, Gisburne," the Sheriff sank a mug of wine with nuptial abandon, "that woman's going to need every ounce of courage to be your wife."

"*Hellfire Sheriff,* you're right! I am as puissant in the fields of love as those of war." Gisburne rose from his seat, about to break into song.

"Whoever heard of a wench being praised for courage?" Muttered Montfaucon, recklessly drunk.

Gisburne deflated from his dramatic pose, and turned an evil eye on his knight.

"What the hell do you mean by that, Ralph?"

"All I'm saying is, Guy, maids are usually prized for being fragrantly discreet and prettily obedient, not spear-witted and stout-hearted."

"Bah, you don't know anything about women. Milady's got the devil's very tongue on her, it can't be denied, but that makes my conquest all the creamier. I'll have her trained to heel before the honeymoon's over, mark me."

"Well said, Gisburne. That maid's been without manly guidance for too long, is all. She's gone back to nature, like any mare left too long without a rider!"

Lady Marian paced her room, high up in Loxley's western tower. The room was guarded, bolted from the outside, and its window looked 50 feet down to stony ground.

Nottingham's seneschal's wife had packed a hasty wedding dress, now laid in nauseating white omen across the bed.

The Lady of Arlingford didn't know what to think. Her bold plan had failed, and she couldn't help but wonder if Robin had been sincere in his love.

Marian's soul trembled.

After her father's death, cozening relatives had connived away the family wealth. The innocent maid had been left with a sack of silver coins, and a small cottage on Arlingford's green. Marian had toughened up, deciding not to trust anyone ever again, until she'd met Robin Hood.

The maid moved to the window, tears twinkling her midnight eyes.

Loxley's summer-rich lands were fading to black. A cold new moon patrolled high and spiked in the sky. Marian knew that without a miracle, the following night would find her in Gisburne's bridal bed.

Hood took every unseen pace with confidence, running the backs of his hands along the walls to guide his passage. The outlaw played the layout of Castle Loxley through his mind, trying to figure where Gisburne would have put Marian.

He stumbled over earth or bones a few times in the lightless tunnel, but reached the castle entrance without any greater difficulty.

A false wall creaked open in the furthest basement of Castle Loxley, and Robin stepped into his family seat. He'd dreamed of this moment for over a year, and the very stones welcomed their rightful master home.

Hood skimmed through the dim store rooms, up a flight of barely remembered stairs, and into the top basement.

Here the ceiling was buttressed by plaster arches, groining in octagonal repetitions. Piled around each pillar were odd crates and bric-a-brac, covered in thickly dusted cloths.

Robin stealthed up three steep steps, and placed his ear against the tall wooden door leading to the castle kitchens.

At that moment, the door opened inwards.

"Bloody *typical*, asking me to get a wedding feast ready in a day." Loxley's head chef ranted. "Only Our Blessed Lady knows where the silver is. Jumping Jehosephat!"

Robin grabbed the chef across the mouth, then drew him at high speed into the far shadows.

The outlaw pressed his wide-bladed dagger to the chef's throat.

"Barry?" Came a short-tempered female voice from the kitchens. "*Barry?* Don't tell me you've fallen down those bloody stairs, you nincompoop!"

Robin suppressed a laugh, causing Barry to wriggle in abject terror, thinking death was upon him.

"Stop squirming, Barry." Whispered Hood, trying to sound dangerous despite his humour. "I'm not going to kill you unless you make me."

"Bar-*ry!* If you don't answer me right now, I'm coming down there. With my rolling pin."

The chef collapsed with despair in the outlaw's arms, believing the last words he would ever hear were his wife threatening to clobber him.

"Actually, mate," Robin leaned in again, "it may go easier if I finish you off before she does, what d'ya say?"

Barry struggled mightily as Robin held back his laughter.

"Calm down, chef. I've come for one thing this night, and it's not your gastronomic soul. Where's Lady Marian?"

Barry stilled again, wonder and puzzlement colliding in his heart.

"Up in the western Tower." Barry replied, his larynx scratching against the dagger blade. "You're Robin Hood, aren't you?"

"Aye, chef, and I-."

"Oi, Millicent!" Barry called. "Get down here! I've something to show you."

Robin almost slit the chef's throat in shock.

"You're not luring me down there you saucy knave! I've got work to do. Get your arse back up here with the bloody silver."

"Women." Barry muttered. "They never listen! Always think we've got sauce on the brain. An', if you ask me, that means *they've* always got sauce on the brain!"

"Listen chef, I'll have to kill you if you betray me, you do understand that don't you?" Robin slackened his grip.

"Oh yes," Barry brushed himself free of dust as he stood up, "that's only fair, isn't it? Don't worry, Millicent knows all your songs. And the merry men helped my cousin Pete's family survive this winter past. She's going to go crazy when she meets you!"

"Er, well, I'm really here *in secret,* chef-."

But Barry was already gone, and Hood had no choice but to go after him, into the candlelit kitchens.

There, a stout-backed lady busied in a deep sink.

"Barry, I hope you found that silver. If you didn't, I'll lock you down there until you do, mark my words."

"Oh Millicent, why don't you turn around, my sweet?"

"*Don't* you sweet me." Millicent scrubbed at her pan with a vengeance. "And unless you've got an armful of cutlery, you nincompoop, I'm not turning around neither!"

"Good matron Millicent," Robin broke in with his suavest voice, "I'm sorry to interrupt your work, but I'm on a daring secret rescue mission, and I vitally need *your* help."

Millicent turned around in astonishment, gaping at the politely smiling outlaw as Barry posed augustly next to him.

"Y'see? Better than cutlery, i'n't 'e?"

"Where on God's good earth d'you find 'im, Barry?" Millicent eyed Robin with a countrywoman's suspicion.

"In the cellar." Barry replied, even prouder. "My sweet, may I present the King of the Woods himself, Robin Hood."

"Blessed Lady!" Millicent dropped her pan with an impressive clatter. "Is it really him? This isn't some idiocy cooked up by your ale-house ne'er-do-wells is it? I'll have your sinews for suspenders if it is!"

"This really *is* him. He had a dagger to my throat and everything." Barry pointed to Robin's blade as definitive proof.

"By the Heavens, come for Marian, 'ave ye?" Millicent narrowed her eyes as she looked Robin up and down. "I was wondering if you'd show up. No doubt she is too! What took you so long?"

"Er, yes. Sorry for the delay, Millicent. Secret rescue missions take a bit of time to cook up."

"Ey! He's funny, my sweet, just like they say! *Cook up*, geddit? I'm a *chef*, right, and he's here in my kitchen *cooking up* a secret plan." Barry chortled.

Robin gave the chef a confused look.

"Shut up, Barry. He's not here to muck about with the likes of you. What d'you need, Robin Hood?" Millicent dropped her voice in bitterness. "There's no love for the new Earl in this kitchen, mark my words. I knew the Old Earl, and his father before him. A fine family, proper, but it ended badly." Millicent tutted severely. "Young Robert always was a jackanapes, and got a large jacksie kick from the King for his trouble." The kitchen wife sighed. "Anyway, I suppose you'll be rescuing Marian now, won't you? Got a plan?"

"Erm, not exactly a *plan*, but-."

"I might have known! You've come in 'ere with a heart full of sauce, and not a thought in your head neither! I heard you were like this, from the songs."

"*What?*" Robin hadn't ever really listened to the outlaw songs, assuming Alan-a-Dale would stick to tried and tested hero shtick.

"Oh yes, we're all familiar with your chicaneries. How the merry man have to rescue you from your... Boldness. And that *poor* Friar Tuck!"

"Poor Friar Tuck, *indeed*." Robin pulled a very doubtful expression, wondering where Dale had got his inspiration from.

Barry chuckled and gazed admiringly at the outlaw.

"Bloody marvellous chicaneries."

"Don't you go encouraging him in his foolishness, Barry! He's almost a married man. Since you don't have a plan, outlaw, here's a serving uniform that'll just about fit. Take up Lady Marian's supper, knock out the guard, and rescue the damsel!"

"Right away, ma'am." Hood lit up the kitchen with his most rakish grin.

Friar Tuck ~ Chapter 34

Three things best not left:
A ship to wind; a woman to rage; a son to ignorance.
Triads of Bardism

Robin Hood eased through Castle Loxley, passing guards unheeded.

Captain Roland had briefed his men to expect a full scale assault, not a lone intruder. In any case, the servant's livery and supper tray put him beneath the soldiers' notice.

The outlaw puffed up the spiral stairs to the top of the western tower, and was about to clobber the guard, when he heard voices close behind him.

"Alright, take it on in." The guard turned back from unlocking the door, and pushed it open.

Having no choice, Robin bobbed his head and ducked into the room.

Marian was staring out of the window, her shoulders bowed with crying.

The outlaw's heart leaped, then plunged as he caught the maid's despair.

"But I really don't see why my fiancée should spend the night in the dungeon." Gisburne's voice echoed up the stairwell.

"It's for her security, my Lord." Montfaucon replied as the pair stepped into the room. "We don't want any accidents, do we?"

"No, I suppose not. M'Lady Marian, overcome at the emotion of the big day? I understand." Gisburne pranced across the chamber with groomly solicitude.

Robin shrunk into his skin, turned his back to place the tray on a corner table, and did his best to blend in with the walls.

"My love, Ralph's had a grand idea. Won't you take your things and come along? With brigands everywhere, I'm sure you'll want to spend your last maidenly night feeling properly secure. Loxley's cells aren't very large, but after tomorrow it'll all be over, and we can settle into wedded bliss."

"I am as much a captive here as anywhere, Gisburne. At least if I'm in the cell, everyone else will know that." Lady Marian gathered a few items, not even glancing at the servant stooping submissively to the side of the chamber.

Montfaucon gave Marian his nastiest smile as she swept by him.

"You see, Ralph, she's already more docile." Gisburne whispered as they followed his fiancée down the spiral stairs.

The King of Outlaws waited five minutes, then headed back for the kitchens, dinner tray in hand once again.

"I've made the cell as comfortable as I can, my love." Gisburne patted a thick quilt and indicated a row of neatly arranged candles.

"I'd prefer the bare walls and stone floor, Gisburne."

"There now, don't you be fretting. It'll all go well tomorrow. The Abbot of Doncaster's riding in to take the ceremony, and our good friend the Sheriff has brought enough vittals for a three day feast. Where would you like to go for honeymoon? I thought London!"

"Hell would be better."

"You're always so witty, my love." Laughed Gisburne. "I'll see you tomorrow, by the altar ... But ... I suppose one kiss before our wedding day would be out of the question?"

Marian's gaze turned incendiary, and her fingers hooked into defensive claws.

"Ah, the sweetness of maidenly chastity! Of course, *you're right* Marian. On the morrow, all will be permitted. Good night, my love." Gisburne slammed the cell door with a happy thump.

"Well, where is she?" Demanded Millicent as Robin reappeared.

"They moved her to the cells just as I was about to-."

"Nincompoop outlaw! Why d'ye take so long about it? That maid is going to be a spinster before she gets rescued at this rate. *Poor* Friar Tuck."

"Now then, Millicent, this *is* the King of Sherwood, and-."

"You be quiet, Barry. You're the knave who delayed his Outlaw Majesty. Playing silly buggers in the cellars!"

Robin Hood couldn't help a shamefaced grin, which Barry echoed a moment later.

"Oh yes, a *right pair* of merry men I've got in my kitchen tonight. You might as well have a bite of dinner, and then for Our Lady's Pity's sake, fetch the damsel from the jail! This time, *bring her back with you*. It's not that complicated." Millicent presented two heaped plates of mashed potatoes and pork sausages, then put her hands on her hips. "And you'd better eat it all."

Properly bolstered in every sense, the Lord of Outlaws set off for Loxley's dungeon.

"Hellfire, *you*, stop. Didn't you already give the Lady her supper?" Gisburne demanded of the servant he encountered on the stairs.

"No, my Lord." Hood kept his head down.

"Dolt." Gisburne gave him a smart slap on the cheek. "No wonder she's fractious, the mare hasn't eaten all day. Feed my fiancée, damn your bones!"

Robin Hood hastened down the stairs as Gisburne headed to the feast hall, cursing the quality of his staff.

Loxley's dungeon accommodated three cells, one of which had no door. The place hadn't been used in Robin's memory and was musty with damp, unlike Nottingham's blood-tanged prison.

The outlaw heard delicate weeping coming from the cell to his left, and peered through the grille.

Lady Marian squatted on the far side of the cell, her wedding dress across her lap, torn to shreds.

A guard stomped angrily down the stairs holding a large key. "Blasted knave! You were supposed to-."

Robin felled the guard with one pop of his metal tray, then unlocked the cell door triumphantly.

Without waiting to see who it was, Marian launched a frenzied attack, tearing at his face with tooth and nail.

"*By Our Lady, Marian stop!* It's me, Robin."

"*Bloody* Robin." Marian turned her claws into fists, and punched the outlaw in the gut. "I thought you'd abandoned me!" Marian swung again, tears flying from her flashing eyes.

Robin deflected the blow and caught the maid in his arms, crushing her to him.

"Dear darling Mawd, I'm sorry it took so long." The outlaw murmured into Marian's ear. "You see, it's all Tuck's fault-."

"*What?*" Marian tore loose of Robin's grip, smiling despite her tears. "Don't you go blaming that pious, hard working monk for your lacksadaisy knavery Robin Hood!"

"Pious? Probably! Hard working? Alright, but what about meddlesome, obnoxious, inebriate-."

"*Poor* Friar Tuck, always getting you out of scrapes, and this is how you thank him. I've heard the songs you know, and now I see they're all true!"

"Getting me out of scrapes? By Our Lady, I'm going have *words* with that minstrel. But darling Marian, dearest Mawd, would you mind escaping this jail before the guards come and kill me?"

"Huh, now you've arrived late, you're all in a hurry."

Robin took Marian's hand, leading her swiftly out of the dungeon and into the servant's quarters.

"You seem to know your way around." Marian commented.

"Yes, I used to play in the dungeons all the time when I was a lad."

"*Oh*," Marian was full of sympathy, "were your parents criminals, too?"

"Er, no, dad was the Earl."

"*What?* Your father was Old Earl Loxley?"

"Yes, bless him."

"But that makes you Robert Loxley."

"Ah. Yes. I suppose it does, or it did."

"The mad-cap Earl!"

"By Our Lady, no-one's called me that for ages."

"*Why didn't you tell me?*"

"I never quite got round to it, darling."

"You're *more* of a knave than the songs say. What other secrets are you hiding from me? A brace of forest girls tucked away in Sherwood's bower, perhaps?"

"*No-one's* got *anyone* tucked *anywhere* thanks to that *poor* Friar Tuck. And please-."

But Robin was cut short.

A monstrously drunk Sir Ralph Montfaucon swayed in the doorway of the next chamber, sword in hand.

"Well, Robin-Robert-Loxley-Hood. You're a traitor as well as an outlaw. That fits." Montfaucon slurred.

Hood accelerated across the room like a bolt of lightning to blast the knight with an iron-fisted punch.

Montfaucon crumpled groundward, so slowed by the drink he hadn't even tried to dodge the blow.

The outlaw jabbed out a few more swift strikes to ensure the knight wouldn't get up in a hurry, grabbed Marian's hand, and raced for the kitchens.

Barry held the cellar door with solemn dignity.

"Your secret tunnel awaits, King Outlaw."

"You have the undying thanks of Robin Hood, true folk of Loxley!"

Millicent's merry cries of "Good luck, Lady Marian!" faded to the outlaws' ears as they descended to the lower basement.

In a trice, Robin had the wall swung open and they were in the tunnel, inching along in the dark.

"I hope you're not scared of spiders." Muttered Robin with mischievous satisfaction.

"Not as scared as they are of me." Came the fierce reply.

"By Our Lady!"

A blooming joy lifted the brooding Little John when he saw Lady Marian's raven curls appear at the trapdoor.

The giant swung the maid bodily into the air, then flung her about like she was a child, both of them laughing outrageously.

"Now then, goodman John, I've only just finished rescuing the damsel, don't you go breaking her." Robin exclaimed as he emerged from the floor.

"*To Sherwood!*" Little John cried in full voice, and without giving his King a chance to protest, picked him up as well.

Friar Tuck ~ Chapter 35

The three to whom it is right to give food:
The stranger; the solitary; the orphan.
Triads of Bardism

Sir Ralph Montfaucon staggered into Loxley's main hall, blood gushing from his re-broken nose.

An awful anxiety gripped Earl Gisburne's heart.

"The devil's bastard ... Devil ... Bastard ... Here. In Loxley. GUY damn you! Loxley *in* Loxley! *Bastard.*"

"Sweeping Hellfire, Ralph!" Gisburne's hands started to shake. "*What devil in Loxley?*"

"*Loxley!*" Montfaucon bawled, then fell to the floor, unconscious.

"By all the over-sauced soldiers in hell's abyss, Gisburne, your man's a bit of a mess." The Sheriff peered over the edge of the feast table. "Stupid bugger."

"I think he was trying to tell us something... ." Gisburne prodded Montfaucon with a toe. "Wake up, Ralph, damn you." The Earl booted his knight hard in the backside. "WAKE UP."

Montfaucon sat in a bleary daze, trying to remember why his nose hurt so much. "*Loxley. Bastard Loxley.*"

"Yes, you're in Loxley, Ralph. What happened to you, man?"

"LOXLEY!" The knight swayed with the force of his cry, then collapsed again.

"Hellfire Montfaucon, are you out of your wits?"

"Leave him, Gisburne. Probably fell over, and now blames your castle for breaking his nose!"

"No, Sheriff. I know Ralph. He's drunk, but something's wrong ... *MARIAN!*"

Gisburne raced for the cells, but tripped at the bottom of the stairs over the guard Robin had knocked out, and crashed face-first into the opposite wall. He peeled himself off the floor, clutching his bloody brow in stupefied misery.

When he saw Marian's empty cell, pain, anger and confusion were catalyzed by the alcohol in Gisburne's blood, and a murderous rage turned everything red.

The Sheriff of Nottingham staggered down to the dungeon after his host, holding onto the walls with both hands for balance.

His drunken, stupid smile dissolved instantly under Gisburne's harrowing gaze.

Suddenly the Sheriff felt very sober, and rather scared. He glanced across at the open cell door, then backed slowly up the stairs, not daring to say a word.

Nottingham was downing a nerve-steadying mug of wine, when Gisburne stalked into the hall moments later.

Without breaking stride, the Earl unleashed an enormous kick at his unconscious knight. Montfaucon slid a good five feet at the blow, but didn't stir.

Gisburne took two paces, and let rip with another huge kick, sending the knight rolling against the wall.

"*By the mad stallions of hell Guy,* you're going to kill him if you keep doing that."

"*Thrice-damned knight,* why did you let Marian escape?" Gisburne yelled, hysterical with fury.

"How d'ye know he knows something?"

"The bastard didn't get all those bruises falling over. Someone gave him a good hiding. If he doesn't get Marian back, *today,* I *will* bloody kill him."

"Today?" The Sheriff cast a look of pity on Montfaucon's tangled form.

Little John carried the lovers on his shoulders into the forest, all three sending victorious peals of merriment into the star-dazzled heavens.

They paraded through the canyon in an upsurge of merry men, Robin and Marian sending regal waves to their cheering crew. Happiness heated every Jack's belly, and haloed every Jane's heart.

Friar Tuck welcomed Robin Hood and Maid Marian from Little John's shoulders, weeping. They were immediately joined by a yelling Will Scarlett, and a hooting Alan-a-Dale.

Little John, overcome by a sense of family he'd thought lost forever, embraced the whole bundle in one clench of his gigantic arms.

"By Our Lady, *what's going on?* John Little! Stop squeezing. Stop! *By Our Lady,* please. Right now!"

The merry men set to getting a feast of a breakfast together.

Tuck watched his flock working in brotherhood, his soul lifted by this most joyous proof of the wisdom in the Holy Spirit.

The hermit burst out of the brake, demanding to know why the camp was uproaring the entire forest, but Tuck hugged him into silence.

"There now, easy brother." The hermit patted Tuck on the back. "Marian's alright, is she? Our prayers have been answered then, yes. Thank the Blessed Mother. Of course, this does give you a bit of a problem."

"Eh? What's that, hermit?" Tuck pulled back from his hug with a suspicious frown.

"Sure, all I'm saying is, it's going to be rather difficult to keep those two apart now, if you know what I mean." The hermit gave Tuck a significant glance. "They may not get up to what-not in the forest … But our Lady of Arlingford's cottage is properly cosy, *if you know what I mean.*"

"Stop saying that. Of course I know what you mean. I'm not totally oblivious to the ways of nature."

"*Aren't you?* Oh. Has Little John had a little word?" The hermit dodged Tuck's swipe with a cackle.

"Anyway, hermit, I'd say it's a problem for you, not me."

"Sweet Mother!" The hermit raised his hands to heaven. "What's crossed that ale-addled brain of your'n now, monk?"

"You're going to officiate at Robin and Marian's hand-fast this afternoon."

"*What?*"

"It's the only answer: We give Robin and Marian a forest wedding. It'll be legal enough for outlaw work. You do the wordy bit, they exchange rings, I slap a blessing on 'em, job done. This way, they'll be married for a year and a day. That should give us time to get them into a church for longer than five minutes."

"The *wordy* bit?"

"Yes. You'll be good at that." This time Tuck dodged the swipe.

The King of Sherwood breakfasted with maid Marian as a glorious sun broke across the edge of the canyon above.

Drifting, translucent waves of July sunlight ennobled the merry men, three score of them, perched on every ledge and boulder, laughing and eating.

Robin turned to Marian, looking more serious than she'd ever seen. "I never imagined a man could feel happiness like this, Marian. It's not even happiness ... There should be another word for this feeling."

"There is, Robin." Marian's eyes were like the midnight coals of a friend's campfire. "It's love."

"*Is this what people actually mean by love?* I never knew!" Robin boomed an enormous laugh.

"Not everyone, my darling, not everyone." Marian replied with a touch of sadness. "But we do. You do. I do. Tuck certainly does."

"Ah yes, *exactly*. Where *is* that poor Friar Tuck and his accomplice, the surely *tragic* Alan-a-Dale. Their King wants a word with those mischief twitch'd jackanapes!"

"You called, my Lord?" Tuck appeared, beaming, the hermit behind him, looking a lot less pleased.

"By Our Lady, I know that look. What's the Friar up to, hermit?"

"Oh, you'll like it, but I certainly don't. *The wordy bit* indeed. Why can't I do the blessing? I learned fine, lyrical blessings in Mayo."

"You're not ordained, hermit, now be quiet. Lady Marian, would you please excuse Robin for just a moment?"

"Of course, dear Friar, I trust your good influence implicitly." Marian smiled sweetly at Robin, who stuck his tongue out in reply.

Tuck led the mystified Robin away, dragging the hermit along by the hand, still mouthing complaints.

"What *is* going on? And did you conspire with Alan to compose corky couplets about me, Friar?"

"Oh, I may have helped with a word here and there. But that's neither here, nor there. Have you asked Marian to marry you?"

"*By Our Lady,* you're slippery today! You've been spending too much time with sly old beardie here. What the blazes are you talking about, Tuck?"

"The Friar is talking about popping the question, you idiot! Weddings. White dresses. Worried grooms. *You know?* Bells, bridesmaids, blessings, bon- , sure, I needn't remind *you* what it all leads to."

"Thank *you*, hermit. Robin, we want to marry you today."

"Erm. That's very nice, Tuck-."

"Sweet Mother Goddess, the boy's complaining! We shrive our souls praying to the Almighty for miracles so he can get his squeeze, and this is thanks he gives us. It doesn't surprise me at all that even *His Omnipotent Peacefulness* gets uppity with these idiots sometimes."

"Now wait just a minute-."

"*Robin!* Have you asked Marian to marry you?"

"Not officially! *By Our Lady,* do you want me to do it right now? Is that it? Will that make you cockahoops happy? FINE."

The Lord of Outlaws pushed past his momentarily cowed counsellors, calling loudly for Marian.

The maid turned, already sensing something afoot from the way Tuck and the hermit were scurrying along behind their distempered King.

"My Lady," Robin fell abruptly to one knee and drew out his neck chain, "I once gave, er, sent you the twin to this ring."

"Yes, my Lord." Marian replied, holding out her fingers to show her oaken band.

"By the love in our hearts and these rings of oak, will you marry me, Lady Marian of Arlingford?"

"Yes, King Robin of Sherwood. I will marry you."

Robin Hood sprang to his feet and wrapped Marian in his arms. Marian gave a great cry of joy, then kissed Robin as sunlight o'er-glowed the air.

The explosion of rejoicing rising from the merry men shocked a thousand blue butterflies from their flowers to flutter up and down the canyon.

Alan-a-Dale appeared, picking out a tender melody on his lute. Will Scarlett leant against Little John, both with tears in their eyes. Tuck and the hermit huddled arm in arm, smugger than maiden aunts.

Shouts of congratulation and celebration rippled out from the Jacks and Janes.

"It's a wedding breakfast!" Robin's battlefield voice surmounted the hullabaloo, chiming the very stones. "John, rig up a nave. Alan, get a choir together. Will, invite *everybody*. Oh, you thrice-blessed crew, Marian and I will be wed today!"

Friar Tuck ~ Chapter 36

The three foundations of Spirituality:
Hearth as altar; work as worship; service as sacrament.
Triads of Bardism

Montfaucon awoke on the floor of Loxley's great hall, his head pounding like the devil's very forge.

Clotted gore glued the knight's cheek to the flagstones as he lifted his head, tearing loose with a gruesome plop.

Tentatively working around him were three or four serving wenches, laying out tables for Gisburne's wedding feast.

Montfaucon gazed dumbly at them for several minutes, his memory a cacophony of pain and confusion.

The knight felt particularly puzzled as to why his nose was freshly broken. He could have sworn the monk had battered him over a week before, but here he was, with his nose flat against his cheek again.

Montfaucon was gumming his torn top-lip when Gisburne stamped in.

"Montfaucon!" The Earl was ready to launch a tirade, but his wind left him in a rush. "Hellflame Ralph, you look *terrible*."

"I feel it, my Lord. What the hell happened last night? What the hell happened *last week?*"

"Damn your bones, Montfaucon, are you still drunk? Let me see now: Last night, you let my beloved be ripped from my arms, not to mention my jail. Last week, you let Robin Hood escape from Nottingham. *Ring any bells?"*

"Oh, hell." The knight groaned as his memory came to boorish order. "Loxley."

"Don't you start that idiocy again, Ralph, or I'll add to your bruises, mark me."

"*It's Loxley,* damn your demented eyes, Gisburne! I swear I won't have your jibes today. Robin Hood is bloody Loxley, Guy. Robert Loxley! Any bloody bells ringing for you?"

"How the hell ... *It makes foul sense* ... Hellflame! *Robert Loxley.* May his soul burn *forever."*

Montfaucon climbed to his feet, and teetered dangerously before getting his legs working.

"I need to go to bed, Gisburne. And would you send for a healer, for pity's sake. I think I might die."

"Bed? *Coruscating Hellfire, Ralph!* You're not going to bed, or doing any dying. You're going to get that harlot Marian back in time for me to marry her *today,* and that's final."

"No need for you to worry at all, brother, but I'm just a wee-tad concerned that doing it this way won't entirely *satisfy* the prophecy." The hermit sounded particularly thoughtful.

"*What?"* Tuck swung round from finishing the wedding-altar.

"Sure, don't fret now, I'm fully confident everything will be fine, if *I* do the blessing."

"*Heaven have mercy!* You better have your bit sorted. The ceremony's going to start in a minute."

The altar was simply a few crates pushed together, but draped in clean yellow canvas, shone deep as gold under the warm afternoon sun.

In remembrance of Divine life, fresh summer fruit crowned the altar-top. Juicy green apples and wildwood pears were stacked in pyramids on a flowing bed of taut redberry and sweet blackberry. Considering the nature of his flock, Tuck felt pleased with the metaphor.

Tuck tweaked the altar's garlands of white flowers, using prayer to lead his mind to the silence of the Holy Spirit. He knelt, bringing a vision of his Saviour to heart. He prayed that his blessing on the couple be empowered by Divine Love.

The pulsing invisitude of Tuck's faith-vision brightened in confirmation.

Little John and his riggers erected a nave of woven branches to welcome the congregation. The Janes threaded a field of delicate-pink flowers into the structure so their heads hung downwards, forming a varipetaled ceiling above the boisterous gathering.

Festivalling Jacks and Janes bantered as they gathered in wait for the bride and groom. Then, Alan-a-Dale's all-male choir broke into a stirring, romantic harmony, and everyone took their places.

The Lord of Outlaws paced regally up the aisle in his finest Lincoln green, casting smiles into all the familiar faces.

Alan-a-Dale gestured, and the choir segued into a soft aria.

Maid Marian of Arlingford appeared, shy as a fawn in her forest-spun wedding gown.

The bride's dress had been tailored at the last minute by Dale. His re-styled monk's robe hung front and back over Marian's riding outfit, nicely showing off her boots as Scarlett had remarked. Sensing something needed adding, Dale had sewn white rose-petals over every inch, transforming the lumpy brown material into a coat of dream-soft chainmail.

Little John took Marian's arm, and escorted her up the aisle, the crowd sighing as she passed.

Marian's hair was fastened high within a circlet of tiny red flowers, her raven locks curling down at the back of her neck in tight bounces of mischief. Her midnight eyes would have wracked an astronomer's soul.

"Good people!" The hermit called out as Little John presented the bride at the altar. "We gather, under bough and under God, to witness King Robin of Sherwood, and Lady Marian of Arlingford, in hand-fast."

The congregation erupted with enthusiastic cheers.

"May God have mercy on their souls. Er, sorry. Heh! Wrong ceremony. *Leave me alone, Tuck.* Erhm. Right. Robin Hood, offer your ring to Lady Marian. Lady Marian, bestow your ring upon Robin Hood."

The lovers exchanged their oaken rings, shining with joy.

"Now, Robin take Marian's right hand with your left, *your other left you idiot*, and the mule-headed monk will do the next bit."

"You've got egg in your beard." Tuck whispered as he came forward.

Tuck settled his mind, then wove a length of cord around the lover's wrists. Over and around, through, under and back, Tuck bound the lovers together with leather and prayer.

He finished with a special knot that left the ends of the cord invisible, as if 'twere never-ending.

"Robert Loxley, do you stand by the one you are hand-fast to, in marriage, for a year and a day?"

"I do."

"Lady Marian, do you stand by the one you are hand-fast to, in marriage, for a year and a day?"

"I do."

"I now declare you hand-fast married. May Our Lady's Love fill your hearts!" Tuck's radiant blessing stirred every soul, the choir soaring to elated climax above the congregation's jubilations.

At that moment, Sir Ralph Montfaucon and Captain Roland were riding out from Castle Loxley with a troop of two score, handpicked men-at-arms.

These were the toughest veterans on the fastest horses.

Gisburne had left no doubt in anyone's mind of their objective: Marian was to be brought back, come hell or high water.

Montfaucon boiled with a hatred he could scarcely contain. He'd been battered to deformity, but worse, his service to Gisburne had been despoiled. Years of work, following often questionable orders, ruined in a week by the outlaw Robin Hood.

The soldiers penetrated directly into the deepwood, knowing from previous hunts that the outer weald was a waste of time. They slowed their horses in surprise when they heard cheering coming from a long way ahead. The troop readied weapons and kicked their steeds into a trot.

The wedding feast wassailed so loud, the outlaws might have flown a flag above the encampment.

Montfaucon and Captain Roland slithered the last few yards on their bellies, and peered downward. Below, the hermit's canyon was riotous with festivalling outlaws.

Captain Roland jealousy observed this company celebrating their leader in sincere comradeship.

Montfaucon narrowed his eyes, scanning for targets. Friar Tuck was the first he saw, sharing a large wine sack with a bearded ragamuffin. The monk's happiness turned Montfaucon's stomach.

Then, Marian and Hood appeared gaily in the midst of the merry throng.

"It's very simple. We get in, grab Marian, and go home." Montfaucon eyed his men-at-arms. "We're going to finish these thrice-damned bandits when the mercenaries arrive. Today, we're just stab and grab merchants. A score of you will ride in at the top of the canyon led by Captain Roland, the other at the bottom with me. *Trample and hack, scythe and wrench! Steal me back that outlaw wench.*"

A late-arriving guest ran into the soldiers deploying at the top of the canyon, and gave one warning yell before being killed.

Little John reacted fast, but was still shouting commands when the mighty charge of Roland's men-at-arms swept in.

Merry men were thrown to the sides or crushed under the monstrous hooves of the iron-shod war-horses. Swords flashed high and flickered low, carving and slicing and barbarously biting into the outlaws.

Most of the outlaw archers were still stringing their bows, the ready few unable to fix targets in the tightly swirling fight.

Roland's troop worked forwards, spreading bloody confusion and blinding chaos, aiming directly for Marian.

At the other end of the canyon, there had been no warning, and Montfaucon impacted with hell's full fury riding on his back. A score of Jack and Janes were downed before Tuck even stood up, skulls smashed, limbs cut in two.

The knight's brutal troop smacked into groups of feasting outlaws like the devil's own war-galley ploughing the high seas.

"Sweet Mother, *NO.*" The hermit's contented expression fell into horror.

The crush and suck of combat swept Tuck and hermit through the canyon like fleas in a tempest.

Montfaucon's black stallion let rip with every hoof, all its evil nature beaming out of its battle-mad eyes. Bodies crunched as the knight spurred for maximum carnage.

Robin held onto Marian as the mass of merry men squashed into the middle of the canyon. The outlaws were compressed on both sides by the wicked attack, unable to form a coherent defence.

The soldiers were stopped in their advance only by the sheer mass of people now trapped in a small section of the canyon. Jacks and Janes were ruthlessly whittled away from the edges of the mob as the invaders pressed ever tighter.

A few men-at-arms were wrenched from their saddles or fell to bow shots, but the outlaws had been taken by surprise, and were still reeling from the shock.

Then, Little John rose above the whirling, churning melee.

"Merry men, *TO ME.* For good King Robin and your very lives!" The giant's roar cracked stones.

The staffmen got organized, sweeping men-at-arms off their horses.

Alan-a-Dale and Will Scarlett were revealed standing by Little John, protecting his back, battling Captain Roland and a pack of soldiers, who were aiming to pass the giant at all costs.

"*Damned monk!*"

Tuck turned in terror as Montfaucon's misshapen features loomed above his stallion's gnashing jaws.

The knight's sword swept downwards, singing as it sliced the air.

Tuck was jammed in the crowd, barely able to breathe, let alone dodge, and had no weapon.

His rational mind warped as it glimpsed eternity.

Peace existed in the line of light skittering along the edge of the descending blade.

The supermarine fathoms of the Truth welcomed Tuck with celestial trumpets.

Then the hermit whacked into him with a tremendous shoulder charge.

Tuck was propelled to the ground, disappearing into the mass of falling bodies, flying blood, rising dust and flailing hooves.

Montfaucon's sword caught the hermit square across the nape of the neck, removing his bearded head in one blow.

With the invaders stalled, outlaw bowmen loosed more accurate arrows, picking off men-at-arms in twos and threes.

Captain Roland, seeing his advantage played out, broke his men away as fast as they had charged in.

Montfaucon was lost in personal hatred. He wasn't sure if he'd hit the monk, and drove into the mob to confirm his kill.

Little John surfaced before him.

Montfaucon's stallion snapped out a deranged, wide-jawed bite. The giant broke the beast's neck with a furious grab and twist.

Even as the horse fell, Montfaucon swung his sword round fast as a thunderbolt, but Little John stepped inside the attack, and hammered his huge fist down onto the knight's helmet.

The blow blasted Montfaucon's brains out of his nose in a fountain of liquefied grey gobbets.

Friar Tuck ~ Chapter 37

The three things all should strive for:
Oneness with Divinity; peace amongst
neighbours; justice in judgment.
Triads of Bardism

Guy of Gisburne stood high on Loxley's western tower, watching distant hills disappear one by one into the dusk of his aborted wedding day.

Drab, stringy clouds splintered across the sky like dust-smothered spider-webs above the hazy acres of Sherwood at the eastern horizon.

Anxiety plagued Guy's bones as much as vengeance tore at his mind. His shires were teeming breeding grounds for criminals, his castle breached, and the most precious gift of his hand in marriage, mocked.

In the cold light of an English summer sunset, Gisburne admitted to himself it hadn't been a good week. Even his sparkling feelings for Lady Marian had sputtered into sullen embers of frustrated lust.

From out of the shadows at the forest's edge came a speeding troop of horsemen. Across the miles, Gisburne identified Captain Roland, and counted more than a score of men-at-arms, but could see no trace of Marian.

Or of Ralph Montfaucon.

"We almost got the girl, my Lords, but ran into two hundred outlaws gathered for wassail, and it was simply too many."

"By the hordes of hell! Two hundred? *Wassailing?*"

"You better not be bloody exaggerating, Roland!" Rage and fear sucked the blood from Gisburne's veins.

Captain Roland turned a militarily filthy look on the Earl, then pointedly addressed only the Sheriff.

"We knew Hood had the shires behind him, but this is no rag-tag peasant band. The outlaw has trained up a cohesive force. They reminded me of my old unit in Flanders. And that's not good news."

"*By the deceptions of hell,* whilst he's let us think robbery is the height of his ambition, the bosky bastard's been building a bloody brigade!"

"Hood *can't* have hidden away two hundred fighting men, even in Sherwood. Roland! *Damn your lies.* You better come clean, and tell us what really happened."

Captain Roland put his hand to his sword. "My Lord High Sheriff, either you control the Earl, or I kill him where he sits."

"Roland, stay calm, please. Gisburne, *shut the hell up*. Roland was leading men in battle when you were dandling on your nursemaid's knobbly knee. If he says there were two hundred, then there were two hundred. If he says we have a problem, then we have a *bloody problem*."

Gisburne clutched at the table until his knuckles were as white as his face, but held his tongue.

"In case you even care, Loxley," Roland's tone was withering, "the knight Montfaucon was killed by a giant. He died well."

Nottingham's Captain marched from the room, his back rigid.

To Gisburne's horror, he found that he did care.

"How will I ever avenge this?" The Lord of Outlaws gestured hopelessly towards the mess of crying, bleeding and dead merry men.

"Robin, please. Let's get the crew settled, then think about what to do." Will Scarlett led his King away from the charnel canyon.

Alan-a-Dale sent the most heartfelt call yet out to the shires. He needed anyone who could nurse, but even more, help to move corpses and dig graves.

Little John hurried every fighter standing into the woods to form a defensive shield. No one knew how much time they had before another attack.

Lady Marian organized first-care, her company of Janes hunting through the carnage to pull the quick from the dead. Under a heap of bodies they unearthed an unconscious, but unharmed, Friar Tuck. Next to him lay the hermit's decapitated body.

Reynold Fitz-Ooth's head had rolled to a stop against the knot stone, right way up. His bearded face smiled as if he'd died hearing the funniest joke in Ireland.

Robin Hood took charge of the injured Jacks, but in truth they weren't capable of much, and there wasn't much to be done. Body and soul, the merry men had been devastated.

Tuck took a team of grave diggers into the forest, searching his deepest heart for the Divine Pattern even as he sought a burial ground.

The outlaws had reached a terrible crossroads. There was only one right path from this place, and three to damnation. How best to help his King choose, occupied Tuck's entire mind. Grief could come later.

That night, half the shires came to mark their respect for the dead. The shirefolk carried candle-lit lanterns, filling the forest with dim orange droplets.

Robin Hood and Lady Marian led the cortege up a long chase to the burying grove. Little John, Alan-a-Dale and Will Scarlett came close behind, faces drawn with misery and exhaustion.

The surviving band of six score merry men followed, each wearing their robbing-cloths of Lincoln green. The mourn-lights of the accompanying shirefolk winked in and out between the trees.

Tuck waited alone in a broad clearing comferenced by holly. Around him lay the freshly dug checkerboard of outlaw graves.

The grove of the dead was silent, but the cruel crunch and sad slap of grave-work still filled his ears.

Tuck reached far into his faith for Holy guidance. His flock faced a worse peril than attack by swords and soldiers. The very spirit of the outlaw band was under threat.

The funeral procession wafted out of the chase to form a ring of mourners, encompassed in turn by a field of flickering lanterns.

"Good children, we gather here, under bough and under God, *to give thanks!*" Tuck lifted his arms to embrace his people, his words deliberately shocking. "Our brothers and sisters gave their lives today, that we may live. We have been blessed by their generosity of soul, as surely as Sherwood will be blessed by their bodies." In the darkened wood, Tuck was aware of his flock as a symphony of overwrought emotion. "Oh my dear ones, know that the Blessed Mother feels our grief. Our Saviour wept for our every pain. Be steady. Our Divine Lord will bring the balance a'right. Today, of all days, do not crush your hearts in anger, or thrash your spirits with bitterness. Remember that today, we celebrated the wedding of our beloved King,

Robin of Sherwood, and Lady Marian, his forest-wife Queen. Remember the Jacks and Janes who lie here, as those merry ones who wassailed with us. They cheered us with their smiles and japes, joined us in vittal and song, rang the very timberland with their o'er-arching joy! Verily, we are at war, but not against Nottingham, or even Guy of Gisburne. *We fight greater enemies.* Tyranny and poverty are the true scourges ruining England, served by ignorant soldiers and their selfish officers. These, our friends who lie in this grove, watched by the trees, welcomed by The Almighty, died in happiness, for liberty!" Almost overcome with emotion, Tuck reached for the silence of his wisdom mind, and found a fanfare. "Tonight, *in this very darkness,* Sherwood holds all England's promise. The heroes of Albion dead today lay down their lives for friendship. Our Saviour said that there can be no greater gift. *This* is why we give thanks along with our tears. We are blessed a hundred times this night by a sacrifice of unbounded love!" Tuck held the heart of his congregation like a broken winged bird, breathing healing warmth with every word. "Let us *raise our spirits* in recognition. Let us *lift our thoughts* with love. Let us *heal our hearts* with adamant resolve! Every Jack and Jane of our most beloved Isle beg us to continue the battle, not in anger, but in love. O, it is right that the memory of our dead stiffen our sinews. Yea, never forget the grief you feel this night, *but do not be o'er-come by it.* In this way, in pain, are our hearts softened. Know this: A soft heart is a happy heart. Our enemy is the hard-hearted. *We are the merry men!* Our Saviour gave his example: By keeping faith in the midst of suffering, we find the truth of life."

A breeze gently rocked the pointed holly leaves, sighing agreement.

Tuck looked about at the true men and women of Robin Hood's crew, and was humbled.

"*My brethren,* we, in heart gentle, in soul ardent, turn our faces to the Merciful Mother. We ask for peace, for the dead, and for the living. We beg the mercy of Blessed Heaven on the blessed dead. And we ask that the bounty of heaven bless this troubled land, that all may prosper, in weal and in faith. In this spirit, we, merry men, will do what must done. *And we will be blessed!* In the name of God, Robin and Sherwood Forest. Amen."

The Lord of Outlaws led his people away, their grief assuaged by the Friar's inspired exhortation.

Alan-a-Dale picked out a dirge, binding every soul in mournful fellowship:

**Would you join a slow marching band?
And take pleasure in your leaving?
As the ferry sails, and tears are dried,
And cows come home at evening.**

**Walk on slowly, don't look behind you.
Don't say goodbye, love. I won't remind you.**

**Could you get behind a slow marching band?
And joy together in the passing,
Of all we shared through yesterdays,
In sorrows neverlasting.**

**Walk on slowly, don't look behind you.
Don't say goodbye, love. I won't remind you.**

**Dream of me as the nights draw cold,
Still marking time through winter.
You paid the piper, and called the tune,
And you marched the band away...**

**Walk on slowly don't look behind you.
Don't say goodbye, love. I won't remind you.**

The waxing moon appeared late in the night, spilling silver light over Tuck as he walked the weald.

Despite his guidance, come the blue light of dawn, the outlaw band would find their grief turned to rage. Tuck knew this because of the temptation to fury churning in his own soul.

Striding along, Tuck thought of his teacher and friend, the hermit Fitz-Ooth.

Tuck stopped in complete astonishment to let out an admiring chuckle. He was unable to attach sad thoughts to the hermit.

The bearded baboon remained as stubbornly contrary in death as in life.

Happy tears leaked from Tuck's eyes as he set off once again, at peace within the clashing elements of his heart. His faith gave him the sure knowledge that this night's anguish would pass.

What he would do in the morning, was another question entirely.

Friar Tuck ~ Chapter 38

The three words of counsel:
Know thy power; know thy wisdom; know thy time.
Triads of Bardism

"London's sempiternal politicking is griping Our guts." King John of England would have shouted, but his horrendous hangover forbade anything louder than a whisper. "Before summer perishes on autumn's sanguineous spear, We need a damn holiday." King John rang for his seneschal.

"How may I serve, Your Highness?"

"What news of Our mercenaries?"

"The High Constable reports the arrival of 200 mercenaries at Dover, last night. They are three days march from Nottingham."

"A fit crew to cheer Our canary cursed bones." King John's eyes regained their cruel spark. "They'll excoriate the outlaws from Sherwood, and We'll celebrate with a Royal hunt! Nottingham's wassail'll do Us more good than London's paunchy priests and pagenting physicians. Make the arrangements."

"At once, Your Highness."

"What news from France?"

"Your Highness, King Philippe is reported to be gathering knights and negotiating mercenaries."

"That wittol wight. We'll wrack his wine-sopped knights with Welsh bowmen, and meet his mercenaries with Our malt-worm Myrmidons."

"Of course, Your Highness."

"Hell's singing maw!" King John clenched his fists. "A war in spring will also occupy those ungrateful idlers who are sprouting like misgraffed mushrooms across this mischievous land."

"Clearly, Your Highness."

"Send in Treasurer Thompson, and Master Focsal."

"Thank you, Your Highness."

Treasurer Thompson's tick beat rapidly as he bowed low. "Your Most Royal Highness, the Exchequer proposes financing the war by recalibrating the fiscal calendar."

"Wonderful. Explain."

"Your Highness, Exchequer experts suggest scutage be halved, but paid three years in advance. The kingdom enjoys an immediate gain in knights and gold; Barons benefit from a relative, long-term, opportunity saving."

"Thompson, the sinews of Mars are tight in your hands. Make it so."

"Thank you, Your Highness."

"Focsal, what news from Portsmouth?"

"My Liege, three war-galleys are complete, and the fourth ahead of schedule."

"England expected nothing less. Roll out your innovations to Our other ports, Admiral! We'll grow ships like a hedgehog does spikes."

Tuck walked, deep in thought.

Robin Hood had once boasted he'd go a long way with 100 men. He'd proved true to his word.

With Marian at his side, Hood's leadership had become incandescent. He'd recruited more fighting men, and established a new, military minded, encampment deep in Sherwood.

A steep hillock thick with yew had been transformed into an invisible stockade, made deadly with concentric layers of obfuscation and ambush.

Hood had taken Loxley's Crusading experience, and honed it with ferocious field-craft. The merry men, stronger than ever, were ready to repel all invaders.

Tuck had always been wedded to Robert Loxley's noble cause, the redemption of his people. Robin Hood was trapped in a struggle for power.

Tuck feared the disguise was becoming the man.

It was Hood, not Loxley who had established the new camp. The Lord of Outlaws had built a base from which he could strike, and strike again, at the enemies arrayed against him.

It was no different in spirit to the hard-faced, cold-hearted, walls of Castle Nottingham.

Robert Loxley had married Marian of Arlingford in a rapture of romance. Hood initiated his men in the ruthless ways of piege, enfilade and trap.

Tuck's rational mind understood the need for strong defence. His wisdom mind recognized Robin was becoming like those he fought against.

Greed and selfishness, as embodied by Gisburne, Nottingham and King John, would always have greater worldly power. For Robin Hood to fight them on their own terms, dominion by violence, led only to ruin. Robert Loxley had to rely on the legitimacy granted by charity and chivalry to stand a chance of achieving his goal.

The merry men were a fearsome fighting company, and Robin capable of raising several brigades more, but ever increasing conflict would serve no-one.

Only peace was victory.

Tuck rove long through the forest, setting aside his burdens to observe autumn's welcome brushing leaf-tips red and gold, then turned for home, accompanied by a breeze as fruity and fresh as the hermit's finest white wine.

Sherwood was a mote of God's ever evolving equilibrium, actualized.

Little John had taken their losses personally. He drilled the men to put up a fight that would shake all Europe.

Alan-a-Dale took Will Scarlett for a high speed tour of the shires. The minstrels' songs sang of danger and defiance chorused with imprisonment, murder and revolt. They found welcome wherever they went, and the merry men were alive in the hearts and pubs of England as August neared September 1202.

Lady Marian watched over the encampment like a tribal mother, anticipating every need. The winter stores had been filled, and a score of nursing Janes trained for first-aid.

The camp was waking up to a damp September morning when a look-out rushed in.

"There's a lone nobleman riding on the main road to Nottingham!"

Distributive justice had almost been abandoned as travellers avoided Sherwood, preferring longer roads to certain robbery.

"Well, now." Hood stood up, his wickedest grin flashing about. "Little John, Friar Tuck, how's about we invite the lucky blighter to breakfast?"

Marian let out a peal of laughter at her husband's good humour. She too had noticed a difference in Robin's demeanour. The hardening of his soul was subtle, but enough that she rejoiced at the return of his old playfulness.

Little John grabbed his ironwood staff, Tuck his new shillelagh, Robin his longbow, and with Marian waving from the palisade, the trio scampered off to greet their guest.

The rider was indeed alone, and dressed in clothes that reeked of old money. Robin gave Tuck a satisfied nudge in anticipation of an easy mark. Then he noticed the noble's piebald horse.

The poor nag was older than the hills, and moved with as much enthusiasm. Looking closer, the animal's shoes were as worn as a beggar's, and its barrel pitifully shallow.

"What ho, wayfarer!" Robin Hood started with his corkiest tone, but catching sight of the rider's face made his voice fade rather abruptly.

Sir Richard of Lees looked so sad, even his long moustaches couldn't hide the double downward curve of his lips.

"By Our Lady," Robin muttered, "this chap looks like he's already been robbed. *Of everything.*"

Sir Richard showed no surprise at the breakfast of bread, boar and beer laid out on a colourful cloth in the middle of his path.

"Crikey," Little John whispered, "that's the first time I've ever seen one of our guests look hungry rather than frightened."

"My fine rider," Robin stepped up, bravely keeping the game going, "looks like you need a good breakfast. You've come to the right place."

Sir Richard glanced disinterestedly across at Little John, who was trying to look intimidating despite his sympathy.

"Oh. Are you going to kill me?" Lees pulled his horse to a stop, resignation etching deeper into his features.

"*By Our Lady!* I've never met such a melancholy aristocrat. No, my thick-eye'd traveller, we're going to get you pissed instead. Goodman Little, help our new friend from his, er, steed, and Friar, broach that beer as quick as your monkish skills permit!"

Lees slid dispiritedly off his horse, and Little John led the beast away.

"Right. *Thank you, Friar.*" Robin applied all his mettle to merriment, thrusting a foaming mug of ale into Lees' unresisting grip. "Drink that quick, and we'd better join you before we all start weeping."

Sir Richard drained the mug in one long pull, sat at the picnic, and set to without further urging.

Robin gave Tuck a look that needed no explanation.

"That's right, dear fellow." Tuck refilled their guest's mug. "You just do the necessary here, and we'll talk after."

While Sir Richard made his way through a worthy quantity of food, Robin concentrated on drinking beer, lest his good spirits drown in their guest's morbidity.

"Thank you for the breakfast, but you may as well kill me now. I have no money to pay you." Lees popped the last morsel of roast boar into his mouth and sat back with a doomed sigh.

"What plagues you, Sir Richard? I must admit I'm tempted to do as you ask, it seems it would be a kindness."

"You're right, Hood." The knight sighed again, a sound to blot out the Sun. "Today, I would greet only my death with joy. I've heard of you, you know. Nobles speak of you with hate and foreboding. But the people love you." Richard turned to Tuck. "And I suppose you are the fighting Friar? I didn't believe the songs, but now, I can see you'd have your hands full with this one!" A flicker of amused understanding darted across Richard's eyes.

For once Robin didn't object. Anything he could do to relieve their guest's gloom was a duty.

"Why would you say such a terrible thing, Sir Richard?" Tuck refilled everyone's mugs in anticipation of his story.

"Today I lose my lands, give up my castle, and kill my son."

The outlaws stared at the knight, not daring to speak.

"Two months ago my son, a hot headed scallion, but a good lad, got into a duel. Stupid really, but he did it for honour." Richard let out a sob. "I taught him honour, and the boy learned it well. More fool me. He was in London for the first time, and by chance came across a lozel knight harassing some fetching maid. My son saw the knave off with a fast bit of swordplay, kissed the wench, and thought no more of it. Until he got to the King's court. Being naive, he reported the story to the King's Constable. To my son's great surprise, the Constable arrested him for murder. The knight he'd fought had died from blood loss, and turned out to be the scion of a family well in favour with cursed King John." Sir Richard offered his mug over to be refilled as he quelled his emotion. "My son protested his innocence, but of course was held responsible. In our modern times, honour and virtue are worth less than fawning favouritisms. They sentenced him to hang. I arrived just in time to intervene. I petitioned the King and courts for clemency on the grounds that the knight had not been killed deliberately ... I spent all the cash I had paying solicitors and other briberies, but managed only to commute the death sentence into a fine. My son was imprisoned, and my lands held in escrow until the payment date. Today."

"Bastards." Muttered Robin.

"Lees isn't as rich as it was, but I thought I'd be able to raise it with the help of friends." Sir Richard gazed into the sky, his moustaches limp with tears. "I have spent the summer discovering I have less friends than I thought. I've not raised half of what is needed, and if I don't pay the Sheriff of Nottingham everything today, my boy hangs, and my lands are forfeit."

"*Thieving* bastards." Hood slammed down his ale. "By Our Lady, how much do you need, dear fellow?"

"Two hundred pounds." Sir Richard's leaden tones showed he'd repeated the figure vainly a thousand times.

"*But that's outrageous.*" Spluttered Tuck.

"Yes. I only agreed to it in despair for my son's life. I was tricked. Being my neighbour, Nottingham stood as guarantor for the fine. At first I was grateful, believing he was helping me, but the knave knew all along I wouldn't be able to find the money. Nottingham's had his eye on Castle Lees for some time, and saw his chance to gut me in my garboil. As guarantor of the unpaid fine, he gets Lees, and all its lands and leases."

"*Does he now?* We'll see about that! You wait here, Sir Richard. Friar, look after our guest." Robin Hood hared away.

The King of Outlaws returned with Little John, the piebald horse, and a pony struggling under the weight of three bulky packs.

"Sir Richard of Lees, God and Sherwood have heard your tale, and told me to tell you they're not best pleased. *No indeed.*" Hood placed his hands on his hips, his eyes black as pits. "By the hand of Providence, my crew came across exactly two hundred pounds a few months ago, and strangely enough, it had your name on it. You really must be more careful with your cash. It's only right it should be returned to you."

"But that's impossible, I've not lost-."

"Extraordinary, I grant you." Interrupted Robin, shrugging. "Perhaps even expeditious! But that's the Lord of Hosts for you. What can I say?"

Friar Tuck helped the dumbfounded knight to his feet with a peal of laughter.

"Sir Richard," Robin applied his boldest parade voice, "regain your trusted steed, take your good fortune, and shove it up the Sheriff's snuffling nose, as far as it will go!"

"God bless Robin Hood!" Sir Richard saluted as he trotted for Nottingham.

"Well, I tell you one thing, when nobles suffer as much as peasants, something is very wrong." Tuck stated as they ambled back to the encampment.

"Ah, Friar, I can't worry about that right now. You know, we are the merry men because of you."

"What? I didn't do anything!" Tuck gave Little John a confused glance, but the giant just nodded his agreement. "How much beer did you have?"

"*Plenty.*" Replied Robin with great satisfaction. "But, you see, it's not so much what you do, it's *who you are.*"

"Eh? You're starting to make as much sense as the hermit. It's *you*, our forest King, who inspires us all."

"Yes, but *you*, and that lovely bearded baboon, managed to drill into my thick skull that I'm supposed to do what's right. I'm starting to realize *why*." Robin stopped them with an impatient wave of his arms. "Don't you see, Friar? If I'm honest, if it wasn't for you, I don't think I'd have helped Sir Richard. I was keeping those two hundred pounds for emergencies ... And in the end, what would it have got me? More weapons?" The Lord of Outlaws looked grave, then smiled radiantly. "Instead, I've bought happiness."

Friar Tuck ~ Chapter 39

The three things a learner must do:
Listen; contemplate; be silent.
Triads of Bardism

Alan-a-Dale and Will Scarlett returned to Sherwood on the first truly cold day of the year.

Their latest tour had been a resounding success, but for all the worst reasons. The shirefolk had welcomed their stories and songs with hearts burdened by trouble and taxation.

The merry minstrels brought bright hope for an evening, but Jacks and Janes everywhere feared the coming winter.

Not only had King John's reign spread destitution, everyone knew spring heralded war with France.

"Robin, on our way back past Nottingham, we saw the mercenaries camped outside new-town." Alan-a-Dale gazed into the late-night campfire.

"How many were there?"

"A good two hundred." Scarlett continued. "The camp was as professional as I've ever seen, and very well guarded."

"We tried to sneak a closer look, but were almost caught, and only luck got us away." Dale tossed a log on the fire.

"They'll fall to our arrows like all other men." Snarled Little John.

"Yes. And we're better prepared than we've ever been." Hood's eyes glittered above the mellow flames.

"When d'you think they'll come?" Asked Tuck.

"Ah. That's the other bit of news. Tell 'em, Will."

"There's a very strong rumour King John is coming from London to visit Nottingham for a holiday hunt."

"*When?*"

"Soon. The Sheriff's stocking up on vittals. He'll want to be rid of us before John arrives, so the Royal hunt can go peacefully."

"With the King visiting, nobles from miles around will converge on Nottingham, along with their escorts." Tuck measured Robin's pacing. "Add that lot to the mercenaries, *plus* the men Nottingham and Gisburne already have-."

"*Bah*, with Sherwood on our side, I'd have a go at Saladin himself!" For once, Hood's confidence didn't scatter the foreboding slinking in the shadows beyond the fire.

"Robin ... I don't know if you understand what you've become outside the forest." Alan-a-Dale raised his hands in appeal as Hood turned to glare at him.

"On our travels, we met a troubadour from Dublin who knew the songs before we'd sung 'em." Scarlett broke in. "He'd even made improvements!"

"Our code of chivalry and charity inspires the people to remember better days." Dale glanced up from the fire to look his King in the eye. "Robin, defending that code makes you the enemy of every crooked noble in Britain."

Hood stopped his pacing. "I've just finished training up enough men to challenge Gisburne, and now you tell me I have to fight the whole country?"

"Ah, er, I didn't mean it like that, exactly-."

"Well, that's exactly what it sounded like. What say you, Friar?"

"The bigger picture is vital. But, we should deal with what's at hand."

"And we won't solve *that* little problem tonight." Little John rallied their spirits with a tough grin. "Let's see what tomorrow brings. It's Wine Harvest after all, and if we're going to be overrun by the devil's own brigade within the week, I, for one, want to celebrate properly!"

The outlaws pretended to be cheered, but they knew the greatest challenge they'd ever faced was bearing down on them like a cracked mountain top.

"When do we go after Hood?" Guy of Gisburne leaned intently across Nottingham's dinner table.

"By hell's vengeance, as soon as possible. Roland? What's your assessment of the mercenaries?"

"They're a robust company, Sheriff. I know some of their Lieutenants. Excellent tactical experience." Captain Roland gave a rare smile. "How's the alchemist doing with our secret weapon?"

"By the bubbling vats of hell, *the mummers have actually done what they said.* The pyrophoria is ready and waiting."

"How many soldiers can we count on to bolster the mercenaries?"

"We've three hundred trained men in barracks." The Sheriff raised his mug in toast. "Enough to eradicate all trace of the sinner Hood and his crew."

"If we can bloody find them." Spat Gisburne.

"I've been thinking about that." Captain Roland cleared a space on the table, gathering cutlery and condiments to illustrate his points. "Going into the forest blind just doesn't work. But, with 500 men, we can change the game."

"Go on, Roland." The Sheriff concentrated his excitement.

"Tomorrow, I'm sending small mercenary scouting units into all parts of Sherwood. Wherever they meet resistance, my men will mark the spot, and retreat." Roland moved table items in a random manner.

"What's the use of that? Your job is to kill them, not play hide and seek." Gisburne demanded, his own failures sharp in his mind.

"The objective, Earl, is to make the outlaws give themselves away." Roland's tone stayed neutral, his mind on strategy. "You see, by necessity, they will fight only for parts of the forest that are important to them. Their new encampment is their most valued area, so it'll be found in the centre of the woodland they defend the heaviest." Roland's eyes sharpened with cunning. "The outlaws will think they're winning every skirmish. But in fact, they'll be betraying themselves." Captain Roland played his cutlery into a loose circle. "By tomorrow night, we'll have defined a broad area to focus on. The day after, we throw a noose of steel around it, and tighten the field of containment." Roland manoeuvred his pieces towards each other. "When we encounter strong resistance, we'll deploy the pyrophoria against their final defences."

"By the devil's wickedest plans, how sure are you this'll work?"

"Nothing's certain in war, my Lord. But this much you can count on: We will find the enemy; and once they're brought to ground, only a miracle will save them from total destruction."

Wine Harvest 1202 dawned with full autumnal ardency over Sherwood, rocking the weald with stiff winds. It seemed overnight the trees had shed half their leaves, covering the ground in a soft yellow shale.

Their harvest tasks complete, most of the merry men gathered in from the shires, anticipating a rollicking end of season party.

Alan-a-Dale and Will Scarlett took charge of the festivities, roasting a row of deer and rolling out broad butts of beer.

Little John boistered through the encampment, blowing away any lingering worries with huge bursts of laughter.

Tuck and Marian tended to the needs of their flock, dispensing money, medicine, food and wisdom in equal measure. Tuck reflected that this was the true duty of those nobly born, the honest price of privilege.

Robin Hood joined the festivities for the morning, but after lunch announced he was going to inspect the fortifications, and headed off alone.

The Lord of Outlaws had spent a sleepless night studying the stars, his oath to the Hilltop Strangers loud in his thoughts. He'd been tempted to forget he owed them a debt for Marian's safety, but every time he glanced at her sleeping form, a diabolical finger tickled across his heart.

Among all the terrifying legends told of men and elves, the worst concerned those who failed to keep their deals. Alban Elfed was the old name for Wine Harvest, and the stars showed Robin his love-debt was due.

Hood spent a while inspecting the camp's defences as he'd said, sharing a cheery word with lookouts as he passed, but then cut away secretly for the Gable of Si'ir.

The forest was quiet as the King of Sherwood made his way to the Strangers' hill, the rustle of fresh leaf-fall sounding loudly under his feet. Sunset came early, the woodland darkening quickly, another sign the seasons had revolved once more.

Robin continued on his way, worrying over the coming battle, and didn't think about what the Strangers could want from him, until he glimpsed the quicksilver moon sailing full above the trees.

Si'ir came into view and a slow, superstitious shudder passed down Hood's spine.

"King of Sherwood." The whisper reached between the trunks of beech and elm to frost the outlaw's ears. "Mount to the crest, and be seated at the foot of the eldritch oak."

Robin Hood gritted his teeth against the urge to run away, and forced his legs to carry him up the smooth sides of the hillock. The earth felt curiously warm through his boots.

From the crest, the shining path of the Milky Way was almost too dazzling to look at. The moon ellipsed at unnatural speed across the blue-black sky.

A tremendous oak towered to the left, its trunk and branches blazoned silver by the moonlight. Robin glanced around, but saw neither Little People nor Hilltop Strangers. A crawling shiver passed over his flesh.

The Lord of Outlaws sent a prayer to the Holy Mother into the whirling skies, then sat against the ancient tree.

It's rough bark radiated a fierce heat into Robin's back, like he was sitting too close to a campfire.

"The process will cause pain." A Stranger appeared out of the night, mist pouring from his mouth with every word. "Do not struggle. We gave in good faith, and so must you."

"What would you have me do?" Robin's voice quaked.

The front of his body prickled with the arctic cold radiating from the elf, and his back burned from the desert heat of the tree behind.

The o'er-arching Milky Way rotated, aligning to a different dimension. The outlaw's old friend, the moon, disappeared.

Robin's control snapped, and he made to leap away, but his feet didn't respond. Aghast, he looked down to find the oak had grown gnarly bindings over his legs.

Then, rope-like roots emerged hot from the earth to encase his arms. Hood gibbered in horror as the tips of the roots penetrated the flesh of his wrists, and began pulsating.

Robin opened his mouth to emit a soul-splintering shriek, but choked as two more tendrils whipped out and darted down his throat.

His last conscious sensation was of these probosci turning his guts to ice.

Friar Tuck ~ Chapter 40

The three remedies of all disease:
Nature; time; patience.
Triads of Bardism

"What on earth are they are up to, Will?" Tuck was some distance from the encampment, perched 30 feet up a yew.

Below, the fifth mercenary platoon of the day scurried away from only two outlaws.

"I don't know, Friar. Maybe they're scared of being ambushed?"

"But these are toughened veterans. I find it hard to believe we've put this kind of fear into them ... Militiamen maybe, but professional soldiers? Do you really think so?" Tuck rubbed his chin in unconscious imitation of the hermit.

"It seems that way. But I'm also wondering why they've split up, rather than coming in force."

"We need someone with military experience to tell us what's going on. Let's find Robin, and quick."

Tuck and Scarlett waited for the mercenaries to disappear from view, made sure the look-outs were back in position, then scoured the woodland for their King.

They returned to the festive encampment late in the afternoon, even more puzzled.

They'd not found a trace of the Lord of Outlaws, but several other look-out posts had reported groups of mercenaries coming close, then retreating at the first arrow.

"John, there's curious business going on in the weald, and we can't find Robin."

"Fiddlesticks!" Cried Little John over a large mug of beer. "The mercenaries are just less trouble than we thought."

"I don't know," interrupted Scarlett, "their reputations are fearsome-."

"So is ours!" Little chomped a mouthful of roast-deer in appreciation.

"But even Marian doesn't know where Robin is." Tuck insisted. "I've got a funny feeling in my waters."

"Don't worry so much, fat badger. Robin said he was inspecting the defences. He's probably out there arranging some new ambuscade to boggle the blighters."

The outlaw Captains decided not to sound the alarm. The merry men were in the middle of their feasting, and there was nothing alarming actually happening.

Scarlett set more look-outs around the encampment, then joined in the wassail with the others.

Afternoon turned to evening, and still Robin hadn't returned.

"Friar, did you find Robin?" Marian asked quietly as Tuck polished off his supper.

"Erm, no, I'm sorry, dear Marian. We think he's probably got enthusiastic with some new defences, and will back by sundown to join in the fun."

Marian gave him a careful look, but said nothing more.

Tuck snuck away from the party as the sun was setting. He had to find a quiet place to meditate.

Countless reports had come in through the day of mercenaries appearing all over the forest, but none had put up even the hint of a fight.

The uncomfortable feeling in Tuck's belly had grown steadily more insistent all afternoon, but the Holy Spirit revealed nothing more.

The noise and bustle of the wassail faded as he headed for the heartwoods.

Feeling out of sorts and a little lonely, Tuck decided to re-visit one of the hermit's old hides. He spent a long time staring up at the full moon, listening to his internal senses.

Still nothing came to mind to explain his disquiet.

He'd almost decided he must have eaten something disagreeable, when the wooden cross hanging around his neck gave a small jump. Tuck pulled the cross out of his habit, and gave it a stern look.

It sat placidly in his hand for a minute, then jumped again, hard enough to jerk its chain taut.

Perplexed, Tuck gave the thing a good shake, then watched it like a hawk. Nothing more happened until he decided it was high time he was getting home.

Within five paces, the cross had jumped again, but this time pulling to Tuck's right. He stopped in his tracks and turned in that direction. Shivers rippled up his neck.

Tuck prayed for guidance, thinking about the Star Dagger hidden inside his cross. He remembered Robin declaring he'd taken some mysterious action, right before Gisburne had suddenly fallen in love with Marian.

Tuck's thoughts went deathly quiet, his wisdom mind locking onto the only possible, if impossible, conclusion.

"Even Robin can't have been that stupid." Tuck muttered to himself, not wanting to believe his intuition.

Then he remembered Robin's desperation at Marian's kidnap, and his waters reversed. "Oh yes he could!"

Tuck was at full speed in three strides, racing through the woodland, not caring how much noise he made.

Every so often the cross pulled on its chain, leaping forwards to confirm his course. It didn't take long for him to realize he was being guided towards the Gable of Si'ir.

Tuck's heart pumped hard as he reached the base of the hillock. The ground felt inexplicably warm under his feet, and black-light diffused the darkness.

The cross-box strained continually against its chain, tugging Tuck towards the oak silhouetted in white on the crest.

Tuck fought against a terrible petrification to keep moving, his knees trembling violently with every step. Everything in him begged to run away, almost defeating the strength of his resolve.

He called his prayers to mind, and drew on his faith, but his body felt as if it belonged to someone else. His most primitive instincts writhed against his will, like he was plunging his hand into a viper's mouth.

Tuck gripped the cross in his right hand, but fell as his legs failed him. Stifling a cry that would have unleashed his panic, he began crawling up the hillside.

Weeping tears of runaway fear, arms rigid and legs like jelly, Tuck forced his mutinous body the last few yards.

On the crest, Robin Hood slumped against the massive tree. Faerie lights pulsed and vibrated behind the bark, the source of the strange glow he'd noticed below.

Only love gave Tuck the strength to cross the final few feet to his unconscious King.

Unearthly, sinewy branches bound Robin to the oak, but most horrible were the smooth green shoots reaching into his mouth.

Tuck tried to gather some wits and clicked open the cross-box.

The Star Dagger flashed radiant blue as Tuck touched the blade to the shoots going into Robin's mouth, and the probosci shrank back into the trunk of the tree.

It was the work of seconds to free Robin completely, but the Lord of Outlaws simply collapsed as the last rooty bonds withdrew into the earth around his legs. Tuck towed Robin across the hilltop sweating, panting and praying, almost unhinged by the sights he'd seen

The tree, if it was a tree, had been unmistakably feeding off Robin, throbbing in time to the outlaw's heartbeat as it sucked at his vitals.

Tuck more slid than crawled down the smooth side of the hillock, arriving at the base in a tangle.

In one hand he clutched the cross-box, the other hugged Robin's drained body to his breast.

"So, priest, you returned." Three tall figures came out of the shadows, but stayed five yards away. "You interrupt our rite, steal away with our guest, and bring a fell weapon to sacred Si'ir."

"*Your guest.*" Tuck's wrath exploded out of his lungs, o'er-coming all his fear. "You've killed him!"

"The King of Sherwood came freely. He was performing a service until you broke the connection."

"*A service?*"

"The Gable needs energy to sustain Si'ir. In return for the May Queen's safety, your King agreed to provide what we asked."

"*Not to his death.*"

"The Gable takes what it needs. For a million years, we have sought the Creator across the stars, using the Rainbow Bridges. Sacrifices are necessary."

"*Sought the Creator?* But you won't find Him amongst the stars!"

"You know nothing of The Pilgrimage. You came here in secret, to spy and to spoil. We let you leave last time. This time, we will not. Even a Star Dagger cannot protect you from all of us."

Other Lords and Ladies materialized from the gloom, ringed by dour-looking Little People.

The temperature dropped alarmingly, mists forming above the ground as the air froze.

"Wait! We do know something of the Creator. A thousand years ago a Messiah came to us. He said the Creator is to be found within us."

"Within *you*, human?" The entire assembly of elves and sprites broke into hysterical laughter.

"Within all of us." Tuck drew on the last of his strength to raise his voice above the tumult. "Your powers are beyond my reckoning, but even you admit you've found no trace of the Most Holy. The Messiah said only with the internal sense, the spirit, can anyone perceive the Creator."

The elves started listening, but the Little People continued their raucous cackling.

Tuck had exhausted every scrap of endurance, and could only finish in a whisper. "The Most Holy is beyond the countless stars, beyond anything we can penetrate with cleverness. Your technologies have brought you further than I can imagine, but will never take you to heaven."

The elves were unnaturally still as they regarded the monk.

"He truly believes this." One stated, mystified.

"Could he be right? Our grandmothers harnessed the void to our search, our mothers traversed the infinitude, yet we have found nothing except more stars, more vastness."

"Are you suggesting we abandon The Pilgrimage?"

"No. This we must continue, for all else is conquered. But the priest's words point to a new direction."

Tuck's tears had frozen on his cheeks, but he wrapped his habit around his King and held him tighter yet.

"*Please.* I didn't come to anger you. I came to save my friend. Please, let us go. We are not your enemies. There are others who love us, who need us. If Robin dies, it will be an appalling loss, not only to his brethren, but to Sherwood, and Albion herself! Please, show mercy."

"*We know your kind*. If you had us at your mercy, you would slaughter us. Why should we let you live? You will attack Si'ir when we are not here to protect the Gable."

"Lords, Ladies, Little People, there are humans who act as you say. But they are our *enemies in-common*. We came to Sherwood to find refuge from them. We have lived here, in harmony with the forest, for nigh on three years. Let the trees be my witness! I love them as I love the Creator, for the forest has illuminated the ways of the Creator in my heart. Robin Hood is King of Sherwood, he loves the weald as if it were his child. Some of our race mean harm, but my people have suffered at their hands as much as yours. We fight them every day, with all our spirit." Tuck collapsed onto his side, no longer able to keep himself upright.

Robin hadn't stirred since being freed, and Tuck knew they were dying.

"Priest. We see you believe what you say, but cannot be sure your faith is true. If circumstances were reversed, your beliefs might change. We require a sign that you mean us, and the Gable, no harm."

"What can I do?" Tuck's tongue was thick in his mouth, his lips solid blocks.

"Give us the only weapon you hold against us, give us the Star Dagger."

Friar Tuck made a final, supreme effort, and opened his fingers to let the cross-box drop to the ground, then passed out.

"The priest is sincere."

"Yes. And the Gable has been replenished. Let this Alban Elfed be remembered as a blessing on us all. Let us go. Let them live."

Friar Tuck ~ Chapter 41

The three things always waning:
The dark; the false; the dead.
Triads of Bardism

Tuck awoke to the sound of a campfire crackling, and the smell of pheasant roasting.

His eyes felt like they were pricked with needles as they opened, but his mouth cracked into a grin when he spied Robin tending the merry blaze.

"Well, good morning, brother Tuck. I don't think anyone's going to believe what happened to us last night. I can't tell you how glad I am you're with me." The Lord of Outlaws gave Tuck a wry smile. "Otherwise Marian'll think I've o'er-nighted with some saucy woodland wench!"

"Robin Hood." Tuck croaked as he struggled to get his legs under him. "I'm tempted to tell her that's exactly what happened, after what you put us through."

Robin laughed uproariously.

Tuck moved as close to the fire as he dared, his bones heavy with the remnants of Elfish cold. Gazing fondly, almost disbelievingly, at his King, he realized a profound change had taken place.

Where Robin's eyes had once been the colour of sunshine on spring shoots, they were now the shade of midnight ivy. His face was gaunt, and the outlaw's expression held the experience of pain overcome.

"Stop staring and eat up, Friar. You look hungrier than I've ever seen you. And that's saying something!"

Tuck laughed, and his heart opened like a thousand petalled flower.

Birdsong filled the forest as the companions ate together, and Tuck gave radiant thanks to the Holy Spirit for their deliverance.

Then he remembered why he'd been looking for the outlaw in the first place.

"Robin, yesterday the mercenaries came to Sherwood, but didn't fight. Whenever they encountered our look-outs, they just ran away."

"If they didn't fight, it's because they had another plan." Hood stared into the distance, assessing his enemy's tactics. "They were hunting for the encampment." The Lord of Outlaws focused back on his friend. "One day you'll explain how you rescued me, but right now, we'd better get back. *They're coming for us, Tuck.*"

Robin Hood and Friar Tuck arrived at the camp to general acclaim and loud questions, which they fended off with cheerful grins.

Lady Marian took Robin in her arms, held him close for a long time, then drew him away for an even longer talk.

"You see, sweet Mawd, I was with our dear Friar, and-." Was the last thing Tuck heard as she marched him off.

Tuck gathered the Captains.

"Robin thinks yesterday the mercenaries were scouting us out, and today they'll attack. John, roust the fighting Jacks. Will, brief your look-outs: They're to retreat and man the defences the moment they see soldiers. We want to keep all our force together. Alan, send out the call to the shires. We're going to need every bit of help we can muster to survive this. If we are overrun, we must have safe houses ready to hide our people. If we withstand the assault, then we'll want re-supply, quick as possible. Brothers, readiness is everything."

With the final preparations complete, the merry men gathered at noon, ready for a decisive battle.

The silence of anticipation o'er-hung the encampment.

Robin Hood and Lady Marian appeared at the top of the palisade, firing the courage of their determined crew.

Friar Tuck, Little John, Will Scarlett, and Alan-a-Dale stood amongst the Jacks and Janes, Captains and troops together.

"Merry men!" Robin's voice rang with the purity of his heart. "Our goal is to free the shires from poverty and tyranny. The men who serve those dark masters have chosen to attack us for what we stand for. *There is no better reason to resist.* Even as we uphold chivalry, they devastate community. Where we share in charity, they grasp in endless greed. On this earth, only might of arms protects us! *This* is why we fight." Robin raised the longbow he held in his left hand, and a swell of lusty yells rose from the outlaw assembly. "The mercenaries know nothing but war. They know nothing of our struggle. To them, we are just another enemy to kill. They will be ruthless. *Today, they come with only destruction in their souls.* But our commitment to each other is worth more than their gold-bought loyalty. WE CANNOT LOSE. Not because God's Might will defend us today, but because *today, we defend God's Right!* All humanity strives for the day every Jack benefits honestly from his industry, each Jane can nurture her hearth in peace. *Merry men*, serve your Captains, charity and chivalry! *Our Lady's Blessing on this day!"*

Like all who heard Robin Hood's speech, Friar Tuck was transported on a wave of quickening that swept from the very earth. Like reverse lightning it chased up his legs, firmed his guts, steeled his spine and shone out of his eyes in a torrent of commitment.

Waves of cheering thundered about the merry men. Standing together in faith, not a man-Jack or maid-Jane feared death.

Robin Hood and Lady Marian lifted their arms, unifying every soul. The eternal blue heavens limned Sherwood's royal couple, the very essence of heroic legend to all who beheld them.

Precisely at that moment of wonderment and power, Tuck was assaulted by a sense of profound disaster.

Once more, his wisdom mind gave him a glimpse of the future effects of their immediate actions. As Tuck looked about, his congregation was turned to corpses, wounds bleeding, women screaming.

Little John was felled, hacked down by a hundred swords. Alan-a-Dale was a figure of bloody despair as he stood above Will Scarlett's bolt-ridden body.

Sick to his stomach, Tuck fled for sanctuary to the peace of his spirit, reciting prayers against the horrific visions filling his consciousness. The relentless premonition followed him even to the inner peace of his Divine connection, revealing to him the most hideous scene of all.

Robin Hood hung from a blasted oak, his body mutilated. Marian lay before him, wailing in devastation.

Tuck clutched his head in his hands, staggered, then fell to his knees, yelling: "IT CANNOT BE."

"Badger, what ails ye?" Little John rushed up.

"Friar, what's wrong? By Our Lady, *speak."* Hood leapt down from the palisade, his face ghost-white.

A wave of fear passed through the merry men. Moments before they'd been ready to face the very devil. Now, the air blew with the metallic taste of doom.

"Robin, *we must not fight.*" Tears of anguish poured from Tuck's eyes. "We will all die! *Nothing will be achieved.* We cannot, *we must not,* fight. For the sake of mercy, send our people away!"

"But, dear friend, wise companion," Confusion clouded Robin's deep-sea gaze, "what's happened? What have you seen?"

"If we fight," Tuck clutched Robin's arm in a death grip, "you will sacrifice these good people, and yourself. *Tyranny will win!* And grow even stronger. The misery! *The pain* ... I can't explain. My God, let it not be ... LET IT NOT BE."

"Tuck, steady old fellow. I trust you, you know that. I've trusted you since I first came to Sherwood. Guide me now, Friar. What do we do, if we don't fight?" The Lord of Outlaws felt the ground tremble under his feet as Tuck locked him in a gaze that reached beyond time.

The courtyard of Castle Nottingham heaved with troops readying themselves for battle.

The Sheriff had summoned Guy of Gisburne and Captain Roland to the ramparts of the highest tower.

The clanking and oathing of soldiers arming carried up to them on gusts of wind rank with sweat and sword-grease.

"By all the bitch-birthed war dogs in hell, that's a sight to warm the cockles."

"Aye, my Lord." Replied Roland with a veteran's satisfaction. "Yesterday's sorties into the weald worked exactly as planned. I'll have our forces in place by noon. Then we'll draw the noose until it's time to burn them out."

"Gisburne, you and your men take charge of the pyrophoria." The Sheriff's eyes gleamed as he imagined the forest in flames. "Give that sinner Hood a taste of hell on earth!"

"It will be a pleasure." Gisburne's gaze ranged hungrily across the distance to Sherwood. "I'll burn that bastard and his doxy, all his thieving crew, and that damned woodland, *to the ground.*"

"Just see that you do." The Sheriff clapped his hands with evil excitement. "Gracious King John is arriving tomorrow, and I am planning to present him roast-outlaw for supper."

Guy of Gisburne watched the Magic and Alchemy team smear pyrophoria generously onto scores of crossbow bolts. The rest of the alchemical preparation was poured into wineskins. The wineskins would be thrown at trees, then set ablaze.

As Kings Justice, the Sheriff had imposed the severest penalties on Robin Hood. By official decree, no outlaw was to leave Sherwood alive.

Their task completed, Alfred Hampstead and his troupe trundled away from Nottingham in their brightly coloured cart.

Once safely outside of town, they let free an argument that had been quietly raging all morning.

"*We had no choice.*" Cried one of the assistants. "If we hadn't done what the Sheriff wanted, he'd have tortured and killed us as well."

"Yes, but *what* have we done? Given awesome power to a man who has too much already."

"But they're outlaws and robbers! The Sheriff's the Law. Alfred, it's his bloody *job* to kill them. And since the Sheriff is the Law, he's in the right, which means we are in the right to help him. Everyone knows that."

"Hood and his crew are undoubtedly on the wrong side of the law. But that doesn't make them criminals! From what I hear, ever since King John seized power, the laws of this land have been abused at every level."

"*For pity's sake Alfred,* I don't need to tell you it's always been this way. The rich exploit the poor, the strong dominate the weak. We can't change that! *You're talking madness.* The only reason we're free of Nottingham, is that he has no more use for us. If he did, they'd be after us with bared blades, mark me."

"Alright, so Robin Hood brought this on himself, but what about the forest? Isn't the forest innocent of all this stupidity? When they immolate Sherwood with pyrophoria, it'll be on our heads as much as theirs. I'm not answering to Saint Peter for that."

"What on earth do you want to us to do? Steal the stuff away from 500 soldiers? *It's too late.* Listen, it was a job. We played our parts. Odd venue, tough audience, tragic script, but that's show-business sometimes."

"Ach, you're right there my friend." Hampstead chuckled. "But being right doesn't change what we've done. I can't leave Hood to face the horror of pyrophoria without warning him."

"Alfred, if we go into that forest today, we'll be killed. They'll think we're mercenaries, and shoot a hundred arrows into our backs before we can draw breath to explain."

"Maybe, and maybe not." Hampstead knew what he had to do.

The players' cart paused on the outskirts of the forest as Alfred Hampstead prepared for his last show in England.

Splendid in his full wizard's garb, the alchemist gathered a few items into his pockets, and tearfully hugged his troupe goodbye.

"If we go in together, they'll be sure to mistake us for soldiers. I'm going alone." Hampstead raised his hands to stifle any argument. "I will meet you at Dover. If I don't arrive to catch the tide, I'll meet you in Paris. If I'm not there before war begins, go to Uri in Wiesbaden, he will guide you. Goodbye, sweet friends. May your audiences' silver fill your bellies, as fully as their applause fills your hearts!" Alfred Hampstead set off on foot into Sherwood Forest, his mummers' mournful farewells a susurrus in his ears.

Friar Tuck ~ Chapter 42

The three things for which thanks are due:
An invitation; a gift; a warning.
The Triads of Bardism

"*But we can win.* Our fighters are ready, our defences strong, and our spirit unbreakable. I've witnessed victory come from far less."

"Yes." Visions of chaos echoed around Friar Tuck's mind. "It is possible, but what do we do then? They'll just come back, with even greater force! The shires plead for peace and prosperity, not bedlam and bloodshed."

"We have a duty to fight for what is right, Friar! Those bastards would bawd Albion herself if they could find a suitor." Robin Hood clenched his fists, personal and patriotic rage double-pounding in his heart.

"You're right, Robin. But we've succeeded so far because we fought for the sake of others. If we fight blood for blood, hate to hate, *they will not stop until the dead pile higher than the trees.* Instead of bringing peace to the shires, we're inviting war into Sherwood. God asks us to use our talents and strengths, yea, *but also our weaknesses* in His Service. I tell you this: It is *a blessing* we do not have the means to fight the war they want."

Hood's eyes turned black under his thunderous brows.

Tuck's words raised the outlaw's most vivid memories of slaughter in the sands, King Richard betrayed by his brother, and Old Earl Loxley pacing his castle like a caged lion.

"So, we just give up? Is that what you're advising?" Hood snarled. "We just hand ourselves over like *little lambs*? Turn our cheeks, and let 'em break us one by one? *Is that what you're saying?*"

"No, Robin." Tuck went eye to eye with his King. "The merry men have always fought for charity and chivalry. We will continue to do so. But the battle they've brewed today is for power, not progress. *This is the vital point:* We have always dictated events, because we put the causes in motion. Today, Gisburne has set the agenda. Make no mistake Robin, Gisburne *wants* you to fight. Mark me: If we contribute to his causes, we will be caught in his consequences."

"But we've been hiding for three years, Tuck. *I'm sick of hiding.* If to live this day means fighting to live this day, then so be it."

"Yes, we must fight to live, but not when they choose. We must overwhelm them, but not with force of arms! Robin, *we must overwhelm our enemies with love.*"

"You've gone completely mad."

"No, Robin. Madness is staying here! It's like waiting for an avalanche. To overwhelm our enemy with love right now means: Care for your people more than you hate Gisburne. Robin, do something he would never do, *recognize your vulnerability.*"

"Captains and crew, the merry men have all chosen to be here, Friar. When our children look to be robbed of every decency, we must make a different future. No matter the cost."

"Many have already suffered injury and death in your name. Today, that number stands to triple. And for no gain. Do you really want that, *Robert Loxley?*"

"*Don't call me that.*" Robin Hood thrust his face up against Tuck's. "I am not Robert Loxley. I don't have his lands, his title, *nor his loyalties.* What I have, has been won by Hood's guile and bow. *Mark me*, my enemies'll find the Outlaw King a crueller foe than ever they did the noble Earl Loxley."

"Robert." Tuck's eyes were gentle. "I know you want to fight for your forest kingdom. I understand that, but it just won't work, my dear friend."

"I've always fought for others, Tuck, and look where it's got me. Maybe I'll do better fighting for myself, for what I want. *It bloody works for Gisburne.* It works for the Sheriff. It even works for King bastard John! *Why shouldn't it work for me?*"

"Because you are not like Gisburne, Robert. To Gisburne, people are objects to be used. This gives him a vicious power, but cuts him off from love, leaving him empty. And just look! Look at what Gisburne has achieved in Loxley since he's been there. *For all his vicious power, he gains nothing.* The Sheriff's frustrated ambitions turn the finest wines to vinegar in his mouth. King John is wracked by enemies at home and abroad. *Do you really think it works for them?* All they have gained is the appearance of success. They know neither wealth, nor victory." Tuck's spirit flowed with the words he needed to find. "You have a choice today, King of Sherwood. Either be a slave to Robin Hood's red rage, or raise Loxley's banner of green and gold. Serve yourself, or serve those you lead!"

Robin Hood stared into his counsellor's brown eyes, noticing for the first time tiny flecks of gold texturing their depthless gaze.

"Tuck. Friar. Friend," sorrow shadowed Robin's face, "the merry men can return to the shires ... But what am I to do? Sherwood is my home. You, Marian, Alan, John and Will are my family. I cannot lose you. I cannot ... I cannot *run* again. My *only option* is to fight."

"Robert, refusing battle doesn't mean abandoning the fight! You must simply use other weapons to win." Tuck rested in his wisdom mind, given up to the guidance of the Divine Pattern. "Since the time has come for the merry men to return to their lives, you must do the same."

"WHAT? *By Our Lady Friar Tuck*, just when I think I've understood you, you make less sense than-."

"Hush, Robert. Hear me out. The people love you. Today, in the face of death, they've proven steadfast. You also have sympathizers amongst the nobility. Many despise John, some loved your father, and a few support our struggle. *You are not alone, Robert Loxley.* The time has come to leave the weald, and bring peace to the shires."

"WHAT? By Our Sweet Merciful Lady, I can't even secure peace in ten square feet of Sherwood! *How am I supposed to do it across the shires?*"

"By having faith."

Alfred Hampstead rambled through the deepwoods with no real idea of where he going, nor what he would do when he got there. This was a most unusual state of affairs for a man of science, and Alfred wondered a little at himself.

The alchemist's disquiet with his work for the Sheriff had started with a song.

He'd been enjoying a quiet pint in a village pub, when a pair of musicians barrelled into the end-of-evening fug. In a blink, the place was resounding with laughing Jacks and breaching kegs.

The green-clad minstrels each downed a preparatory jug of ale, then whisked the night away with their music.

Hampstead had innocently joined the stirring choruses until he realized they celebrated the very criminals he was helping to destroy:

Robin Hood, Robin Hood,
riding through the glen,
Robin Hood, Robin Hood,
with his band of men.
Feared by the bad, loved by the good;
Robin Hood, Robin Hood, Robin Hood!

The outlaw melodies had played inside Alfred's head ever since.

One morning, he'd woken in a stark sweat from flickering, tortured dreams of a sylvan church in flames. The final straw was the Sheriff's inspection of the pyrophoria store. Nottingham's glee at the destructive virtues of alchemy had turned Alfred's stomach.

Will Scarlett was patrolling with the look-outs who first spotted the alchemist wandering purposefully, if aimlessly, through the weald.

"*Who the blazes is that?*" Scarlett muttered in astonishment.

Alfred had chosen simple robes of aqua-blue, but made of silk so densely woven it seemed to generate its own light. Above the robe's tight collar, the alchemist's unlikely moustaches quivered stiff as antennae.

A conical hat hung with carved knucklebones topped off the costume.

"It's a bleedin' wizard." Whispered the first look-out, fascinated.

"It's bleedin' Merlin!" Exclaimed the other.

"It *can't be* bleedin' Merlin. Everyone knows 'es bin frozen for eternity by that corky witch o' his."

"Merlin or not, what's *any wizard* doing here, and now?" Superstition swept elastically around Scarlett's legs.

"Shall we shoot him quick, just in case?"

Scarlett ignored the temptation, and stepped out from his concealment.

The pair of look-outs stayed hidden in the brake, longbows ready.

"Ah, perfect!" Cried Alfred as Scarlett appeared, scowling down his short sword. "I've been looking for you."

"*What the blazes do you mean by that, wizard?*"

"Actually, I'm an alchemist. And, you are an outlaw, if I'm not mistaken?"

In his shock and suspicion, Scarlett gave no reaction.

"Ah, oh, sorry, indelicate question, I know. But time is short, so I'll take that as a *provisory* yes, shall I? Ahem. Good." Not wanting to startle the chap further, Alfred employed his politest tones. "Good, er, woodsman, I'm looking for Robin Hood. I have a rather dire warning to deliver."

"*What?*" Scarlett's guts turned to water. "What evil d'you bring clinging to your back, alchemist? You'll not harm Robin whilst a man stands in Sherwood."

"Ah, no. Sorry, you've misunderstood. I've come to *warn him* of trouble, not *bring him* trouble. Very similar concepts *in practice*, I agree, but collaterally different *in principle*, if you see what I mean."

"I say we kill 'im now Will." Came a shaky voice from the bushes. "He looks like a wizard, an' talks like a lawyer!"

"Thank you, but only on my command." Scarlett called back. "What's this warning? Tell me. I can tell Robin."

"The Sheriff is readying his troops for attack even as we speak!"

"Well, thanks, but we already know that." Scarlett glared, hefting his blade. "Now, go back to where you came from. The warning is welcomed, *but you aren't.*"

"Gisburne's planning to burn the forest down around your ears!"

"Impossible." Scarlett snorted. "Sherwood's too green to burn at this time of year. And it's too big. Get out of here you crack-pot."

"*Oh, they have a dread new weapon, outlaw.*" Alfred suddenly applied his most dramatic tones. "It is an *alchemical preparation* that ignites greenwood as 'twere kindling. *Oh,* know that it burns so terrible hot, that to see it blinds the unwary!"

"Stop your nonsense." Scarlett narrowed his eyes in real anger. "For the last time, *be on your way.*"

"Oh, dear. I had hoped I wouldn't need to do this." Alfred swung his right arm high, lobbing a handful of walnuts into the air.

Each broke apart to release clouds of dense, dirty smoke. The look-outs yelled in terror and let fly a brace of arrows.

There was a silence as the yellowish mists eddied ominously.

"Did we get 'im?"

"I can't see him... ." Scarlett peered through the wispily clearing clouds.

"That's because I'm behind you. Now, if you don't take me peacefully to Robin Hood, I'm transmogrifying all of you into *particularly ugly toads*."

A short time later, a nervous Will Scarlett escorted a blindfolded and doublebound Alfred Hampstead into the encampment.

"By Our Lady, today's not the day for fancy dress, Will!" Robin Hood interrupted his discussion with Friar Tuck.

"I'm sorry, Robin, but the, er, alchemist wanted to see you."

"Well, I'm glad courtesy hasn't been forgotten as we face invasion and death, but I am *rather busy*."

"Erm, yes, I tried to explain that ... But he was quite persuasive ... And anyway, he says he carries a dire warning."

"Even more reason not to bring him." Robin threw Tuck a long-suffering look. "Very well, let's hear what he has to say. With the way he looks, it's bound to be worth hearing."

"Ahem. Thank you, Robin Hood, Lord of Outlaws, King of Sherwood." Alfred took a deep breath and deployed his most rolling basso profundo. "FLEE OUTLAWS. *Oh,* flee whilst you can!"

Robin Hood and Friar Tuck each staggered back a step at Alfred's words, their expressions etched with shock.

"They are coming for your *carcasses*. Oh! They will drive you out of hiding with alchemical fire born of all hell's fury!"

"*By Our Lady,* have you staged this mummery, Tuck?"

"No, I most certainly have not. *Who are you?* What's this about alchemy?"

"I am a messenger, sympathetic to your cause." Alfred stared about with apocalyptic conviction. "Nottingham has gathered 500 soldiers, but knows valiant Sherwood protects you. Captain Roland will surround the wood," Alfred flung out his arms in ominous embrace, "then vengeful Gisburne will conflagrate the weald!" Alfred's arms shot skywards mimicking flames. "Those not immolated, will surely be impaled." Hampstead thrust his hands groundward, stabbing and burying in the same motion.

"Well, you do sound impressive, but frankly, there's no way to set Sherwood on fire at this time of year."

"Ah. I *knew* it would come to this. Do allow me to demonstrate." Alfred flung a small pouch into the centre of the campfire before anyone could stop him.

Every outlaw froze in fearful expectation.

WWWOOOOOOOOMMP!

Stunning white-yellow flames detonated 15 feet into the air, sending a heat wave withering leaves for 20 yards.

Little John reacted first, jumping bodily onto the alchemist.

"*By Our Lady,* fetch water!" Robin ran for the nearest bucket.

"Mph. Mphh. Mph mph!" From underneath Little John's bulk, Alfred Hampstead frantically pounded his one free hand on the ground.

"I think he's trying to tell us something."

"Don't let him go, but do let him breathe, goodman John." Tuck called as he joined the fire fighters.

Little John shifted his weight enough for Alfred to free his head.

"*Don't put water on the fire!*"

WOOOOOOOOMSSSSSHHHHH!

The first outlaw had already flung a good bucket-load.

The campfire bloomed to double its size, spattering sticky little flaming gobbets in every direction.

"*What evil is this?*" Little John slapped Alfred with one hand, and at his burning clothes with the other.

"How do we put the fires out, alchemist?" Cried Robin as the encampment grew ever more frenzied.

"St ... op ... stop ... sla ... slap ... slapping me ... please ... Heaven have mercy! You don't."

"WHAT?"

"Erhm, do let me explain." Hampstead took on his tones of lectureship. "Pyrophoria's *primary alchemical characteristic* is that it will burn almost anything. Even water. In fact, my, er, informants suggest only an extreme temperature change has a chance of interrupting the reaction."

The campfire blazed like a demon in torment.

Around the camp, the scattered drops of flame produced by the explosion were proving incredibly difficult to extinguish, burning on green bark like it was oil.

Robin Hood divided his dazed glare equally between the alchemist and the Friar, his imagination vivid with prophecy and pyrophoria.

"MERRY MEN. *To me.*" The King of Sherwood's call blasted across the encampment like a hunting horn.

The outlaw band hastened in from their defensive positions, bows and staffs held steady.

Tears came to Hood's eyes at their vitality, their humanity, the noble purpose o'er-coming all their fear. He recalled crossing the Channel with a similarly fervent band, and knew he'd made the right decision.

His people would do more good alive across the shires, than dead in Sherwood.

"Outlaws! By pitting your lives against tyranny today, you have earned the approval of Arthur, and the love of Albion. *But the struggle must continue tomorrow.* Merry men! Return to the shires and spread the word: *Resist everywhere.*" Hood swept the band with his invincible gaze. "And *by Our Lady*, be ready for when I call you again. Brothers, I will call you again! Alan-a-Dale! Prepare the escape route. Will Scarlett! Spy out the enemy. Little John! Assemble a rear-guard of two score fighting Jacks. Lady Marian," Robin took Marian's hands for a single moment, "guide my people to safety in the shires. Friar Tuck! Bring the alchemist, and come with me to the barricades."

Friar Tuck ~ Chapter 43

The three things that avert calamity:
To be worshipful; to be upright; to be strong.
The Triads of Bardism

Scarlett reported back much quicker than expected.

"Robin, we're surrounded. The forest north, east and west is already thick with soldiers. Alan is preparing a route south. The terrain means the mercenaries are still spread thin in that direction. Our best chance is to punch through early, before they get close enough to tighten up their ranks."

"How are they arrayed?"

"With everything short of mounted knights! There's at least 500 of them with swords, spears and crossbows, closing with awful speed."

"Good work. Send me a score of fighting Jacks. You and John take the second score, and make that break south. Marian will lead the escapees through Sherwood. Alan will prepare safe havens across the shires." Hood clasped Scarlett's arm. "I'm heading east to create a diversion." Robin sent his gaze deep into Scarlett's eyes. "Do look after each other, eh? And, Will? Thank you."

Scarlett fought back tears as he realized his King was saying goodbye.

Unable to respond with words, Sherwood's Captain sprang away to follow his orders.

"Right, Tuck. We're now on the run, and rather than facing a heinous enemy, he's clawing at our back. What do you suggest we do?"

"Ah, Robin," Tuck gripped his shillelagh, "now we fight for all our tomorrows." Then he couldn't help a shy grin. "How we do that, however, is up to you."

"*By Our Lady!*" Robin Hood uproared with laughter. "If I die with you beside me, Friar, I'll be a happy man. Whatever sin we carry to the Pearly Gates, there's no way you'll not talk us in!"

"Well, don't get us killed just yet. I'd like a bit more practice before we have a go at Saint Peter." Tuck shot back, causing Alfred Hampstead to let out a guffaw.

A score of fighting Jacks appeared around their King.

Their eyes glowed with bravery above their Lincoln green scarves as the Lord of Outlaws welcomed them with a tight-lipped smile.

"You and me, *we're going to make a lot of noise.*" Hood's expression went dark with determination. "We attack east, *but so scathingly,* they'll be forced bring reinforcements in from the north and south. That'll give the escapees a chance to break away. We're going to do it proper underdog style: *Confuse at a distance, and kill up close.*"

Earl Guy of Loxley rode at the head of the largest troop of fighting men he'd ever led.

The array of sharp edges eager for his enemies' flesh pleasured his heart with spikes of power. Everyone was finally getting everything they deserved.

Captain Roland slung his steel noose around the forest with well practiced gestures. The mercenaries responded with disciplined eagerness, looking forward to easy blood against these bush-trained peasants.

The weald remained deathly quiet beneath the clamp and stamp of the armed men as the siege-line was secured. The mercenaries were stretched wide at first, but quickly drew together as the noose closed.

No look-outs were spotted, no resistance met, but Roland knew this simply meant the trap wasn't yet tight enough to make the enemy squirm.

Gisburne rounded in from the east, shaking with the desire to unleash his flaming furies. His crew of pyrophoriacs trod carefully, a company of almost silent mercenaries creeping alongside to the left, another to the right.

SHHHHHHHEEEEEEEEKUNCH!

The first outlaw arrow hammered through the air like a giant hornet, slamming half its length through a mercenary's chest plate.

Volley after volley followed, swarming with fury.

"Advance to battle!" Commanded Gisburne.

The mercenaries raised shields, and shifted into a running assault. Moving fast made each man a harder to hit, and the sooner they overran the archers, the safer they would be.

All along the line to the east, small teams of merry men attacked as if they were ten times their size.

Few of their frenziedly shot arrows found live targets amongst the charging mercenaries, but the invaders felt like they faced every outlaw who'd ever lived.

"We've found their nest. Send for reinforcements! *Ready the pyrophoria!"*

The pyrophoriacs loosened winesacks and loaded cross-bows.

The mercenaries pressed their attack, blades braced to the fore.

The first rank of Robin's diversionary teams fell back in the face of the lighting advance. Fleeing, the outlaws couldn't shoot, and the pyrophoriacs darted out into the lull, alchemical weapons ready.

To the south, Little John and Will Scarlett vanguarded the escapees a half-mile to the banks of a deep stream.

Alan-a-Dale had left signs guiding them to an almost invisible ford, an ideal place to cross. The fighting Jacks settled quieter than shadows amongst the tall reeds.

Scarlett glimpsed a glint of sword through the dense copse of oak. Then, a line of mercenaries appeared, advancing with slow menace.

Yells and cries rent the forest in the east as Robin's team went to work.

The mercenaries to the south, 15 yards from Little John's balled fists, halted and held a whispered conference.

The sounds of battle in the east grew fierce, calls for reinforcements coming through the trees.

As hoped, many of the mercenaries broke away to provide support. Those remaining in the south formed a looser, but still formidable barrier.

Lady Marian appeared at the head of the escapees, and nodded their readiness.

Will Scarlett flanked left with five archers. Little John formed a tight wedge with his staffmen.

Five yards distant, the mercenaries reached the far bank of the stream. After some cursing, they broke formation to find a way across the water.

Whilst most were struggling against the fast current, a group of three found the ford by chance. They paused at the edge, then came quickly over the crossing stones.

To the east, Robin Hood's second line of defence was instantly put to rout by the first wave of Gisburne's pyrophoria-dipped crossbow bolts.

Their alchemical tips ignited as they tore through the air, arriving as exploding fireballs.

The pyrophoriacs followed up by hurling their wineskins. The heavy bundles snapped through low branches, splattering their contents in wide sprays of wildfire.

With staggering speed the forest was shimmering under torrents of flame.

The mercenaries accelerated into their advantage.

"*Fall back.* Fall back to the first defences!" The King of Sherwood loosed arrow after arrow through the mounting conflagration as his crew scrambled away.

Robin's beard was singeing by the time Friar Tuck pulled him after them.

At the stream, Little John waited until the mercenaries were almost in his arms before mowing them down.

The fighting Jacks dashed over and established a bridgehead on the far side.

Lady Marian had the escapees moving through the breach in a trice.

It took a good few moments for the remaining mercenaries to realize what was happening at that little stretch of the stream.

Then they raced in, yelling alarums and oaths.

From high out of an oak, Will Scarlett and his men sniped the first mercenaries to get within 10 yards of the escape route.

Lady Marian used these precious seconds to hie the escapees into the heartwood.

The mercenaries regrouped and shot four outlaw bowmen out of their trees. Will Scarlett and his remaining man dropped from sight, leaving a score of mercenary swordsmen to close in on the rear-guard.

Little John roared invocations to the Holy Mother as his crew readied to withstand the counter-attack. They had to give Marian enough time to reach Alan-a-Dale.

Captain Roland's troops in the west let out a cheer when they saw the forest to the east go up in flames. It was the signal Gisburne had found the main band of outlaws.

Anticipating a bandit encounter at any second, Roland drew his sword. The attack was going exactly as planned.

The fire raged into the treetops and caught across the canopies. Ash, elm and yew creased like sandcastles at high tide, crumpling as the heat sucked them dry, then dissolving in liquid flames.

Robin Hood, Friar Tuck, Alfred Hampstead and the diversion team gathered behind a now useless enfilade east of the encampment.

Crackling white tongues of elemental destruction flickered everywhere.

"Tuck, go to Little John. Tell him to get everyone away, and go with them. I'll meet you noon tomorrow, at Saint Mary's in Edwinstowe. Our diversion is going to last about five more minutes at this rate."

"But Robin-."

"MOVE IT FRIAR."

Tuck reached for his internal silence as the inferno intensified in every direction. Despite the immediate danger, his spirit was buoyant.

The merry men would have been helpless against this apocalypse. As it was, most of his congregation had every chance of escaping.

Tuck grieved for Sherwood as woodland animals began streaming past, predator and prey running together to escape the fire. He was leading Alfred to the stream, staying just ahead of the blaze, praying hard, when a cool breeze blew into his face.

Within a few paces, the breeze had mounted to an erratic draft moaning in from every direction.

"*By Melchior,* the pyrophoria's triggering a firestorm!" Alfred yelled above the booming cacophony of the woodland in full burn.

The tallest tongues of flame, now reaching double the height of the trees, were propelling superheated air high into the atmosphere. At ground level, the wind swept in to fill the gap, feeding and fanning the burn from below.

"A firestorm of this intensity could consume the entire forest." Alfred stopped to point out the blue heat scorching around each tree. *"And I mean the whole damn thing."*

"What can we do?" Tuck shoved Alfred into motion as a frightened family of wild boar hurtled by. "You said yourself nothing will stop this stuff."

"Yes, nothing will stop it." Guilt wracked Alfred's guts. "Nothing except extreme cold."

"WHAT did you say?" Tuck grabbed Alfred's face in his hands, suddenly sure of Sherwood's only hope.

Little John's fighting Jacks were almost crushed under the first mercenary charge. Only the giant's tremendous strength saved them from instant defeat.

The mercenaries lashed in from all sides, their swords stabbing and slicing like lizards' tongues from between their disciplined shields.

Will Scarlett and his remaining bowman circled in from the flank. Their deadly arrows took several mercenaries in the back, giving Little's crew a moment's respite.

Just as it looked like the outlaws were rallying, a pair of mercenaries appeared out of the weald directly beside Scarlett.

The outlaw swung his bow round to deflect the first cutting swipe, but the second mercenary lunged in with a grinding stab to the ribs.

Scarlett scrabbled for his short sword, determined to keep fighting, but blood bubbled from between his lips, and his strength failed him.

"For charity, chivalry, and Robin Hood!" Scarlett sobbed in triumph and agony as the mercenary stabbed again.

Scarlett's bowman tried to defend his Captain, but was beaten back.

Will Scarlett dropped to the ground, mortally wounded.

The bowman gave a sad cry, then scrambled away to Little John's side for a last stand.

Lady Marian led the escapees through Sherwood by the most secret routes. Palls of smoke rose above the forest, the chill ring of combat chiming through the trees.

Tears rolled down Marian's cheeks as she prayed for all the outlaws, but especially Robin Hood.

Flocks of displaced birds wheeled into the darkening skies, their calls clogged and hoarse. The Lady of Sherwood hastened her people the last mile with eyes as fierce as an eagle's.

In a fallow field at the forest edge, Alan-a-Dale met the escapees with a fleet of wagons. The merry men had to get far from Sherwood before slipping back into shire life. When Gisburne realized the outlaws had escaped, he would be sure to scour the area.

Alan-a-Dale was loading the third wagon when rats, rabbits, badgers and voles began pouring out of the forest. This carpet of small creatures was soon joined by deer and boar, wolves, wildcats and foxes, snakes and even a pair of bears.

Not a single creature made a sound as they pattered, skittered and slid for safety.

Marian stared into the trees, her heart seeking her husband.

Captain Roland narrowed his gray eyes.

Having detected and disarmed several ingenious traps, he'd reached the well concealed western palisade of the enemy encampment.

The total silence beyond the walls told Roland it had been abandoned.

The sounds of engagement came crisply from both east and south, riding the crunching washes of flame-heated air. The burn had spread wider, as they'd planned, pushing in a solid wall from the east, and jumping tree to tree across the north and south. The outlaws seemed well trapped, but the empty encampment bothered Roland in his bones.

Robin's handful of merry men retreated before the onslaught of fire and mercenary swords, until they collapsed against the eastern wall of the encampment. They could go no further, and already the palisade was charring above their heads.

Higher still, a towering cloud of black ash mushroomed over the forest, shaped by the howling gales chorusing the firestorm.

Hood remembered this feeling from the battlefields of Egypt. His crew's eyes were all on him, hungry for leadership in the midst of unthinkable chaos.

The King of Sherwood's concern for his men opened a well-remembered wellspring of puissance in his belly.

Surrounded by flames fit for hell alone, Robin Hood's fearless features fed his crew with an inspiration only the battle-shocked soul can savour.

Out of the brake thundered a herd of deer.

The animals ignored the men, leaping north in confused bunches, escaping like everything else.

"O happy crew! Get amongst the deer. Let them shield you as they guide us out." Robin gave a great laugh, his eyes reflecting bronze in the inferno. "I wish the Friar was here. *For once, acting like animals might actually save our souls!*".

Friar Tuck ~ Chapter 44

Three characters that please the Divine:
Those who love everything living with all their heart; those who protect everything beautiful with all their strength; those who seek knowledge with all their understanding.
The Triads of Bardism

Guy of Gisburne was in raptures at the effect of the pyrophoria. This was power enough to satisfy even his ravenous soul.

Trees twenty feet from the flame front were now spontaneously combusting into roaring pyres. As the firestorm moved, it left total desolation as its trail. Even the rocks had shattered.

Gisburne gazed fondly at the bare blasted woodland. His enemies would soon have nowhere left to hide.

The blaze harried Tuck and Alfred Hampstead to the banks of the southern stream. They arrived in time to witness a heavily wounded Little John at the last gasp of a losing battle.

The mercenaries had killed all the fighting Jacks, and were readying to bring down the giant.

Hampstead threw one his pouches into their melee.

Catching on a raised sword, the pouch blew open and scattered a purple powder into the air around the fighting men. In a blink, the mercenaries were convulsing under seizures of violent sneezing.

Little John, whose height kept his nose out of trouble, smashed his way free of his attackers, and hot-footed it across the stream to his rescuers.

The trio scampered into the smouldering heartwoods.

"Well met, Friar. Where's Robin?"

"We're to meet him noon tomorrow, at Saint Mary's. What of Marian?"

"She'll be at the outskirts of Sherwood by now."

"Thank the Lord. And Scarlett?"

"Will's dead, badger." Little John's voice broke. "He was defending me and my crew when they ... When they got 'im."

"Oh, John, I'm so sorry, for all of us. Will Scarlett was the best Captain we had. He will be missed terribly. May The Blessed Lady Herself welcome his soul." Tuck stopped in his tracks and exchanged a long look with Little John. "You'll have to reach Marian and Alan on your own."

"I'll do it. But what about you?"

"Me and the alchemist are going to see what we can do about saving Sherwood!"

Robin Hood clenched his teeth against the blistering heat, pushing his men onwards amongst the herd of deer. The air had become thick and slippery, like they were underwater. The ash cloud was blotting out the sun, the incredible noise swamped their senses, and the wind blew ever harder. Man-high whirlwinds of fire chased through the weald like infernal festivallers, turning every trunk they touched into columns of charcoal.

The animals were losing their sense of direction, doubling back as the paths to freedom were cut off.

Still not having seen one outlaw, Captain Roland swung his troops north. The bellows and shrieks of the blazing woodland sent worse shivers into his mercenary heart than any enemy ever had.

Roland encountered Gisburne leading his men up from the east.

"*By Hellfire, what a day!* Did the bastards fall mewling into your arms Roland?"

"No."

"*But that's impossible.* I engaged the entire band on the eastern flank, and sent them fleeing towards you!"

"The entire band? Are you sure?"

"I had them coming at me *by the dozen*. The mercenaries did a fine job, and pyrophoria did the rest. I need more of that stuff. The outlaws must still be in there, *roasting.*"

"I didn't find anyone defending the main encampment. I hope you're right."

"*I know I'm right.* From the moment we attacked, I had the bastards trapped between you and the burn."

"I heard fighting to the south before the fire cut it off." Mused Roland, a chill in his bones despite the heat striking at his face.

"*What the hell are you saying?*" Demanded Gisburne, eyes turning deadly.

Just at that moment, scores of deer careened out of the flames and capered north, their coats charred and smoking.

"Gisburne, don't you get it?" Roland laughed in scorn. "They fooled you with a diversion. *You lit the fire in the wrong bloody place.*"

Gisburne whipped out his sabre. "I saw them. I fought them. *And you lost them!*"

Roland eyed the Earl's threatening blade. "Are you going to use that, or get it out of my face?"

"What are *you* going to do, if I leave it right there?" Gisburne's features were dense with rage.

In reply, Roland gave a short nod.

Three mercenary swordsmen stepped up and stabbed Gisburne smartly in the back.

Earl Guy of Loxley stared in disbelief at the blades piercing out of his chest.

Captain Roland watched dispassionately as Gisburne's eyes went wide with infinite fear, then drooped with death. He'd seen the same look on every battlefield he'd ever blooded.

In his day, they'd called it the thousand hell stare.

"Get the troops together, Lieutenant." Roland ordered, his voice husky. "We're moving out."

The veteran knew he'd won the fight, but lost the day.

"Where are we going?" Asked Alfred as he tagged along behind Tuck.

"You wouldn't believe me if I told you."

"Try me."

"We're going to see the Elves of Sherwood. If anyone can save the forest, it's them."

"Right now, finding forest fairies sounds like an entirely sensible thing to be doing, Friar."

"Don't call them that!" Tuck replied with a laugh.

Billowing ash and black smoke smothered the skies in low, choking clouds as Tuck and the alchemist arrived at the Gable of Si'ir.

"Now what?" Asked Alfred, gazing about with interest.

"I'm not sure." Muttered Tuck, his wisdom mind blankly silent. "Somehow we need to call the Lords and Ladies before the fire gets here."

"Summoning sprites, eh? Hmmm. Tricky stuff. I've read books about it, of course."

"What d'they say?"

"Usually the summoner ends up dead. Or worse."

"This oak has got something to do with it." Tuck used a cautious foot to prod the eldritch oak.

Hampstead gave Tuck a troubled look.

In the absence of anything better, Alfred had gone along with the Friar's unlikely idea. However, the Gable of Si'ir was disappointingly bare of anything antediluvian. Not a standing stone, long barrow or lowly mushroom-ring marked the spot.

Watching Tuck poke uselessly at the oak brought all Alfred's guilt rushing to his heart. Not only was he sure that stopping the pyrophoria was impossible, the Friar seemed to have misplaced a few of his marbles in the trauma.

The best thing they could do was keep running.

"Erm, Tuck, I'm sorry to interrupt, but the fire's getting closer, and-"

"*Excellent idea, Alfred.*" Tuck spun around and raced off towards the leaping flame front.

Alfred dashed after him, scared the Friar had completely lost his wits.

Tuck had to shield his face from the heat as he broke a blazing bough free from a beech. Alfred helped him drag the flaming log up the hillock.

They lent it against the oak and took a step backwards.

"Desperate move," Tuck stated approvingly, "but we *are* in desperate times."

"Well, to be honest, I didn't mean for you to-."

"I only hope they don't kill us before we can explain."

"What? I *arrrrgghhh!*"

Directly from the centre of the eldritch oak erupted two tall figures.

Every feature of their faces was set at sharp angles, hatred shining in their silver eyes. Each held a black-bladed longsword, raised high to strike.

A shocking blast of cold knocked Alfred instantly to his knees.

"*Betrayer.*" The elves swung their weapons in for the kill.

"Friends! Sherwood has been set ablaze by alchemy. I came to warn you. *Look to the east!* Si'ir is under direct threat."

The elves took in the firestorm consuming acres of the weald, and lowered their weapons.

The first elf slipped back into the trunk of the oak, as if passing a curtain.

The second, wispy curls of steam rising from all over his body, sniffed the smoke-laden air. "*Who has done this?*" A terrifying fury possessed the Wild Huntsman.

"Our enemies came to burn us out-."

"NO priest, *who gave humans the alchemy?*" The elf snatched Tuck into the air with one hand.

"I don't know-." Tuck almost fainted at the elf's freezing touch.

"I did." Alfred Hampstead spoke from where he knelt. "The Friar's done nothing but try to warn you. I'm responsible for this."

"You *are?*" Tuck gasped as the elf dropped him. "But *why*, Alfred?"

"I wasn't given a choice." The alchemist's eyes lowered with shame. "My Lord elf, pyrophoria can only be stopped by an extreme drop in temperature. It has to be *very* cold. What do I mean by-."

Three more elves, heavily cloaked, emerged from the oak.

"We know what devours the forest." The first stated. "Priest, once again, you prove our friend. You may go. The alchemist remains."

"But-."

"Go now. If you are caught in our magic, you will die."

"Tuck, do as they say." Alfred gripped Tuck's hand. "God knows I deserve whatever judgment they pass on me."

"But, Alfred-."

"*Go.* Good luck." Alfred pushed Tuck firmly away. "And long live Robin Hood!"

Not knowing what else to do, Friar Tuck backed away down the hillock.

Little People poured out of the oak to form concentric rings around the Lords and Ladies. The assembly weaved in time to their otherworldly music, dancing up a vortex of spell power.

Above the Gable, an opening appeared in the firestorm's ash cloud.

Tuck turned and ran as fast as his legs would take him.

A low humming filled his ears, then came a black flash, like negative lightning.

Tuck was knocked flat on his stomach by the titanic shock wave that blew past him a moment later.

A total absence of sound clanged around Tuck's skull as he struggled to his feet. He blinked and rubbed at his eyes for several seconds, before realizing the air itself was clouded with mist.

Everything else sparkled under a thick layer of crystalline ice.

Friar Tuck ~ Chapter 45

The three witnesses of Divinity:
Infinite power; infinite knowledge; infinite love.
The Triads of Bardism

"My Lord, the outlaws have been smashed and routed from the forest." Captain Roland, covered in fine white soot, stood to attention in Nottingham's private study.

"Not a moment too soon. King John arrives tomorrow, and I don't need *any more distractions*. I've invited every noble I can think of in honour of our gracious Liege, and now the sinner is dead, to witness my elevation to the highest ranks."

"We lost only few men, but Gisburne was among them, my Lord."

"Oh, what a shame! I'll miss him at wassail ... I wonder what the King will do with Loxley, now the seat is vacant?"

"My Lord, to guarantee security, I advise a sweep of the shires to round up any sympathizers."

"Find me three criminals to hang on Sunday. Always makes a good impression." The Sheriff gripped Roland's arm. "Roland, *nothing* must interfere with the King's visit. Make sure the peasants understand there will no mercy for *anyone* involved in *anything*."

Friar Tuck had gone to Rubygill for the night, then reached Edwinstowe at dawn.

Too anxious to pray, he'd spent the morning hovering in the nave of Saint Mary's church.

At just before noon, a poorly disguised Little John thrust his bowed head through the open double doorway.

"Fish!"

"Badger!"

Lady Marian dashed past the giant, closely followed by Alan-a-Dale, and the outlaws fell into a joyous huddle.

Then they broke apart, each trying not to be too obvious as they waited achingly for their King.

"You must be very happy, Friar!" Called Robin Hood merrily as he bounded in through the priest's entrance. "You finally got us all into a church."

"Heaven have mercy Robin Hood, I'd be glad to see you even if it was in a brothel. Err, sorry Lady Marian."

Marian's laughter shimmered like veils of light through the old stone church.

Soon enough, the outlaws had settled in the snug of The Royal Oak pub, situated with traditional wisdom only a step from Saint Mary's.

"To Will Scarlet! Brave Captain and beloved friend." Robin cried slow tears as he lifted his pint of ale.

"*Will Scarlett, Captain and friend!*" The merry men waked Will Scarlett with full outlaw honours.

Round midnight, Robin Hood settled both elbows drunkenly onto the table, and pulled a serious expression. "Right. We need to figure out what to do next."

"Have another beer!" Yelled Little John.

"I second that motion." Alan-a-Dale raised his jug unsteadily.

"Do we have a third?" Robin cast about as if in senate.

"*Aye.*" Lady Marian carried the day.

"The beers have it! Is three rounds enough, do you think, Friar? Or should I order four, in case they try to close the bar?"

"The hermit taught me three things that always close too early: The casket of a sinner; the purse of a miser; and the bar of a drinker."

"By Our Lady." Robin Hood stood from the table, his deep-forested eyes staring wide. "*So many* have fallen in the struggle." The Lord of Outlaws hung his head in honest humility. "I thank Our Lady for our escape yesterday." Robin's voice grew so quiet, the merry men stopped breathing. "Friar, if not for you, today, my soul would be wracked with the weight of our dead. To be spared that burden is a blessing I cannot express."

"You made the brave decisions, Robin." Tuck responded in his most gentle tones. "All I did was relay Scripture's teachings."

"Hmmm." A glimmer of Hood's humour glinted in his emotional eyes. "Maybe, but I'll wager you're the first churchman to tell the parable of Jesus and the outnumbered outlaws."

"Wai ai badger!" Little John cheered above the exuberant laughter that shook the snug.

"Speaking of which, the Prioress of Rubygill wants to meet us tomorrow."

Everyone except Marian immediately lost their humour.

"By Our Lady," Robin pulled an unconvincingly sober face, "*I hope you lot have been washing behind your ears.*"

"Who's the Prioress of Rubygill?" Asked Marian innocently as the crew cracked up again.

"*No, Friar.*" Robin's anguished cry rose over the tumult. "Sweet Marian *can't* meet the Prioress. They'll compare notes, and it'll be the end of me!"

King John's Royal Progress entered Sherwood Forest from the south.

The September sun peeked pale rays through plump clouds, layering the land in shades of cool green and elegant gray.

A few miles in, the healthy woodland became a landscape from the devil's own nightmares. A choir of stark charcoal columns heralded the area of devastation. Within, the weald was swept clean for two crow's miles.

The forest floor had become a smooth brown crust that lay like a stagnant lake.

"Hell's *blackest* teeth." John breathed in bewildered shock to his High Constable. "Has there been a fire?"

"My Liege, there must have been, but I've never seen anything like this."

"I'm sure Nottingham will have an explanation as to why *Our* forest has been allowed to go up in flames. If We can't hunt tomorrow, whoever's responsible will rue the day. Drive on!"

The surface of the roadway was thick with ash under the horses' hooves as the Royal train made all speed for Nottingham.

"My most gracious Liege, welcome, welcome, and welcome once again to Castle Nottingham. It's been too long since your last visit." The Sheriff bowed low.

"Thank you, Nottingham. We hope your hospitality will chase the doldrums of London away from Our spirits."

"Most Majestic King, we will wassail like never before! We have canary wine to doctor the turgid palette, and country wenches to nurse the jaded appetite."

"Very good. We wish also to hunt, what has happened in the Royal Forest?"

"Most Noble Majesty, with Your permission, it is a tale unfitting for Your welcoming party-."

"Do We need to ask you twice, Nottingham?"

"Ah, no, Gracious King. My most sincere apologies, the matter is simply a little indelicate. The truth is, the Earl of Loxley got carried away whilst serving justice on a band of forest-dwelling outlaws. The Earl started a fire to smoke them into the open, but clumsily let it get out of hand."

"Where is this bumptious Earl now? Loxley always was a seat of trouble!"

"Ah, my Liege, the *former* Earl of Loxley died in the forest, killed by that very same fire. Unfortunately, he left not a single heir."

"Hmmph. The fellow might well count himself lucky, not to have survived his stupidity. And Us, that the fool had no progeny."

"I couldn't agree more, Your Majesty. In some recompense, the outlaws are dead, and Sherwood teeming with game."

"I've had a full report from Brother Tuck." Prioress Brighid of Rubygill presided over the outlaws in her refectory. "You did well to survive the mercenary attack, but the question is: Where do you go from here?"

"Excuse me, Mother Prioress, but why does it concern you what we do? Why do you care?" Robin asked, albeit meekly.

"The Church was established in the interest of humanity," Brighid replied with conviction, "to strive for peace and decency. What you call chivalry and charity, we call virtue. *You do know what virtue is, don't you Robin Hood?*"

"Er. Yes."

"Hmph. If you do, someone must have knocked the concept into your corky head since the last time I saw you!"

"*But-.*"

"Don't interrupt." Brighid shook her head at Marian with every feminine sympathy. "Now, for better and worse, the Church's other great interest is politics, the struggle for power. Circumstances are such that both humanity and politics are served by you and your band of outlaws, Hood."

"*By Our-,* erm, how is that so, Mother Prioress?"

"The Bishops have just finished a conclave at Lincoln. King John was the hot topic. The coming war with France is ill-conceived, and donations to the Church are suffering because of these new taxes. Before taking action, the Bishops need to gain the trust of the Barons, and you're the key."

"*Now wait a minute-.*"

"Robin, listen to the Prioress a little longer." Tuck made soothing motions with his hands.

"Quite. If you're willing to meet him, the Bishop of Ely will be here tomorrow. He dearly wishes to speak with you."

"Well, that's easy enough. Bring the fellow in! Why wouldn't I want to meet him?"

"Because the Bishop has asked to meet Robert Loxley, *not* Robin Hood."

The Lord of Outlaws narrowed his eyes as the atmosphere thickened with fate.

"What say you, Tuck?" Robin gave his counsellor a direct look.

"The Bishop of Ely could be a powerful ally. The problem is, the Bishop can't meet the King of Outlaws. It would put him in a difficult position. But, it must be your decision. Once you return to being Robert Loxley, you will have to face what he escaped by becoming Robin Hood."

"Marian, what say you? I'll no longer be a King, and may end up in jail."

"Ah, we've both been in jail, my love. And we both got out." Marian smiled with her dark eyes. "When I think of the future, I see only you. But the you I see will not be satisfied by the life of an outlaw. On your deathbed you will be Earl Robert of Loxley, why not live as him?"

"I will love you beyond death, darling Mawd. Alan?"

"You were forced to become Robin Hood. And you've played the part brilliantly! But this is a chance to return to your rightful life."

"Were Sherwood a theatre, Alan-a-Dale, *all* the players have been exceptional. John?"

"Ach, I don't know anything about politics, and don't care what you call yourself! What's important is the man, and the struggle. Tell me you'll be the same man. Tell me you'll continue the struggle. You'll have made the right choice."

"*There's the rub.*" Robin struck the table with the flat of his hand. "The Earl of Loxley can't fight tyranny and poverty, he's part of the problem."

"Ah, here's where things get interesting." Prioress Brighid almost smiled. "If we succeed in, ah, rehabilitating you, *we want you to continue to champion charity and chivalry.*"

"Now this I have to hear!"

"We want you working *inside* the established order. Our interests require friends amongst the aristocracy ... A noble who credibly urges compassion, and cunningly influences progress."

"I won't become the pawn of Rome."

"My superiors know that. Obviously, you cannot be coerced. We're offering to support you in your chosen quest. That it serves the Church's purposes, both humanly and politically, is only to be expected."

"Oh, for the simplicities of Sherwood. But they belong to Robin Hood, and already I see I am no longer he. So be it." The King of Outlaws stood from the table, his features soft with sweet melancholy. "I relinquish the crown of Sherwood Forest. Our Lady bless the weald, and all who dwell in her."

"*Our Lady Bless the weald, and all who dwell in her!*" The wend of the deepwood touched the outlaws' hearts as they chorused their King for the last time.

"You have made a good choice, Robert." Sister Beatitude appeared in the doorway of the refectory.

"Mum!" Robert Loxley hugged his mother. "Come and meet Marian."

That night, Rubygill hosted a dinner that went down in its history. It was even said the Prioress had been heard laughing.

Friar Tuck woke Robin Hood the next morning with a firm poke in the ribs.

"*By Our Lady* Tuck, what the-."

"Robert, come on. We've got business to take care of." Tuck hustled his half asleep, and wholly unwilling, friend into the lavatorium.

There, grinning behind a chair, stood Alan-a-Dale, sharpening a pair of shears.

"Morning, sir." Dale called musically. "Do take a seat. With you in a moment."

"Eh?" Hood sat, trying to catch up to events, but then Little John waltzed in, holding an armful of expensive garments.

"Well, I'm glad to see you got 'im 'ere early, badger. In the light of a civilised morn' our boy do look right *unsavoury*. Anyone would say 'es bin sleepin' rough these past few years!"

"*What are you cockahoops up to?*"

"How would you like it styled today, sir?" Alan-a-Dale made a few experimental snips. "I'd say the European fashion would favour you. You've certainly got the nose for it!"

Lady Marian almost choked on her breakfast when Robert Loxley entered the refectory.

The Lord of Outlaws had been shorn of his rakish woodland chic to reveal a handsomely featured nobleman, with sensitive eyes and a strong chin.

Standing from her seat in welcome, Marian reflected that it was the first time she'd seen her husband wearing anything other than Lincoln green.

His attendants looked a lot like Alan-a-Dale, Little John and Friar Tuck, but years younger and decades fresher.

All had new clothes, shaved chops and groomed hair.

"Now I see why the Prioress filled you all with fear." Marian laughed in delight. "*It's a miracle!* You're actually clean."

The merry men, who had looked so proud, crumpled at Marian's teasing.

"We didn't do this for the Prioress." Robert replied, a little too quickly. "It's so we can properly discuss very important matters with the Bishop."

"Of course it is, and quite right too, and *oh,* a more handsome group I've *never* seen. Come and have breakfast my darlings, and let me have a proper look at you."

"Robert Loxley! May the Heavens preserve us, I thought you were dead." William Longchamps, the Bishop of Ely greeted Robert with wonder shining in his eyes. "When the Prioress told me you may yet live, I couldn't believe it. Where have you been these past three years? I looked for you everywhere, even in Europe."

"I, ah, had some errands to run. Why were you looking for me, Your Grace?"

"Because of this!" The Bishop motioned Robert towards a battered cedar chest sitting on a tabletop.

"What is it?" The tips of Loxley's fingers tingled.

"It's yours, Robert." The Bishop's voice dropped in reverence. "It's from King Richard."

"*By Our Lady,* how can it be?" Robert reached out to touch the chest.

"I was Richard's Justiciar during the time he was on Crusade. Until John usurped the throne, I acted for the King in everything. The Lionheart sent this chest from the Holy Land, to reward your exceptional service. By the time it arrived in my hands, events had overtaken us all, and you were missing."

"What's inside?"

"Money, of course. But there's also a letter. You should read it."

Robert opened the chest and lifted out a roll of thick parchment. Beneath gleamed a fortune in gold coins:

My Noble Knight Robert Loxley,

We would reward your valour on the battlefield, but you would protest it as the duty of any English knight.

We would reward your loyalty to Our crown, but you would protest it as the duty of any English man.

Therefore, We reward the care you have shown Our soldiers. On the field, your blade and bravery have saved many a blighted company from obliteration. Off the field, your good offices encourage Our fighting lions, while this damnable desert ceaselessly saps their strength.

Robert Loxley, by Decree Royal, We bestow on you the fief of Huntington. Huntington and Loxley are hereby joined together, in toto et perpetuam.

It is right for England to promote those who will serve in peace as well as they do in war. In this spirit, We ask you to accept this token of Our highest esteem and goodwill,

Richard, King of England, Lionheart.

Friar Tuck ~ Chapter 46

The three candles that illume every darkness:
Truth; nature; knowledge.
Triads of Bardism

King John's Royal hunt rode from Castle Nottingham into the warmth of a forgotten summer's morning.

The soft-edged September sunlight settled in golden drifts over the grassy meadows. The burnished red and bronze canopies of Sherwood shone on the horizon.

The day passed like one from yore.

Game proved plentiful as promised, and a few hours in the saddle shook John's distempers from his shoulders.

The King laughed and joked with his courtiers as they made their slow way home, the air sliced with a delicious chill, the skies stupendous with sunset.

"Damn fine country you have here, Nottingham." King John drew off his hunting gloves as the gillies lined up the day's trophies.

"Your Majesty is *most* gracious to say so. Of course, I've been tireless in looking after Your forest."

"Of course. Now, what entertainments have you for Us tonight?"

"If it pleases Your Majesty, this evening the Castle presents a troupe of Spanish dancers."

"Dancers, you say?" The King's eye quickened. "You really are a most *convivial* host, Nottingham."

"Always a pleasure to be of service to Your Majesty."

That night, Nottingham's wassail hall was riotous with music and banter. An extravagance of torches lined the walls above the Spanish dancers as they stamped and span, their movements dense with passion.

Three score courtiers and nobility toasted the King with loyal abandon.

The Sheriff sat to the King's right, deeply pleased at John's loud enjoyments of the evening.

"My Lord." Nottingham's seneschal sidled up with a look of abject misery.

"*By every cock-eyed curmudgeon in hell.*" The Sheriff fitted his full fury into a whisper. "I told you not to disturb me, seneschal."

"I am most terribly sorry, my Lord, but there's a group of nobles arrived in the courtyard, insisting on paying their respects to the King."

"*What?* I'm not having His Majesty interrupted now, it's going too well. Give 'em a mug of wine and bloody tell them he's busy."

"Er, thank you my Lord, but they said the King would want to see them."

"Who the hell are they?"

"The Bishop of Ely leads them, my Lord."

"*Ely?* What's that sly conniver doing here?" The Sheriff shifted uneasily. "*Damn his bones.* I can't deny a Bishop ... Very well, show them in, show them in. I shall inform His Majesty."

"At once, my Lord."

"Your Most Worshipful Highness... ."

"What is it, Nottingham? Eh? We'd forgotten what country air does for Our humours. Marvellous show you put on! Well? Speak up."

"It seems the Bishop of Ely wishes to pay his respects to Your Majesty."

"*Longchamps?*" King John's face drew tight with suspicion. "Why's that old fox roving so far from home?" Then John laughed. "Never mind! This night, England is magnanimous. We will welcome him like a friend. Prepare a seat for my brother's keeper here, by my side."

"Ah, Your Majesty, I really don't think-."

"Nonsense Nottingham, it's time Ely and the Crown were reconciled. Show him in. And bring more wine!"

Bishop William Longchamps of Ely and his retinue entered the hullaballoo of the hall, bowing with formal elegance.

"Your Grace." King John called above the noise. "Welcome, come, sit here, next to Us. Let past differences be forgotten for the good of the Kingdom."

Longchamps was taken aback by this effusive greeting.

The last time John Plantagenet had spoken to him, was to threaten death.

"May the Lord bless Your Majesty. I can only thank you, and admire Your Kingly wisdom."

It was John's turn to be taken aback.

This kind of praise from any Bishop, let alone Ely, was rare as rubies.

The King's good humour grew ever larger.

"Who are your companions, Ely? We welcome them to Our wassail with open arms. The more the merrier!"

"Your Majesty, may I present Robert Loxley, the Earl of Huntingdon."

"By the blackest fangs of Hades." King John's cry instantly silenced everyone in the hall. "Loxley lives!"

"Seize him!" The Sheriff yelled.

"Hold fast!" Longchamps' command stalled the guards. "Your Majesty, I would beg a boon."

"First a surprise, and then a boon? Ely, you are as audacious as We remember. *Tread carefully.*"

"My Liege, I ask only that you hear Loxley's petition."

"Loxley's *petition?* We want to hear what the mad-cap has been up to! And why you boldly present him as Earl of Huntingdon. The last time We looked, Huntingdon belonged to the Crown."

"Your Majesty, Loxley carries a Decree Royal from Richard, adding Huntingdon to his ancestral lands."

"Does he, now. Well, We wonder where he got that from. *What the hell are you up to, Longchamps?*"

"In emulation of Your Majesty, I seek only to mend past differences for the benefit of the Kingdom."

"In emulation indeed!" King John laughed with surprising satisfaction. "Ah, We've missed your sparring in court, Ely. Very well, the dead shall speak. Come forth Loxley, let's see if you've learned anything during your time underground."

"Your Majesty, thank you for hearing my petition."

"That man is an outlaw!" Shouted the Sheriff, his features puce with rage and outrage. "Your Majesty, *he led the outlaws of Sherwood.*"

"Nonsense," Ely cut in with easy confidence, "it is well known a fellow named Robin Hood led that band."

"But Robert Loxley *is* Robin Hood!" Squealed the Sheriff.

"And my auntie said she was the tooth fairy." Ely pulled an incredulous expression. "My Liege, I think we can safely say a castle full of soldiers is the last place an outlaw would walk into ... *Not to mention in the company of Bishop!*" The assembly fell about laughing.

"But *I know-* ."

"*Do* stop wittering, Nottingham. You told Us all the outlaws were dead."

"Err, that's right, Your Majesty."

"Then how can their leader be standing in your wassail hall?"

"Err, I don't know, Your Majesty."

"You're drunk, Nottingham. *And so you should be.*" King John raised his mug. "We're wassailing!" Every man in the hall cheered and toasted their Liege.

"But-."

"But, do shut up."

"*But-.*"

"Immediately." The King's eyes flared hard, and the Sheriff sat.

"Well? What *have* you been doing, Loxley?" John gave Robert a penetrating look.

"Tending my flock, Your Majesty." Robert Loxley replied humbly.

"*Tending your flock!*" King John rose from his chair in total astonishment, then pealed with laughter. "You *are* a mad-cap, Loxley."

The hall had been stunned by Robert's answer, but now instinctively followed the King's example.

Three score nobles, and two score assorted servants, serving wenches and soldiers, exploded with merriment.

"Oh my! Oh my! I haven't laughed like that for *years*. Tending your flock." The King chortled. "And where was this flock, Loxley, which you *tended?*"

"Your Majesty, my flock was where I found it."

"A true shepherd's answer." John giggled. "And did your herding bring you *rich rewards?*" The King cast his eyes around the room to share his marvellous humour.

"Yes, Your Majesty, more than I could ever have hoped for."

"*Enough to pay my scutage, boy?*" The King snapped, jutting forward.

Every eye turned on Robert.

The only movement came from the torches flaring and ebbing against the walls.

"Yes, Your Majesty." Robert placed a leather sack on the floor.

It settled with the thick clink of heavy coins.

King John seemed like a spear poised to strike, his face thrust far over the table, his right arm outstretched, finger extended to point with dreadful exactitude.

"Everything I owe is here, Your Majesty." Robert's respectful calm was unshakeable.

King John reeled himself back in, stupefied at Loxley's answer.

"You must have worked hard." King John made a closer inspection of the man standing before him. "*Very* hard. What is it you want?"

"My Liege, with the payment of what is due, my petition is for the return of Loxley, to be joined with Huntingdon as Richard decreed."

"And what have you got to say about this, Ely?"

"Your Majesty, my pure desire is my duty to the Crown of England. Richard's Decree Royal was put in my hands three years ago, but since Loxley had, ah, sought alternative employment, I failed to deliver it until now."

"My brother would thank you for your dedication, Ely." John replied, narrowing his eyes.

The King sensed everything was not quite as it seemed, but couldn't put his finger on what.

"In law, a Decree Royal stands above any other consideration." John mused. "And with Loxley's finances in order, there certainly seems no impediment to Our granting your request." The King sounded eminently reasonable. "What say you, Nottingham? How's about some clemency for our mad-cap?"

"*Never.* My Liege, I swear the man's a scoundrel of the worst order. And I can prove it."

"My dear Nottingham," the King glanced across to the visibly nervous Robert Loxley, "you do shock Us."

"Just look to his gold!" Nottingham jeered. "It's all been robbed. The sheep story was *very amusing*, but the coins will prove the *terrible truth*." The Sheriff strode to the centre of the room and picked up the sack. "Since these coins have been stolen from travellers, they will carry the marks of ten different mints and a hundred different hands!" Nottingham opened and upended the sack.

The gold coins formed a brief cascade of chiming light as they fell, then scattered everywhere.

One rolled to the feet of King John, who raised his eyebrows ironically as he reached down, then brought it up in his closed fist.

"We hadn't thought to expect an entertainment of this quality." The King raised his fist high, and every eye followed it. "In the balance hangs the fate of the man before us. Scoundrel or shepherd, we shall see... ." King John opened his hand, and heaved a great cry: "*It holds the head of Saladin!*"

The wassail hall uproared with delighted shock.

One or two knights actually drew their swords, as if the Great Sultan had appeared in person.

"This *is* a night for surprises." King John couldn't have sounded more pleased. "Are they all the same, Sheriff?"

"Ye ... Ye, yes, my Liege." Nottingham held bunches of coins in his dumbfounded hands.

"You certainly went a long way for your flock, Earl Loxley!"

Friar Tuck ~ Epilogue

Earl Robert of Huntingdon and Loxley formally married Lady Marian of Arlingford at the Church of Saint Mary in Edwinstowe, on the anniversary of their hand-fast.

Robert worked tirelessly for the people of England both in his fiefs and in London. The Earl's charisma ensured chivalry and charity became popular amongst the aristocracy once more.

Under Dame Marian Loxley's affectionate stewardship, the shires sprouted prosperity like a well tended herb garden. The Earl's wife also found time to bear her husband four sons and a daughter.

Despite these riches, what truly filled Robert's heart, and Castle Loxley, with happiness, was Marian's endlessly bubbling laughter.

Little John officially became the Castle blacksmith, but spent more time accompanying Robert on business than he did hammering metal.

Alan-a-Dale returned to Loxley every winter with tall tales and new songs.

Brother Michael Tuck was appointed Loxley's confessor. In this role, he counselled the Earl, but also worked within the Church as an ambassador for compassion and common sense.

In his spare time, Tuck liked to walk the fields, fens and forests of Loxley. Farmers at dawn would sometimes come across him sleeping under a tree.

After many years, the people said wherever the merry Friar passed, blessing was sure to follow.

King John's war with France lasted 12 years. Throughout this time, he clashed continually with the Church.

The years of turmoil and hardship ended with a French victory, and the Barons turned firmly against their King.

Then the Pope excommunicated him.

Then the Welsh rebelled.

Assailed on all sides, in 1213 King John assigned the Kingdom of England to the Pope in the Bulla Aurea. In return, Rome supported John against the Barons, but even this extraordinary move came far too late.

In 1215, the Barons of England forced King John to sign Magna Carta, the first step towards democracy in the history of the modern world.

"We've finally done it, Friar!" Robert Loxley bounded up to Friar Tuck. "By Our Lady, all Albion's children will toast this victory over tyranny forever!"

"Ah Robert, my heart feels like it did on those early mornings in Sherwood, do you remember?"

"Aye, Tuck." Loxley chuckled. "I dream of the weald. Sometimes, I see Robin Hood, and forget we were once the same man."

"I know what you mean." Tuck grinned. "Sometimes, I think of the hermit, and forget we were once different men!"

Robert Loxley laughed up to the sunlit Heavens.

Friar Tuck ~ Glossary

Word	Meaning
Abashed	ashamed or embarrassed.
Abominable	very unpleasant, loathsome.
Accession	coming into the possession of a right, title, office.
Acquiesced	to agree; consent.
Actualized	to make into reality or fact.
Actuated	to put into motion, activated.
Adversary	enemy, opponent.
Aggrieved	emotionally injured by injustice or wrong-doing.
Agog	full of excitement or interest.
Ails	to bother or hurt.
Airily	in an unconcerned manner, often with a hint of sympathetic humour.
Alarums	alarms.
Alban Eilir	see *Lady Day*.
Alban Elfed	see *Wine Harvest*.
Albion	ancient name of England.
Ambuscade	to attack suddenly and without warning from a concealed place; ambush.
A Mhuire Mháthair	Mary, the Sacred Mother.
Amiably	in a good natured manner, friendly.
Antediluvian	pertaining to the time before the Flood; otherworldly.
Apoplectic	anger intense enough to threaten or cause apoplexy.
Apostolic	pertaining to the early Church fathers.
Apparated	to appear.
Appeased	to make peaceful.
Arboreal	of or pertaining to trees.
Arboraceous	of or pertaining to trees.
Arcadian	rurally idyllic.
Arcane	complex and mysterious to the extent of seeming magical.
Ardent	expressive of intense feeling.
Ardour	intense feeling of enthusiasm, experienced as heat.
Argent	silvery white.
Arrayed	set out, usually in quantity.
Arthur	King Arthur Pendragon.
Ascetic	one who commits to significant self-denial for spiritual reasons.
Assuaged	to relieve; ease.

Askew	tilted.
Astutely	of keen penetration or discernment.
Asylum	an inviolable refuge.
Atonements	acts that reconcile a sinner with the Divine.
Audacious	recklessly bold.
Augustly	with notable masculine dignity.
Auric	possessed of a golden aura.
Avarice	excessive or insatiable greed.
Avowal	frank admission.
Avuncular	characteristic of an uncle.
Bacchanal	an occasion of drunken revelry.
Ballow	to cudgel, beat about the head.
Balm	soothed, healed.
Banding	bending in an uncontrolled manner.
Bantam	a breed of small, proud, quarrelsome chicken.
Bantered	to exchange lively, joking, remarks.
Bard	one of an ancient Celtic order of composers and reciters of poetry. In Wales, they formed a part of the order of Druids: Bard, Ovate, Druid.
Barful	difficult.
Basha	rudimentary outdoor shelter.
Basimecu	from the French.
Basso Profundo	bass voice of the lowest range.
Battening	to eat voraciously.
Bawd	to sell for sex.
Bawdy	Indecent, lewd.
Bawled	to shout or exclaim loudly.
Bay	reddish-brown colour.
Beard	to challenge.
Beleaguered	plagued with misfortune.
Bellicose	aggressively hostile.
Beltane	1st of May.
Be-mete	to thrash.
Bender	semi-permanent shelter often made of branches.
Beneficence	gift derived from active goodness.
Bestow	to give, present.
Bilbo	using a sword. *From:* Bilbao, where high quality swords were made.
Biliously	extremely unpleasant or distasteful.
Billow	to swell, surge and roll.

Bint	female criminal associate .
Blatted	to make a raucous, percussive sound.
Blazon	coat of arms, as displayed on a shield.
Blazoned	to highlight or display conspicuously.
Bodkin	dagger.
Boggle	destabilize.
Boggler	unstable person.
Boistering	roistering in a boisterous fashion.
Bole	trunk of a tree.
Boon	favour or blessing.
Boorish	unmannered, crude.
Boosting	slang for theft.
Booty	slang for gains from criminal activity, and buttocks.
Bosculating	repetitive, agitated movement.
Bosky	with trees and undergrowth.
Boadicea	celebrated warrior queen of the Iceni tribe, who led an uprising against the invading Romans in ancient Britain.
Bored	to drill a hole in.
Brace	2.
Braggarts	boasters.
Brake	undergrowth.
Breeches	riding trousers that reach just below the knee.
Bric-a-brac	collection of miscellaneous articles.
Brigand	robber based in mountains or woods.
Broach	to break open.
Brooked no quibbling	to have no patience with argument.
Brusquely	abrupt, rough.
Bubuckle'd	warty.
Bucolic	suggesting an idyllic rural life.
Bulla Aurea	a document giving the Kingdom of England up to God and the Saints Peter and Paul. Effectively, this was John recognizing the Pope as his superior.
Bullseye	centre of a target.
Bumpkin	an awkward, simple rustic.
Bumptious	offensively self assertive.
Buoyed	encourage, keep afloat, support.
Bustled	to move with an abundance of energy.
Buxom	cheerful and well bosomed.
Cack-handed	clumsy.
Cacophony	a loud, discordant mix.

Camaraderie	good fellowship, positive brotherhood.
Camelot	the seat of King Arthur.
Canary	sweet wine.
Candlemass	1st or 2nd February. The last feast in the Christian year dated by reference to Christmas, marking the end of Epiphany.
Cardinal & Sub-cardinal points	The four directions, and eight diagonals.
Carnelian	rich mineral red.
Catso	the lowest of thieves.
Ceiling-beams	long structural members supported at each end, often of wood, that hold up a ceiling, joists.
Changeling	an evil fairy substituted for a human, usually when a baby.
Chafe	an irritating friction.
Charnel	a place of dead bodies.
Chastened	admonished, reproved.
Chastity	unselfish sexual abstinence.
Chase	a long hollow, typically a wide dry stream bed.
Chicaneries	trickery or deception.
Chief Justiciar	King's representative when absent from Court, regent.
Chivalry	the moral code of a medieval knight, including: courage, courtesy, generosity and sensitivity.
Choler	anger.
Cinched	to bind firmly.
Cinereal	blackish gray.
Clap	sexually transmitted disease.
Claret	deep purplish-red colour.
Cleave	to divide.
Clemency	mercy, leniency or forgiveness.
Climes	literally climates, areas of land.
Clodded	made up of clods of earth, lumpy, uneven.
Cockahoop	person unbalanced by over-excited humour.
Cock-eyed	squinting, or with a strange set to the eyes.
Cocking-a-snoot	a rude gesture.
Cockles	from the expression 'to warm the cockles of the heart', meaning to give a visceral feeling of satisfied wellbeing.
Codger	old person.
Coenobite	member of a holy house.
Coerced	to compel by force or trickery.
Colubrine	snake like.
Comferenced	loosely surrounded.
Commendations	positive reports.

Complacency	self-satisfaction with an existing situation.
Conclave	a private meeting, especially of those with power in a particular sphere.
Confounded	perplexed to immobility by a surprising combination of events.
Conflagration	a large, hugely destructive fire.
Connived	to cooperate in wrong doing.
Consternation	a sudden amazement that results in utter confusion.
Contrition	sincere remorse.
Convivial	talented at feasting.
Copious	abundantly supplied, bountiful.
Corky, corkily	cheeky, humorously shallow.
Cortege	a ceremonial procession.
Coruscating	emitting vivid flashes of light.
Countryman	an unsophisticated, but capable and canny rural dweller.
Courteously	with fine manners, polite.
Cowering	to crouch in fear, usually trembling.
Cozening	obtaining something by cajoling, deceit or trickery.
Cranked	to turn a mechanism, which for crossbows drew the string for firing.
Crucible	a place or time characterized by a gathering of powerful influences; a container.
Cupid	the Roman personification of erotic love and beauty, son of Venus (Roman Goddess of Love).
Curmudgeon	person of unhappy humour.
Dam	dame, consort, wife.
Dandling	to cause a baby to move lightly up and down.
Darkling	subtly menacing, near darkness.
Daunted	to be subdued through intimidation.
Debauched	a corruption of the soul brought on by indulgence in perverse sensuality.
Deboshed	debauched.
Declaiming	to speak in an dramatic manner.
Denizen	local inhabitant.
Depraved	lewd, corrupt, evil.
Derogate	unworthy.
Despoiled	stripped of worth.
Despondent	feeling or showing profound discouragement.
Deviltry	reckless or diabolic wickedness.
Dexterity	skill in physical movement, particularly the hands.
Dilly dally	hesitation or time wasting.
Dirge	a funeral song.

Disconsolate	hopelessly unhappy.
Disembowelled	to have the abdomen cut open, so the stomach and guts come out.
Disgruntled	displeased and discontented.
Distemperate	inclement, forerunner of trouble.
Dizzard	person of extremely dull stupidity.
Doldrums	a listless mood; low spirits.
Doltish	foolish.
Dorter	sleeping chamber.
Doughty	steadfast; valiant.
Doxies	female acquaintances of low repute.
Dudgeon	feeling offense or resentful anger.
Dulcet	pleasant to the senses; melodic, soothing.
Dusk	the darkest part of twilight.
Dusky	given to shadows.
Ecclesiastical	of the Church.
Efreet	desert living spirit.
Effusive	unrestrained, exuberant.
Eldritch	eerie, uncanny, Elfish.
Elongated	to make longer or taller, usually resulting in thinning.
Embowered	enclosed by trees.
Emulation	imitation.
Ensorcelled	to be under the influence of magical spells.
Enfilade	a position from which troops can inflict a sweeping arc of fire along the length of enemy forces.
Enlistment	joining of a group, usually militant.
Environs	the surrounding parts or districts.
Eostre	ancient goddess of the dawn, celebrated at spring equinox.
Epiphany	January 6. Celebrates the shining forth of God in human form.
Ergo	therefore.
Escrow	a contract where the first party depositing something with a third party, with the promise of fulfilment on a condition with the second party.
Exchequer	medieval office in charge of the royal revenue, tax collection and issuing coinage.
Excoriate	to remove the centre.
Excruciating	unbearable.
Exhortation	an urgent address.
Exorbitant	exceeding the bounds of custom.
Expansive	wide-ranging, generous.
Expeditious	done with speed and efficiency.

Experiential	from direct experience.
Exuberant	uninhibited enthusiasm.
Fealty	loyalty, fidelity.
Faeces	excrement.
Fecund	fruitful, productive.
Fell	fierce, cruel and savage.
Festival of the Trees	see *Lady Day*.
Feudally	the ruling political/economic system of the Middle Ages.
Fief	a set of inheritable lands.
Finagle	to convince by manipulation.
Finesse	disingenuous handling of a sensitive situation; artful management.
Firmament	the vault of the sky.
Fiscal	pertaining to the public treasury or revenues.
Fisticuffs	fighting.
Flabbergasted	overcome with astonishment.
Flambant	of flame.
Flatulence	foul gases generated by inefficient digestion, uncommon farting.
Flotilla	several squadrons of ships.
Foppery	over-concern with appearance or manners.
Foreboding	a powerful feeling of approaching misfortune.
Foreknowledge	knowledge of something before it happens.
Forested	characterised by shades of dark green.
Fracas	fight.
Frankish	French.
French disease	see *clap*.
Fret	to feel and express worry.
Frisson	a sudden, passing sensation of excitement, usually felt along the skin.
Frittering	to squander piecemeal.
Frivolity	carefree; lacking serious purpose.
Frolicking	rapid, playful movements.
Fructifying	to make fruitful, fertile.
Fug	thick but warm atmosphere, usually with an element of wood-smoke.
Full mail battle-armour	a long chainmail shirt with hood, worn with greaves to protect the legs, plates to protect the arms, and a metal helmet.
Furlong	220 yards (0.2 km).
Gage	a token of challenge, thus the challenge itself.
Gaia	the Greek goddess of the Earth.

Galliard	French person, and a dance. *From:* Galliart: an improvised, leaping dance, done in triple time.
Gallopin	an under-servant in a kitchen; a cook's unskilled assistant.
Gambolled	frisky frolicking.
Garb	outfit, set of clothes.
Garboil	disturbance, misfortune.
Gasting	frightened.
Gastfreundschaft	the ancient art of treating a guest as a friend.
Gastronomic	of the art & science of fine foods and eating.
Gawdy	gay trifle.
Gehenna	place of extreme suffering, hell.
Giglet	a wanton.
Gillie	a hunting guide.
Gingerly	with extreme care and caution.
Girned	Extraordinary, often humorous, contortion of the face.
Gladius	short sword used in ancient Rome.
Glowering	staring angrily.
Gobbet	a lumpy mass or fragment.
Goodfellow, Robin	a trickster spirit or non-malicious wood sprite.
Greensward	open grassy area.
Groining	intersecting.
Groomly	in the solicitous manner of a bridegroom.
Guile	insidious cunning; artful deception.
Gyrovague	wandering monk.
Harangued	to launch a scolding verbal attack.
Harlot	lady of easy virtue.
Harridan	a scolding, belligerent woman.
Harried	to harass by repeated attacks.
Havering	hesitating.
Haymaker	a particularly powerful blow with the fist.
Hazed	obscure with dim light.
Hefted	hoisted.
Heinous	wickedly abominable.
Hemp dancers	criminals. Hemp rope was used for hangings.
Hie	hasten.
High Constable	medieval commander-in-chief of the King's army.
Holt	wooded area, usually hilly.
Hugger mugger	secretly and without due form; law breakers.
Hurly-burly	noisy agitation.
Huswife	lady of ill repute.

Ignoble	of selfish and cynical character.
Illumined	brightly illustrated.
Immanent	held or living within.
Immutable	changeless.
Impartially	not showing preference or favour.
Impertinence	unmannerly insolence.
Implicitly	implied understanding.
Imploring	To beg urgently and piteously.
Imposthume	septic swelling.
Imprecations	curses or maledictions.
Impregnable	too secure to be taken by force.
In concord	agreed.
Incongruous	out of place.
Incredulous	disbelieving.
Indomitable	cannot be subdued or overcome.
Inducing	lead into, persuade, de-repress.
Inebriated	drunk.
Inertia	the tendency to keep moving once in motion, or to remain at rest when immobile.
Inficete	serious, humourless.
Infinitude	beatific sense of endless multiplication.
In toto et perpetuam	entirely and forever.
Invisitude	beatific sense of the infinite not perceived by the 5 external senses.
Irascibly	easily provoked to anger.
Ire	spiteful anger.
Irreverent	lacking respect.
Jabbler	someone who talks a lot.
Jack	any man.
Jacksie	backside.
Jaded	ruined by overindulgence.
Jane	any woman.
Jape	joke.
Jaunted	to walk in a sprightly, self-confident, manner.
Jauntily	in a buoyantly genteel manner.
Jig	a fast, usually playful, tune, accompanied by erratic dance movements.
Jounced	to move up and down in a jolting manner.
Jovial	full of joy and happiness.
Jubilations	celebrations.
Keened	to wail a lament.

King's Justice	a sheriff, or the punishments a sheriff imposes.
Labyrinth	a complex arrangement of paths, traditionally walked to induce meditation.
Lacksadaisy	idiotically thoughtless.
Laden	loaded down.
Lady Day	20-23 March. Spring equinox. Festival of the Trees.
Lammas	1-2 August. First Harvest.
Languid	lacking in vigour.
Languishing	lingering.
Languorous	a dreamy, lazy mood or quality.
Larks	childish games; and a type of forest bird.
Lavatorium	washing room.
Leery	alertness caused by an unexpected event.
Legitimacy	genuine authority, lawful in the broadest sense.
Levitated	to move vertically in defiance of gravity.
Licentious	unrestrained by law or general morality.
Lily-livers	cowards.
Limned	outlined with light.
Liturgy	religious ritual.
Livery	distinctive uniform, worn by the servants or staff of nobility or an organization.
Livid	appearing strangulated because of strong emotion.
Loam	highly fertile soil.
Lofty	high in style.
Lozel	rascal.
Lumbars	lowest 5 vertebrae of the spine.
Luminescent	emission of light not caused by incandescence.
Lustily	with vigour and overt presence.
Maitre D'	*Maitre D'hôtel*, manager of a dining room, head waiter in a restaurant.
Malachite	mineral green.
Malapert	presumptuous.
Malt-worm	boozer.
Malus libri	the debilitating condition of having read too many books.
Mark	take note of.
Mayhem	rowdy disorder.
Meath	County of Ireland containing the Hill of Tara.
Melee	fight.
Merlin	the druid / wizard of King Arthur.
Mettle	courageous disposition.

Michaelmas	29 September. Holy day of obligation in the Middle ages.
Midsummer	19-23 June. Summer solstice. Alban Hefin. Mother night.
Mincing	taking small, dainty steps.
Misgraffed	unsuitably mated.
misplaced a few marbles	to have lost some powers of rationality.
Morphed	transformed.
Motes	small particles.
Mummer	actor.
Mur Ollavan	the City of the Learned, a druidic college.
Muster	to gather.
Myrmidons	the followers of Achilles, an ancient Greek hero.
Nay-say	contradict, oppose.
Nayward	tending toward ill.
Neapolitan bone-ache	see *clap*.
Necromantic	magic to do with the dead.
Nigh	nearly, almost.
Nine-pins	the game of skittles (pin bowling).
Nips	small sips.
Noisome	disgusting.
Nonchalantly	with obvious lack of concern.
Nonplussed	puzzle completely.
Nor'easter	a strong wind from the northeast.
Nuance	subtle difference.
Nuptial	to do with weddings.
Obnoxiously	annoying or objectionable.
Occulences	that which can be seen by the way it obscures something else.
Ochre	earthy colour ranging from pale yellow to orange or brown.
O'er-	over.
O'er-brimming	full to spilling.
Oft-time	frequent.
Omnipotent	all-powerful.
Ostler	one who is employed to tend horses.
Out of nick	beyond reckoning.
Outlandishly	freakishly strange or odd, having a foreign appearance.
Overscutch'd	well whipped.
Pagenting	show, with notion of unreality or deception.
Painted	attractive but false, lacking any depth.
Paree	City of Paris.
Pate	the crown of the head.

Patronage	the distribution of jobs or favours on a political basis.
Paunchy	with a swollen belly.
Parhelion	optical effect in the sky, caused by sunlight refracting through ice crystals in the high atmosphere. Usually bright spots on either side of the sun, sometimes arcs or bands.
Parity	Equality obtained through supposing equivalence.
Peachy	splendidly sweet.
Pell-mell	every which way.
Penance	action undertaken to merit forgiveness of sin.
Peristalsis	the progressive wave of contraction and relaxation of a tubular system.
Pernicious	causing ruin.
Perturbed	to disturb greatly.
Pervading	to be spread throughout.
Pestilence	an evil influence, or virulent disease, decay.
Petard	device, trick or trap, explosive or unpleasant.
Petrification	process of turning to stone.
Pervading	found in all places.
Pewter	alloy of tin and lead, silver-grey in colour.
Phantasmagoric	a shifting series of deceptive appearances.
Phantasmic	spectral, nightmarish.
Piebald	of several colours.
Piege	trap, pitfall.
Pissant	a person or thing of no value or consequence.
Pious	having a dutiful spirit towards, and earnest wish to fulfil, religious obligations.
Placidity	collectedness, calmness.
Plantagenet	medieval noble family, rulers of England from 1154 to 1485.
Plashing	when a beam of sunlight falls like water to splash against an object.
Pleurisy	infection of lungs, characterized by a dry cough.
Plumes	a rising feather-like pattern of dust, water or smoke impelled by agitation.
Plunked	to move or drop something suddenly and heavily.
Pomp	ceremonial extravagance.
Precepts	a rule prescribing a particular course of action.
Precocious	mature unusually early.
Preposterous	contrary to common sense.
Preternatural	beyond what occurs in nature.
Prevarication	to speak falsely.
Primped	to minutely adjust one's appearance in a self-regarding and excessive manner.

Privvy	toilet.
Prodigious	amazing, wondrous, oversized.
Profligate	recklessly extravagant.
Progeny	offspring.
Providential	resulting from Divine providence.
Puce	dark purple.
Pugnacious	given to quarrelling or fighting.
Puissance	physical strength arising from moral strength.
Quailed	loss of moral courage.
Quash	subdue, negate.
Queased	a sickly motion.
Quelling	subduing.
Quench	to completely satisfy a thirst.
Quietude	quiet stillness.
Ragamuffin	raggedly dressed, disreputable, person.
Rakish	dashing and debonair with strong indications of mischief.
Rambunctious	turbulently active and noisy.
Rampant	prevailing in action, dominant. *In heraldry*: a figure standing upraised, and in profile.
Ramping	to assume an aggressive stance.
Rapscallion	rascal.
Rare earths	Minerals that hold uncommon elements, amongst which are pyrognomic crystals that become incandescent at low temperature.
Raucous	loud and disorderly.
Ravening	voraciously seeking prey.
Ravenous	intensely, vastly hungry.
Reave	to take away.
Recoiled	to move swiftly in extreme reaction away from an event.
Recolt	harvest or vintage.
Redress	righting a wrong.
Refectory	a dining hall.
Refutation	example proving a contrary opinion incorrect.
Reifying	manifest a thought or internal state in external reality.
Relics	objects closely associated with a sacred personage, often thought to embody blessings.
Reneged	to deny or back out of.
Renunciate	person who has given up certain things voluntarily.
Resplendent	splendid.
Revenant	ghost.
Revoked	to take back.

Ribald	vulgar, mocking, indecent.
Ribbing	to joke with a mocking manner.
Roiling	to move in a turbulent and disturbed manner.
Rollicking	extreme telling off, featuring dramatic gestures and despairing, angry words.
Roan	chestnut coloured horse, sprinkled with gray or white.
Rue	to regret bitterly.
Sable	very dark brown.
Sabre	Heavy, single-edged sword, favoured by cavalry.
Sallied	to move briskly, an energetic movement.
Sallow	having a sickly complexion.
Sanguineous	of, pertaining to, or containing blood.
Sapphire	bright blue, from the gemstone.
Sardonic	characterized by mocking derision.
Saucy	lively, pertaining to sexiness.
S'Blood	a foul oath.
Scallion	a young man.
Scant	less than seems indicated.
Scintillating	to sparkle and flash like gemstones.
Score	20.
Scouted	reconnoitre, seek and observe.
Scriptorium	a room where manuscripts are stored, read, or copied.
Scroyly	rascally.
Scrumping	to take fruit from a tree, usually without permission.
Sculled	the action of an oar in water.
Scutage	a tax paid in lieu of military service.
Seanachie	traditional Irish storyteller; teacher at the hedge school (seanchaí).
Sempiternal	never ending.
Seneschal	the officer having charge of a dignitary's household.
Sentinel	person or thing that stands guard or watches from the perimeter of an area.
Sessile oak	large deciduous tree. Age 1000 years or more.
Seven league boots	legendary footwear giving the power to travel 7 leagues (approx. 20 miles) with a single stride.
Shale	layered matter.
Shanty	sailors' song, sung in rhythm with work, or the sea, or both.
Shillelagh	wooden club.
Shrive	to make enthusiastic confession.
Shtick	an acting routine.
Sidhe	the place whence fairies come, often seen as hilltops or mounds in this world, *Sidhe*.

Simian	ape-like.
Simpering	with the manner of a happy idiot.
Sinews of Mars	supplies needed to make war, esp. money. *From:* Mars, Roman god of War.
Skellum	rogue guilty of a plague of crimes.
Skulking	to be present but avoiding attention in a stealthy & suspicious manner.
Slated	slate-like, a flat darkness.
Slivered	split into slender slices.
Smitten	struck with love, as if by a hard blow.
Snaggle	roughly curved.
Solar plexus	the centre point of a radiant network of nerve fibres, situated at the upper part of the abdomen, just below the sternum.
Solicitude	an attitude of excessive attentiveness.
Sooth-sayer	fortune teller.
Spangly	glittering caused by a sprinkling of many small reflective objects.
Spayed	without ovaries.
Spectral	of ghosts and the undead.
Spinney	an area within a forest.
Splay	to spread out, often at oblique angles.
Sprightly	vivacious, spirited, upbeat.
Sprog	a new military recruit.
Stag-headed oak	tree in its old age.
Stalled	being kept at a stop.
Staphyline	grape like.
Stave	short staff.
Steed	a horse, usually understood to be impressive or high-spirited.
Stoically	characterized by austere fortitude.
Stump	the step of something heavy.
Stupefied	stunned amazement.
Sturm and Drang	literally 'storm and drive' : The quality of a person driven by pure, unfettered and overwhelming emotion.
Sublime	supreme or outstanding.
Sub-prior	3rd in command of an Abbey.
Succubbi	female devils.
Sulphurous	fiery, acrid, suffocating odour, commonly associated with the fires of hell.
Sunder	to break open.
Suffrage	sisterhood.
Sumptuous	luxuriously fine.
Supermarine	vibrant turquoise.

Svelte	gracefully slender.
Swathed	fully covered or closely wrapped.
Sylvan	of trees and forests. *From* Sylvanus, Roman god of the woods.
Tallow	animal fats used to make candles.
Tally-hoo	a hunter's cry.
Tara	the Hill of Tara, *Teamhair na Rí*, Meath, Ireland. The seat of the High King of Ireland, Árd Rí na hÉireann.
Tardy	given to lateness.
Tempestuous	turbulent, given to storminess.
Thick-eye'd	sad.
Tam Lin	legendary character trapped into making a pact with the Elves.
Temperance	moderation.
Theosophy	any inward-focussed spiritual practice that unifies man's spirit with the Divine.
Thunderhead	massive tower of cumulus cloud, characterized by its density and high definition, indicating good conditions for a thunderstorm.
Tipsy	a light, happy inebriation.
Tirade	an outspoken, long, angry and bitter complaint.
Titubantly	the light and unbalanced motions of the very drunk.
Tonsure	the shaven part of a cleric's head.
Transmogrify	change shape into something grotesque or bizarre.
Treasurer	a key post, 'without portfolio', in the Exchequer (see *Exchequer*).
Trepidation	fear felt in the body.
Trews	close fitting trousers.
Trice	very short period of time.
Trilled	to make rapid, repetitive musical sounds with a wind instrument, often vibrato.
Trouncing	beat severely.
Tuatha Dé Danann	a magical race, the First People, living in the pre-history of Ireland.
Tumescent	swollen.
Tumultuous	marked by disturbance and uproar.
Tunicle	a vestment worn by Bishops.
Turgid	bloated or distorted through excess.
Turpentine	resin derived from coniferous trees, used as disinfectant in the middle-ages.
Twined	twisted or woven together.
Uisce beatha	Irish distillation renowned for its near-miraculous medicinal effects on body and mind, closely related to the Scottish Usige beatha, anglicised as *whisky*.
Uncouth	unmannerly.

Unheeded	not noticed.
Unredeemable	incapable of being fulfilled.
Unruly	not conforming to rule.
Unwary	not cautious.
Unwarranted	without authority or sanction, lacking hierarchical support.
Uppity	aggressively self-assertive.
Uprearing	to lift or elevate.
Vacuous	characterized by a lack of intelligence; empty.
Vanguard	to protect the front, usually of a moving group.
Varipetaled	of many different types of flower.
Vassals	subjects or subordinates.
Venal	able to be purchased, as by a bribe.
Venerable	commanding respect due to impressive age, dignity, character or sanctity.
Verdant	usual meaning: flourishing with life, particularly greenery. A subtler implication if talking about a person can be innocence to the point of naivety.
Victuals	food.
Viridian	a bright shade of deep bluish-green.
Virulent	intense, acidic.
Vitatic	with relevance to Saint Vitus' dance; causing involuntary convulsive reactions including laughter.
Vittals	alcoholic drinks.
Vocative	a form of speech used to formally address, call or specify.
Wai ai	expression of delight, from northern England.
Warded	to protect, or take care of, an area.
Wassail	party, feast.
Wayland	legendary British metal-smith of eldritch skill.
Wayward	turned away from what is right.
Weald	wooded or uncultivated country.
Wee-tad	a little a lot.
Welter	agitated flurry.
Wend	movement, path, way.
Whiffling	breathe in fitful puffs.
Whipping cheer	served with the lash.
Whorl	a circular arrangement of like parts.
Widdershins	anti-clockwise.
Wide	in reference to clothing: over-styled, brash, cocky.
Wight	thing, creature, demon.
Wimpled	a woman's head cloth drawn in folds about the chin.
Wine Harvest	19-23 September. Autumn equinox, Harvest Home.

Wittol	complacent cuckold.
Wold	an elevated tract of wild or open country.
Wrack'd	tortured.
Yakking	conversing avidly but lightly.
Yelp	to emit a short, exclamatory sound.
Yield	surrender.
Zephyr	a gentle breeze.

Friar Tuck ~ Notes & Credits

Note on songs:
Alan-a-Dale's songs by Jethro Tull. www.j-tull.com

Songs From The Wood
Words & Music by Ian Anderson
© Copyright 1977 Ian Anderson Music Limited/Chrysalis Music Limited.
All Rights Reserved. International Copyright Secured.
Used by permission of Music Sales Limited.

Jack-In-The-Green
Words & Music by Ian Anderson
© Copyright 1977 Ian Anderson Music Limited/Chrysalis Music Limited.
All Rights Reserved. International Copyright Secured.
Used by permission of Music Sales Limited.

Cup Of Wonder
Words & Music by Ian Anderson
© Copyright 1976 Salamander & Son Music Limited/Chrysalis Music Limited.
All Rights Reserved. International Copyright Secured.
Used by permission of Music Sales Limited.

The Whistler
Words & Music by Ian Anderson
© Copyright 1977 Ian Anderson Music Limited/Chrysalis Music Limited.
All Rights Reserved. International Copyright Secured.
Used by permission of Music Sales Limited.

Slow Marching Band
Words & Music by Ian Anderson
© Copyright 1982 Salamander & Son Music Limited/Chrysalis Music Limited.
All Rights Reserved. International Copyright Secured.
Used by permission of Music Sales Limited.

Unter der Linden, by Walther von der Vogelweide. (Traditional).

Robin Hood Riding Through The Glen, by Carl Sigman.

Note on historic dates, places, events and characters:
Most are real and accurate; some are real, but not accurate; a few are accurate, but not real.

Note on *The Triads of Bardism*:
Across Europe, Bards were respected by both Church and State. The Triads are distillations of British wisdom in this tradition.